ELIZABETH WILSON is a resear⸛ her books on feminism and popu⸛ ntly Visiting Professor at the London⸛ . Her novels *The Twilight Hour* and *War D⸛* ⸛so published by Serpent's Tail.

Praise for *The Twilight Hour*

'This is an atmospheric book in which foggy, half-ruined London is as much a character as the artists and good-time girls who wander through its pages. It would be selfish to hope for more thrillers from Wilson, who has other intellectual fish to fry, but *The Twilight Hour* is so good that such selfishness is inevitable' *Time Out*

'A vivid portrait of bohemian life in Fitzrovia during the austerity of 1947 and the coldest winter of the twentieth century' *Literary Review*

'A book to read during the heatwave to keep you cool. The observant writing ensures that the iciness of the winter of 1947 rises off the page to nip your fingers ... [An] exciting, quirky story and a gripping evocation of an icy time' *Independent*

'Fantastically atmospheric ... The cinematic quality of the novel, written as if it were a black and white film with the sort of breathy dialogue that reminds you of *Brief Encounter*, is its trump card' *Sunday Express*

'An elegantly nostalgic, noir thriller; brilliantly conjures up the rackety confusion of Cold War London' *Daily Mail*

Praise for *War Damage*

'[A] first class whodunit ... The portrait of Austerity Britain is masterfully done ... the most fascinating character in this impressive work is the exhausted capital itself' Julia Handford, *Sunday Telegraph*

'[Wilson] evokes louche, bohemian NW3 with skill and relish' John O'Connell, *Guardian*

'The era of austerity after the Second World War makes an entertaining and convincing backdrop to Elizabeth Wilson's fine second novel ... A delight to read' Marcel Berlins, *The Times*

'This book is as stylish as one would hope. An evocative, escapist tale of murder and secrecy in post-war London, *War Damage* paints a picture of a city that, way before the '60s (even in the rubble of the Blitz), was swinging' Lauren Laverne, *Grazia*

'*War Damage* captures the murky, exhausted feel of post-war London. Buildings and lives are being reconstructed and shady pasts covered over. The atmosphere of secrecy and claustrophobia is as thick as the swirling dust of recently bombed buildings. Wilson excels at a good story set in exquisite period detail' Jane Cholmeley

'Cultural historian Elizabeth Wilson used post-second World War austerity Britain as the setting for a crime novel in her atmospheric *The Twilight Hour* (2006), set around bohemian Fitzrovia and Brighton in 1947. In this loose sequel, she again brilliantly evokes that bleak world of bomb sites and food shortages ... Wilson presents a nation struggling to get back on its feet, but she does not overdo the period detail ... Regine is an idiosyncratic, vivid protagonist' Peter Guttridge, *Observer*

'[A] sleek and vivid period piece' *Gay Times*

The Girl in Berlin

Elizabeth Wilson

First published in 2012 by Serpent's Tail,
an imprint of Profile Books Ltd
3A Exmouth House
Pine Street
London EC1R 0JH
website: www.serpentstail.com

ISBN 978 1 84668 826 3
eISBN 978 1 84765 808 1

Designed and typeset by sue@lambledesign.demon.co.uk

Printed by Clays, Bungay, Suffolk

10 9 8 7 6 5 4 3 2 1

For John and Katherine Gieve with thanks
for all your support

one

⊂✦⊃

May 1951

JACK MCGOVERN'S GLANCE swept the scene as he
stepped off the Glasgow train. A beam of sunlight pierced
the grimed glass roof. Steam billowed upwards from farting
engines. Wrapped in the solitude of the crowd, he watched
as his fellow passengers fanned out across the concourse and
scattered, drawn towards the exit like lemmings.

The rush and echoing noise exhilarated him. The anticipation never failed, was always like the first time: he'd come to
conquer London. Cast off the past. London was the future,
his future, a place of light and brightness after the dark, rain-
soaked north. London was freedom.

He'd had a seat on the journey south, but his long legs had
been cramped and he'd had nothing to drink but one bottled
beer. The carriage, crowded with dozing passengers, had been
draughty and at the same time sweaty, and the best he'd
managed was a feverish doze. Now exhaustion was replaced by
anticipation as he stood on the platform and took his bearings,
quietly, from habit, observing those who hurried, and those
who loitered or looked round, uncertain, caught between the
excitement and anxiety of travel. Especially those who loitered.
They were usually the interesting ones.

The pale, wolfhound eyes that missed nothing seemed unexpected, set in his dark, saturnine face. He'd read somewhere that olive skin and black hair came from the ancient Picts, the men who'd lived in the glens before the red-haired, pink-faced Vikings arrived, but perhaps his height came from the Norsemen, as he was tall for a Scot, five foot ten. Any hurrying passerby who glanced at him would have thought him a fine figure of a man, but few noticed him, because he had the art, so necessary in his job, of fading into the background. His trilby shaded his face, his tweeds were unremarkable, his movements smooth and subtle. In London he could disappear in the slip-stream of seven million lives pouring through the labyrinth of the great city.

Had his left elbow not been shattered at Alamein, he might have stayed in his native land, but he could no longer lift his arm to shoulder height and that had ruled out both the army and the shipyards where his father had worked. So the injury had been a blessing in disguise, providing the opportunity to get away from the city and family he loved, but who constrained and oppressed him with their demands, their customs, their assumptions.

Nobody in the police force knew – and it continued to surprise him that they hadn't bothered to find out – that his father had been a communist. In the tenement kitchens of his school mates you often saw the Virgin Mary, the Sacred Heart or a reproduction of *The Light of the World* beaming down, but in his home it was Uncle Joe, Comrade Stalin who watched kindly over them.

McGovern senior had swelled with pride when his son got the scholarship to grammar school, but the education he so strongly believed in had gradually placed a wedge between him and his son. Jack McGovern hadn't followed his father into the shipyards. Instead he'd found an office job, but he was bored, so he enrolled at night class to study law, and somehow got in with a bohemian crowd from the Art School. Among them was Lily. She and her middle-class, arty friends from Pollockshields and Hillhead had fascinated him and to them a worker's son from Red Clydeside was exotic, a romantic figure in these socialist times.

To old McGovern the new friends were tempting the son away from his working-class roots. Father and son had argued fiercely and things came to a head when McGovern told his parents he was marrying a coloured girl. For Lily was half Indian.

Like Jack McGovern, she didn't quite fit in. That – and because he wanted a different life – was why McGovern had left Glasgow, left Scotland, come to London and, almost on a whim, or to defy his father, joined the police.

He soon became a detective and now was seconded to the Special Branch. To be part of the state apparatus that spied on the workers was the ultimate act of a class traitor. And just as the Branch knew nothing about his background, so his father still didn't know the whole truth about the path he'd chosen: that he was dedicated to crushing subversion in every form, whether it was striking workers, trades unionists, or even militant tenants' movements. It was a secret he had to keep. His dad would have disowned him and he didn't want that, although in fact he'd disowned his father, or at least his class. Yet he still respected his father and didn't even know himself just why he'd rejected Glasgow and its fierce, proud working-class way of life.

McGovern stood for several minutes, no longer surveying the crowd, but suddenly longing for Glasgow after all, not because of his residual love for the blackened tenements, the dark streets and the stunted, shrunken men in their flat caps trudging through the sooty fog that passed for air, but because Lily was still there.

He squared his shoulders and made for the exit. He was keen to get down to the Yard.

♦♦♦♦♦

Three members of the Vice Squad were seated in the canteen and as McGovern closed in on them they were talking about the impending Messina trial. Gangsters; they loved that.

'The defence'll be bribery.'

'Get away with you.'

'Tell that to the marines.'

Hilarious. Then they looked up, slightly disappointed to see him back, but made room and were friendly enough. 'Here's the Prof.'

McGovern had to join in the laughter, but held himself superior to them. Most of them were bent: taking bribes, running toms. The bribery joke was only funny because everyone knew the gangster Messina had certainly had Vice Squad coppers in his pay at one time or another. Their double standards reeked of English hypocrisy. His methods, by contrast, were justified by their ends: to protect the state.

'How's Uncle Joe?' That was a joke too. They scorned the Special Branch as much as he held their lot in contempt. He was alien to them. He was a boffin, wasn't he, with all the stuff he knew about Commies, Nazis, the IRA. Not that people cared about fascists and republicans these days; it was all about the Reds now.

'Comrade Stalin is well, thanks for the enquiry.' He went along with the joke, although he knew, and they knew, it had a sting in its tail. It wasn't the Branch, but MI5 who dealt with communist subversion. MI5 were in the saddle these days and his colleagues liked to remind him.

Behind that also lurked the suspicion that perhaps it wasn't a joke at all. There was something about being a copper; you got tainted with what you were supposed to be fighting. Just as the Vice Squad were up to their necks in pornography and prostitution, so all the extremist ideologies they were supposed to suppress contaminated McGovern and the Special Branch. It was a contagious disease and they were at risk from the infection because they were too close to the enemy. Furthermore, the Branch was distrusted on account of the aura of conspiracy that surrounded its officers. Their work took on the methods of their enemies: entrapment, blackmail and covert surveillance. To their fellow policemen, accustomed to the more straightforward methods of physical violence and bribery, they seemed sinister. Information, knowledge, after all, rather than the fist and the boot, were their professional weapons.

Above all they were just too brainy. They thought too much, were too clever by half. Such men were dangerous. Also, as McGovern freely admitted to himself, you had to be a bit unhinged to do the job. Men were drawn into this neck of the woods by some kind of obsession. He himself was fascinated by the conspirators he encountered, fanatics in thrall to a single obsessive idea.

He soon tired of sparring with his fellow detectives and escaped up to his poky office on the third floor. It got little daylight, because it looked out on a light well at the centre of the building, but McGovern liked it because it was out of the way and seldom attracted visitors. His assistant was seated at a desk against the wall, laboriously hand writing what McGovern assumed at a glance was some kind of report.

'I thought you weren't back till tomorrow, sir.'

Manfred Jarrell showed no surprise, but then there was little that surprised him. His accent suggested a privileged family or at least a public-school education, but he was as cagey as McGovern about his background. His hair, worn too long, was a violent shade of carrot orange, the contrast with which made his white, almost greenish, spotty complexion look even more sickly. Yet no-one ribbed him about his morbid looks or poncey accent.

'Another bleeding *hin*tellectual! He's going in with you,' was how Superintendent Gorch had introduced the lad. McGovern still didn't know quite what to make of Jarrell, but had an uneasy feeling that the younger man had *him* worked out.

'I'm officially on leave till tomorrow, but Gorch wants to see me.' He knew he was scheduled for bodyguard duty, looking after some middle-grade visiting American. Escort duty could theoretically be dangerous, but in practice was almost always a ticket to unbearable boredom.

'What's been going on while I was away?'

Manfred Jarrell shrugged. He blinked and pushed his round glasses up his nose. 'Electricians' Union,' he said, 'riddled with Reds. The British Electricity Authority want something done about it. All the leading officials are members of the Communist Party. They've smashed the wages freeze—'

'Okay, okay.' This aspect of the work made Jake a little uncomfortable. 'We all know it's run by Frank Haxell. That's nothing new. Why the sudden emergency?'

Jarrell shrugged and pushed his glasses up again. 'Because the wages freeze has gone west, I suppose. They've kind of won, haven't they.'

'Maybe for the moment, but one wee victory for the workers doesna' make a revolution.'

'Oh – and there was a message. *He* called yesterday. You're to meet him tomorrow evening.' Jarrell handed McGovern a torn-off sheet of paper on which was written the name of a pub and the time, 6.00 p.m. McGovern folded it into his pocket and stood thinking about it, interested, excited even. Jarrell looked at him. 'You'd better cut along to the boss, sir. He doesn't like to be kept waiting, does he.'

McGovern looked quizzically at his subaltern, who seemed to lack a proper understanding of his subordinate position. 'I'll do that,' he said.

Detective Chief Superintendent Gorch was one reason McGovern stayed in the job. He'd not seriously considered cutting loose, but on dark days, on boring and frustrating days, and there were quite a few of those, he flirted with the idea of some wholly different life. He dreamed of living with Lily on the edge of Loch Fyne, scene of childhood holidays with his mother's crofter family. Lily would paint and he would ... but what would he do? That was the problem. He would fish. Like surveillance, fishing required patience. You sat there for hours, waiting, not a twitch on the line until suddenly ... But he knew he'd never be able to survive the pure air of the glens. He needed the smoke-soaked atmosphere of a great city. And Lily wasn't exactly wedded to the beauty of the Scottish landscape. She longed for the sun beating down.

He sat down in a leather chair near Gorch's desk.

'How's your father-in-law, then?'

'It's bad news, I'm afraid. My wife may be up there a while.'

'I'm sorry to hear it.' Gorch always spoke quietly. The vast jowls and flat, thick lips, the overgrown eyebrows, beefy cheeks and overall his great girth and weight encased in an old-fashioned, three-piece suit of dark grey birds-eye cloth, the waistcoat near bursting over his bulging stomach, added up to an air of reassurance rather than menace. He might have been a clergyman from years gone by or possibly a head game-keeper, or even a benevolent workhouse master. He did not seem to belong at all to the modern era, to the rapid pace of the thrusting postwar world. But he would have been only two or three years old when Queen Victoria died.

Gorch's words sank in a friendly silence. After a while he added: 'They've got a job for you, lad.'

They – MI5; McGovern's pulse quickened.

Another pause. 'Kingdom thinks very highly of you.'

'Thank you, sir.'

Gorch eyed him cannily. 'I suppose you think they're a bunch of public-school pansies.'

McGovern smiled faintly, but shook his head.

'Kingdom is a clever man. He had a very good war record in intelligence. Some of them may be, let's say, amateurish, but he knows the score all right. Some say he was the best inter-rogator we had. Thing is – this is confidential – they are in a lot of trouble. In fact, they're in very big trouble indeed.'

'Sir?'

'They know there's a mole, known it for some time. And now – well, Kingdom will put you in the picture.'

'I'm meeting him tomorrow evening. There was a message.'

'Report back to me.'

Without Lily the flat was dusty and lonely. He longed to ring her, but telephone calls were expensive. It still surprised him she was his wife, that he'd ever dared ask her to marry him and that she'd accepted. She wasn't like other women, that is, like the women from his childhood. She didn't gossip with the neighbours, didn't clean and scrub everything in sight. On the contrary, she came from a wealthy family and she had a career.

She wouldn't have much time for her painting up there, looking after her father, now he was so ill … he pictured her at the easel, wearing her dirty, grey smock and frowning at her work, motionless for minutes on end, staring, her long, black hair caught up in a rough knot at the back. Her skin was pale and people often didn't realise her father came from India, especially as her name, Lily, seemed quite British – although she'd told him early on that it was also an Indian name, and chosen by her parents for that reason: that it was both Indian and Scottish, like her.

Her family, the wealthy Campbells, who ran one of the big Glasgow department stores, had been no more pleased than

McGovern's about the marriage. They'd shaken their heads and pursed their lips and whispered that Lily was going the way of her mother – because it wasn't the first time for them, for Lily's mother, Jean, had gone off to India and married a native. That Lily had married a working-class lad was hardly a scandal to compete with that. Yet it still amazed McGovern that he, brought up in a working-class tenement, should have married into such a clan.

When India was torn apart by Partition the Campbells, in spite of the scandal, had taken in Jean, her gentle, harmless husband and their daughter. How lucky it was, they used to say, that Lily was so pale. Really, you'd never know she was a half-caste.

He'd brought home a beer and tuned into the Home Service. As he relaxed he started to think about tomorrow – not about the day's work in the wake of some minor American dignitary, but of the evening's rendezvous with a spy: Miles Kingdom.

two

ALAN WENTWORTH HAD spent the afternoon with his mistress, Edith Fanshawe. As a result he hadn't returned to Broadcasting House until teatime, with masses of work still to do. This was ironic, since usually when he rang his wife to explain that he had to work late, the real reason was a rendez-vous with Edith, but on this occasion he could give the excuse with a good conscience, as he was telling the truth.

It was well past seven when he left the building and his imagination slipped back to Edith. Her cries of pleasure – her declarations – I'm addicted to you, you beast ... He pushed open the swing doors and turned left, his hat pulled down, hands in the pockets of his corduroy trousers. As he walked along, frowning, he wasn't thinking at all, he was mentally revisiting the pale, softened marble of her thighs, the look in her violet eyes as she incited his desire, grasping him so greedily – he could not shake off the obsession.

He bumped violently into an oncoming pedestrian. The disagreeable shock, the blunt jerk of a stranger's body against his, unleashed an unreasonable anger. 'What the hell! Can't you look where you're going?' he said, although it had been his own fault.

Then he looked again. The man was carelessly dressed, hatless, his raincoat flapping open, but – the bony face, the shock of hair.

'*Colin*! It *is*, isn't it? Good God!' Astonishment wiped out all thoughts of Edith.

A wary look crossed the face of the man who'd once been his friend. He seemed ready to bolt, run for cover.

'This is extraordinary. What the hell are you doing here?' Alan knew the question was ridiculous, but the words just burst out.

'Alan—' Colin Harris just stood there, seemingly stunned.

'Where on earth have you been, old chap?' That sounded even sillier, as though Colin had been gone for a few hours rather than three years.

Colin shrugged, held his hands wide as though he didn't know himself. The twisted grin suggested his disappearance might have been a bad joke.

Alan looked at his watch. He was so late. But if he was going to be late home anyway ... and now he had an excuse. 'We have to have a drink – there's a pub round the corner—'

Colin shook his head, put up a hand as if warding off a blow.

'Oh come on – can't just pass by on the other side, you know—'

Colin fell into step beside him.

They found a seat by the stained-glass window of the pub across the road. Alan insisted on buying the drinks. They'd barely spoken, yet he could tell just by looking that Colin was hard up, that things were going badly for him. He placed the glasses on the table. 'Just going to phone Dinah,' he said. 'You remember Dinah, don't you?'

'Of course I remember Dinah.'

'We've got a kid now. Little chap, he's a year old. Thomas – Tommy.'

The telephone booth was near the bar and there was a lot of noise.

'You'll never guess who I've just bumped into! Colin!' he shouted.

And Dinah immediately responded with: 'Oh, you must find out what happened to him – bring him up here immediately.'

Pleased with the convenient excuse he returned to his seat in genial mood.

'So, tell me what – what you've been doing – what *happened* to you?' Cigarettes helped to ease the tension. The beauty of a cigarette was not just the nicotine but that it also gave you something to do with your hands. All the business of it – matches, hands to lips, inhaling, exhaling, it was quite a little drama – masked unease.

Colin stared into his glass. 'I – I was just coming to see you. On the off chance. Heard you were working at the Beeb.'

'You didn't seem all that pleased to see me, though.'

'I – it was a shock. I wasn't – I hadn't geared myself up – it's taken a while to decide to get in touch. You're one of the only people … I was going to get up a bit of Dutch courage first. And I left it late – thought you wouldn't still be there at this hour – easier really, if you weren't. The thing is—' He stopped abruptly, mid-sentence.

'After the trial you just bloody disappeared. What happened?'

'I don't know where to begin.' He frowned into the distance. 'Well …'

'We even wondered …'

'If I'd fled behind the Iron Curtain?' The sarcasm Colin managed to convey with these words stirred the embers of Alan's guilty feelings towards his old friend. He should have done more. He should have *cared* more. But before he had time to form his confused feelings into words Colin said in a different, defiant tone of voice: 'Well, you'd be right.'

'Really?' Alan managed to sound merely mildly interested, as though Colin had said: 'I went to ground in Wales for a bit', but he felt nervous. He dreaded what was coming next.

'I was angry. With all of you. With bloody everyone. You – the Party, the comrades – my mother – I don't know why. You stood by me, after all, didn't you. But I just wanted to see the back of everyone who had anything to do with the whole bloody mess. I stayed with my mother for a few weeks while I tried to decide what to do. But she drove me mad. At first I thought things would get back to normal, but the fact is I had hell's own problem getting work here after the trial. British justice! I got off in the end – didn't I? Well, you wouldn't think so. Prospective employers wouldn't look me in the eye. You know – no smoke without fire. Do we really want someone who might be a criminal sitting in our cosy little office? One of them even suggested I go and start a new life in New Zealand. New Zealand! Do I look like a sheep farmer, for Christ's sake? The Party wasn't much help either. I thought the comrades would stick by me, but I was a terrible embarrassment. Bugger me if they didn't suggest I left the country too! Someone put me in touch with some friends in Germany, nothing official, just some people they knew; communists, of course, communists who'd survived. They said if I disappeared for a bit, I could come back later when everyone would have forgotten about it. So I went to East Germany. Not that it was East Germany then. I went to live in the Soviet sector of Berlin.

'These friends fixed me up with a kind of semi-journalism job, but ... it's been difficult. I've never really belonged, I don't fit in. I mean, I wasn't a defector, so in a funny way that meant I wasn't *on their side*. I'm in a sort of no man's land – in Berlin – and Berlin's a sort of no man's land of its own. And God, it's depressing ... I mean, we had the Blitz and the doodle bugs and all that, but it's nothing to Berlin. And as for boys – ' he said, looking anywhere but at Alan, 'well, that was depressing too. When I first got there in '48, it was still – people would do anything for food, cigarettes, money. It was all rather degrading. Anyway ... oh, God, it's such a long story ...' He didn't finish the sentence. Instead he smoked hungrily, flicking ash off the coal with a nervous tic, staring away in a corner of the saloon bar, oblivious of the drinkers refreshing themselves after work, the cheery drone of male voices and laughter. Then he straightened up. 'At least what they're trying to do is create a better Germany. West Berlin is just a little outpost of American imperialism. I know that sounds like propaganda, but it's true. All they care about is keeping the Soviet Union at bay. But it's all … it isn't how I imagined …'

Alan thought of himself as a man of the world, but he was not a cynic. He was still capable of being shocked to hear that Colin, a defendant in a big trial, who had been convicted and then had the conviction quashed, should nevertheless have been treated with suspicion. No smoke without a fire.

Deep down Alan had known all along that Colin had gone east. Colin had always been such an idealist. Over the years when Alan had thought about Colin, which wasn't, frankly, that often, he'd thought it was a good solution. He was a communist, wasn't he, so it was logical to go and live and work in a communist country.

Colin did not sound so enthusiastic now. Well, there were hordes of disillusioned communists littering the place these days.

The knuckles of Colin's bony hand stretched tight round his glass. He took a long gulp. 'The thing is – I'm trying to come back. I need a job, here, I mean. That's why I was on my way to see you. I just wondered if there was some slight chance you'd be able to get me something … I don't know what exactly you do at the BBC and I know it's a long shot, but—'

'I work for the Third Programme. Features.' Alan spoke gruffly. Even to state the plain truth somehow sounded like boasting, as if he were deliberately contrasting his own success – or luck, or both – with Colin's blighted fortunes. He frowned. 'You must have oodles of contacts.'

'Well … not necessarily,' replied Alan cautiously, hoping he didn't sound as dismayed as he felt. Alan was adept at avoiding emotional discomfort, but this conversation was becoming awkward. He was experiencing a mixture of guilt at his own success and irritation that Colin was always his own worst enemy.

'I've tried so hard to make a life for myself there, but it's not easy.'

Alan looked at Colin's bent head and felt an unwelcome surge of pity. The trouble was Colin *always* tried too hard. He'd actually fought in Spain, when so many just talked about it. He'd actually stayed in the Communist Party when so many had left. He'd actually gone to live in an outpost of the Soviet Union, when so many found it easier to sneer at tarnished idealism. Like Alan himself. Out of guilt he said heartily: 'I'll give it some thought. Three years in Berlin isn't going to help, of course,' he added more brutally than he'd intended, 'unless – were you able to do any filming …?'

Colin shook his head. 'I did investigate the possibility of getting work at the German studios in East Berlin, at UFA, but …'

Alan controlled his impatience. What a fool Colin was, really. He'd been in documentaries once, he could surely have got something. But as soon as the thought formed itself Alan felt he was being a bit of a cad. 'Perhaps if you could write something on spec … I mean, if you've been doing journalism over there – that might be a subject, well, East Germany, that's a subject in itself, of course, although there isn't much sympathy for any of those countries at the moment …'

'You surprise me.' Colin's tone was bitterly sarcastic.

There was an awkward silence. Colin stood up. 'I'd better be off. I'm … you'll be late home. I mustn't keep you.'

Alan jumped to his feet too. 'You can't just bugger off like that – look, I'll do what I can, you know I will.'

'Trying to get your black sheep commie friend some work. It'd be embarrassing, wouldn't it.'

'Colin! Please. Sit down. Don't be so touchy. I do want to help.'

And, to Alan's surprise, Colin did sit down. But the silence was heavier than ever.

'Couldn't the Party find you something?' Alan was feeling a bit desperate, and also it really was getting late.

Colin smiled grimly. 'I'm not in the Party's good books these days.' He drank again. 'I'm an embarrassment to them, like I said. There are too many bureaucrats in the Party now and not enough revolutionaries. There as well as here. Of course it's really difficult, actually coming to power and running a country. Especially a divided country.'

Alan looked at his watch. 'Look, why don't you come home with me and have something to eat. Dinah'd love to see you.'

Colin shook his head.

'At least let me get you another drink.'

Colin shook his head again. Then: 'Oh, all right.' He sank back in his chair. 'Can't stay long, though.'

Returning with the beer, Alan was tense with curiosity. 'Have you left the Party, then?'

'No ... no ... it's not like that ...'

Silence.

'Well then?' said Alan impatiently.

Colin leaned forward and suddenly became more animated. 'I'll tell you one thing you'll be pleased to hear.' And now his grin was hostile. 'I fell in love.' He stared angrily at Alan, daring him to react. 'The bit that'll please you is it's a girl.'

Alan swallowed his astonishment and managed an encouraging smile. He'd always tried to appear liberal and tolerant, but underneath ran a current of repulsion and Colin hadn't been fooled after all.

'A German girl. Her name's Frieda, Frieda Schröder. We

want to get married, but there've been so many problems. And King Street haven't been helpful. They don't think anyone should be encouraged to leave a socialist country.'

Alan hadn't thought about King Street for centuries. He'd been there, the Covent Garden headquarters of the British Communist Party ... in the very cold winter, when Colin had been in frightful trouble. It all seemed so long ago ... lost youth ... He sighed.

'How could they help you bring her over here?'

'Oh ... I don't know. But anyway, they'd just rather I stayed disappeared, I suppose. At first I thought we'd just get married and stay in Berlin, but then   well, Frieda doesn't want to stay there. She wants to get right away, so that meant my getting a job back here – and there's still quite a lot of red tape if you marry a German ... it's easier than it was just after the war, but – as I said, it's a bit awkward for the Party – an East German girl who wants to defect just as the socialist dawn appears over the horizon. That's not what they want to hear.'

He can't bear to look me in the eye, thought Alan, and didn't understand why.

'The main thing is, though, I have to get work. If I am going to come back, that is.'

'Look – you *must* come back up to Hampstead and have something to eat. Meet Dinah again and my son.' (With what pride Alan spoke the last two words.) 'I insist. I'm not taking no for an answer.'

Dinah heard the key in the lock and when the door opened she saw with real joy the tall figure looming behind her husband.

'Colin!'

She flung her arms round him as he stepped forward. 'How wonderful to see you!' But she felt his body go rigid at this unusual display of emotion and her arms fell back to her sides.

They sat round the table in the basement kitchen and it was just – almost – like the old times before Colin's trial. She eked out the shepherd's pie with baked beans and there was some Scotch in the cupboard to supplement the bottled beer the men had brought.

Whether it was the drink or the warmth of the kitchen or Dinah, something was freed in Colin. He talked and talked. When Dinah heard about the German girl she clapped her hands. 'Oh, that's marvellous!' – although as soon as she'd said it her hand flew to her mouth, for of course it sounded as if she'd disapproved of his being queer in the first place. To tell the truth she'd never really understood that – the queerness – and this was so much better. Except that his fiancée was still in Berlin.

'She's ... you've no idea what she's been through ...'

But he was talking more about Berlin than about the girl. 'It's so hard to describe what it's like ... the bomb damage – so much worse than here – just miles of rubble—'

'Worse than *London*?'

'Of course, much, much worse. They've started to build again now, but in 1948 it was still ...' Colin smiled grimly. 'I don't think I'll ever enjoy going round ruins again. You remember, Alan, that Cambridge trip to Italy and Greece before the war? How we loved wandering round Pompeii and all those ruined temples and cities and villas? Well, in Berlin I thought: it's just like that. It's like wandering through the ruins of some ancient civilisation, a long-dead culture. The difference was people were still living there, in cellars, in ruins, in cemeteries. As if all the corpses in Pompeii had risen from the dead and were living some macabre kind of after-life. And they're still there, some of them. Five years after the war.'

The kitchen was filled with their cigarette smoke. 'I can't bear the Cold War,' Dinah burst out. 'The Bomb – it's all so terrible.' She knew her words sounded trite, but that was because there were no adequate words for the horror that loomed behind everything in life: nuclear warfare; Hiroshima. She was suddenly afraid she might burst into tears. It must be the Scotch. Her thoughts skidded back to safer ground – not that it was that safe, as Colin seemed so twitchy. 'What are you going to do now, Colin? What are your plans?'

'I was saying to Alan, I want to come back, with Frieda, of course, but I need a job and that isn't going to be easy. And there's an awful lot I've got to do first – visas and so on. The red tape makes it all so difficult. At both ends.'

'Can't you just marry her there? You'd be able to bring her back then.'

'It's not that simple. She'd still have to apply for British citizenship.'

'But that wouldn't be difficult, would it, if she were married to you?' Alan was genuinely puzzled.

Dinah knew there was more, that there was much Colin hadn't told them. 'What's she like? Tell us about her. How did you meet her?'

Colin smiled, more relaxed. 'When I first got there I stayed with some friends of friends, a Party connection. They were living in a derelict apartment in the Prenzlauerberg – still are, for that matter. There wasn't really room for me, but they were very kind ... I have a sort of hotel room now ... but that's expensive.' He frowned. 'It's difficult to explain what life's like over there. Frieda, for instance, she has a job in West Berlin. I'm not clear what happened to her right after the war. I think they were in West Berlin for a bit. But anyway, if a German woman could get a job with the Allies, it didn't matter what kind of job, waitressing, cooking, cleaning, it was a godsend for them, it meant they got more food, some cigarettes, chocolate and other things like that. Frieda did cleaning in an Allied officers' club. But she's been lucky and managed to progress to office duties. She still works in the British sector, but far fewer people are crossing over now. It's becoming a bit of a problem ... I have a snapshot of her. It's not very good.' He fished it from his wallet and held it out awkwardly.

Dinah looked at the small, creased photograph. You could hardly see the face of the young woman trying to smile as she squinted into the sun. She wore a print dress and her hair hung in waves to her shoulders, the front pinned back in a wartime style. There was something poignant about the snapshot, perhaps there was always something poignant about the way people looked when they were photographed like that, it would always be a hopeful moment, and yet already it was locked in the past. She handed it back and Colin tucked it in his wallet.

'As I said, she's desperate to get away from it all, so I'll have to find something here.'

'I'm sure you will, sooner or later.' But Dinah knew her words were empty ones.

Colin pushed his shock of hair back, a familiar gesture. 'I'd better get going.'

'Stay,' ordered Alan. 'It's after midnight. The tube shut hours ago.'

So Dinah made up a bed on the sofa in the sitting room, and they left Colin unlacing his shoes.

three

❦

A FEW LIGHTS PRICKED THE DUSK along the Kurfürsten damm. Frieda had worked late, because Herr Schneidermann insisted. There was no point. The canteen provided lunches for those British personnel and a few Germans with cushy jobs, attached to the occupying forces. There were no customers after six in the evening, but he kept her there, gave her silly clerical jobs and now and then ran his hand over her bottom. He would have liked to go further, but she'd long ago perfected a chilly hauteur that froze off men like Herr Schneidermann. The veneer was brittle. She had no power to prevent men from doing whatever they wanted, but it usually worked.

Herr Schneidermann knew how she'd got work in the British sector, of course: through her British friend. The British were less interested in women than the Russians and the Americans. It was said they did not much like women, their educational system saw to that, but Colonel Ordway had been kind to her. Stiff and unattractive, with sparse, mousy hair, a fierce toothbrush moustache and staring blue eyes, he had helped get her through the bad time, at least until ... Only too soon he'd gone back to England and his wife and anyway *der Vater* had insisted they move into the Russian sector. But she'd kept the job.

Herr Schneidermann had got *his* job as canteen manager by more dubious means, she felt sure, but it was not done to ask too many questions. Even the seemingly harmless 'Where do you come from?' was often too much. Yet Schneidermann couldn't resist dropping a hint from time to time of his importance before 1945. Frieda didn't care that he might have been a Nazi supporter, or even an active Nazi, and that denazification had left him unscathed. Anyway, Nazism hadn't been purged or cleansed, it had simply subsided and disappeared, seeping silently into the ground like poison from some chemical factory site, polluting the environment in a different, quieter way.

What wore her down was the way Herr Schneidermann hated everyone: the Amis, the Russians, the English, the German refugees from the East, and the Poles. This universal hatred found expression in his low-grade bullying of her. He found petty ways to annoy, he criticised her work and he even sneered at her shabby clothes, although his weren't much better. But it was work. It might not last that much longer, but she was determined to hang on until the place finally closed down. There were definite advantages to living in the Eastern sector and working in the West.

Frieda kept her bicycle in the storeroom at the back of the canteen. The bicycle was the only tangible memento of Colonel Ordway, other than the job itself. He'd found it somehow for her when they moved to Prenzlauerberg. This evening as she bent to unchain it, she saw the back tyre was flat. How could that have happened? She suspected Schneidermann, but surely even he would not be that spiteful.

Now she must wheel the heavy machine right across the city. That meant she would be late, which in turn would mean trouble from her father. He would shout and scream at her for being so careless with the precious machine. It would just have to be endured. Her experiences for the past six years, since their shattered arrival in Berlin in 1945, had taught her stoicism. The Colonel, too, had unexpectedly given her strength. It was what they called the stiff upper lip. 'Chin up, old bean. Things won't look so bad in the morning.' When he was worried about something he hummed or sang a quaint song from some previous war: 'It's a long long way to Tipperary' or '*Après la guerre*, there'll be a good time everywhere'. A hymn, 'Time, like an ever rolling stream bears all its sons away' was another favourite. It was soothing, especially when she was exhausted after one of those evenings when she'd been out scavenging for her father.

She had learned to put things in perspective. In those first days you couldn't plan; mere survival took up all your time and energy. Was that why she'd stayed, hadn't fled? Colonel Ordway had told her of a scheme, the North Sea Scheme, that could get her a job in England. But her father had moved them back to the East, which made it more difficult. His threats and bullying had frightened her.

Now, however, she had a plan.

four

ONCE A WEEK TOMMY'S nursemaid, Mary, arrived from Camden Town on the dot of nine and set Dinah free to spend the day at the Courtauld Institute. The first time Tommy saw her leave his face turned beetroot. There was a moment's silence, like when the V2 dropped, as he apparently stopped breathing, before the explosion of yells. Alan's horror at the sight of his son in paroxysms of rage and despair had led him to tell Dinah to give up the whole idea of the Courtauld. That was their second worst row ever. Dinah didn't know quite how she'd won. In fact, she hadn't won, she'd simply run away, leaving solid Mary to calm father and son. It was the first time she'd ever directly flouted her husband's wishes.

Once she'd disappeared, it was out of sight, out of mind for Tommy, as Alan had had to admit, but ever since then Dinah had been careful to slip away while Tommy wasn't looking, to avoid a scene. That didn't stop Alan from reverting regularly to the subject of Dinah's Mondays at the Courtauld. (He didn't dignify them with the term 'work'.) He never objected in abstract or moral terms, did not on principle disapprove of working mothers. It was more along the lines of: 'I don't understand why you keep it up. Surely you have enough to do here at home? I'm earning a good salary now. You've got your friends,' and lately, 'now Reggie has the twins ...'

Sometimes Dinah suspected that Alan was jealous of the Courtauld, or, more likely, its director, Dr Anthony Blunt, whose assistant she liked to think she'd unofficially become. Alan did not admit to jealousy, of course, and in fact he was not jealous. It was rather that it had simply never occurred to him that Dinah could possibly have any needs or aspirations that did not revolve directly around his own and, now, that extension of himself, Tommy. But Dinah stood her ground and continued quietly to work at the Courtauld, with the not-quite-defiant reminder to herself: I can't just be a housewife.

Today, however, as Dinah walked down Fitzjohn's Avenue from Hampstead to Swiss Cottage, where she would catch a bus to Portman Square, she was not thinking about Alan or Tommy at all. She was puzzling over Colin's reappearance. He'd seemed so tense, so anxious and worried, not that there was anything new about that. He'd always been tense and nervy, and when she'd known him before, he'd had reason to be, but he hadn't been defeated. Last night he had seemed just that: as if it was all too much, the stuffing knocked out of him. And he'd looked shabby in a different way from his bohemian disarray of old. But perhaps that was just due to conditions in Germany.

And then to disappear without saying goodbye ... Tommy had woken her soon after six and by the time she got downstairs, Colin had gone, leaving just the blanket and eiderdown neatly folded. Poor Colin. He always seemed to run into bad luck. He was one of those for whom nothing went right ... 'I was born under a blighted star' ... who had said that?

He'll find his own level, Alan had said with careless complacency as they'd lain in bed discussing their friend on the sofa downstairs – though it was all a bit awkward, the stuff about a job.

At least, thought Dinah, walking down the hill, Colin had found a girl. It was rather a pity she was German, but if he succeeded in bringing her home to England then he had every chance of settling down and making a happier life for himself. Surely it couldn't be too difficult, not now? Dinah decided to write to her father, a prominent lawyer, to ask his advice. He'd know exactly what Colin ought to do.

The Courtauld Institute was a temple, a shrine. Every Monday when Dinah crossed the threshold, she thrilled to its atmosphere, which from the very first day had taken hold of her. As soon as she'd walked up the magnificent double staircase rising to the rarefied realms above she'd known this was the place for her. It was a place of freedom and at the same time of dedication. And over it all presided the great geniuses – Michelangelo, Poussin, of course, and Raphael. They were tangible presences in Portman Square, not ghosts, but living members of this community devoted to their art.

The arrival of Tommy had interrupted her degree, but Dr Blunt had kindly allowed her to 'intermit' and from time to time encouraged her to return as a full-time student. 'You don't have to come in every day, you know.' Dr Blunt had also suggested she take time off from library duties to attend lectures at least. Don't give it up completely, he'd said. Meanwhile she worked in the library under Miss Welsh, but she also assisted Dr Blunt, by checking references and clearing copyrights.

In this way she felt she was still part of the great enterprise that was the study of Western Art. Art had become a passion and she was determined to pass her love for art on to Tommy, above whose cot she'd pinned coloured photographic reproductions of *The Birth of Bacchus* and *Landscape with Diogenes*, both by Nicholas Poussin, the artist to whom Dr Blunt had devoted so much scholarship.

Alan had laughed when she put them up. 'Is Bacchus really more appropriate than the Infant Jesus?' Not that Alan was religious or anything like that, but in some ways, Dinah was discovering, he was more conventional, or was becoming more conventional, than when they'd first met. But then he'd added kindly: 'At least it's not Walt Disney.'

The Courtauld Library would have looked out over the square, had not its long windows been obstructed by its metal bookcases. Miss Welsh always wore gloves, whether to protect the books or her hands was not clear, or perhaps the gloves simply signalled her conception of the Institute as a kind of ongoing social event. Her manner was that of a hostess rather than a keeper of books. Fresh flowers appeared every day and cakes or buns and tea were served in the afternoon.

Dinah usually stayed until five, but her fellow library assistant, the Hon. Cecily Barrington-Smith, seldom put in a full day's work, pleading more pressing social engagements. Cecily had been a debutante and done 'the Season' the previous year, but had yet to find a husband, although Dinah – who might have been forced into debdom herself had it not been for the war – had always assumed the whole purpose of being a deb was to meet eligible young men and end up with an engagement ring. Cecily and Miss Welsh discussed these matters in murmured conversations from which Dinah was excluded. Miss Welsh had hinted that she disapproved of someone lucky enough to be a wife and mother even entertaining the idea of paid work. Actually, Dinah was not paid, but she hadn't told Alan that.

It did not occur to her that Miss Welsh was jealous of her privileged relationship with Dr Blunt, Miss Welsh being only one among many women at the Courtauld, young and middle-aged, who simply adored the Director. Dinah, on the other hand, was not in the throes of a crush, but simply liked and admired Dr Blunt for his dedication to art and for his good-mannered kindness towards her. Nor did Dinah flatter herself that Dr Blunt was especially interested in her. He just wanted her to have the enormous benefit of studying at the temple of art he'd virtually created, and you simply could not exaggerate what he'd brought to the Courtauld.

This lunchtime Dinah found her friend Polly and together they made for the nearest ABC teashop. They'd started out at the Courtauld together, but Polly was now a postgraduate.

Dinah deeply admired Polly's perfectly achieved, bohemian Juliette Greco look. Her dark, pageboy hair was cut with a fringe, her white shirt had the collar turned up and she cinched in her black, drainpipe trousers with a wide red belt. Her nail varnish was invariably perfect. Life with Tommy meant you were always somehow untidy, nail polish an impossibility.

'I was in the laboratory this morning,' said Polly, 'it's absolutely fascinating. You can see where an artist has made alterations.' She described the developing X-ray techniques that could penetrate layers of paint. To Dinah it was strange and thrilling that the appreciation of art could take on aspects of detection and that after hundreds of years it might be possible to learn a new truth, X-ray an artist's intentions, his mistakes and his changes of mind, or even the economy with which he'd re-used his canvases.

The waitress cleared their plates and Polly asked for coffee. 'Do you think one can care *too much* about art?'

'Why on earth do you say that?'

'I was just thinking – it's almost as if it's like a religion to Dr Blunt, you know. And I feel it myself. I'd almost rather be here than anywhere. Yesterday evening I went to the cinema with David and you know I found myself thinking, tomorrow's Monday, tomorrow's Monday and I was more excited about getting back to work than about spending the evening with David. Yet he's my fiancé! I'm supposed to be in love with him. The film wasn't very good, of course, but all the same ...'

'Nonsense, Polly – of course we all love art. It's Dr Blunt's lecture this afternoon. Are you going?'

'It's been cancelled.'

'Cancelled?' Dr Blunt's lectures were an event. He never cancelled them.

The director's lecture was a high point of Dinah's week. Now an afternoon in the library stretched drearily ahead.

'He'll be back tomorrow, I think. Perhaps he'll give the lecture on another day, later in the week or something.'

'But I won't be able to go to it then,' wailed Dinah. 'You'll let me borrow your notes after, promise.' But the day was ruined by the disappointment. And it did seem extraordinary. What on earth could possibly have led Dr Blunt to do something as drastic as cancel his lecture? It was, as he put it, an immoveable feast.

They returned to the Courtauld together and Polly followed Dinah into the library. Miss Welsh stared in refined horror at Polly's drainpipes. Her faint frown conveyed the idea that a woman in slacks was an appalling inversion of the natural order. Dinah returned to her re-ordering of the books in the medieval section.

Dinah had intended to report back to Dr Blunt about a reference he'd asked her to look up. His absence was even stranger in that he'd particularly asked for her to have the information ready for this Monday. Disappointed not to speak to him about it, she gave the reference to his secretary. Then, to compensate for the disappointment, she decided not to stay on, but to visit her friend Reggie in Kensington.

Seated on the top deck of the 73 bus, travelling west instead of north, she thought of Alan, rising steadily up the ranks of the BBC features department, and soon destined, he felt sure, for television. He had contacts. 'That's the future, Dinah, it'll be back to making films.' He'd again be doing what he'd done in the war, making brilliant documentaries. She was so pleased for him. He was so talented. And surely he could find some sort of job for Colin?

Dinah's friend, Regine, who was now – finally – Mrs William

Drownes, opened the door herself. She looked, if anything, more bohemian than ever these days, her red hair longer and more consciously pre-Raphaelite. But since the birth of her twins she'd been looking a bit too thin, even haggard.

'How are you feeling, Reggie?' asked Dinah as they sat down in the drawing room with their tea and cigarettes.

'Having twins at my age is no joke,' said Regine. 'Thirty-seven is just too old for children.'

'Oh, Reggie, but it was worth it, wasn't it!' Dinah knew it had been difficult, with life-threatening complications, and three months later she hadn't fully recovered. There'd also been The Scandal, of course, which, if such a thing were possible, had been even worse. And the twins had arrived such a disgracefully short time after her marriage.

'How are they? Can I see them?'

'If you like. Later. Nanny's feeding them at the moment.'

Reggie had a real nanny, referred to simply by her surname, Holt, with a proper grey uniform and a round felt hat, not just a Mary, who was Camden Town Irish. Nanny Holt frightened Dinah, who didn't think Tommy would have got on with her awfully well, but of course Nanny Holt did everything the proper way, and would have considered Mary – and Dinah herself – dreadfully lax and lacking in routine.

'Now tell me what's going on at the Courtauld,' and Regine leaned forward, more animated now. 'William's heard some rumours.'

Dinah shook her head, frowning, puzzled. 'Nothing's going on. Why should anything be going on?'

'I've no idea, darling, it's just that one of William's authors – he's written some book about being in the intelligence in wartime, well, it's a thriller, actually, but William says it's based on real life – well, he was hinting at ... I don't know what, really. Dr Blunt used to be in intelligence, of course. In the war.'

'I haven't heard anything.'

'Oh, darling, but then you're not much good at gossip, are you.'

'He did cancel his lecture today.'

Reggie was one of those women who somehow acquired lots of husbands. There was a mystery about her first, pre-war one, met in Shanghai. Then, while still married to her second, she'd no sooner taken a job at Drownes, the long-established publishers, than she'd ensnared or fallen for (according to your point of view) the son and heir. To the conservative hierarchy of the firm, this was more than enough to cast her as the scarlet woman. To make matters worse, her second husband had caddishly divorced her, citing William Drownes as 'co-respondent', something that was simply not done, when he should have behaved like a gentleman and faked a weekend in Brighton with a prostitute to give Reggie grounds for divorcing *him*. It was appalling for a man to drag his wife through the courts as an adulteress and harlot, even if she was the guilty party. Almost everyone condemned Neville Milner as vindictive and small-minded, but that didn't help Reggie, who had to leave her job and languished for months in a moral no man's land, a fallen woman, living in sin, until the decree 'nisi' finally became 'absolute'.

Dinah, who had never much liked Neville Milner, completely took Reggie's side, as did Alan. Alan, however, had been a little more worldly about it: Reggie's a bit of a hell-raiser, you know. Never one to leave a heart unturned. But Dinah had loyally pointed out that Reggie was, well, not exactly beautiful, but so fascinating with those long green eyes and white skin.

'How is William?'

'He's very well – very busy, of course. He's so sweet to me, you know, and he adores the twins. I'm so lucky really.' Yet her manner was tinged with melancholy. 'He has to work so hard. Drownes is doing awfully well, but it takes a lot out of him. And I do get bored, staying at home alone all day.' It quite suited Regine to feel a little sorry for herself; she said it with a little moue that was almost a smile.

'You're not alone, though. There's the twins!'

'They're only three months old, darling, of course I *adore* them, they're simply wonderful, but they're hardly ready for stimulating conversation or a good gossip.'

'You'll have to make do with me, then,' said Dinah, while reflecting that, after all, Reggie, having Nanny Holt, could go out at any time. 'We could go to the cinema,' she said, 'if you'd let Tommy stay here with Nanny one afternoon.' Although, even as she said it, she wasn't sure she could bring herself to leave poor Tommy with the grim, grey-clad one.

'That's a lovely idea, darling. We'll do that – but please do tell me about the Courtauld. I'm desperate to hear about the glamorous Anthony Blunt. He's going to be a Drownes author, you know. William's frightfully chuffed. That's why he's so keen to know what's going on there.'

'Why should anything be "going on"? I didn't see him today. I told you. He cancelled his lecture. He never does that,' said Dinah.

'Well, there you are. So something is going on.'

Anthony Blunt was at that moment seated in another English garden whose lawn ran down to the bank of the Thames at Sonning. His hands clasped between his knees, he sat forward bonily in his deck chair, and made his arguments as limpidly as if he'd been leading a seminar, but with mounting frustration, as he tried to persuade his host – a man he had always disliked, although they kept up a pretence of friendship – not to speak to the authorities about their common friend, Guy Burgess.

'I've *known* for a long time, Anthony. Guy even hinted … he as much as *confessed*.' And now that Burgess had disappeared along with his unbalanced colleague, Donald Maclean – now was surely the time to speak to the police.

'To *rat*, Rees. Is that what you're saying?' Even as Blunt spoke the words he was conscious of the irony. He himself had inwardly ratted or lapsed or just lost his faith or whatever you wanted to call it long ago. His instinct to still protect the friend to whom he was devoted had nothing to do with saving the Cause; it was simply about saving Guy. And possibly himself as well.

five

M CGOVERN HAD MET Miles Kingdom at some official police event, but he could no longer remember exactly when. Such occasions blurred into a general memory of boldly decorated hotel banqueting suites with glaring lights. In the early stages senior officers in important suits chatted pompously to colleagues in whom they saw a mirror image of themselves. Later on, they retreated to the bar or danced to hackneyed big-band music with wives who had spent the evening meekly on the sidelines. Lily had only once accompanied him to a police 'do' and after the sniggering looks the wives cast at her sari, had vowed never to go to one again. He too did his best to avoid them. And if it harmed his career to have a wife who was part Indian, then so be it.

Kingdom had approached McGovern casually, but it soon became clear that this was no chance meeting. 'They say you're good at your job,' was the clue that Kingdom had specifically sought him out. Kingdom would never otherwise put in an appearance at an event like that. He'd appeared to talk casually, but dropped more than a hint that he knew all about the incident that made McGovern's name: an IRA bomb plot, intended to disrupt the war effort, had been prevented, thanks to his surveillance and flair.

Promotion had been the result, but recently McGovern

had begun to feel vaguely dissatisfied with the Branch. So Kingdom, taking his leave with a carelessly spoken, 'Let's be in touch,' had intrigued McGovern. And intrigue was the word, the possibility of work more exciting than the Branch routine, of deeper secrets.

Since that first conversation there had been meetings, hints, suggestions, instructions. McGovern had shared information and investigated suspect individuals for the man from MI5. He'd thought he should mention the ongoing contact with Kingdom to Gorch, but when he did, he found that Gorch knew about it already. Still, McGovern could not rid himself of the feeling that the arrangement – informal though it was – was what Kingdom would have termed 'left field', but that made it all the more exciting. That it was slightly irregular gave it an extra frisson. If it furthered his ambitions, so much the better, but for the time being it was enough that it held out a tantalising promise of new and expanded horizons.

This evening the two men met in an anonymous bar near Victoria Station, where commuters downed a quick pint to get rid of the taste of the office before the homeward journey. Lonely men stared into their drink; over-hearty groups of colleagues snatched a half-hour of freedom between the demands of work and those of the little woman.

McGovern nodded almost curtly at Kingdom and muttered a greeting, but his apparent surliness arose out of uncertainty as to how to address his companion. Clearly 'Miles' was out of the question, but as between 'Sir', 'Kingdom' or 'Mr Kingdom' he had no idea. And the ambiguity was part of the relationship itself. What, after all, was Kingdom? Colleague? Superior? Agent?

This uncertainty was part of McGovern's more general ambivalence, an ever-fluctuating attitude that unsettled him, as he tried not to admire the agent too much, but to keep his sceptical detachment. He even feared it might be deference or snobbery (feelings he'd certainly not learned in childhood) as he looked across the small wooden table at his companion. For Kingdom's father, as McGovern had taken the trouble to find out, had been governor of Madras, his mother a society girl, Lady Vanessa Pyke. One ancestor had been a Nabob, another an officer in the Indian Army. There were landed connections as well.

As if that wasn't enough, Kingdom was also good-looking. Melancholy, greenish eyes stared out of a ruddy face with the daunting inherited arrogance bestowed by two hundred years of imperial rule. He wore his thick blond hair effetely long, to McGovern a gesture of startling bravura, almost anarchistic. On this warm evening he wore a light grey suit and a black tie striped with blue. McGovern was sure the tie meant something, but what – a school, a regiment – he didn't know. What impressed him most and against his will, however, was the man's unshakeable sangfroid. It seemed as much part of him as his elegant suits, his crested signet ring, his heavy watch and his silver cigarette case, the outward signs of that inner sense of entitlement.

Kingdom entertained McGovern with tales of secret-service cock-ups and wartime disasters. His persona of raconteur and connoisseur of black farce seduced McGovern because it spoke to the Scot's own deep scepticism. But Kingdom was more than a sceptic. He appeared to be blessed or cursed with the nihilistic view that life was inherently absurd. His careless cynicism shocked, but that was part of his spell. They were two men of the world, Kingdom implied, who understood the infinite folly of human nature and the futility of hoping for a redemption of mankind. That was, ultimately, the fatal flaw in communism, was it not, its naive belief in human betterment.

Above all, the charm was potent because Kingdom represented a conduit to the hidden world where, McGovern was convinced, the engines of power throbbed and the wheels that changed the world turned. Every meeting with Kingdom was a rendezvous with power.

Now Kingdom brought out the cigarette case. 'How was Glasgow? Your father-in-law's ill, I understand.'

McGovern accepted a cigarette, although State Express wasn't his favourite brand. It flattered him that Kingdom took a personal interest. It also slightly worried him, but Kingdom had never hinted at any knowledge of McGovern's Red Clydeside connection.

'All hell is about to break loose down here,' murmured Kingdom. 'You have absolutely no bloody idea of the fucking catastrophe. Was this the face that launched a thousand ships and burnt the topless towers of Ilium?' He laughed at what seemed to be a quotation, but it meant nothing to McGovern. 'The Trojan horse, anyway. Yes, I think we can say there was a Trojan dobbin. The shit hitting the fan, as the Americans would say, will be as nothing to the Krakatoa of evacuated material that is about to engulf us. I won't divulge the sordid cloacal details, you'll know soon enough. And it's not what I wanted to see you about.' He looked at the tip of his cigarette. 'Although it's all connected.' And he sipped his gin and tonic, a beverage McGovern considered effeminate.

'I need some information about a man called Colin Harris. He's living in East Berlin, but he's over here at the moment and it might be useful to find out what he's up to. I'd like him placed under surveillance. I don't want that stupid police unit, A4 in on it. They're such bumbling fools.'

'You want me to shadow him?'

'I don't care how you go about it. Shadow him, possibly. You might even find some way of getting to know him. Under cover. It's up to you.'

They had been speaking quietly, their conversation drowned in the general noise, but Kingdom lowered his voice still further to add: 'He has a record – a rather odd one.'

McGovern looked round carelessly. They were just two men seated at a table in a pub, alongside other similar men. Yet whenever he met Kingdom like this he felt an invisible field of energy surrounding them, and it astonished him that the strangers who brushed past them were not jolted by its electricity. In no other aspect of his work did he feel this self-consciousness, this excitement.

'Ready for another?' said Kingdom.

Normally McGovern would have refused, preferring to get home to Lily. Tonight with no Lily to go home to, he was happy to carry on drinking.

Kingdom returned with their drinks. His mask was proof against all the slings and arrows outrageous fortune could throw at him. At the end of the day, old boy, it's water under the bridge.

Today, however, there did seem to be a bit of tension.

'Why is this particular subject of interest?'

'Just curious to know what he's doing over here. Might even have something to do with our other little problem.'

'Doesn't sound as if it is so little,' said McGovern casually, hoping to hear more.

'We've been such bloody fools. We've known there was a mole, or moles, for months. We were getting so close. And now two of them have done a bloody runner.'

McGovern stared, trying to take it in. 'Done a runner?' he repeated stupidly. 'You mean – defected?'

'There's no point going into the whole story now. You'll find out soon enough. I just want to know what Harris is doing over here. Bloody poofs – the bloody poof mafia, he must be mixed up in it somewhere. He's staying in one of those dumps in Paddington that's not quite a brothel. We've put a tap on the telephone, but that won't get us far. He'd use a public phone for anything sensitive. He's over here from Berlin. For how long, I wonder. How would you feel about going to Berlin?'

'Berlin?'

'You speak German, don't you? How did that come about, by the way? An unusual accomplishment for a policeman.'

'Policemen aren't all thick.'

'That's not what I meant. I'm sorry if you thought that. I meant *German*. Why that particular language?'

McGovern's olive complexion never flushed red, but his face felt hot. It was so difficult to explain. In part it had to do with his father's communism, a confused compulsion to understand the other side. At one stage he'd even been obscurely attracted to the dark glamour of it all, although he'd soon got over that. He'd gone to German classes as part of his project of self-education. 'I thought it might come in useful,' he said. 'I've studied Russian as well.'

'How very prescient.' Kingdom stared around the hot smoky saloon. Then his gaze returned to his companion. Impenetrable.

'Well ... we might send you off to Berlin. Though actually it's all too bloody late, of course.'

On the day they were to shadow Harris, McGovern reached the office at seven-thirty, only to find that Jarrell had beaten him to it. Indeed, Jarrell looked so pale and dishevelled that McGovern wondered if he'd not gone home at all.

'You've been here all night, have you? You're a wee vampire, are you, Jarrell? That would explain the name. Manfred. Well, the cock's crowed now, you'd better get back to your coffin.'

'My parents – well, my mother – called me Manfred after a work by the poet Byron,' said Jarrell sniffily.

'Oh, really.' And trying not to laugh, McGovern made his way to the records department. MI5 might be in charge of all things communist, but the Branch had records as well. It wasn't difficult to find what he was looking for.

Colin Harris: card-carrying communist; fought in the Spanish Civil War; distinguished World War Two record, fought in Italy; briefly in films after the war. From a police point of view, however, the strangest information was Colin Harris's conviction for the murder of some painter of whom McGovern had vaguely heard – Lily must have mentioned the name. The conviction had been quashed on appeal. The way the report was written subtly suggested that the whole thing had been botched and the prosecution was a mistake based on tenuous evidence – or something more sinister. Either way, whoever had been in charge of the investigation must have been wiping the egg off his face ever since. McGovern didn't recognise the officer's name, but he did now recall the case. It had been big news at the time. After the trial, Harris had reappeared in East Berlin, where he'd been since 1948. A mug shot was attached to the file: bony face; a shock of hair – fairly distinctive, a recognisable face.

McGovern returned to his office with the file and handed it to Jarrell. 'We're to investigate this character. He's in London just now.'

Jarrell read with amazing rapidity. 'A practising *homosexual*. That makes it sound like a religion, don't you think, sir? Practising – like practising Christian. And a Red as well. I shouldn't have thought the two would go together.'

'You'd be surprised, Jarrell. And the right wingers think all the Reds are perverts and the communists think the same about the fascists.'

Unlike Alan Wentworth, McGovern wasn't repelled by deviant sex, it seemed merely puzzling. His colleagues in the Vice Squad, cheered on by the Director of Public Prosecutions, had embarked on a crusade against queers, hunting them down in urinals and posing as perverts themselves. He found that pointless and stupid, a distraction from the efforts of law enforcers who were struggling to contain the Messinas, the gangs, or the real perverts like Neville Heath, who'd raped and murdered a girl while posing as a war hero, or George Haigh, the acid bath killer.

'It says nothing here, sir, about any kind of contact with the Soviets.'

'East Germany's more or less the same thing. It's a puppet regime. They *are* the Soviets.'

'Some people think communism is a virus, a disease, spreading everywhere. But if it's a mental illness, can you catch it, sir? Senator McCarthy thinks so. It's what he said at the House Un-American Activities Committee in America.'

So Jarrell had been doing his homework and now wanted to show off about it.

'But the *Daily Worker* describes what McCarthy's doing as a witch hunt,' continued Jarrell. 'D'you think that's fair? Is communism really a kind of epidemic?'

'You're a wee swot, aren't you, Jarrell, a troglodyte.' Troglodyte was one of Kingdom's words.

'I'm interested, that's all.'

'Good lad. I was only joking. But you can answer the question yourself.'

'I want to know what you think, sir.'

'I don't. Our job is simply to crush subversion. The cause is immaterial.'

'That's Gorch's line. But you don't believe that, do you.'

'No.'

Gorch, like most of McGovern's fellow policemen, was anti-intellectual. Deeds, not thoughts, were what mattered. A villain could believe anything he bloody well wanted to, so long as it remained inside his head. That was all very well, but the seasoned policeman, for all his common sense and practical wisdom, seemed not to understand that ideas were the motor for action. That was another of Kingdom's attractions. He did understand.

'I think communism is more like an obsession than measles,' said Jarrell. 'Or I suppose it could be rather like a hobby. Only not quite the same.'

McGovern thought of his father. 'For many ordinary communists it's just a sense that life is unfair. They want an equal chance. And why not.'

Yet he himself had rejected the faith in equality. He wanted to get ahead.

'D'you think this Harris is a spy, sir?'

'Do you?'

Jarrell shook his head. 'Someone working for the Soviets wouldn't be openly a Communist Party member, would he? The opposite, if anything.'

'On the other hand, he's in Berlin. And Berlin's the front line of the Cold War, and the world capital of spies, and it's also where the Third World War is going to start. But now he's here. So today we're to follow him around London and see if that throws up anything interesting. If it doesn't, we might try something else. We'd best look sharpish, if we get down there right away we should catch him before he goes out.'

That was the point of the early start. Of course, you never could tell. A suspect might stay in his bolt hole all day long and never venture out at all. Unlikely in this case; the man must have business of some kind in the capital, otherwise he wouldn't be here.

Outside in Whitehall, McGovern considered Jarrell's appearance. 'You need a hat. Your hair is a wee bit conspicuous.'

Sussex Gardens was a seedy avenue running parallel with Praed Street, adjacent to Paddington Station. The whole area was pocked with cheap eateries and tearooms where sad transients stared into nothingness. There were newsagents, and barbers' shops where you could buy rubbers. One side of Sussex Gardens itself was lined with dingy mansions. Most of the houses on the opposite side had gone, leaving an overgrown bomb site.

The hotel where Harris was staying was simply two of the tall houses knocked into one. The peeling stucco was grey with dirt. The columned portico – its pretensions so at odds with the squalid façade – was chipped and three steps led up to a door from which the paint had worn away. Grimy net curtains veiled the windows. It was only a few rungs up from a dosshouse or the sort of place where you could hire a room for an hour.

The two policemen stood on the opposite side of the road, although there was little cover. McGovern lit a cigarette. Jarrell didn't smoke.

For half an hour they waited in vain for anyone to emerge. It seemed much longer and every time McGovern looked at his watch he was dismayed to find that only two or three minutes had passed. But at last the hotel door opened. They knew at once the man standing on the steps was Harris. He carried his height well and walked like a soldier. He certainly didn't fit McGovern's vague idea of a homosexual as a womanish fop.

Their quarry strode away in the direction of the Edgware Road and entered the underground station. They kept him in sight through the rush-hour crowd, down the stairs and onto the thronged platform. When the train arrived, they entered by separate doors, so that Harris was between them, halfway along the gangway.

By the time they followed him out into Charing Cross Station, McGovern was feeling the familiar tension that this sort of work involved. You had to be so careful and so quick. The concourse was crowded with commuters heading in from the suburbs, but they kept Harris in sight as he bought a ticket and stood looking up at the indicator board.

At the ticket office McGovern flashed his identity card at the man behind the grille. 'Your last customer – where was he going?'

The clerk stared in surprise, but answered meekly. 'Deal, sir.'

That was that then. Shortage of resources meant they were strictly forbidden to stray beyond the capital. In any case, it was usually suicidal to follow a target out into the country-side. The train leaving for Deal against the rush hour would be carrying few passengers. Harris would almost certainly realise he was being followed.

'No use, Jarrell. He's going to the Kent coast. We can't follow him out of London. Stay here a minute.' And Jake left his companion looking crestfallen while he made for a telephone kiosk – there was a line of them along one wall of the ticket hall – to ring Kingdom.

Kingdom took the news quite casually, but McGovern had the feeling he wasn't pleased.

six

C⚬⚬⚬

H E WOKE SUDDENLY. Bewildered. A gap in the curtains
let in a shaft of dim light from the street, saving the room
from total darkness. Then he remembered. It was the first time
they'd been away together. The only sound, apart from Edith's
breathing, was the sigh of waves against the shingle beyond
the front, as if the sea were sleeping too.

He couldn't see his watch, but somehow knew it was the
dead pit of 2 a.m. He buried his face in the pillow, seized with
the insomniac's terror of unending hours of wakefulness. He
turned over, but he was too hot. He turned over again, but
found no comfortable position. He lay on his back for a while,
rigid as a crusader on a tomb, but his mind had wound itself up
and the interview was ticking away remorselessly in his head.

Konrad Eberhardt had turned out not to be the lofty, serious
European scientist and intellectual Alan had expected. The old
man had been rude, for a start. He'd agreed to the interview
over the telephone, but when Alan arrived on the doorstep the
unkempt, grizzly old bear of a man had claimed to remember
nothing about the appointment.

'I've come to interview you about your work. You were
going to talk to us about it.'

'What is that you say? You're interrupting my work.'

'The BBC, sir. You agreed to talk to us—'

'Agreed to talk to you? Did I? I don't remember this, I don't know who you are—'

Eventually, however, Eberhardt had grudgingly allowed Alan across the threshold and led the way into a cluttered front room, furnished with items that had been modern in the thirties. Alan followed, aware of the old man's smell, the odour of neglect, a mixture of tobacco, ear wax and even, faintly, urine.

While Alan had fiddled with his hefty recording machine Eberhardt had watched him. 'Visitors! I don't need visitors. I had a visitor ... you've been to see me already, haven't you? Didn't you come here yesterday?' He peered at Alan, surly and suspicious. 'Or was it the day before?'

Alan plugged his machine into a dangerous-looking power point that hung off the wainscot. 'May I sit down, sir?'

Eberhardt gestured vaguely at a heavy cubic armchair. He stared bleakly at Alan and then abruptly sat down himself.

'In the current political climate there is a great deal of interest in your scientific work,' began Alan. 'And on your philosophical reflections on that work.'

The old man continued to peer at him suspiciously.

As the intellectual permafrost of the Cold War settled over public discourse, Eberhardt the physicist had become an obscure, half-forgotten figure in postwar Britain, a semi-recluse since the death of his wife. He was still tenuously attached to a Cambridge laboratory, but was not thought to be doing new scientific work. Then, when his friendship with Klaus Fuchs, the convicted atomic secrets spy, became known, an aura of the vaguely sinister had got attached to him, although he had nothing to do with atomic research. Journalists had tried to interview him about Fuchs and hadn't been satisfied by Eberhardt's response. He was tainted by association.

Eberhardt's past in Germany was also mysterious. He'd had a reputation as a Marxist, but one too lofty ever actually to have joined the German Communist Party, the KPD. Yet he hadn't left Germany until 1938 and hadn't spoken out against the Nazis, who in turn left him alone, at least to begin with. This was surprising because Alan had discovered that the old man *had* been a KPD member, but he always denied it and since the war he'd tacked sharply to the right of the political spectrum, swimming bravely, like many others, with the tide.

Then unexpectedly he'd written a book of essays, part science, part philosophy, in which he'd set out some unusual and controversial – even contradictory – ideas.

'Your recent book of essays aroused a lot of interest.'

'Essays?' The old man's eyes seemed to cloud over behind the thick spectacles and he gazed blankly at Alan.

'*The Role of the Scientist: Secrets, Lies and Truth.*' Alan repeated the book's title gently, but with sinking heart. He hadn't expected it to be this difficult.

Yet his mention of the title unlocked something in Eberhardt's brain and in a moment he was in full flow, brushing aside Alan's attempts to cut in with a question, as Alan tried desperately to stem this pouring out of words. At one point Eberhardt talked of a united, neutral Germany, at another of air strikes launched against the Soviet Union. Now he was talking about Germany and being a German, now he had strayed into garbled maunderings about Marxism-Leninism, then moved on to the role of the scientist and finally even entered dangerous territory in denouncing McCarthy as well as Stalin.

After enduring this for some time, accompanied as it was by clouds of smoke from Eberhardt's pipe, Alan managed to drag the interview – not that it could be dignified by such a name – towards safer ground, to Eberhardt's earlier life, his exile in Britain, his family. But just as Alan felt things were going better Eberhardt stood up. 'This is enough,' he said. 'I have no more time. Already I had one visitor. Why do these people want to interfere with my life? He also said he was a journalist. They want me to return to Germany, you know.'

'Return to Germany? Are you considering that?'

'That cynic Brecht went back East. They wouldn't have him in West Germany.' For the first time Eberhardt laughed, a laugh that turned into a rude noise as he blew a mock fart. 'East, West, home is best.' He stood up, was moving around as if looking for something. Then suddenly he turned round and made an abrupt, almost threatening gesture, leaning forwards towards Alan and saying, too loudly, 'You've been here long enough. I've got to make up my mind. Too many interruptions. I don't need visitors. I don't want any more visitors. You'll have to wait for my autobiography. I've written my autobiography, you know. I think that's what could be called in English "spilling the beans".'

Alan moved against Edith's flank and began to be aroused. Only sex would enable him to sleep again. He stroked her buttock and, as she stirred, entered her from behind. The bed creaked, but that was exciting too. By now he knew how to elicit the harsh, urgent gasps she made as she came. They never failed to excite and soon he was groaning too, sounds that faded to a dying whisper along the empty corridors.

But he still couldn't sleep. The Eberhardt interview had been a disaster. Editing would be a nightmare. And it had unsettled him. The incoherence, the anger, the repetitions, the conflicting ideas – this was not the magisterial intellectual émigré he'd expected. His frustration made him more restless than ever. When eventually he dropped off, as dawn whitened the gap between the curtains, his dreams were confused and sinister.

Breakfast, surrounded by the shabby remnants of grandeur in what was reputed to be the town's best hotel, was a dispir-iting experience. The windows were shrouded in sallow net curtains, the florid carpet was threadbare. The coffee was awful, the toast leathery. Edith, however, went at the bacon and eggs with a will. Their affair had hitherto included few shared meals and this was the first time Alan, slightly taken aback by it, had noticed how greedy she was. Then he reflected that he shouldn't have been surprised, for he already knew all about her greed for sex, for attention and, above all, for fame.

'Did the interview go well?' She'd waited for him in the hotel bar while he was interviewing Eberhardt, but on his return, they'd wanted only to get upstairs, gripped by the compulsion of lust.

'It was a disaster! How on earth I'm going to edit it ... he said one or two things ... I began to think he might be paranoid, but I suppose some of these old émigrés have plenty to be paranoid about ...'

Edith asked the right questions and listened dutifully for a while, but Alan sensed she was not really interested. As if to prove him right, she suddenly interjected: 'Why is he living in Deal? It's such a dead end sort of place. You'd have thought Hampstead or Golders Green would have been more congenial.'

'He's not Jewish, Edith. Look – we'd better hurry if we don't want to miss the train.'

'Do we have to, darling? There'll be another one. Let's stay a little longer—'

She moved her hand against his thigh under the prim table cloth and then further into his crotch.

'For God's sake, Edith, this is a provincial hotel—'

But she knew how to excite him and of course they went back upstairs. She'd had her hair cut short so that it fluffed around her sharp face. He'd preferred her in her Evita Peron incarnation, ash blonde hair pulled tightly back into a sort of bagel. Yet there was a curious frisson in making love to this gamine. Her body was voluptuous and not gamine at all, but that contrast only added to the piquancy.

Afterwards he regretted it. It was weak to have let her entice him into the sagging bed and its crumpled sheets again, especially as she became triumphalist, demanding and imperious. 'Don't you think it's time you broached the subject to your wife? Does it all have to be such a secret? Wouldn't it be fairer to tell her the truth?'

He was straightening his tie in the triple mirror, three images of himself multiplied to eternity. 'What is truth, said jesting Pilate and would not stay for an answer,' he quoted, lightly enough, but trying to slam a metaphorical door in her face. Marriage to Dinah suited him very well and he was not about to have that disturbed.

'You know what I mean.'

'We mustn't miss another train. We need to get going. I have to get to the Beeb at least before lunchtime. I want to start work on the interview as soon as possible. It's going to be a nightmare, getting anything usable out of it.'

The wind tossed them about along the front.

'This is exhausting,' said Edith. She took his arm. They had no fear of being recognised here.

At the London terminus the sense of licence illogically persisted, so it was a shock when Alan heard someone shout his name. He looked round at the passengers on the busy concourse – it was well past the rush hour, but people seemed to have become addicted to travel since the war – and recognised the owner of the voice with a mixture of surprise and dismay.

'It's been a long time, Wentworth! When did we last ... 1945, was it? How are you? Good to see you. You're looking extremely well. And Miss Fanshawe – I heard your poetry reading on the Third Programme. The one about the girl in the park was particularly moving.'

'Kingdom!' Alan was completely rattled that Kingdom knew who Edith was, but there was no way out of this situation. It was already too late. They'd been rumbled.

'I'm so glad we've run into each other like this. I was going to get in touch with you anyway. I have an idea for a programme ... Have you time for a coffee?'

'I'm late for work already. I don't—'

But Edith interrupted him. 'Just a quick coffee, darling, I'm dying to hear more about what your friend thought of my work.' She glanced flirtatiously at Kingdom.

Alan had no choice. 'I'm sorry, forgive my rudeness. This is Miles Kingdom, Edith. Miles – Edith Fanshawe, the poetess. But perhaps you've met already.'

'No, but I know and admire your work, my dear. There's a tearoom in the station.' Kingdom strode purposefully ahead of them towards it and inside motioned them to a free table. Seated, he turned to Alan, 'I loved the production of that Jean Paul Sartre play you did. Three people in hell for all eternity. The ultimate vicious circle. Fantastic idea. Sartre's a genius. The ingénue loves the man, the man lusts after the lesbian, the lesbian wants the younger woman. What a sensational play. "Hell is other people!" It was the absolute essence of French cynicism, or was it really nihilism.'

'Existentialism,' said Alan mechanically, but aware only that this was another triangle of hell, the man, his mistress and the friend who knew too much. Not that Kingdom could be described as a friend. Sullenly he watched Edith, who less than two hours ago had put away porridge, bacon and eggs and toast, but was now demolishing a fat Bath bun, while Kingdom tried to draw him into a conversation about the Beeb. Of course he didn't have an idea for a programme. It was just a fishing expedition, to try to find out how many Reds there were in the Corporation. He was subtle about it, but Alan wasn't fooled.

In a futile attempt to scotch any idea Kingdom might have had about dirty weekends by the seaside, he said: 'We were in Deal, interviewing Konrad Eberhardt, the writer.'

'Really?' Kingdom was smoking. 'That's what they call it at the Beeb, is it, a trip to the seaside?'

Edith laughed.

'Remind me who he is,' said Kingdom (but surely, Alan thought, he must know perfectly well) '... some clapped-out, old mittel-European warhorse? Scientist of some kind? Altogether rather passé, I'd have thought. What was the point of interviewing him?'

'He wrote that book of essays about philosophy and the role of the scientist, don't you remember? We thought it might be interesting to find out what someone like that really feels about the Cold War. It didn't go that well, actually. He spoke very oddly at times. Confused, paranoid even, to tell you the truth. Talking about spies and people being after him. He seemed to be thinking of going back to East Germany.'

'Really?' Kingdom glanced from under his lashes and laughed drily. 'Well, he must be insane then. No-one in their right mind would ever do that.'

'He was rambling on about some autobiography as well. Claimed it would reveal all, "spill the beans" was his exact phrase.'

'So you may have a scoop on your hands.'

'I think that's very unlikely.' Alan could bear the situation no longer and stood up. 'I have to go.' Edith rose too. He'd half hoped she might stay behind – but on second thoughts, no, that would have been fatal. She'd have hinted like mad about their liaison.

'Just before you go – piece of luck, meeting you like this. I wanted to have a word about a friend of yours. Colin Harris. I believe he's back in London.'

Another unpleasant surprise; Alan said curtly: 'What about him?'

'I wondered if you'd seen him at all.'

'I have as a matter of fact. Why?'

Kingdom shrugged. 'Nothing, really. I just wondered why the sudden return. We thought he'd settled down behind the Iron Curtain.'

'He's completely harmless, Kingdom, surely you're not suggesting he's a security problem.' Alan's bad conscience about Colin now translated itself into outright hostility towards Kingdom. 'Is this all part of your lot's idiotic belief that all queers are traitors? If that's the case, you can stop worrying. He's getting married to some German girl. Frieda someone. They're thinking of coming back here to live. That's what he said, anyway.'

Kingdom raised an ironic eyebrow. 'A change of direction! I wonder if there's been a political change of direction as well.' He raised his hat and said: 'I'll be in touch,' as they parted outside the tearoom. 'I'm delighted to have met you, Miss Fanshawe.'

'What does your friend do? I thought he was rather a charmer. Quite glam, actually.'

'He's a spook.'

'A what?' Edith looked baffled.

'A spy, secret service.'

'A real spy? How exciting!'

'He's saving us from communism.'

Edith missed the irony. 'My goodness,' she said solemnly. But then Edith was a Catholic. Yet, in spite of knowing that Catholics and communism were chalk and cheese, Alan had been shocked when Edith had declared herself an admirer of General Franco, Spain's fascist dictator. This – a terrible political faux pas in Alan's social circles – did nothing, of course, to cancel out the gripping compulsion of those hoarse gasps, those contortions in the creaking bed, those clenching orgasms. On the contrary, it added to the excitement to be pleasuring a Catholic crypto-fascist, whose groans must bear witness to the knowledge that she was committing a mortal sin.

'Why is a spy called a spook?' enquired Edith. 'What an odd word for it. A ghost.'

Alan had never thought about this. 'That's a good question. I suppose ... well, they're invisible, aren't they; spies, like ghosts.'

'A lot of people don't believe in ghosts and perhaps not in spies either. I believe in ghosts. Actually, I find them easier to believe in than spies.'

'Hmm, spies as apparitions – I like that. A spectre is haunting Europe. A secret, invisible world of conspirators that most people don't know exists and probably, like you, don't believe in. But unlike ghosts, they certainly do exist.'

'Haunting's always a premonition of something bad, isn't it? Who's to say that those who knew us in life don't come back to try to protect us or perhaps do us harm?'

'Well, I hope Kingdom isn't going to haunt us.' But Alan had an unpleasant feeling he might.

They didn't kiss on parting, but he said, as he always did: 'When shall I see you again, darling?' As he hurried towards the underground station he was, however, feeling rather sick of Edith. Too demanding, too ... enveloping. And she never thought about anyone except herself.

Back at work he began the daunting job of trying to edit the farrago of nonsense spouted by Eberhardt. As he listened to the interview before getting it transcribed, he felt increasingly depressed. Perhaps he could splice a few extracts from the material into some wider programme about the pre-war intellectual diaspora from the continent, but he wasn't sure he'd be able to sell that idea. Eberhardt hadn't had too hard a time. He'd never seen the inside of a concentration camp, and had got into England with relative ease, unlike so many of his Jewish compatriots. Yet perhaps even exile itself was enough to blight a life, or perhaps the pain of being a German, a citizen of that disgraced, dismembered land, whose crimes were so frightful, could send you a little insane.

Possibly a programme about scientists ... the scientist had become a sinister figure these days. But with all the atomic stuff that was a hot potato, too much security and secrecy around all that ... And what Eberhardt's political views really were was anyone's guess, so there wasn't much mileage in that sort of approach: Reds who saw the light ...

Alan's own leftish enthusiasms had waned, as he admitted to himself without much regret. He was just another parlour pink, he supposed, whose vaguely socialistic leanings combined quite comfortably with a Hampstead home, a convivial social life and the best of most things money could buy in these austerity times. Perhaps at the end of the day the political fevers and passions of his youth were simply less important than he'd once believed them to be. Certainly, these days he was more interested in Tommy than in atomic warfare, keener to build his career than fuss about communism. But he still didn't like the anti-Red witch hunts, avoided the fashionable anti-Soviet extremes. Which was why he worked for the rest of the day on trying to see how Eberhardt the scientist could be used to demonstrate that it was all more complicated, that it wasn't black and white. His task wasn't easy.

Eberhardt stood in the middle of the room. He was looking for something, but what was he looking for? He was all of a muddle.

His pipe had gone out. He pulled it from his mouth and dug at the bowl with a pencil. By the time he'd got it alight again he'd forgotten that he'd forgotten what he was looking for.

He went for a walk. He went for a walk every day. Sometimes it seemed as if one walk ran into the other with only a blank in between. People saw him as he hunched along the front, a dark figure who'd become familiar, yet who didn't look as if he belonged. Sometimes he muttered to himself, like a tramp.

The plaintive shriek of the gulls as they launched themselves into the wind above the waves surprised him, because he kept forgetting he now lived by the sea and would often turn into a side street, taking a route from his past and becoming bewildered when familiar landmarks failed to appear. The High Street was reassuring, since it wasn't that different from the one in Norwood, where he'd lived in London. Sometimes, on the other hand, he looked up expecting to see the Frauenkirche and then dimly remembered the bombing of Dresden.

The gulls were a puzzle, though.

His routine was still just about intact. After his walk he had something to eat and then got down to work. Ideas crashed about in his brain and untangling them was an arduous labour.

seven

⌒✳⌒

'So they've got rid of that ape, General MacArthur,' said Kingdom, as he and McGovern walked across St James's Park. 'His idea of dropping a nuclear bomb on North Korea wasn't *quite* the move to thrill Uncle Joe, was it. Or Chairman Mao. Just a *tiny* bit of an adventurist, our general. Fortunately our esteemed prime minister has talked the Americans out of the idea. So that's all right. One up to us. All the same, the North Koreans did it – crossed the partition – so why not the Russians in Berlin? That's what you always have to remember about Berlin. That's where they'll invade.'

'Would that no be a wee bit risky?'

'An optimist, eh.'

'Just realistic. The Russians are no so very reckless, would you say.'

'The Red Army has five million men – five times the size of the US army. They're sitting there, across the border, twiddling their thumbs. But you may be right. You probably are. What's in a way more interesting is that Berlin is a hotbed of … how shall I put it? There are thousands of madmen, informers, spies, opportunists, each of whom has his own agenda. That's why someone like Harris is dangerous. Especially now.'

McGovern knew something was wrong. He didn't know how he knew, as Kingdom's demeanour never changed, but know he did, as if he sensed an inaudible batsqueak vibration, an electrical tingle you could barely feel. 'Why d'you think he went to Deal, sir?' He'd finally fixed on 'sir', because you couldn't go wrong with that.

Kingdom did not reply. The chilly spring wind whipped round them. The trees, thick with bursting green foliage, the lilac hanging heavy and scented and the long laburnum tails of sickly yellow, all this vegetation was sinister with new life, aggressively sap green, the grass almost emerald, the sky a blinding white-grey, the flowers garish in a direct clash between new growth and the cruel denial of warmth. Nature green in tooth and claw. McGovern found it oppressive and suddenly wished he were back in Scotland. On a day like this it'd be properly wet, raining in Glasgow, but the vegetation wouldn't be so far in advance of itself and the weather.

Kingdom pulled a copy of *The Times* from under his arm. It was folded to show the obituaries page. 'Take a look at this.'

The early death – from alcohol, illness or both – of Bill Garfield, the writer famous and admired for his stand against tyranny of all kinds, the socialist who'd denounced Stalin, had already caught McGovern's attention. He'd read his books and liked them, if not quite as much as he'd hoped to.

'I thought you might think of going to the funeral. Funerals are so interesting, don't you think? You never know who may turn up at a funeral. When my father died, three of his mistresses put in an appearance. Mamma wasn't too pleased, as you can imagine.'

McGovern swallowed. The scenario was so alien he almost laughed, but that would have been inappropriate. Or so he thought until Kingdom added: 'I thought it was rather amusing, myself. Might be useful to see who turns up at this one. Harris is sure to be there, so you should go anyway. You remember I said we put a tap on his hotel telephone? It was just on the off chance. We thought he'd be careful not to use it. On the contrary. He rang some leftie mate of his. They're going to it together. What does that tell you about Harris?'

McGovern wasn't sure whether the question was rhetorical or not. 'He's careless, or stupid or naive.'

'Exactly. The latter I think, don't you?'

'I suppose he knew Garfield in Spain.' McGovern was guessing, but Kingdom said:

'Good man. You'll know they were on the same side and yet on opposite sides – of the same side, so to speak. Harris was a communist, but Garfield supported the Trots and the anarchists. Most discouraging, the way comrades fall out, don't you think? Must be very tiring.'

McGovern smiled. He was thinking of his father's occasional tirades against Trotskyists, 'ultra leftists' and others who deviated from the party line. 'I liked Garfield's essay on Englishness,' he said.

'Appealed to you as a Scot, did it? I thought it was unutterable crap.'

'We're going to a funeral, Jarrell. Famous writer. Died of drink. Probably.'

'How very sad, sir.'

'Bill Garfield. Heard of him?'

'Of course, sir.'

They alighted from the Bakerloo line at Kensal Green and at once saw the cemetery stretching back alongside the Harrow Road, flanked by a high wall, which shielded it from the general decay of the area. Inside, however, they found a different kind of decay in the flat but uneven sprawl of monuments to the dead. The place seemed deserted. The two of them loitered uneasily along the nearest path.

'Won't we be noticed? Won't they think it odd, complete strangers at their friend's funeral?'

'They'll not be bothered,' said McGovern, and quoted Kingdom: 'You never know who'll turn up at a funeral.' But he wasn't wholly convinced. After a moment he added: 'Your hair's awfully conspicuous, Jarrell. Even with the hat.'

'I'm sorry, sir.' Jarrell tried to squash his new trilby even further down on his head, but the red hair still stuck out.

'You'll have to get it dyed.'

'*Dyed*?'

'Dyeing it will nae turn you into a fairy.'

They had obviously taken the wrong path, because before long it led them to an ivy-covered bank and beyond that rusted railings, and what must be the Regent's canal, so they retraced their steps and started again, this time turning right along a wider avenue. The neglected mossy graves, interspersed with vaults, stood all unevenly on either side. It was a peaceful place, rather as McGovern imagined an ancient ruin would be peaceful.

'The crematorium must be at the far end,' said McGovern uncertainly, but they walked forward and eventually found that it was.

A large group – a small crowd even – had gathered at the entrance. It was easy enough for McGovern and Jarrell to loiter at the edge. At the funeral of a known figure like Garfield, there would be quite a few unfamiliar faces and hangers-on, different groups who didn't know one another.

A hearse crawled along the avenue, followed by a Daimler. Pale, indistinct faces stared blankly from its windows, as if the chief mourners were bewildered to find themselves in this situation. Funerals seemed always to take place in slow motion.

'Keep your eyes open,' muttered McGovern unnecessarily to his sidekick, 'look out for Harris.' He recognised some of the more famous among the gathering mourners, observing them as closely as he could from the discreet standpoint he and Jarrell had chosen. More beards and unconventional dress than you would usually find at a funeral, he thought. There were some homburg hats and bowlers, but a good proportion of the men were defiantly bareheaded and along with the formal suits there were corduroy trousers and even a tweed jacket here and there. The clothing of the female mourners was even more varied, some outfits startlingly flamboyant.

As the mourners began to file slowly into the chapel he noticed two latecomers striking along the avenue. He nudged Jarrell.

Harris was of the bareheaded brigade, but wore a heavy herringbone overcoat and carried a briefcase. His companion was shorter, slighter, and even thinner. His handsome face with high cheekbones and dark eyes was shadowed by a showy fedora. Not something you'd wear if you were trying to be inconspicuous.

'I don't think we'll go in,' said McGovern. 'We'll wander a wee way away and wait for them to come out.'

He smoked to pass the time and he and Jarrell walked among the gravestones peering at the names of the dead. When the mourners emerged the two policemen strolled cautiously nearer. Harris appeared, still with the man in the fedora. Now they were talking to a short, heavy, elderly man, walking slowly forward, one on either side of him. The old man was carrying a holdall and stopped to pull a weighty-looking package from it. This he handed to Harris, who put it in his briefcase. All three then wandered away in the direction of the canal. The detectives followed them at a distance.

At first they kept the trio in sight without too much difficulty, but the back end of the cemetery adjacent to the canal was quite overgrown with richly sprouting ivy and tangled brambles bursting fiercely out of the earth, fertilised by so much human bone meal, and abruptly Harris and his two companions disappeared behind a wall of undergrowth and shrubs. 'Where the hell are they?'

Jarrell shook his head. 'They must be there, where it's all overgrown.'

'Can't follow them there. They'll hear us even if they don't see us and they can't get far because of the canal. We'll hang about nearer the chapel, catch them again when they come back.'

Knots of mourners were still chatting on the path, with that sense of dislocation only a funeral can induce. It was some time before Harris and his companion reappeared, walking briskly past the chapel and towards the exit.

The old man was no longer with them.

That was strange, but McGovern knew they had to follow Harris. However, the two men outpaced them and when they reached the exit they were only in time to see them in the distance as they jumped onto a number 18 bus, and to watch as it lumbered away towards Paddington.

'Actually sir,' said Jarrell, 'I think I know who the old man is. I saw a photo of him in *The Listener*.'

McGovern hadn't thought anyone read *The Listener*, a digest of radio programmes. How typical of Jarrell.

'There's a programme about him this evening, an interview. His name's Konrad Eberhardt. He's some German scientist. Came over here before the war.'

'That's very smart of you, Jarrell. Sharp eyes and good memory.'

'Thank you, sir.'

That evening at home McGovern switched on the wireless to hear the Eberhardt interview. But it had been postponed.

eight

ᴄ⊶ᴐ

THE PALLOR OF THE evening sky was rapidly deepening to a mysterious blue. Searching along the railings, Charles Hallam found a rusted gate and stepped out onto the edge of the water. Beyond the canal, the backs of warehouses and derelict buildings, junkyards and gasometers loomed and the solitude of the canal was only enhanced by the murmur of traffic from the great city beyond, like the breaking of waves on some distant man-made shore. The canal stretched ahead of him, a bend obscuring the way forward as it blurred into dusk.

But the towpath was not this side. It was on the opposite bank. He could not walk home along the canal from here. He advanced on a ledge of land alongside the water, pushing past buddleia and hawthorn, but met a tangle of brambles. There was no way forward. He would have to turn back through the cemetery, now thick with twilight. To gather his courage before venturing back among the graves, Charles stopped for a moment to gaze at the black water. It shivered sullenly, bearing slowly along its flotsam of bits of wood, a creamy foam gathering against planks, a tangle of metal caught on a branch. Then he saw something bigger and heavier in the water. It rolled slightly, sickeningly large, an indistinct shape that, as he watched, heaved slowly sideways to reveal a pale blur. A face, like a swimmer coming up for air, then once more submerged.

A body.

He stared transfixed, paralysed, trapped between the water and the cemetery at his back, where the graves gleamed in the fading light. They unnerved him. Gathering in the dusk they'd developed a silent half-life, patiently waiting as if for those they sheltered to emerge. Then, acting without thought, instinctively, he swung round and launched himself towards the rusty gate, knocking against it as he fled past, running madly towards the exit.

But the entrance gates were locked. His heart pounded in his chest, he was sobbing for lack of breath. He forced himself to stand still, take stock. There must be a way out. There had to be. The wall was high, too high to climb. He followed it, forcing himself not to panic, to move slowly, to calm himself with the thought that there *was* a way out. He followed the wall, stumbling through shrubs, tripping over loose gravestones and imagining a night among the graves, a nightmare, the horror of hours in this uninhabited yet peopled graveyard.

But where the wall ended was the driveway to the crematorium. Its wooden gate was easily climbed.

The relief of finding himself in the Harrow Road exhausted him. He leaned, shaking, against the cemetery wall. What an idiot to have panicked like that. After a few minutes he started to walk mechanically along the road.

The slowly turning body ... should he go to the police? But they'd think he'd imagined it. They'd want to know what he was doing in the cemetery. As he walked on it began to seem like a dream. Perhaps he *had* imagined it. That made it worse. The image had swelled out of his mind, some sick, haunted thought, a secret he could share with no-one.

He walked until he came to a part of the town where the lights were brighter and there was noise and laughter and life on the streets. Of the men, many were black. Some hurried, some loitered, some walked with white girls. It was a different, unfamiliar world, but he was too drained to feel curious about a scene he might otherwise have explored. Only then did he think of a bus and rode the 31 back to Camden Town. After that there was the final walk to Primrose Hill where the canal ran alongside their house.

The body; he shivered. It might be floating closer and closer to this very spot, rolling and heaving towards him. He stood on the little bridge next to the house and peered along the darkness of the water, lit just here by the light from the kitchen. The canal was flat and still, but he stood there for ages, unable to tear himself away.

It was an effort to go in. His mother, Vivienne, whose life had seemed to lose all purpose since she ceased dancing, was back in the mental hospital. In her absence his father had seen fit to invite his widowed sister and her daughter, Charles's cousin, to stay with them. Their visit, and especially its indeterminate length, unnerved and irritated Charles. Luckily he himself was only home for forty-eight hours. He stood in the hall and took a deep breath.

'You're late, Charles. We were wondering where you'd got to.'

'I'm sorry, Aunt Elfie. I lost track of the time.'

'This is Mr Kingdom. He was a friend of your uncle's.'

From the doorway Charles took in the tableau. The stranger was standing with his back to the marble fireplace, smoking, with a glass in his hand of what looked like whisky. He was tall and attractively sleek. He stared out opaquely at Charles, and he was almost but not quite smiling. And wasn't he wearing an Old Etonian tie? Without doing anything, he dominated the room. Aunt Elfie and Judy looked tentative beside him, almost apologetic, but Kingdom was the sort of man who would never apologise for his presence. 'Your aunt tells me you're doing the Navy Russian Course.'

'That's right, sir.'

'Enjoying it?'

'It's very interesting.'

'What made you choose it?'

'Well … it seemed better than doing a lot of square-bashing and then going to Germany or Cyprus or somewhere. I mean, going to Germany would be interesting, of course, but not as a conscript.'

'Germany certainly is interesting, but you're right. Everything depends on the circumstances. You're good at languages? Reading modern languages later on? Elfie says you're going up to Oxford.'

'I'll be reading Greats at Oxford. Obviously Latin and Greek aren't the same as a living language, but the principle's similar.'

'He's very young, you know, Miles. He's so in advance of his age. He did Higher Certificate in one year. So precocious. He was even allowed to join the Russian course early.'

By the way Aunt Elfie smiled, Charles became suddenly and astonishingly aware that she was proud of him. It had never occurred to him that she cared one way or the other.

'Just luck, really.'

The conversation was probably longer than any he'd had since he'd arrived the previous day, silently resentful of the unwanted guests in what he thought of as his mother's house.

Poor Aunt Elfie; even her appearance annoyed him. She wasn't in mourning of course – it was years since Uncle Tony had been killed – but her pleated, dull tartan skirt and hand-knitted grey cardigan subliminally expressed her bereaved status, as did the diamond and sapphire regimental badge brooch she wore at the collar of her blouse. Her wavy, dark hair (shared with both her brother and Charles – the beautiful family hair) was going grey and was rolled up round the back of her neck. Strands escaped at the sides, but not in the graceful way Charles's had, until shorn for National Service, of course.

'We're having a sherry. Would you like one?' Aunt Elfie gestured him towards the sofa. It was as if she owned the place, Charles thought, but he hid his resentment as he sat down, making sure to smile in a friendly way at his cousin.

Judy smiled back at him nervously. Charles was sexually indifferent to women, but not to beauty. Had the girl been lovely, he'd have admired her as he might admire a painting or an animal. But Judy hadn't inherited the family looks. She was a pudding and her ugly school uniform of pleated serge gym tunic and checked blouse didn't help. Navy blue did nothing for her translucent skin and her hair and eyes were the colour of snails, he thought.

He took the sherry his aunt handed him, but he'd have preferred whisky; sherry was a girl's drink. Aunt Elfie treated him like a child, but he couldn't be bothered to make a fuss. It would have been beneath him to show his feelings.

'You really are awfully late, Charles. I was beginning to get quite worried.'

How she fussed!

'I *am* sorry.'

'Where were you walking? It must have been interesting to keep you away so long.' How knowing was Kingdom's smile! Had he thought Charles had been looking for men? Had he somehow guessed ... was *he* ... but Charles didn't think so. Unfortunately.

The body – he'd forgotten for a moment, impaled by the man's stare. Now he remembered it sickeningly turning. He swallowed.

'Not specially.' He smiled faintly, his lids lowered in the manner he'd perfected until it ceased to be conscious and came automatically.

'Supper's ready. We waited for you. My brother is at some

dinner,' she explained to Kingdom. 'He won't be back until late.'

Over fish pie and stewed rhubarb Aunt Elfie and Kingdom discussed the activities of various friends. It was gossip, and didn't interest Charles. All these people they talked about were so old and unknown to Charles. Yet he knew the stranger was watching him, was clearly interested in him. Accustomed to men's interest, Charles knew, however, that it wasn't *that* sort of interest. And, although his thoughts were still queasily in the cemetery, he managed to respond gracefully when they'd exhausted the gossip and Kingdom started to ask him questions, about his interests, his future, even his thoughts on the various crises rocking the world.

'Things in Korea are very sticky. Thank God at least they've sacked General MacArthur.'

Aunt Elfie looked at her late husband's friend with an anxious frown. 'I read in the *Telegraph* they're talking about another war. Surely that isn't going to happen, is it, Miles?'

'The Red Army's right there in East Germany, Elfie. Stalin hasn't given up his plans. Communism's spreading westwards.'

Aunt Elfie said abruptly: 'Shouldn't you be getting on with your homework, Judy? Just help me clear away and then you can work in here.'

Obediently the girl stood up and started to help her mother clear away. To avoid having to be alone in the drawing room with the guest and make conversation, Charles assisted them.

'I'll help you with your homework if you like,' he said.

'Oh – would you?' Judy looked so delighted that he felt sorry for her – so easily pleased.

He began to feel better once he was again seated in the gloomy dining room, which the shadowless glare of the single overhead light did nothing to dispel. Judy placed her books on the table. Charles looked at the Latin. She was only twelve; it was all pretty easy.

'You got it almost all right,' he said carelessly. 'I expect you're good at Latin. Dad says you're very clever.'

His father had not actually said that, but flattery was for Charles a standard weapon. Flattery could get men who thought they were straight as hell into bed with you. It could get you off being disciplined. It helped you get away with things, and getting away with things was Charles's speciality. Lard it on, and everyone was eating out of your hand. Except Christopher, his fellow conscript, with whom Charles was hopelessly in love.

It certainly worked with Judy, who grinned with foolish pleasure. The homework done, she became animated and chatty, but Charles was unprepared for her question about his mother.

'Mr Kingdom said he saw her dance *Giselle* once. It was wonderful, he said. Will she be better soon?'

She couldn't have known it was the wrong thing to say.

Charles stood up and walked towards the window. 'She suffers from depression. It's a – a recurring thing. They treat it with electric shocks.'

'Electric shocks!' Judy sounded horrified.

'It works for a while, but then the effect wears off again.'

An awkward silence filled the room. The overhead light cast an oppressive, shadowless glare.

'I don't remember an awful lot about my father,' said Judy, 'I was only three when he was killed. Mummy thinks I'm heartless, because I don't seem to miss him more, but I was so little.' She was desperate to talk, Charles could see that, and he felt trapped. That was the pitfall of flattery. When followed through, it could ensnare you in other people's feelings.

'I wish Mummy would get married again, but she was quite angry when I said that.'

'Perhaps she'll marry Mr Kingdom.'

'Oh, Charles, d'you think so?'

The eagerness in her voice surprised him. He turned to stare at her. 'Would you like that?'

'He's awfully nice,' the girl said. 'And then, you know, she'd be – she'd be happier, I suppose. She says nobody cares about widows, they don't have a proper place in life.'

Charles wasn't going to discuss the sad lot of war widows. But Kingdom interested him. 'What does he do?'

'Mummy says he's a journalist.'

A journalist. Charles wondered. Kingdom had an air of ... importance, of weightiness.

Judy looked shyly at Charles. 'Mummy says you seem rather bored.'

'Does she? Well, National Service is boring, it's just marking time, really. I'm not at school any more, but I'm not at Oxford either. In between. But I have a project,' he continued, hoping to shock her. 'I'm visiting at least one cemetery every time I come home on leave.'

It had started with Brompton cemetery, where a man who'd once been important to him was buried. No-one knew he'd visited that grave, and his father would have been surprised and shocked if he'd found out.

'Cemeteries!' She was round-eyed.

He smiled. 'D'you think that's rather morbid?'

Now he was thinking about the slowly turning body again.

nine

C⫯⊃

INAH HEARD THE BUZZ of voices even before she saw
the gathering on the pavement outside the entrance to
the Courtauld in Portman Square. She must have forgotten,
she thought, or hadn't been told – being in only on Mondays –
that some famous visitor was expected. There'd been talk of the
king paying a visit, until he had bronchitis (the Hon. Cecily had
hinted it was something much worse, but then she was continually showing off about knowing royalty and aristocrats) and
the visit had been postponed. But someone *must* be expected.
There were photographers in front of the building, banked
up near the door. As she pushed her way self-consciously past
them she could feel the tension, *smell* the seething expectancy.
The jostling and calls of the crowd were quite violent, even
threatening. Not for nothing were they called news hounds.
They'd smelled blood.

Someone detached himself, stepped out and touched
her arm just as she thought she'd reached the safety of the
threshold. 'Dinah! What are you doing here? Gerry Blackstone.
Remember me? Back in the old days – the Wheatsheaf, the
Fitzroy?'

Her wits had deserted her. She stared blankly at him.

'I'm with the *Chronicle* now.'

'Of course I remember.' They'd all been friendly back then,

it was around the time of Colin's trial. But – a *crime* reporter
here, outside the Courtauld ...

'What brings you to this neck of the woods?'

'I'm a student here. What's happened? What are all these
people doing?'

'Be an angel, go inside, see if you can find Blunt.'

'*Dr Blunt?*'

'Don't tell me you haven't seen the papers. You must know
– the Missing Diplomats – he knew them, didn't he? There are
rumours going round he helped them get away. They've done
a bunk – it's all over the *Express*.'

'*Who's* done a bunk?'

Gerry Blackstone grinned. 'Be a sweetie, Dinah, get us the
lowdown – my paper would love an inside story—'

'I couldn't possibly.' She removed herself smartly from his
touch. 'I haven't the faintest idea what you're talking about.'

'Please, Dinah! Come on. I need a scoop.'

But she fled into the building, ran upstairs and into the
library. 'What on earth's going on?'

Miss Welsh was by the bookshelves, trying to sneak a look
out of the windows. She turned, startled, as if guilty, towards
Dinah, who saw that a mottled flush had crept up Miss Welsh's
cheeks. 'I don't know why they're here.' She moved away from
the window. She was doing something Dinah had never seen
anyone do before; she was literally wringing her gloved hands.
'It's terrible. Terrible.'

Dinah squeezed against the bookshelves so that she too
could peer from the window. The pack of hungry journalists
had already grown larger, like a flock of ravens. They darkened
the pavement and spread across the square, holding up the
traffic. 'Where's Dr Blunt?'

'I've no idea.' Tears trembled in Miss Welsh's voice.

'There was someone I know out there, a reporter. He says
it's something to do with – I don't know, I couldn't make

head or tail of it, someone's gone missing, two diplomats or something—'

Miss Welsh made a strangled choking sound as she brought out a creased copy of the *Daily Express*.

'Yard Hunts 2 Britons – On Way to Russia' screamed across the front page. Guy Burgess and Donald Maclean, two diplomats, were missing. They'd crossed the channel on a holiday cruise ship on Friday, 25 May and had last been seen when they took a taxi from St Malo to Rennes. After that they had just vanished into thin air. The photos of the two men at the centre of the mystery fascinated Dinah as they stared blandly out from the page.

Polly pushed open the library door and Dinah turned round to see who it was. 'What's going on? Have you seen Dr Blunt?'

Polly almost danced across the room – insofar as it was possible to dance between the shelves and the table in the centre. She was even more animated than usual. 'He's hiding in his flat, I believe. Isn't it *exciting*!'

'How can you be so frivolous!' cried Miss Welsh. 'Exciting! You silly little girl. Don't you see what this means?' She was close to hysteria, her face now a quite disturbing shade of red.

'Let's go outside,' muttered Dinah. She stood with Polly on the stairs.

'God, she's in a flap,' said Polly unnecessarily.

'I saw a reporter I used to know out there. He said it's to do with these men who've gone off. But how can it possibly have anything to do with Dr Blunt?'

'Dr Blunt was in M15 in the war, didn't you know that?' said Polly importantly.

They lit cigarettes and as Dinah breathed in the smoke she began to inhale Polly's excitement too, but she said: 'So were lots of people,' trying to bring them back down to earth.

'But he knew this Guy Burgess awfully well. And he was – you know – *queer* as well.'

'D'you think ...?' Dinah couldn't even formulate the question.

However, Polly finished it for her: 'They might have been lovers—'

'How do people know they're not coming back?'

'Why should they just disappear? Jeremy says Guy Burgess didn't even tell his mother.'

'Does he know Jeremy's mother then?'

'His *own* mother, idiot.'

'How does Jeremy know that?'

'Oh, you know Jeremy. He always has all the gossip.'

'Well anyway, I'm sure Dr Blunt hasn't done anything wrong.'

'Of *course* not!' agreed Polly. 'But would you say it was wicked to help your friends if ... even if you knew *they'd* done ... something?'

'I don't know.' Dinah spoke slowly. 'But why should they have done anything – anything wrong?' The whole thing was so unimaginable, although, of course, Colin ... they didn't really know what he'd been up to for the past three years.

'I wouldn't report a friend to the police.' Polly was adamant.

'That day he was away. Dr Blunt. The day he cancelled his lecture. You don't think—'

But Jeremy, their fellow student, came running up the stairs before she'd had time to formulate the thought. 'Have you heard the news, darlings! Isn't it frightful – all those vultures out there, hounding poor Dr Blunt. What are we supposed to do? Dr Simon said lectures are to go ahead as normal, not Dr Blunt's, of course, but I simply couldn't do any work. How can anyone settle with that braying gang out there? I'm going to Selfridges to have a cup of tea.'

They dashed down the marble staircase and out by the back way to avoid the reporters. As they hurried towards the department store, the whole extraordinary business began almost to seem exhilarating, an adventure, like playing truant from school. Yet, once inside the store, it was as if nothing had happened. The jostling hysteria a hundred yards away no longer existed. Women in couples or alone were seated at the square tearoom tables, drinking tea and eating cakes and biscuits at ten o'clock in the morning. Women going shopping: that was reality, surely, not this Dick Barton fantasy.

'He's still upstairs apparently,' said Jeremy, referring to Dr Blunt's flat at the top of the Courtauld building.

'Have you seen him?'

'No,' admitted Jeremy, 'but I might sneak up this afternoon, to see if I can get him to talk to me.'

Jeremy, with his mop of curls and warm brown eyes, was loved or lusted after by everyone. He was Dr Blunt's favourite of the moment: not that he intended to do anything about it, he assured them. I only like girls, I'm afraid, he would say, as if that were a failing.

'Perhaps they're in love and ran away together,' suggested Polly.

'Maclean's married,' said Dinah stoutly, having picked up that much from her rapid glance at the *Express*. 'It was his wife who reported him missing.' But of course it wasn't as simple as that. Oscar Wilde had been married. 'I don't *really* understand why everyone is going on about it so.' For in her heart of hearts she did not believe in spies and spying. It seemed like something out of a novel or a film, a fantastic fictional world, both impossible in itself and entirely unrelated to her life of ordinary domesticity. The idea they could be Russian agents ... 'I can't really believe that. That would be – well, extraordinary.'

'It's rather frightening, actually,' Jeremy was looking away, across the tearoom, 'that's there's so much that's hidden.'

'It can't *really* be anything to do with Dr Blunt, though, can it?' asked Polly, but it wasn't a question.

They returned as they had come by the back entrance, but it was simply impossible to do any work. It was not long before Jeremy poked his head round the library door and beckoned Dinah.

'Don't be long, Dinah,' said Miss Welsh, her voice like a wince as if it hurt her to speak. 'We're still very behind with the cataloguing.'

But who cared about cataloguing now? The cataloguing was the least of the Courtauld's problems. There was an air of suppressed panic about the place. The wheels were spinning, but the vehicle wasn't moving. And Dinah didn't know what to do with the new set of references Dr Blunt had asked her to look up.

'Guess what.' Jeremy's eyes were darker than ever with excitement. 'I've just seen him. I went into the office and Miss Lefebvre said he'd rung down saying he had terrible toothache, he simply had to go to the dentist. He wanted someone to go with him. What an opportunity! Of course I said I'd go. We left by the back entrance. We walked round the side and up Baker Street together. Somehow we managed to avoid the reporters. When we got to Baker Street station he said I could turn back. He'd got away from the vultures.'

'How did he seem?'

'How d'you think! Pretty edgy. Tense. And he didn't look well. White as a sheet. He'd been drinking.'

'Poor Dr Blunt. But how did it help, you being with him?'

'Gave him a bit more Dutch courage, I suppose. It gave him the nerve to leave the building. But the main thing was they still haven't realised there's a back entrance.'

'That was stupid of them.'

'Very.' Jeremy leant against the stair rail. 'At one point I thought he might be going to say something – you know, about it all. He sort of cleared his throat and I thought – but all he did was ask me how my work was going. Nice of him to think of that in the circs.'

Day after day the headlines shouted, the rumours grew: 'According to a friend they planned the journey to serve "their idealistic purposes"'; 'Police in Berlin and West Germany have been asked to be on the lookout'; 'Boatloads of police landed in Ischia where they interviewed W.H. Auden, the poet. It was rumoured that his white-painted villa on this sun-soaked island was to have been the end of the line for Burgess'; 'Burgess knew atom spy Alan Nunn May'.

Day after day reporters gathered in Portman Square.

The Missing Diplomats even cropped up at Dinah's peace group. This consisted of just a group of half a dozen women to whom Dinah had been introduced by a local Labour Party friend. Until she joined the group she'd felt alone and isolated in her horror of the atom bomb. To find other women who felt as she did had helped her get a grip on herself. You felt so much better when you were at least trying to do something. They'd been meeting for some time, but only now were they ready to plan their first action: they were going to leaflet a shopping centre.

Instead of discussing this, however, the meeting was swamped in speculation about the Missing Diplomats. It was always the same conversation, Dinah thought. It always circled round the possibility that the two men were Russian agents, communists, spies. The unthinkable. One member of the group said that Guy Burgess was obviously unstable. Surely the Secret Service would have more sense than to trust someone like him – and so would the Russians. A second dismissed all the stories, convinced the men were just a couple of rogues playing a practical joke. A third mentioned Klaus Fuchs, who'd been convicted of treason, but he only gave secrets to the Russians because he believed that science should have no national boundaries, that knowledge belonged to everyone and that the world would be safer if both sides had the bomb.

If only there were real peace instead of the Cold War there wouldn't be any need for atomic weapons, nor for spies. Sometimes when Dinah thought about it all she felt anxious and close to tears. Sometimes she did cry, alone in the evening, seated by Tommy's cot as he slept.

Peace was so important. You'd do anything to stop another war.

Alan meanwhile said the BBC was also awash with gossip. He was burning with impatience to have his say, like everyone with the slightest claim to acquaintance or inside knowledge. All joined the stampede for their moment of notoriety, desperate to have their second-hand moment in the spotlight.

They went to a party the first Saturday after the news had broken. Guests from broadcasting, journalism and the arts drifted through the rooms of a dilapidated house in Maida Vale near the canal. Everyone was talking about Burgess and Maclean.

Dinah stood beside Alan as he argued with some colleagues, speculating about what could have happened, where the two men really were. But not only was she sick of the mystery, it also didn't do to look too dependent on your husband. It was never good to cling; better to roam around until you found someone who was willing to talk to you. And soon enough she found a rather jolly young man with tousled hair and a Fair Isle jumper, who was also bored with the Missing Diplomats and told her instead about the history of cinema he was writing. Later they danced to Jelly Roll Morton and Humphrey Lyttleton records. When there was a slow blues, the jolly young man (the name's Frank, he told her) held her close and she enjoyed that, but then she said: 'It's awfully late – I'd better find my husband.' As soon as she'd said it she wished she hadn't, but it *was* late.

She looked round for Alan and saw him standing with a little group of men and one woman by a marble chimneypiece. The woman was about thirty and was holding court, one arm resting along the chimneypiece.

'Who's she?' she asked Frank.

'Edith Fanshawe; she edits *Poetry Now*.'

Edith Fanshawe's pale, fluffy hair curled round a pointed face in which the features seemed too large. Her eyes were light and there was something imperious and mocking in the way she gazed at her audience. The black dress accentuated her curves in an attractive way, so that you did not notice that she was really rather too plump. When Alan saw Dinah he put his arm round her waist and said: 'There you are. Come on. We're going.'

Dinah was pleased enough to leave. They took a taxi home and during the journey Alan leaned back moodily in his corner. She knew him like that; he was usually thinking about work.

'I enjoyed the party,' she offered, but he merely grunted and she was content to doze in the enclosed space as it carried them through the quiet streets. When they reached home his mood changed again and in bed their coming together was as passionate as it had once always been. He was insistent and demanding, almost angry in the way that both excited and unnerved her.

ten

C✦✦✦Ɔ

MCGOVERN COULD NOT REMEMBER when he'd last stood like this beside a dead body. One of the advantages of working for the Branch was that death was not a piece of rotting flesh on a slab, but an abstract event which had happened somewhere else. Visits to the mortuary were rare.

Every sound that echoed in the white tiled chamber – a dropped instrument, a visceral squelch, the drip of water from a tap – underlined the silence it interrupted. The smell of decaying human offal, blood and stagnant canal water leaked through the lime-juice odour of disinfectant.

The sterilised façade of normal life was pulled away in the mortuary. This was the real event, and an obscene contrast to the good manners of gentlemanly discussions with Kingdom and the colourless boredom of watching and waiting for conspiracies that seldom materialised.

When the canvas sheet was rolled back, a sharp intake of breath from Jarrell hissed through the silence, but Jarrell, whose curd-white skin looked greener than ever in the harsh light, turned not a single carrot-coloured hair at the gruesomeness of his surroundings and the body on the slab (his first, he said). The corpse was not in good shape: a flabby, slack, over-used body; the sallow skin as if pickled in nicotine; the bony cage of ribs and shoulders contrasting with the swollen belly; short, skinny legs like a toad. The coarsely sewn-up cut down the length of the torso reminded McGovern of Frankenstein's monster. There was a pathos about the body, neglected by an owner who'd been more interested in things of the mind.

'It's Eberhardt,' said Jarrell.

'You recognise him?'

'Yes, we recognise him,' said McGovern. 'Any identification?'

The pathologist gestured to a wallet and a bunch of keys. 'These were found at the side of the canal. No money, so robbery could be a possible motive. He died from drowning,' he continued, 'but there's also a nasty blow to the side of the head. The skull's fractured. He was probably tipped into the water while he was unconscious, but he might have fallen in when he received the blow. Impossible to tell, really. He was also ill. He had very early signs of lung cancer, but I don't expect he knew that. I'm not sure he was murdered, but it's a working assumption. And I should say he hadn't been in the water for more than … oh, not much more than twenty-four hours, certainly not more than two days. The body had got caught on a plank near that old cemetery in Paddington.'

'Yes. We saw him two days ago, so it couldna be longer than that.'

It could indeed have been robbery with violence, an assailant who didn't even mean to kill him, who either tipped him into the water or else just hit him and then fled and afterwards the unconscious man somehow rolled sideways off the edge of the towpath and into the canal. But McGovern remembered that there was no towpath on that side of the canal. No robber could have come that way.

'One other thing,' added the pathologist. 'The brain wasn't normal. He was suffering from signs of dementia.'

It was Kingdom who'd instructed him to get down to the mortuary. It shouldn't have been a Branch case at all, and was in fact assigned to DI Slater of the CID, but now it was McGovern's case too, because Kingdom wanted it to be. Kingdom had somehow known about the dead man, but didn't know his identity. This was bound to be awkward. Slater would have to accept there was a security angle, if that was what he was told, but he was bound to resent a Branch colleague muscling in and interfering. It was irregular and could be construed as insulting. But McGovern could tackle that. What he didn't understand was why Kingdom was so interested. It wasn't an interesting case. A body in the canal wasn't unusual. Accident or foul play, it could be either. Even suicide, although someone bent on self-destruction would hardly choose a method that involved hitting himself on the head before jumping into the canal without weighing himself down. Slater might prefer to be able to put it down as an accident, but it ought to be treated as a suspicious death because of the head wound.

Back from the mortuary, McGovern called in at Gorch's office.

'It's a tricky situation. Go carefully,' advised the Detective Chief Superintendent. 'Kingdom's preoccupied with the Burgess-Maclean affair. Everyone's tearing their hair out over there. I'm not too happy he's dragged you into this business, but I suppose they're so stretched ...'

'He wants me to keep an eye on this suspicious death. An old man's body dredged up from the canal. Turns out it's an old émigré scientist.'

'Did Kingdom know that?'

McGovern shook his head.

'Is there some sort of connection with this person of interest he's got you shadowing? The whole thing's tricky. I don't like it. But there you are. We'll just take it step by step. Easy as she goes.'

McGovern returned to his office and began to examine the contents of Konrad Eberhardt's wallet, but he was interrupted.

DS Monkhouse was a tight-lipped young man. McGovern had him as one of the new postwar breed coming into the police force, but then reflected that he himself was more or less one of them too. 'I've been sent to request the return of the dead man's effects, sir. They shouldn't have signed them off to you, sir, with respect. DI Slater wishes to remind you that they constitute evidence, which we need in pursuance of our investigation.'

McGovern leaned back in his chair, swivelling it round at the same time. He loved his swivel chair, a new acquisition. 'You may not know this, but I also happen to be involved in the investigation.'

'Yes, sir, but you are not authorised to be in possession of them.'

'A wee stickler for protocol, I see, DS Monkhouse. Well, how can we arrange matters so that I can carry on going through them? I don't need them for long. Twenty minutes will do.'

'Sir, if you return them to me you can then report to the investigation room and sign for them there.'

'That's a waste of time.'

'It's the procedure, sir.'

'I'd prefer you to go back and tell them I'll be right over with the stuff, in half an hour at the outside.'

'DI Slater says I'm to return with the material, sir.'

'All right. Wait outside in the corridor and when I've gone through it, I'll hand it over.'

'It's needed right away, sir.'

'Yes. By me.'

'It's against protocol, sir.'

The man should have been a bank clerk. 'There's the door. Go. I'll no be more than half an hour.'

'I'll have to file a report.'

'Do so.'

McGovern immediately regretted his rudeness, but the

interruption had ruined his train of thought. Then again, he'd been pretty stuck anyway. He looked at the objects laid out on the table. The large black wallet was shabby, worn at the edges and the inner pockets coming away from their moorings. There were the two keys, one a Yale. There was the identity card, with Eberhardt's address in Deal. There was a card advertising the Polish Club in South Kensington. There was a letter, folded tightly into four. He opened it out, and saw the writing was German. The paper was yellowed. He started reading and realised it was an old love letter. Nothing.

The door opened and McGovern looked up, expecting a further protest from Monkhouse, but it was Jarrell. 'Who's that bloke in the corridor? He looks cheesed off.'

'He's waiting for me to give him back the canal stuff, which he says we have no right to. CID don't like us nosing about in their cases. But it's our case too. I'm keeping him hanging about so you can take the keys and get copies cut. Be as quick as you can. When you get back he can take the stuff away. It'll not be telling me anything more.'

Slater would probably take the trouble to search the old man's house, but he'd not think it important and the search would be superficial, a going through the motions exercise. In any case, he wouldn't be looking for what McGovern and Jarrell would hope to find.

It was less than half an hour before Jarrell returned with the keys. McGovern slipped the originals into the large envelope with the wallet. He opened the door and handed them to Monkhouse. 'Sorry I was a wee bit curt earlier. Please thank DI Slater. Apologies for the delay.'

'Sir.'

McGovern turned back into the office and said to his sergeant: 'D'you feel like a day at the seaside? We're taking a trip to Deal tomorrow.'

♦ ♦ ♦ ♦ ♦

The Yale key opened the door. McGovern sniffed a smell of stale tobacco smoke underlaid with the smell of dry dust, paper. It wasn't the sour smell of a house used to too much cooking and not enough cleaning. There'd been little of either in this house. He stood still for a moment, getting his bearings. A door to the left was ajar and led into a living room. He walked slowly in with Jarrell following and looked round: books on shelves that lined three walls; a rather angular utility sofa placed against the window wall; and a desk near the back wall, on which stood a fairly new Underwood typewriter, a battered wooden in tray, a bottle of ink, blotting paper, a writing pad and some pens and pencils. A kitchen chair was drawn up to the table, tidily tucked in; and everywhere, on chairs, on the table, on the floor, piles of papers. 'Have a look out the back, Jarrell. And upstairs. I'll do this room.'

It would take hours to go through all the books, let alone the papers. People persisted in hiding money or documents between the leaves of books. It was not particularly safe, because the trick was known to burglars and a determined one would do what McGovern was doing now, take each book out, shake it, look behind it and return it to the shelf. His hands were soon covered with dust. There were many scientific books in German and English. There were also German editions of Marx and Engels, of Lenin and Trotsky, of Hegel, Kant and Feuerbach. There were other authors he'd never even heard of. There were also volumes in English and French: novels by Balzac, Dickens, H.G. Wells, Arnold Bennett, Thomas Hardy, Jean Paul Sartre, thrillers by Simenon and Dashiell Hammett. Had the man ever done anything *except* read? McGovern worked his way through them mechanically, trying not to look at the contents. He was familiar with some of them. In his line of work a superficial study at least of the political ideologies he was paid to combat was, if not mandatory, at least desirable; or so he told himself to justify his extensive reading, which he was able to pass off as 'research'.

Eventually he became so bored that he turned to the papers. And halfway through the second pile he at last found something interesting. It was a letter typed on headed writing paper; the address was the Progressive Travel Agency, near Baker Street.

> *Sehr geehrte Herr Dr. Eberhardt,*
> *Die Fahrkarte sind bereitet. Sie können die abholen, oder wenn*
> *Sie lieber will, kann ich sie auf dem Postweg schicken.*
> *Mit freundlichen Grüssen, Alex Biermann*

It wasn't much. But it was something.

eleven

⤙✦⤚

THE TRAVEL AGENCY stood in a side street off West-
bourne Grove. McGovern had never been inside a travel
agency before, was barely aware of them. It was taken for
granted that Lily and he went home to Glasgow for their
holidays and they were quite happy with the arrangement,
which included trips into the countryside, to Loch Fyne and
as far as the Mull of Kintyre. But a travel agency was a sign of
the times, he supposed, that people were travelling more now,
going abroad, currency restrictions lessening. He looked at the
alluring poster in the window, illustrating azure skies and a
turquoise sea, and allowed himself to contemplate the idea of
continental hedonism.

'Have you ever been to the Côte d'Azur, sir?'

'If you look closely, you'll see it's the Black Sea, Jarrell.
Sochi. But yes and no, if you count the desert as a Mediterra-
nean holiday. And yourself?'

'I've been to Brittany.'

The door clicked softly behind them. The man facing the
detectives from across his desk looked as though he was wearing
make-up, his high colour as if rouged. The flowing chestnut
hair and purple corduroy jacket suggested an actor. The smile
and booming greeting seemed equally exaggerated. The young
woman, seated at a second desk tucked into a corner, was also

brightly dressed in a flowered cotton frock and red-rimmed spectacles that matched her lipstick.

'How may I help you? Please take a seat.' The man was like a master of ceremonies, thought McGovern, dazzled by the elaborate gestures and flashing smile.

'I believe a Mr Alexander Biermann works here.' The travel agent frowned. His manner was so theatrical that McGovern decided the surprise was genuine. Or was it more than surprise? McGovern thought a touch of panic flickered across the highly coloured mask. The woman in the corner scraped her seat against the floor as she rustled through a folder of papers.

'Alex ... Mr Biermann. Yes, he's employed here. Or rather – he was. He's just left us, I'm afraid. May I ask in what connection ...?'

'May I sit down?' McGovern felt he would be less threatening if seated.

'Of course – of course—'

McGovern sank into one of the wicker basket chairs provided for clients and gestured to Jarrell to do likewise.

'It's in connection with a drowning. A body was found in the canal. Among the dead man's effects we found a letter from Mr Biermann to the dead man from this agency concerning some tickets.'

The travel agent cleared his throat. 'As I said, Mr Biermann is no longer here, in fact I believe he's away from London at the moment.'

'On holiday? On business, Mr ...?'

'Harvey Lefanu. Director of the ProgressiveTravel Agency.' He leaned forward and held out his hand. McGovern disliked its clammy feel.

'He's on holiday in Yorkshire, I believe. He left yesterday, as a matter of fact.' Harvey Lefanu looked down, away, anywhere but straight at McGovern. He blinked, batting his lashes.

'Do you know anything about this letter Mr Biermann

sent?' And McGovern pulled Biermann's letter from his inside pocket, unfolded it and handed it to Lefanu.

The travel agent took it. 'Dear Dr Eberhardt—' He looked up. 'You're investigating *Eberhardt*'s death? I saw *The Times* obituary yesterday. A shocking thing ... but surely—' And he looked questioningly at McGovern.

'The circumstances of death aren't clear.'

'"The tickets are ready. You can pick them up at any time, or, if you prefer I can post them to you,"' read Lefanu. 'This is what we do, Inspector. Arrange holidays. Provide tickets.'

'Presumably the tickets are still here somewhere.'

Lefanu gestured vaguely. 'Do you know anything about this, Doreen? Where did Alex keep his tickets for collection? In his desk, I suppose.'

'Of course, Mr Lefanu, where else.' The young woman stood up and walked over to an alcove at the back of the agency, where a third, smaller desk was located. She opened each of the three drawers and looked through the contents. 'They're here,' she said, but made no attempt to hand them over.

'I'd like to have a look at them, if you don't mind.'

The young woman handed them to him and continued to stand beside him. She smiled brightly at Jarrell, who appeared to be admiring her.

McGovern glanced at the tickets and passed them to Jarrell, who murmured: 'Destination Dresden.'

McGovern had got it into his head that Alexander Biermann was the man in the fedora who had been with Colin Harris and, at one point, with Eberhardt, at the funeral. It was so obvious. It hit you in the face. Those two must be responsible for Eberhardt's death. Yet he knew how dangerous it was to jump to conclusions. It was reasonable to have suspicions about Harris and his companion, but there wasn't a shred of evidence that that companion was Biermann. You had to go by the facts. Facts, facts, facts. Don't invent your own conspiracy theories,

Gorch always said. There are enough of those around already.

'When will Mr Biermann be back?'

'He's only away for a few days. He's back next – Wednesday, is it, Doreen?'

'Yes,' said Doreen, 'but he won't be here. He's starting a new job. Why are you so interested in him?'

'We're investigating what may be a suspicious death,' McGovern said cautiously.

'You're not suggesting Eberhardt's death had anything to do with Alex!' protested Lefanu. He looked horrified.

'We're simply trying to find out everything we can about how he died.'

'But why all these questions about Alex? He hasn't done anything wrong.' Now Doreen sounded rather shrill.

Lefanu was looking alarmed. 'The police are only doing their duty, Doreen.'

'We're interested in why Mr Eberhardt was planning to travel to Germany,' said McGovern soothingly. 'We have hardly anything to go on. These are simply routine enquiries. We just wondered why the deceased would have used this particular agency. He lived in Deal, seemed something of a recluse. We just thought there might be some connection. I'm not even altogether clear what the work of a travel agency involves. I've never even been abroad myself. Except to North Africa with the Eighth Army, but that doesn't count.'

Lefanu still looked anxious, but he answered politely: 'We arrange tickets for rail and coach, also air tickets. We organise hotels, we can arrange special trips. Effectively, a travel agent undertakes all the arrangements for a holiday, relieving the client of the work and anxiety involved in doing it for himself.'

'And people mostly travel where – within the British Isles, to France, Holland, further afield sometimes, to the colonies for instance?'

'We specialise in slightly more adventurous destinations,'

put in the young woman. 'We're trying to open up the market in Yugoslavia, Hungary. We organise peace tours.'

'And Germany too? Does anyone want to travel to Germany now?'

'Mr Biermann was exploring that possibility.'

'It's a German name, Biermann. He's a German national, is he?'

'Oh no,' said the girl, 'he came here as a child. His parents had to leave Germany because of the Nazis. They're all British now.'

'You don't have a photograph of him, by any chance?'

'No. Why should we?' Lefanu's smile revealed obtrusive teeth. He suddenly reminded McGovern of Little Red Riding Hood's wolf.

'I assume you have his address, though. I'd be grateful if we could have that.'

'Well – is that necessary?'

'It would be helpful. Mr Biermann's not in trouble. But he might be able to clear up one or two things about Konrad Eberhardt.'

'Yes, yes ... of course ... Doreen?'

The young woman wrote out an address on a notepad and handed the sheet to Jarrell with a bright smile. As the detectives left, Jarrell looked backwards.

'Nice to meet you, miss.'

Outside he commented: 'Quite a looker.'

McGovern bought a midday edition of the *Evening Star*. The 'Missing Diplomats' again. Day after day it went on. They'd been seen as far apart as the mid-west and southern Italy. The speculation ranged from the sinister to the grotesque. McGovern was keen to talk to Kingdom about it, but he was unreachable.

They found a café, where they ordered cheese sandwiches.

'That place is a front, Manfred.'

'A front, sir?'

'A laundering outfit.'

Jarrell frowned. 'Money laundering?'

McGovern shook his head. 'Laundering people. That's what a front like that is for, or partly. Nothing criminal. It's just a useful way of giving Party workers a veneer of respectability. Peace tours – that gave the game away. Whenever you hear about peace tours, Women's International League for Peace and Freedom, that sort of thing, you know it'll not be a million miles away from the Communist Party.'

'But how is it a front? Aren't they really a travel agency?'

'They certainly *are* a travel agency, but of a special kind. Holidays for comrades eager to travel to the Eastern bloc to see socialism at first hand; trade union tours to the Soviet Union. But they do something else more important. Say there's someone who's been working for the Party, been a Party bureaucrat, but now he wants a change, or he wants out, or the Party wants him to do something else, then when he applies for a job it'll not look so good if all he's ever done is work for the Communist Party. He'll not get many job offers that way. So instead he works his passage via the Progressive Travel Agency or some other similar organisation. Then when he applies for another job, no-one will know he's ever worked for the Party. He's just been employed by a travel agency.'

'Oh.' Jarrell looked rather blank as he sipped his squash. After a while he said: 'The girl, sir. Suppose I hung about and got her on her own. Would she talk some more, d'you think?'

'She probably wouldn't, Manfred, but I suppose it's worth a wee try.'

When Jarrell returned to the office the following morning he looked rather pleased with himself. He hung his hat on the hook behind the door and sat down. 'Well, I saw Doreen Smith yesterday evening.'

'You've seen her already? That was quick.'

'I hung around outside the travel bureau at the end of the afternoon and waited till she came out. She was on her own. The owner didn't seem to be there. We went for a coffee and got on like a house on fire.'

'I'm thrilled, Manfred. Tell us about it.'

'There's no need to be sarcastic, sir.'

'I'm not.' But McGovern had been, he knew, and the reason was that it was difficult to imagine his assistant chatting up a girl. But he swallowed his grin and tried to look serious.

'She's the friendly type, you know. Bit of a flirt, if you know what I mean,' said Jarrell primly. 'Turns out she was stepping out with Biermann. She said she knew he had a serious girl-friend, but she didn't mind – it was just a flirtation, they weren't going steady or anything. But I think she must be a bit sweet on him because I asked her if she had a photo of Biermann and she had. And Biermann *is* the bloke who was at the funeral with Harris.'

'Good. Did you find out anything else useful, apart from about Biermann's love life?'

'It wasn't difficult to get her talking. I kind of explained we were only interested in Eberhardt, we weren't after Biermann and I think she thought telling me about him would persuade us he was really, you know, okay, in spite of being a communist. It was all about how marvellous he was, an idealist, wants to make the world a better place, that sort of thing. He used to be on the *Daily Worker* but then he decided he wanted to do something different, not sure what. I tried asking about Eberhardt and according to her Biermann knew him pretty well. His family knew him back in Germany, and they stayed in touch over here. Biermann visited him a lot. She said they used to discuss things, politics, mainly. Talkative young lady.

The only thing she was a bit evasive about was his holiday in Yorkshire, she wouldn't say much about that.'

'You'll be seeing her again, I hope? You could maybe find out more. No mention of Harris, was there?'

Jarrell shook his head. Faint colour appeared on his cheeks. He was blushing. 'I'll do my best, sir. We didn't make a definite arrangement, but we sort of left it I'd get in touch.' He stood up and took a little turn round the room. 'I tell you one thing, sir. The Alexander Biermann she was talking about sounded like a thoroughly good sort.'

'Idealists *are* good people, Jarrell. Haven't you discovered that yet? They're always working for the betterment of mankind. The trouble is, mankind just wants to go to the dogs in as pleasant a way as possible.'

twelve

ᑐᖏᑐ

TOMMY'S BATH WAS READY, but when Dinah tried to remove Tommy's vest he stiffened his body and started to yell. The sound of the doorbell was both a relief and a nuisance.

'Who on earth can that be, Tommy? Did Daddy forget his key?'

But Alan never forgot his key.

She hurried downstairs, still holding the child. 'Colin, how lovely ... unexpected—' Tommy, hoisted against her shoulder, had forgotten to cry now. He stared at Colin and stretched out a hand as if in blessing.

'Is Alan around?'

'No, he'll be back in a while, I'm not sure when ... You'll have to make do with me, I'm afraid.'

'I'm sorry, I'm disturbing you.'

'Of course you're not. Tommy's just having his bath. Come upstairs. You can watch. We can talk. And then I'll get you a drink.'

Colin perched on the lavatory seat lid in the steamy bathroom, while Dinah knelt and rubbed soap over Tommy's slippery body. Tommy sucked his rubber duck and then bounced it on the water.

'Big splash Tommy!' Dinah looked up at Colin. 'He loves the water.'

'He's a dear little chap.' It was the first time she'd seen Colin smile.

Dinah wrapped Tommy in a towel. 'Why don't you go downstairs? I'll just get him into his pyjamas. He can play a bit more. It's really his bedtime, but it won't hurt him to stay up a bit later for once.'

Colin seemed bony and huge in the crowded bathroom. When he stood up he nearly knocked over the pail of dirty nappies. It was better once they were downstairs in the sitting room.

'Is a cup of tea all right? I don't think there's anything stronger.'

Once they were settled with their tea she sat back in the armchair with Tommy on her lap. 'You seem a bit worried, Colin. Is something the matter?'

'I think I'm being followed.'

Dinah stared at him. She did not believe him. He wasn't seeing things in the right perspective. He must be exaggerating.

'I can see you don't believe me, but it's true. I'm sure of it. I've seen this red-haired man more than once. Carroty red. Unmistakeable.'

'Are you sure?'

'I wondered if Alan – I mean, I know he has contacts. He knew this Guy Burgess character, didn't he?'

'Not really. He'd met him once or twice, that's all. But what are you saying, Colin? What has that got to do with it? And how could Alan help?'

'I don't suppose he can. It's just that I thought he might know one or two chaps in MI5 and could find out what's going on.'

Dinah was jigging Tommy on her lap. She played with his toes. 'This little piggy went to market, this little piggy stayed at home ...' But all the while she was thinking and thinking, thoughts winging through her mind in a dark cloud of dread.

'He doesn't know the first thing about MI5, Colin. He'd never even mentioned Guy Burgess until all this happened. Anyway I don't understand. Why should anyone from MI5 be following you?' She observed Colin from over Tommy's head. He hadn't changed. He'd always been so troubled and unhappy. She'd had endless sympathy for him back then, but now with her adult life, a wife and mother, she was a little impatient. Colin just had to grow up and not go around endlessly trying to save the world.

After a bit Colin said: 'Of course I've been in touch with Party members in Berlin. Germans I mean. Why shouldn't I? It seemed quite a normal thing to do when I arrived. But now I'm beginning to wonder if … does MI5 think I'm some kind of spy? I suppose it's a crime to be a communist these days. This bloody Cold War.'

Dinah loved the feel of Tommy's warm little body close to hers. She kissed his ear. 'Oh, Colin, why should anyone think you're a spy?' She hugged Tommy and felt sad herself and weary with all the talk of war.

'Well, I'm sure I'm being followed.'

If only Alan were here. He might have been able to talk some sense into Colin. Colin was over-dramatising everything and feeling sorry for himself. She wished he'd go away. She couldn't stand pitying him. It made her feel hopeless and impatient because it was all so wrong and so stupid.

Tommy wriggled and wriggled. He began to rub his eyes. He was tired. He needed to go to bed. Dinah hoisted him up against her shoulder and rocked and patted him quiet. 'So you're in touch with the communists over there?'

He sat up straighter. 'Why shouldn't I be? They're running a legal government. I'm *living* in East Germany anyway.'

'I'm sorry. I didn't mean to imply you shouldn't be.'

'No, I'm sorry, I shouldn't have snapped. And anyway I

don't see much of any – well, activists, you know. Everyone's too busy rebuilding the country.'

Tommy had started to grizzle. 'He's tired. I need to get him to bed.' Dinah stood up, the child balanced against her shoulder.

'I mustn't keep you. I'd better be off. Alan won't be back till later, you said.'

'I suppose you could try the Stag's Head – near Broadcasting House. He sometimes has a drink there after work. Or the Gluepot. That's another pub he goes to.' Alan had said he'd be back around eight. Dinah didn't want to say that, in case it was taken as an invitation to stay for another hour or so, but guilt forced her to add: 'You're welcome to wait here, of course.'

'I think I'll push off. Thanks all the same.' Now he sounded annoyed, resentful, but it wasn't her fault that Alan was late. She didn't like it either. Once Tommy was in bed she felt lonely, but loneliness was better than Colin in this mood.

She stood on the doorstep. By the little gate he paused and raised his hand. 'It was lovely to see you, Dinah. I'm sorry—' But sorry for what she wasn't quite sure as he disappeared along the alley that led to the road by the churchyard. She put Tommy to bed and then started on the dirty nappies.

Edith was often to be found these days in the pubs around Broadcasting House frequented by the Third Programme crowd. Even when there was no hope of going back to the flat with his mistress (he often wondered why that word was in itself exciting), Alan found it enjoyable in a masochistic way to be there with her, their secret liaison carefully concealed, he hoped, from the circle of men that invariably surrounded her. Of course it was true that the conversations in the saloon bar usually focused on Third Programme matters and so could at a stretch be described as work by other means, but Edith was a more pressing reason for his presence.

He'd noticed that she seemed especially to fascinate older men, and this made him wonder if he himself was getting old, but that was stupid, he was only thirty-five and hadn't even reached his prime. Actually their affair, while not exactly common knowledge, wasn't quite as secret as it ought to have been, yet that also excited him. He was the one who had been chosen. On the other hand, when the affair went through moments of tedium and irritation, he reflected that it was hardly a triumph to have been preferred above a bunch of scruffy intellectuals.

On this particular evening they were gathered in the familiar saloon bar of the Stag's Head with its oak panelled walls, inlaid rather strangely with squares of tartan, each different, and the name of the clan to whom the tartan belonged written in gilt gothic lettering. He wondered if the decor was meant to reference the monarch of the glen.

Edith barely looked at Alan, she was holding forth about T.S. Eliot. He sometimes felt she was a little too keen on playing the role of dedicated poetess. He'd secretly have preferred a woman who was more muse than genius and as he listened to her views on Eliot, he was longing to kiss the pink neck where it rose from her blue angora jumper.

A group of car salesmen nearby discussed the economy and the price of petrol. Alan realised he felt bored. He finished his drink and decided to leave. There was no point in lingering here. He placed his glass on the mahogany counter and bade a casual farewell to the company in general, careful not to single Edith out.

As he approached the door it was pushed open.

Colin saw Alan at once and grabbed his arm. 'Were you just leaving? Glad I caught you. Dinah said I might find you here.'

'Dinah did?'

'I've just come from Hampstead ... I need to talk to you—'

Alan looked round furtively. Perhaps Dinah knew more

than she let on. Perhaps she'd guessed ... but surely not. She knew he had a drink from time to time. There was nothing to fear. 'Well ... I don't want to be too late – Dinah's awfully good about my long hours. But as you're here – of course. What can I get you?'

They found a corner away from Alan's friends, although Alan noticed out of the corner of his eye that Edith and one or two of the others looked across inquisitively. 'What's this all about then?'

Colin, smoking furiously, poured out a confused story, which Alan found hard to follow. The main point seemed to be that Colin thought he was being followed.

'I just don't understand why anyone should be following you,' Alan said. 'What would they think you're doing?'

Yet he remembered Kingdom's interest in Colin and began to feel Colin was not being straight with him, that he was holding something back. Nor was it clear to him what was driving his friend away from Berlin and back to London. 'Why are you really marrying this German girl?' he asked. 'Are you really in love with her? I mean ... in the old days ...' He couldn't bring himself to be explicit.

Colin shrugged. 'Old Schröder, her father, is very unpleasant. Frieda's desperate to get away from him. She just wants to leave, and ... it just seems better, that's all. Or – that's what I thought, although now I'm not so sure. You see, there's been a complication. Someone I met – well, he's died. You must have seen it in the papers. Konrad Eberhardt. He was very well known.'

'Eberhardt! I interviewed him only a week or so before his body was found. I didn't know you knew him.'

'Well, *they* know I knew him, I'm sure of it. And ever since he died I've been followed. And actually I didn't really know him, not exactly, but a friend of mine ... it's all rather involved. Only now they seem to think he was murdered, don't they, and

I'm just afraid that somehow they'll pick on me, that they'll try to pin it on me.'

'Don't be crazy – that's all in the past.'

'But they tried to frame me then, so why not now?'

'For God's sake – look, don't start getting a persecution complex. No-one's interested in you. All they can think about is Burgess and Maclean.'

'Then why am I being followed?'

'Colin.' Alan tried to keep his temper. 'Look, calm down. Let's talk about this sensibly.'

'You think I'm raving? I tell you, I've seen him. Following me.' He stood up jerkily. 'I'd better be going. It's hopeless talking to you.'

'Come on, old chap. Don't be like that. I'll walk to the underground with you.'

Colin strode furiously along Oxford Street, so that Alan found it hard to keep up with him. 'D'you think you're being followed now?'

Colin also glanced back. 'I don't think so. I don't know. But you don't believe I am anyway, do you? I only came looking for you because I thought you might be able to help.'

'Look, I do want to help, but—'

'I don't like to keep asking you for favours.' Colin was slowing down a bit now and seemed calmer. 'It was just that I wondered – if you did know anyone – whether you could find out what's going on. You knew Guy Burgess, didn't you?'

'Very slightly.' Alan's reply was icy and intended to be. In the first days of journalistic hysteria he'd rather exaggerated his acquaintance with Burgess. Then there'd been a self-important thrill in discussing it. To think that men you'd known socially, had even worked with, could all along have been cloaking their real beliefs and secret activities by inventing a false self, an alternative personality. Extraordinarily interesting! At first everyone had wanted a piece of the action. However, as time passed and it seemed more and more likely that the missing diplomats really had been spies, the boastful voices fell silent. One didn't want to be smeared by association.

The last thing he wanted now was to give Colin some crazy idea that he had anything to do with spies and spying. That Colin had even mentioned the name annoyed him. And you never knew what Colin in this insane mood might do – go blabbing to someone...

'You see, I can't help wondering – they might think I had something to do with all that, that I helped them get away.'

If this was a confession, Alan knew he absolutely didn't want to hear it. They stood by the underground entrance. The crowds pushed past them, heads down, weary, self-absorbed.

'What on earth makes you say that?' He searched in his pocket for his cigarettes and shuffled one from its pack. 'Sorry—' and he offered the packet to Colin.

Colin was not so far gone in his anxiety as not to respond to Alan's tone of voice. 'Oh, don't worry. Of course I didn't have anything to do with it. But ... oh, what's the use? You wouldn't understand.'

'No,' said Alan, irked by the bustle around them and raising his voice against the grinding sound of a bus turning the corner, the bronchitic wheeze of brakes, the general traffic rumble. 'I don't understand. I don't understand what you're up to or what you're doing in East Germany.'

'Well, no, people like you never understand, do you?' And Colin turned towards the mouth of the underground station.

Alan grabbed his arm. 'Hang on. It's just that – look, when I saw you I assumed you wanted to know if I'd done anything about – about seeing if I could get you some work. And the fact is, I have tried, but it isn't easy.'

Colin stared. 'I didn't expect anything to come of that.'

'Well, I am trying. Have you got a phone number where you're staying? There are one or two leads—'

'I'm going back to Berlin the day after tomorrow.' But he gave Alan the number of the Paddington hotel.

A few evenings later Kingdom rang to suggest a drink. Alan suggested the Stag's Head, but Kingdom preferred an obscure bar in Soho, which Alan immediately understood. The Third Programme crowd would have been sure to ask questions.

Miles Kingdom was in an affable mood. 'Oh, don't stick to beer, old man, I'll sock you a gin and tonic.'

'Thanks. I'd rather have a whisky, actually.' The sudden reappearance of Kingdom was slightly disturbing, but he thought he might as well get what he could out of it.

'You're looking well, Wentworth. You remind me of a Jewish joke I heard recently. "When you're in love, the whole world's Jewish."'

'I'm not quite sure I get the point.' But Alan knew it was a reference to Edith. Only he wasn't in love with Edith ... was he?

'How are *you*, Miles?'

Kingdom smiled. 'Well, you know, old chap, the best of times, the worst of times.'

'I can hardly see how it's the best of times.'

'Every cloud has a silver lining. And at least *now we know*.' He looked calm and icy cool as ever, but, of course, Alan thought, he must be bluffing. They knew for certain, then, that the diplomats really were spies? Perhaps not, for Kingdom added: 'Or do we?' He drank. 'I'm wondering if you can do me an awfully big favour.'

'If it's about Guy Burgess, I hardly knew him. I wasn't even at the Beeb when he was.'

'I know that. And what more is there to say about him? Far too late. No, it's your friend Colin Harris who interests me.'

Alan felt slightly dizzy. It couldn't be the result of just one whisky. It must be nerves. But he wasn't going to let bloody Kingdom wind him up. 'Yes. You said. What about him?'

'I wondered if you'd seen him again.'

Alan swallowed more whisky. 'What if I have? In the first place I ran into him quite by accident. I mean ... I hadn't seen him for years. We drifted apart, well, he left the country ... just disappeared. I don't know if you know, but there was this trial. He was very bitter.'

'Of course I know about the trial. Very odd business. It almost seemed as if he'd been framed.'

Alan looked sharply at his companion. Could it possibly be? Did Kingdom know something about it? In which case, Colin wasn't so crazy to be afraid. But no, he didn't believe that. Because if it were true, Kingdom would never have hinted. He was just teasing.

'But you've seen him again? Didn't you say he wants to come back here? Is life in the People's Republic not living up to expectations?'

Alan shrugged.

'And with a wife or a girlfriend, you said?'

Remembering the more harmless parts of earlier conversations with Colin, Alan became more expansive. If he tossed Kingdom a scrap of useless information, perhaps he'd stop asking so many questions. 'The girl doesn't get on with her father or something. She wants to get away from Germany, come over here. He showed us a snapshot – she looks nice enough. Frieda Schröder, I think that's the name. But I did rather wonder if he's doing it out of kindness ... pity. He never cared much for women in the past.'

'So I gather.' Kingdom stood up. 'I think I'll have another.'

'My round. Another gin?'

'Make it a double.'

Kingdom sat down again and extracted a cigarette from his case. When Alan returned Kingdom seemed to have lapsed into a contemplative mood, but after a while he said: 'I'd just be awfully interested to know what Harris is up to over here. And over there. Amazing him getting married. I suppose one ought to applaud any effort at normality. Everyone always assumed he was a dedicated homosexual.'

'Everyone?'

'Well … you know what I mean.'

'You really can't expect me to spy on my friends.'

'Christ, no! Whatever gives you that idea?' Kingdom smoked in meditative silence for a while. Then: 'And how's the lovely Edith Fanshawe? Very talented woman. I heard her on the wireless again the other day. You're a lucky man.'

'Lucky?' Alan spoke indifferently, but silently stiffened with a mixture of anger and alarm. He suddenly hated Edith. If he hadn't let her entice him back to the bedroom that morning in Deal they'd have caught the earlier train and he wouldn't have run into Kingdom at the terminus. In which case he wouldn't now be in this awkward situation.

Kingdom smiled. 'I see what you're getting at. I've always thought it would be bloody complicated, trying to run two women at the same time. Never went in for it myself.'

Alan tried to remember if Kingdom was married. He had been, he recalled, but something had happened. That's it, she'd committed suicide.

Kingdom drained his glass. 'Don't worry about Harris. I don't suppose he's done anything he shouldn't have done. It's just that one can't trust anyone these days.'

Which was pretty rich, Alan thought, coming from a spy.

thirteen

❀

THE COMFORTABLE LOUNGE OF the Hotel Am Zoo with its deep chairs and panelled walls was closer to luxury than McGovern had ever been before, other than on two visits to Lily's grandparents' house. The foyer had Turkish carpeting and was decorated with fake-looking portraits of nineteenth-century statesmen or businessmen, as if trying to imitate a stately home. Outside the revolving door the porter, a pantomime figure in a pale blue and silver uniform, patrolled the pavement. McGovern found it ironic that he should have been introduced to this pompous performance of the good life in Berlin of all places.

It had also surprised him to have been provided with a room at such a grand hotel. After settling in he had explored as much of the place as he could, roaming down empty corridors, investigating laundry rooms and looking for emergency exits in case he needed to get away quickly. He'd searched his room for hidden mikes. He'd moved outside and walked all round the building and through the immediate neighbourhood. He had to be prepared for the unexpected.

In fact, there had already been something unexpected: the note that had been waiting for him when he'd arrived the previous evening. A Dr Hoffmann welcomed him to West Berlin and begged permission to meet him the following morning at

10.00 a.m. Kingdom had given McGovern the names of two contacts, but neither of them was called Hoffmann, and no-one had answered the telephone number McGovern had dialled.

As he waited for the unknown Dr Hoffmann his thoughts reverted to Lily. He'd made a brief trip to Glasgow to see her before he left. She'd wanted to know all about his mission, as she called it, to Berlin. They'd walked through the Botanical Gardens. McGovern had his arm tightly round Lily. She'd said how exciting it sounded and hoped it wasn't dangerous. And wasn't his job to stop enemies of the state in Britain, not follow them abroad? She'd hit on exactly the nub of it. He'd tried to explain it as a kind of special mission. And no, it wasn't what he'd normally do. To check up on Harris once he'd left the country was certainly outside the parameters of the work of the Branch. Berlin must be stuffed with secret service personnel who were perfectly capable of keeping tabs on the Englishman.

Kingdom had said: I trust you. I've squared it with Gorch. What he hadn't explained was who he *didn't* trust, why it was necessary to have McGovern instead and how he'd managed to square things with Gorch, who was normally both a stickler for the correct use of his men and mindful of expense. He'd have expected Gorch to say it was out of the question for a member of the Branch to take unofficial leave in order to undertake some ill-defined assignment overseas.

McGovern had tried to explain to Lily that in the confusion and panic over the missing diplomats, unusual measures had had to be taken. He'd also wondered if it was something to do with the fact that MI5 and MI6 didn't get on anyway. Kingdom had given him the name of an MI6 man he was to see in Berlin, but had given the impression he'd no great faith in him. He didn't seem to trust anyone and had told McGovern to keep as quiet as he could the reason for his being in Berlin.

Lily had worried and he'd had to reassure her. He'd miss her so much, he said.

At the same time he couldn't wait to go. It would take him further from Lily, even if it was only for ten days or so, but it would be the first time he'd ever been to the Continent. That his first trip to Europe was to Berlin of all places brought a rush of adrenalin. It might be his chance to spring free of the stagnant waters of the Branch and find a new sphere of action.

The tension that fizzed through him was a strange heady mixture of loss at leaving and excitement for what lay ahead.

'*Guten Morgen*, Herr Roberts. You are David Roberts, I presume? Hoffmann. At your service. You received my message, I hope.'

Miles away, McGovern had momentarily forgotten his new name and looked up, startled, at the stranger, then scrambled to his feet and confusedly held out his hand. The German smiled glintingly, eyes shielded behind rimless spectacles.

'Herr Dr Hoffmann. I was surprised to find your note waiting for me. I was expecting Theodor Feierabend to contact me.' He watched Hoffmann to see how he reacted.

'Unfortunately he wasn't free today,' said Hoffmann smoothly. 'I am here instead.'

'*Sehr freundlich.*' But McGovern was uneasy. 'I wasn't expecting a reception committee,' he said. His nervousness made him sound rude, but that couldn't be helped.

'You speak excellent German, Herr Roberts,' said the stranger, although McGovern had uttered only a few words. 'But we can speak in English if you prefer.'

'I welcome the opportunity to practise my German.' That he spoke German was, of course, one of the excuses Kingdom had given to justify sending him here. But it was a flimsy one, because there must be hundreds of agents who spoke the language.

'I understand you're a journalist on a roving reporter expedition. You want to write articles about our new West Germany and particularly the new American-supported economy of West Berlin, the "showcase of the West". Is that not correct?'

His ironic tone surprised McGovern. He wondered what it meant. It seemed to hint at something: a disavowal of sympathy for the new German state perhaps, a hint he might be on the other side?

'I can show you something of the new West Berlin. It really is something close to a miracle,' continued the German, 'if you remember the blockade in 1948, when we were on our knees. If the Allies hadn't come to our rescue then – if we hadn't had the airlift—' He shook his head. 'We'd have been finished. As it is, the phoenix has risen from the ashes. So – if you're agreeable – I thought I might show you some of the sights of the new Berlin, if that suits you, Herr Roberts. Our new Germany. This is what you will require for your articles, I believe.'

McGovern saw no alternative to accepting the offer. They walked out onto the Kurfürstendamm. McGovern's eyes smarted in the gritty wind that swept down from the cruel white sky.

Dr Hoffmann pointed out the bland modern office buildings along the Kurfürstendamm, with a showy façade of shops and cafés at ground level. Trams clanked past and cyclists flowed by, alongside a surprisingly large number of new and expensive-looking cars. This part of Berlin looked impressively prosperous, compared, thought McGovern, with London, still so shabby six years after the war.

Yet the new prosperity of the Kurfürstendamm was a façade. They walked east, passing the ruined Gedächtniskirche, with its fang-like surviving spire, where glimpses of the mosaics inside could still be seen through the holes in the gaunt remaining walls. On the far side of the road stood men and women in blue capes, who, Dr Hoffmann informed him, were selling tickets for the lottery that would help rebuild the church.

Then, as soon as they left the wide avenue, they found they had wandered into a necropolis. They traversed bleak, windswept spaces of cleared land, hills of rubble and gaping caves that had once been basements and cellars, alternating with neat piles of bricks where rebuilding was soon to begin. Dr Hoffmann launched them down streets shaded by the shells of buildings with gaps for windows staring sightlessly and walls pockmarked with bullet holes. At one point they passed a whole neo-classical façade that had fallen backwards and reclined, cracked and broken, at a crazy angle. They walked through the battered landscape as if through a dream.

Yet, as over any ruin, moss, grasses, weeds and even pink and purple flowers had grown up to lend a rural air to what must once have been the most urban of cities. McGovern marvelled at how life continued at all costs. And although some of the streets, or what had been streets, were deserted, elsewhere men – many missing a limb, but stumping grimly along nonetheless – and women hurried by through the shattered city, bent on their unknown purposes. He stared at them in fascination. Survival – these people had survived. He sensed none of the humour that was supposed to have helped the British get through the war. It was grim determination that kept them going here. The results of their ruthless resolve were already visible along the Kurfürstendamm and also in the cleared spaces, but most of all it showed in their faces, flinty, pale and obdurate.

Dr Hoffmann led McGovern right to the end of the Western sector. When they stopped he gestured towards the red flag ripped by the wind over the Brandenburger Tor. 'Here, East meets West.' He glanced sideways at McGovern. 'The East Germans are rearming, you know,' he said suddenly.

McGovern nodded solemnly.

It was a long walk. They retraced their way back through the Tiergarten. 'You know this was a beautiful place before the war,' Hoffmann said conversationally. 'There were trees and shrubs. Now the trees have all gone, as you see.'

McGovern cleared his throat. The pointless pleasantries, which had been going on for over two hours by now, were seriously frustrating him.

'What work do you do, Herr Dr Hoffmann? If you don't mind my asking.'

'I'm a lawyer. I live here in West Berlin – in Charlottenburg to be precise – but I have a legal office in East Berlin. There's a shortage of lawyers over there. On this side of the great divide we have numerous lawyers from the previous period in our history.'

'Presumably they've all been through the de-Nazification process?'

'Oh ... de-Nazification.' He paused. 'That has been rather overtaken by events, I fear. It is more important, as I'm sure you appreciate, Herr Roberts, to ensure that communism does not take hold. Our little island of Western values here is really very fragile.'

'Of course. But your work, in particular. What exactly is it you do? The legal system there, is it the same? I should have thought it might be rather different. In the East, I mean.'

Dr Hoffmann didn't answer the question. 'You shall visit me there, tomorrow perhaps, or the next day.'

'I'd like that. What kind of law do you specialise in?'

'It varies. I also act,' he said with a smile, 'as a kind of employment exchange. As I said, there's a shortage of lawyers in the East; I can sometimes create opportunities for those who are willing to work there.'

McGovern did not understand this. 'So people – Berliners – can move freely between the sectors?'

Again Dr Hoffmann didn't answer, merely made a vague, expansive gesture. Then he said suddenly: 'Herr Feierabend tells me you wish to meet the Englishman, Harris.'

At last! McGovern was relieved that Hoffmann had been the first to mention the reason for their meeting.

'It so happens I am acquainted with him – through his fiancée. I know her father, you see. As a matter of fact, you could meet the young lady. I could take you to lunch where she works. I'm sure she'd be delighted. She's crazy about all things English.'

'I'm Scottish, as a matter of fact.'

'Really? But ... well, you live and work in London, I believe. For – which newspaper was it?'

Did the German really not know that he was an agent and not a journalist? Surely he must have been told he was no journalist. Was he simply teasing?

'The *Scottish Herald*.'

'Ah yes. Sometimes I imagine the Scots as being a little like the East Germans.' He laughed at what seemed intended as a witticism.

'In what way?'

Herr Dr Hoffmann laughed again. 'Oh, being more socialist, I suppose. But what do you think if we have lunch at, say the Kempinski – yes, I think that would be better and then we can meet Fräulein Schröder later today when she leaves work. If you are free later on, Herr Roberts.'

Did that mean they were to spend the afternoon together? McGovern's heart sank. He wasn't sure how long he could keep up the polite façade, when he was so uncertain of Hoffmann's motives and what the meeting was about, or whether it would actually lead to Harris. But certainly he must accept the offer of an introduction to the fiancée.

McGovern assumed the Kempinski tearooms had been recently rebuilt, but the interior harked back to a time before Weimar, to before the First World War, with its stuffy over-decoration, its red walls and brocaded chairs. They had lunch among prosperous-looking businessmen and a sprinkling of solid, unglamorous women. In a single morning McGovern had already picked up the strange Berlin atmosphere. In the

Kempinski the bonhomie rang false. McGovern looked at the Germans at nearby tables and wondered: where were you in 1945? How did you vote in 1933? How many guilty secrets? How many buried memories? What did you do in the war, Herr Dr Hoffmann? Yet he had the feeling that the Germans were not thinking about the war at all, that they'd buried their memories and forgotten where the corpses were. Yet it was as if the effort of forgetting was itself a heavy burden. That, surely, was what caused this indigestible atmosphere: the wearisome work of repression.

McGovern felt it impossible to bring up the subject of the war directly, and what Hoffmann's role in it had been. On the other hand, the German was more than ready to describe the hunger years right after the war's end: 'Today Berlin looks at least clean. After the war for months, for years even, a grey dust hung over everything, the air itself was grey dust rising from the rubble being frantically cleared; it hung in the air like a kind of visible catarrh. And as you see, in spite of all the clearance, we still have a long way to go. But now since the end of the Blockade, we have a future. Our Mayor, Ernst Reuter, has seen to that. And the Marshall Plan money is helping us so much, of course: the American money that has saved Europe from being entirely overrun by communism.'

Again the mocking tone baffled McGovern. In a curious way it reminded him of Kingdom's.

Dr Hoffmann accompanied McGovern back to the Hotel Am Zoo. They were to meet again at six. In the meantime McGovern was at a loose end. He found a kiosk in the hotel foyer where Kurt, who said he was the night concierge, sold postcards and American reading matter – Mickey Spillane thrillers and the *New York Herald Tribune*. He was a friendly character and McGovern chatted to him. It was always possible he might turn out to be a useful contact. After listening to an account of the Eastern Front, he chose a postcard of the

Gedächtniskirche, taken before the war. He wrote the postcard to Lily in the lounge and then sat down with *Our Mutual Friend*. Charles Dickens was a great favourite of Lily's father, but McGovern was finding it heavy going.

At half past six McGovern was standing with Dr Hoffmann across the road from the canteen in the British sector. They waited and watched. The place looked empty and shut.

Then suddenly she was there. She stood on the pavement, which was not really a pavement, and she was one of those tall women with long thighs and a willowy twist to her waist that her faded dress enhanced as it clung to her legs. Her dark hair blew out in the wind and whipped across her face. She was wearing a red cardigan.

They crossed the road. Dr Hoffmann lifted his hat: 'Fräulein Schröder. How nice to see you – I hoped to catch you as you left work. I want you to meet an English friend of mine, Herr Roberts.'

McGovern also raised his hat. The young woman did not look especially pleased to see Dr Hoffmann.

'I hope you have time for a drink, Fräulein Schröder. You could even practise your English a little bit.'

She looked doubtfully at the two of them and said in German: 'I need to get home. I don't have my bike at the moment.'

'We'll see you home safely, don't you worry. Just a quick drink – I know a bar nearby.' His arm stretched out behind her in an encircling, avuncular gesture. He led them along the street and soon McGovern realised that they were still quite near the Kurfürstendamm.

The name of the *Lokale*, Chez Ronny, snaked in red neon over the door. Downstairs, tables encircled the small dance floor. A four-piece band was playing 'In the Mood for Love', but no-one was dancing. Dr Hoffmann gestured towards a free table. 'In the early years after the war this place was a favourite of the English and Americans. As you see, Germans are beginning to be able to afford it now. Some Germans, at least.' He glanced around complacently. 'What can I get you?' And he clicked his fingers at the waiter.

McGovern felt beer would be a safe bet. Frieda Schröder asked for lemonade. The drinks came accompanied by a plate of sliced sausage.

'I mustn't stay long. *Der Vater* will be annoyed if I'm late.' Frieda Schröder looked round the room.

They made stilted conversation. The girl said hardly a word as Dr Hoffmann expanded on the opportunities of postwar Berlin. 'Herr Roberts lives in London – perhaps he'll be able to help you when you get there. Tips about renting a flat – I believe you have almost as much of a housing problem as we do?'

'It's not anywhere near as bad as here, I'm sure,' said McGovern. He turned to the girl. 'You're living in the Eastern sector, I'm told.' Not a good ploy; her face was closed in, she didn't want to talk about it. 'What can I tell you about London?' That didn't work either.

Now the band was playing American jazz. If the customers here were the wealthier Berliners, what must the others be like, McGovern wondered. Like the clientele of the Kempinski tearoom, the drinkers were not badly dressed, but even the smartest looked self-conscious, and a similar air of joyless-ness hung over the bar. Could the clientele really all be newly successful businessmen and their wives or secretaries? Or was the place floating on black-market money? McGovern suspected it was the latter.

'I thought it would be a good idea, Fräulein Schröder, to set up a meeting with Herr Roberts and your fiancé now he's back from London.'

McGovern bit into a piece of sausage. It was extremely salty.

Frieda Schröder sipped her lemonade. 'That would be good,' she said in a low voice, 'but Colin—' She broke off and stared downwards as if at some mesmerising object on the floor.

'Colin ...?'

'Oh nothing, Herr Dr Hoffmann.'

Something was wrong, but Hoffmann appeared not to notice her unease, or chose to ignore it. For a girl who was supposed to be so anxious to reach Britain, she was making a good job of concealing it. He was obviously going to have to get her on her own and Hoffmann, perhaps deliberately, had made that possible by taking McGovern to her place of work.

She distrusted Hoffmann; that seemed clear. And who was Hoffmann, anyway? McGovern had so far failed to reach either of the contacts, whose names, real or fictitious, Kingdom had given him. That in itself was worrying. He sat in the smoky bar and tried to act as if he were enjoying himself.

'What do you say to a drink tomorrow evening? Then we can show you the Eastern sector, Herr Roberts.'

'I'd like that.' It was true. He was curious to see the socialist part of Berlin, to meet Harris, but above all to embark properly on his mission.

A frown drew Frieda's narrow, winged eyebrows together. Beautiful eyebrows, McGovern thought, at one with her pale skin, her mobile mouth. But then she was altogether beautiful.

On an impulse he asked her to dance. He'd expected her to refuse, but at once she brightened up. He felt self-conscious as they took to the empty floor, as he was no expert dancer, but she moved easily against him and their slow, rhythmic movements lulled him into an unexpected sense of ease, so that for the first time he forgot about his suspicions and anxieties as they swayed together, circling in space, their surroundings forgotten.

fourteen

∾

THE STAIRCASE CURVED ROUND the wall, to the second floor. Of its iron balustrade only the sockets remained and the stone steps were chipped and cracked. Frieda kept her hand on the wall as she climbed and tried not to look down. Everyone knew the building was unsafe. Her key rattled in the lock and the door creaked as she pushed it. At once Herr Vogel opened his inner door and peered out. She flinched at the sight of his long nose and sinewy lips, his sour expression and spiteful eyes.

'The rubbish was not taken out this morning.' He moved further into the passage, barring her way.

'I'm sorry – I was late for work, and—'

'That's no excuse. It is your responsibility to take out the rubbish, that was agreed. That you are too lazy to get up for work on time is not my problem.'

'I'll take it down now,' she said meekly.

'Are you joking? This is a ridiculous idea. The rubbish must be taken down in the morning. You know that perfectly well. So my wife has had to take it down two flights of stairs. With her bad back that's not funny.'

Suddenly Frieda had had enough. 'Couldn't you have taken it down yourself?' But as soon as she'd spoken her stomach contracted with fear. She couldn't afford to anger him. She was afraid, always so afraid. It was hard to always have to be so careful.

'Is that meant to be a joke?' he barked. 'Is that all you have to say?'

She looked down like a child being admonished.

'We did not want you here in the first place. You know that, I think. All you refugees – you were billeted on us, we were forced to take you in – my son lost his room, you made my wife sick with your mess in our kitchen. And now this impertinence.'

Frieda swallowed back the lump in her throat. 'I'm sorry.' She forced the words out.

'I don't know how long this can go on. We all know what your father got up to in the war. He wouldn't want the bureaucrats in Pankow to find out too much, would he? And why did you come running back over to this side? Things get too hot in the West?'

She said nothing. The silence lengthened as the recognition dawned on Herr Vogel that he'd spoken recklessly, that he might have gone a bit too far. Everyone had to be careful what they said these days. Frieda allowed herself a half smile. Improbably, her father had made quite a few friends in the Communist Party. He could well make life unpleasant for the Vogels. Perhaps they might even be turned out of the flat altogether, leaving it free for her father and herself.

But soon none of this would matter – these quarrels that were part of daily life and would never change. Nothing would ever change here. The threats and counter-threats signified little, because there simply weren't enough dwellings. The apartments on the Stalin Allee were not even begun, the area was still being cleared by the cohorts of voluntary labourers. Frieda and her father were condemned to live on top of the Vogel family in this kind of hell for the foreseeable future. Or rather, *they* were. But not she. She would escape. The only

solution was to get away. She would. She *must*. And there had
been a new surge of hope today when Hoffmann had introduced her to the Englishman. Another Englishman! It seemed
almost too good to be true. It was a little bit of insurance, just
in case Colin couldn't find a way.

'I'm sorry,' she repeated and moved forward and now Herr
Vogel moved back to let her pass. She turned the key in the
lock of her room, shut the door behind her and sat listlessly
on the bed which also served as a sofa. She took some bread,
margarine and cheese from the cupboard. This room was their
life. Her father had the divan, of course. She had to sleep on a
camp bed at the back of the hall.

She put the food on a plate, but then left it on the table
and went to the window. The view of the square with the water
tower at its centre was the best thing about the room, the only
good thing. But now Colin was back. He was coming to see her
this evening. Perhaps he would have good news.

The government didn't like East Germans trying to leave
the Democratic Republic. It was unpatriotic, anti-socialist. You
weren't even supposed to travel into West Berlin – there were
all sorts of inducements not to. She didn't care.

It would be wonderful to get away. But could she – *could she*
– really marry Colin? He was so sweet, correct and chivalrous.
He was kind to her – not unlike the Colonel in a way. Unlike
the Colonel, though, he had never made love to her, had never
even tried. It seemed unnatural. He was manly and not bad
looking, yet – but perhaps it was the English school system,
again, that suppressed his inclinations or made him unable
to express them. Or perhaps it was part of that famous British
'fair play' that the Colonel used to refer to. Perhaps Colin was
just chivalrous and scorned the idea of taking advantage of her
until they were legally married.

She had tried, but if an embrace became too prolonged
he had always withdrawn with a gentle smile. She sometimes

suspected he only pitied her, in much the same way as he'd pitied the orphaned puppy they'd once found whimpering in the ruins. But perhaps it didn't matter that she was not loved, but only pitied, so long as she reached England.

The door banged open. She looked up, anxious, but her father seemed in an unusually good mood. She feared his violence almost as much as ever, but with the hope of escape she was these days observing him with growing detachment. She'd known for a long time that she had no love for him, nor he for her, but her fear was beginning ever so slowly to fade, replaced by hatred, or something that would have been hatred had it not been so cold, so dispassionate. She watched him as if from far off. He was no longer even her father, but just an unpleasant, uncouth bully. But until she got away, cut loose from him, she would never be free of the past.

'I'm hungry. What is there to eat?'

'There's some stew,' she said, 'left over from yesterday. I'll heat it up.' She fetched the saucepan and took it into the communal kitchen. When she returned she said: 'I met an Englishman today, Herr Dr Hoffmann introduced us. I thought you might know something about it.'

'*Another* Englishman? Why should I know anything about this, stupid bitch?'

She already wished she hadn't mentioned the meeting. Any encounter with a foreigner, and English at that, was naturally suspicious. It was also a possible opportunity. She sighed. She was too tired to explain. What was the point?

She ladled the stew, which was actually a potato and cabbage soup with some pork knuckle floating in it, into bowls and father and daughter sat and faced each other as they ate.

'Well – go on. Tell me. What was he like? Getting anything out of you is like getting blood out of a stone.'

He was always so angry, always had been. She tried to remember what he'd been like before he got the job ... but she'd been so little then and couldn't remember a time when their home hadn't been filled with his rages. Her mother used to say it was because of the work, that it had changed him, he hadn't quite known what he was letting himself in for when he'd applied, but in the SS you obey orders. Frieda didn't accept that excuse. He'd *loved* his work. And loved what came after too. When they'd fled the Russians he'd managed to cast off his job and all that it meant, but he hadn't shed his violent temper.

'Tell me!' he shouted now. His good mood had evaporated.

'I don't know, there's not much to tell. He was a journalist, that's all.'

Der Vater didn't beat her so often these days, but he bullied her with words, with his shouting and with his threats. At first he'd opposed the marriage. He'd shouted she wouldn't get a passport or a visa, he'd see to that. A daughter had no right to leave a parent. And what of her duty to her country, to the fatherland?

Then one day he'd abruptly changed. It might not be such a bad idea after all, for her to get married and move to England. He could follow her eventually. She'd swallowed that terrifying threat with the thought that once she was there, once she'd reached the promised land, she'd make sure he never did.

He glared at her. 'I'm going back to Saalfeld next week,' he said. 'For Hoffmann. Hoffmann wants me to go and have a look down there. See what's going on.'

'For Herr Dr Hoffmann? But why?'

Her father grinned. 'Never you mind,' he said, 'and don't go talking about it either, or you'll regret it.'

Later that evening Colin called round.

'How lovely.' She didn't dare fling her arms around him, but instead carefully took his arm.

'Let's sit in the square,' he said, 'it's a nice evening.'

They walked across the street and sat in front of the water tower. It was very quiet. Occasionally a bicyclist whirred by.

He put his arm round her. He looked at her with his kind look – but that look dismayed her, for it often preceded bad news. 'I'm not sure, you know, it's such a good idea to go back to England.'

She felt faint as the words sank in. She was mute with … it was dreadful, a great void opened up inside her—

'What would you think if I stayed here? We could still get married.'

'But you said … what are you talking about?'

'I'm not sure it's such a good place to be.'

'Colin – please – don't say that—'

Colin stared ahead. She thought the silence would go on for ever.

'I can't bear living here,' she muttered. She remembered what had happened during the day. 'I met another Englishman,' she said. 'Herr Dr Hoffmann introduced us.'

Colin sat up sharply. 'What did he look like? What was his name?'

'Herr Dr Hoffmann wants you to meet him. He says you could meet in his office tomorrow afternoon, late afternoon, or evening.'

Colin frowned. 'I don't trust Hoffmann.' He'd brought cigarettes from England. He offered her one and they sat smoking in silence. The taste was subtly different from the cigarettes you got, if you were lucky, in Berlin.

'While I was over there,' said Colin eventually, 'I wasn't only sorting out visas and trying to find a job. I met one or two old friends. Things don't look that good so far as work's concerned, but I decided not to worry too much about that. I could probably get some freelance assignments … anyway … I also thought I might get some work through the Party. I met up with someone I used to know. His family's German but he was brought up over there, they were exiles. He's a British citizen and all that. He'd been seeing someone – another pre-war refugee – a well-known scientist.'

'What has this to do with our getting married, getting away from here?'

'Hang on, I'm coming to that. This man, his name's Konrad Eberhardt, had written his autobiography, so my friend said, but he needed someone to help with the finishing touches. Alex thought it might be just the thing for me.' Colin paused. He ground out his cigarette and flung the stub away. He'd been leaning forward, staring at nothing, but now he turned towards Frieda. 'To cut a long story short,' he went on, 'Alex thought it would be a wonderful propaganda coup if Eberhardt's autobiography could be published. Eberhardt had been a communist before the war, then he moved to the right, but Alex thought he'd come to see things differently again. He even thought he migh persuade him to come back to live over here. Alex is a committed communist, you see. I was sceptical about it all, but I ended up agreeing. It sounds a bit strange, but Eberhardt was to hand over the manuscript at a funeral we were all going to. And he did. But a few days later we found out he'd been murdered. The news of his death wasn't such big news as it probably otherwise would have been because there's a huge scandal going on over there. You probably haven't heard about it, they seem to be playing it down over here. It's about some spies who were probably double agents. But you see, I'm worried they might connect me with the murder.'

He stopped. Frieda realised it was the end of the story, but she didn't understand it. After the silence had lasted for a minute or two, she said: 'What has this to do with us? I simply don't understand. Why would they suspect you of his murder?'

'I've been in trouble with the police before. I don't want any more trouble. It's better if I stay here – at least for a while.'

'In trouble with the police?'

'I wasn't guilty. I got off in the end. I'm sure I was framed, you see. So I'm scared they'll try it again.'

'They?'

Colin shook his head. 'It's too complicated to explain. I just got the wind up, that's all. I'm – well, I'm frightened to go back.'

Frieda stood up. 'No, Colin,' she said. She was scared, but determined. 'You mustn't be frightened. I'm not going to go on living here. You promised. I won't let you back out of it now.'

He looked sadly up at her, then stood up himself. 'It's so difficult, Frieda. Let's see what happens. Maybe they'll find out who killed him. If they arrest someone ...' The sentence petered out in a shrug.

Frieda wanted to scream. But she controlled her feelings. She was good at that. 'My father says he's going back to Saalfeld next week, you know, where we used to live.'

'Is he? What for?'

'I don't know. Something to do with Hoffmann. Something bad.' She braced herself. She had to be decisive. 'Colin, I won't stay here much longer. I *won't*.'

Colin lit another cigarette. 'Please don't be upset, Frieda. Look, nothing's definite either way – about London,' he said. He put his arm round her shoulders as they walked back towards the apartment. She felt a little better then. Besides, there was now the other Englishman. It was strange of Hoffmann to have introduced them, but it might be a different opportunity.

fifteen

❡

LIFE RETURNED TO SOMETHING like normal at the Courtauld. Dr Blunt resumed his lectures. With no further news of the missing diplomats the crowd on the pavement slowly dwindled and after a few weeks only a couple of loitering journalists remained. Yet with nothing to feed on, press speculation about the missing men grew wilder, although all that could actually be said was: Guy Burgess and Donald Maclean had completely disappeared.

The journalists and photographers might have decamped from the pavement outside, but they still pestered Dr Blunt with calls, badgering him for interviews and revelations. His secretary, Miss LeFebvre, acted as chief front-line protector, fending off all comers from her office in what had once been a bathroom, her desk to one side of a magnificent marble bath, now used as a receptacle for parcels and stationery. The telephone rang ceaselessly, but Dr Blunt was always unavailable for comment.

Everyone at the Courtauld was naturally appalled at the way the press had pursued the director. It was shocking and indefensible that the fallout from the madness of politicians should have crashed right up to the doorstep of the Courtauld to torment Dr Blunt: Dr Blunt *of all people*, the most distinguished art historian of his generation, a patron saint of high-classical art and prophet of its beauty and importance. Indeed, he looked more saint-like than ever, with his papery face and fragile build. He was as insubstantial as ectoplasm. Yet, willowy he might be, but his was the thinness of fine steel. He appeared both tough and vulnerable and it was this combination, together with his wit and charm, that inspired the adoration of every individual who frequented the cathedral of art.

'You haven't really explained why you think he's so wonderful,' complained Alan, when Dinah described the iniquities Dr Blunt had suffered. 'He was very close to Guy Burgess. He surely must know where he's gone.'

'That's unfair!' But when challenged, Dinah found it hard to pinpoint the source of the director's charisma. Finally she said: 'He has – I don't know what it is – a lightness of touch – he's amusing – and he's so passionately dedicated to what he's doing, to art.'

'Art with a capital A,' said Alan.

'Charm's too elusive to explain.'

'Charm … isn't charm a bit treacherous? Doesn't it always disappoint in the end?' As Alan spoke he was thinking of Kingdom and whether he could be described as charming. No; there was something more determined and steelier about Kingdom. Charm was too lightweight a word for the spy.

'Dr Blunt isn't disappointing. His lectures are wonderful.'

Alan laughed. 'I know he can do no wrong, darling, as far as you're concerned.'

They were relaxing in the little sitting room in the late evening light. Dinah was knitting a jumper for Tommy. She bent over the needles and the bright yellow wool. Thinking about Dr Blunt, she'd dropped several stitches.

'They definitely think Eberhardt was murdered,' said Alan. 'You know, the old chap I interviewed in Deal.'

'Reggie said something. How awful.'

'It'll probably mean we can't broadcast the interview, but it was all such a mess anyway.'

'Have you heard from your Berlin friend at all? The communist?'

Dinah was sitting with Regine in Regine's walled garden. 'We think he must have gone back to Germany. Though he seemed awfully disillusioned when we saw him. But then he didn't seem to like it here either.'

'William says some people enjoy being disillusioned. He's still getting all these manuscripts written by Reds who've seen the light. He says it's quite a little genre. I can't understand why people always look on the dreary side of things. I always try to look on the bright side.'

'Even you seemed rather depressed—'

Regine swept depression aside. 'Oh, that was when I still wasn't feeling well, darling. I'm feeling much, much better the last week or so. I think I've finally recovered from the birth of the twins.'

'You're looking wonderful.' Dinah spoke rather wistfully. And indeed Reggie was looking wonderful again. Post-birth blues had evaporated. Her wild red hair stood out in corkscrews and her pale green linen dress set off her eyes.

'My tummy's still sagging a bit.'

'Oh, nonsense, Reggie, you're thin as a rake.'

'It's not fat, it's the muscle tone, darling.' She twisted her green jade necklace between her fingers. 'How is your Dr Blunt bearing up? The scandal just goes on and on, doesn't it?'

'It's got awfully boring, don't you think,' said Dinah. 'Alan was talking about some old chap he interviewed who's been murdered or something – the missing diplomats business quite knocked it off the front pages. And yet he was quite well known, a scientist, I think.'

'You mean Konrad Eberhardt? But there was a long obituary

yesterday and the papers are picking up on it now, the *News Chronicle* had a big report today. And shall I tell you something? Don't mention it to anyone, will you, not yet, but it looks as though he's left his copyrights, his estate and all that, to Drownes. So William will make lots of lovely money. Drownes published his book of essays that made such a stir last year.'

'Who'd want to murder an elderly scientist?'

'That's just the thing, darling. William says it might have something to do with atomic secrets, you see.'

'Good heavens! Alan never said anything about that.'

In fact Regine's version was a highly imaginative embellishment of what her husband had actually said, but that was how rumours started. Dinah had nothing to cap it with and after a friendly, lazy silence Regine spoke again. 'I'll tell you what else – Drownes is doing so well just now. We're going to publish one of your Dr Blunt's monographs. So I'll meet him at last and decide for myself whether he's really as wonderful as you say. I'll have him round to dinner. You and Alan will come, won't you?'

'That would be lovely,' said Dinah.

There was a little sound from the lawn where the twins lay sleeping in their double pram and Tommy was playing on the grass. She gasped. 'Oh look – Tommy – he's walking.'

Her son staggered forward, then fell to his knees on the grass. But as she ran forward to stop him from crying he looked up at her and shouted with laughter.

Dinah looked at the papers on Alan's desk in his little study, the second bedroom, upstairs behind their own. This would soon have to become Tommy's room, and then Alan would have to move either to the attic or to the dining room, or else they would have to move house.

She was looking for the gas bill, because this morning an

unpleasant letter printed in red had arrived from the Gas Board. Alan must have forgotten to pay it – they weren't too hard up at the moment.

As she leafed through the mess of papers on the table she came across the stuff on Konrad Eberhardt. Alan had cut out *The Times* obituary. It was a respectful and admiring piece beneath an unprepossessing photograph. It must have been taken some years ago, but Eberhardt was already balding, and she didn't warm to his face with its lines carved down either side of his mouth and prominent, shining nose. And while his clothes weren't slovenly or neglected exactly, his dress managed to convey the impression that to think or care about his appearance was beneath him, that the Thinker had no time for such trivial matters. The Thinker, Eberhardt seemed to suggest, was essentially a mobile brain, which unfortunately for the time being had to be encased in a vulgar fleshly casing and the less attention paid to this the better.

Some of Alan's friends had that sort of attitude. The way they complimented her on her appearance, on the rare occasions they bothered to notice, conveyed the view that only a woman would stoop to the trivialities of fashion. In their eyes it was part of what made women so generally unsatisfactory. And some of their wives and girlfriends were worse, with wrinkled or laddered stockings (they even wore *lisle* stockings, which surely wasn't necessary any more now that clothes rationing was a bad memory from the past, even if nylons were still in short supply and so expensive). They had wiry hair that had never seen a hairdresser, naked, scrubbed faces and dreadful, peasant dirndl skirts that seemed to have been made out of curtain material. She sometimes feared she was slipping into the same low standards – she had so little time for herself – and it wasn't that she minded if some women preferred to dress like that, but their looks at her efforts at smartness conveyed a surely unmerited air of superiority.

Of course not all Alan's friends were like that. Some, both men and women, were really quite smart. Edith Fanshawe, for example, always looked well turned out and glamorous.

Underneath the press cutting was a manuscript annotated in both pencil and red ink, which must be Alan's interview with Eberhardt and beneath that was an edited transcript of the interview itself. It was covered with more notes and crossings out in red ink and as Dinah read it she understood why. It barely made sense. The first bit was better: the drama of his flight into exile followed by internment. She tried to imagine that wandering life, the fractured sense of identity, the shock of facing extermination or expulsion from your own country, the country of your birth. How complacent the English are, she thought, how complacent I am, yet she didn't understand some muddled remarks on the importance of identity. Who cares if I'm English? I never think about it. I'm just me, she thought.

She laid the transcript aside and continued her search for the missing gas bill, but she was distracted again by seeing a copy of Eberhardt's book. She picked it up, seeing the Drownes logo on the spine and as she opened it a scrap of paper fell out. It was part of a cigarette packet, torn off and now evidently used by Alan as a book mark. Scribbled on it in a stranger's writing were the words, 'See you by the seaside!'

Dinah turned the scrap of card over between her fingers. It puzzled her for a moment, but she replaced it and continued her search for the bill. By the time she found it she'd forgotten about Eberhardt.

sixteen

⊂₩◡

THEODOR FEIERABEND'S FLAMBOYANCE was a startling contrast to Hoffmann's ultra-correct appearance. He wore a royal-blue satin shirt with full sleeves and a floppy collar and had tied a green neckerchief round his throat in lieu of a tie. A long lock of his already receding dark hair fell forward over his domed forehead, emphasising his large, dark eyes, rosy face and lips and fleshy nose.

'Things are much better in Berlin these days,' said Feierabend, looking round the Hotel Am Zoo lounge. 'The cultural life here is truly amazing.' He gesticulated with large red hands that poked incongruously from his satin cuffs and laughed in a friendly way. His teeth gleamed white, unlike those of so many Germans.

'I myself work for the East German Opera,' continued Feierabend. 'I sing in the chorus.' He smiled. 'It is difficult for me – I have more than one job. Opera is my dream, but in the daytime I do various jobs and then some evenings I work in a cabaret. You should come and see my show before you leave. You should come this evening, in fact. Why not? I sing at the Eldorado. The Eldorado is great fun – I think so, at least. Come this evening – unless you have something better to do.'

The friendly and seemingly artless introduction unsettled McGovern. His British contact, Victor Jordan, was briefly in

Bonn, so McGovern had been unable to do what he would have preferred, which was to see Jordan first and get the lowdown on the German scene in general, and his German contact in particular.

Feierabend did not seem like an agent. Actually, he was not exactly an agent. He was, McGovern supposed, one of the hundreds – thousands – of individuals who, Kingdom had warned him, played an ambiguous role in the floating world of Berlin, men, and no doubt women too, who acted in various ways as go-between, messenger, and who knew useful individuals on both sides of the divide. It occurred to him that, downtrodden as she appeared, Frieda Schröder could also possibly be one of those individuals.

The long mirrored bar of the Eldorado was set off by wood panelling and the room was furnished with sofas heavily upholstered in faded brocade, and leather chairs which looked rather new. The chandeliers certainly were new and altogether this was an interior McGovern had already come to think of as – similar to the Hotel Am Zoo – heavily opulent in the Germanic style. At the opposite end of the room from the bar was a small stage on which a band was assembling.

Dolores the singer was ushered in with a chord from the three-piece band. The drummer brushed the cymbals. Dolores, who was very tall, wore long diamanté earrings and a sequined dress. It took McGovern several minutes to recognise her heavily made-up features as those of Theodor Feierabend.

'*Ich bin eine Frau die nie nein sagen kann*' came the throaty tenor. McGovern, stunned, didn't immediately realise the song was the familar 'I'm just a girl who can't say no'. Feierabend's feminine coyness was parodic, he winked at his impassive audience and gestured with his large, meaty hands. McGovern found the performance hideously embarrassing. He felt even more embarrassed when at the end of the set Feierabend swayed to his table and sat down.

'Did you enjoy it? You did look surprised,' said Feierabend with a roguish laugh. 'But, of course, I'm a happily married man, you know. I just do this to earn some money.'

'You sent Dr Hoffmann to meet me,' said McGovern.

Feierabend's smile became almost coquettish. 'I hope you found him useful,' he said. 'He knows everyone, even your Englishman.'

'Yes, Dr Hoffmann has arranged a meeting.'

'Dr Hoffmann can arrange anything. He has so many contacts. He will be extremely useful so long as you remember that you cannot actually trust him.'

Across the naked expanse of what had been Alexanderplatz a gigantic photograph of Stalin stared out. The slogan in German beneath it read: 'The unshakeable friendship of the Soviet and German peoples is a guarantee of peace and freedom'.

McGovern had passed without difficulty from West to East, but now he was actually in East Germany, in the Russian sector, he felt apprehensive, unsure how to handle the imminent encounter with Harris. Harris might recognise him from the funeral in Kensal Green Cemetery, but that was easily dealt with: McGovern in his persona as a journalist had known Garfield – that would be his line.

More troubling – as it had been from the beginning – was the vagueness of his mission. Kingdom had not fully explained why Harris was so important. Although he'd suggested that Harris might have had something to do with the Burgess–Maclean affair, he'd seemed more interested in the reasons for Harris returning to London and, not only that, was keen to keep him away. He can't do much damage in Berlin, said Kingdom, but we don't know what he might not get up to over here.

Harris must be important, otherwise Gorch would never

have sanctioned McGovern's highly unorthodox trip. Perhaps Kingdom had some sort of leverage on Gorch. He'd hinted as much and he'd certainly succeeded in twisting his arm. McGovern didn't want to think about that, because he needed Gorch to be straight. He couldn't do the job he did for someone he didn't respect.

He looked round Hoffmann's office to distract himself. It was large and spacious, but sparsely furnished. Just an old desk and filing cabinet and a few upright chairs stood forlornly around on the splintered wood floor.

Hoffmann himself had made good, strong coffee – he appeared to have no secretary, which seemed odd – and offered Camel cigarettes. He entertained McGovern with stories of the complexities of the black market, told with an ambiguous detachment, before asking McGovern about his background. McGovern was rather enjoying expanding on his fictitious youth in a provincial Scottish newspaper office, his big scoop – a postwar miners' strike – and his transfer to the London office of the *Herald*, but Hoffmann started to ask some very probing questions and McGovern was relieved when the doorbell rang.

Hoffmann answered it himself and returned, followed by Colin Harris. When Hoffmann introduced the two men Harris smiled and shook hands. He had a firm grip. He smiled in a perfectly friendly way and showed no trace of recognition, still less suspicion.

'Dr Hoffmann tells me you're on an assignment to report on life in Berlin for the British press. He didn't say which newspaper.'

'The *Scottish Herald*.' It was a pretty safe bet that Harris didn't read the Scottish press. 'But I also hope to sell an article to one of the weeklies.'

'The British press has a very negative view of life over here.'

Dr Hoffmann said to Harris: 'I thought that you would be well placed to give your fellow countryman a fair picture of the German Democratic Republic. It does not surprise me to hear that the British press paints a dismal picture, an ideologically tainted picture. You could redress the balance. I was in any case going to suggest a little tour of the East Berlin scene. We could start at the Kleine Melodie, perhaps. And then on a later occasion you could perhaps show Mr Roberts where all the work is going on to create the new Berlin that is rising on this side of the border.'

'I'd be very interested in that,' said McGovern politely – and truthfully.

Dr Hoffmann had a car – unusual, or so McGovern assumed, in the East – and they set off through streets that were eerily silent, even emptier than most of those in the West. Here there had been no attempt to produce the phoenix of a thriving commercial centre. The bar, down a side street, was also quieter than Chez Ronny or the Eldorado, and dirtier too. An accordionist squeezed out a barely recognisable rendition of 'La Ronde'. The room was stuffy and smelled of dust and beer.

Dr Hoffmann ordered vodka. McGovern had never tasted it before. It had a kick, so he knew he must be careful not to drink too much. But a second round came swiftly. This time McGovern attempted to pay, inadvertently bringing out a Western banknote. When the waiter saw it, he warded it off with a gesture of alarm. Dr Hoffmann smiled and produced his own East German money. 'Currency smuggling is severely punished here. You can understand the difficulties. The situation is so complex.' McGovern apologised and stuffed his note back in his pocket.

There was certainly something uneasy about the whole atmosphere of the Kleine Melodie, its sparse sprinkling of drinkers and dismal surroundings. The place depressed McGovern profoundly, but Harris didn't seem to mind. He talked freely. There was something innocent and guileless about the man. He enthused over the new socialist Germany. 'My fiancée wants us to live in England, and I've put out a few feelers for work over there, but – I've been back recently, and … I don't know … there's more hope here, more sense of purpose, less war-mongering. I found London quite dispiriting. I was shocked by all the propaganda, all the talk about rearmament, the Cold War has got such a grip—'

McGovern bit back the startled question about Harris's future plans that had almost escaped him. Instead he said mildly: 'We try to report the news honestly, without bias.'

'You imagine there is such a thing as objective, unbiased news?'

McGovern had expected that response, but he continued: 'I think it's important to find areas of common ground.'

'Common ground, eh.' Harris laughed and swallowed his vodka in one gulp. 'How can there be common ground when there are irreconcilable contradictions in capitalist society.'

'Herr Harris, our British visitor wants to learn about Germany, not listen to tired old arguments about perennial political differences.' And Hoffmann called for more vodka from the surly, elderly waiter, who limped towards them with the bottle in his hand. At close quarters it became clear he wasn't elderly, it was rather that his grey face was lined with suffering and privation and a kind of ingrained resentment.

'I'm sorry.' Harris smiled. 'It's just that I get annoyed with the lies peddled in the West. By the way, I can't resist asking you, Mr Roberts, what you think of the disappearance of the two diplomats?'

McGovern's pulse quickened, but all he said was: 'It's a complete mystery.'

Harris had reddened and became animated, starting forward in his seat. 'I think it's extraordinary. It's no secret I was a British communist – still am – and there was never any talk of spying – I never heard of such a thing. In my view, it's an attempt to smear the Party – I shouldn't be surprised if they even try to get it banned. And it's simply ridiculous, isn't it, to believe that these two upper-class characters could have been secretly spying for the Soviet Union since *before the war*. I simply don't believe it. Spying and socialism – they're two completely different things.'

'You seem very sure that's what they are. We can nae be certain that's the case. All that's known is, they've disappeared.'

Harris subsided. 'I'm sorry. It's just … well, I don't believe it, that's all. And there's so much cynicism.'

'Not here as well, surely. Isn't East Germany trying to do something different? I hoped you could tell me about that.' The reality of life in East Germany was something about which McGovern had a genuine curiosity, but the news that Harris had decided not to return to London left him completely deflated. His mission had largely succeeded before it had properly begun. He might perhaps be able to claim that it had been he who'd succeeded in dissuading Harris, but the truth was he hadn't even had to try, and now he was unsure whether there was still any point in delving into Harris's activities in Berlin. However, for the time being he had no choice other than to plough on. 'You see, I'm not political. My job is just to describe the world as it seems to me. I don't have an axe to grind. I'm just trying to be truthful. I'm trying to find out what the new Germany, both halves of it, is really like. I'm sure there's so much you can tell me. Our readers will be particularly interested in having an objective outsider's view.'

As the evening progressed and more vodka was drunk, Harris's mood changed. McGovern had the feeling he didn't normally drink and, from being open and enthusiastic about East Germany, he became gloomier with each shot. Several times he attempted to continue the conversation about Burgess and Maclean and reiterated his views on the iniquity of spying and its anti-socialistic nature.

'I'd never do a thing like that.'

'Well, I should think not, Mr Harris,' said Dr Hoffmann drily, 'but then you're not a spy, are you.'

Yet the very fact that Harris so emphatically rejected the morality of espionage paradoxically sowed suspicion in McGovern's mind. Hadn't Harris denounced spying a little *too* emphatically?

This only made McGovern's own situation, or rather his mission, more ambiguous. Perhaps – the thought occurred to him with a lurch of anxiety – Kingdom *hoped* Harris would turn out to be a fully committed agent himself, working for the East German communist government. It could be that McGovern's mission was to discover something of that kind – maybe even to *invent* it – in order to give Kingdom some sort of leverage over his colleagues. Was he caught up in some inter-departmental act of war? That surely wouldn't do his career any good.

'I think we should move on,' said Dr Hoffmann. 'We will go to the Hotel Nordland for dinner.'

A short drive and they emerged from Hoffmann's automobile onto another empty square. Opposite the cliff-like hotel a toyshop sent a dim beam of light across the pavement. The blue neon sign of what seemed to be a cooperative restaurant, H.O. Gastronom, gleamed eerily in the surrounding gloom.

The lobby of the Hotel Nordland was by contrast all too bright. They went upstairs to a restaurant. Apart from themselves only two other tables in the high-ceilinged room were occupied and they sat amid a sea of pink tablecloths and gilt chairs. The food, when it came, was elaborate, with game and pork in rich sauces, and there was caviar and Russian champagne, but the conversation was increasingly awkward as Harris drank steadily and Hoffmann began to show signs of impatience. McGovern wished the evening were over and was thankful when coffee was brought. But then his interest was aroused by what appeared to be a delegation of some kind, who entered and seated themselves at a larger table in the centre of the room. McGovern looked over at the badly dressed men and women: 'Who are they?'

'Trade unionists, minor party officials from the government here,' said Hoffmann.

'They're just having coffee and sandwiches,' observed McGovern.

'Of course, for the vast majority of East Germans these Nordland prices would be utterly beyond their means, but they are well fed. There has to be a place like this for foreign delegations and so on – for distinguished visitors such as yourself,' he added with a smirk, 'but it cannot be a priority.'

Harris was looking around him with a certain disgust. 'This isn't the real socialist Germany,' he said. 'Despite what I've been saying, they've got their priorities right over here. Here in the Democratic Republic they put first things first: industry, housing, production. Consumer goods will be the icing on the cake when the real foundations are laid. West Berlin sickens me. I never go there. Their so-called economic miracle will come a cropper sooner or later. But there are problems here too. Very big problems.' He nodded owlishly. He was quite drunk now.

Dr Hoffmann was watching him closely. 'It is time to go I think.' He turned to McGovern.

As they came out of the hotel a battered tram clattered past them, the violent noise only re-emphasising the silence that returned in its wake.

'I'm going to walk home,' said Harris. He seemed to have sobered up a bit in the chilly air. 'Glad to have met you, Mr Roberts.' And he held out his hand.

'Can we not meet again? Your perspective interests me. Tomorrow, perhaps, or the next day? In the afternoon?'

Harris hesitated. Then he said: 'Why not? My work is freelance and there isn't that much of it at the moment, so I have plenty of spare time.'

'You could pick me up from my hotel, if you're prepared to break your rule of not setting foot in the West. I'm staying at the Hotel Am Zoo – you know, it's actually opposite the Zoo, hence the name, I suppose.'

'Very well.' And Harris walked away quite steadily, his footsteps echoing on the pavement.

Hoffmann drove McGovern back to the Am Zoo. En route they crossed a square where an enormous model of a candle had been erected, topped with a naked flame that flickered in the wind.

'That's to remind West Berliners of all the million German prisoners of war still missing in Russia,' explained Dr Hoffmann in his perennial tone of tolerant irony. 'You can't see, probably, in the dark, but there's a booth underneath, where someone from the Red Cross sells candles for a few pfennigs. The people who buy them have them lighted in the window – it all goes towards the continual Red Cross efforts to search and negotiate to bring more *Spätheimkehrer* home, the ones who are so late coming home.'

'Are there still so many prisoners of war who haven't returned?' McGovern had not known that and was shocked, but he had already learned that there was so much he didn't know.

In his hotel room, he lay on his bed without undressing. It had been a strange evening. The whole atmosphere had been odd. There was Harris – sincere and naive, but conflicted and unhappy.

And there was Hoffmann. Hoffmann was the enigma. He was living in the West, yet had an office in the Eastern sector. He seemed friendly with Harris, the uprooted communist, who seemed happy nowhere – and yet had spoken enthusiastically

about the new East German republic. And there was Feierabend. What on earth was one to make of him?

But it was to Harris that McGovern's thoughts repeatedly
returned. He'd liked the man. And he believed him when he
said he had no time for the spies.

The idea that he'd had something to do with the Burgess
and Maclean disappearance was not credible. McGovern simply
did not believe it. Therefore he must look elsewhere for the real
reason Kingdom had had him sent here.

The obvious reason was that he was to find out what Harris
was up to: why he wanted to get married to Frieda Schröder;
and why he wanted, or had wanted, to return to England. But
that information could surely have been obtained from agents
already on the scene. Perhaps therefore the underlying purpose
of his visit was to check up on the contacts themselves.

Amid all the ambiguities, however, Kingdom had given
him one very clear message about what he wanted. I don't
want Harris back in this country, had been his parting shot.
The problem with that was that McGovern had no way of
preventing him.

Unless …

Unless he himself had been sent as the agent of
destruction.

No: that could not be the unspoken message. There were
sure to be plenty of assassins in this city. Someone would know
who they were and how to get hold of one. Also, he could
surely not have been meant to deduce such an order from
Kingdom's ambiguous instructions. Yet: I don't want him back
here, Kingdom had said.

seventeen

ᑕ᙭ᓇ

DINAH AND ALAN WERE sitting in their basement area. To make the subterranean yard seem more like a garden Dinah had placed tubs of hydrangeas and roses in the corners and trained a clematis up the wall as far as the railings.

Alan was in a mellow mood. He'd had a good week. He hadn't been blamed for the Eberhardt interview debacle, and since Eberhardt's mysterious death everything had changed anyway. He had got the go-ahead for one of his cherished projects, a history of documentary film, in spite of doubts about whether such a visual subject would work on radio. Edith had gone to visit a friend in Suffolk, and this was a relief, because although her voluptuous hold over him had far from diminished, her demands were becoming difficult to handle. Finally, this evening he had come home at a decent hour and played with his son after his bath and, as he lifted the wriggling, laughing, shouting infant out of the water, he knew he loved him more than anything in the world. Dinah, towel held out, had said: 'He looks so like you.'

Now Alan was outlining his plan for the documentary series, to include, he hoped, an interview with the famous documentary maker and producer, Edgar Anstey, when the telephone rang from upstairs.

'Is that you, Wentworth? Terrific. You know it's Wimbledon

next week? I've got a couple of spare tickets. Centre Court of course. Care to come along with your wife – or your mistress if you prefer? I think Jaroslav Drobny might win this year, don't you? Should be a good afternoon. Provided it doesn't rain, of course. We'll have a spot of lunch beforehand.'

Outside again, Alan sat heavily in his seat and drank back the rest of his beer.

'Work, darling? You look a bit glum.'

'Chap I used to know – I saw him again quite recently, didn't I tell you? Miles Kingdom – he's invited us to Wimbledon next week. God knows why. Do you fancy it? I'd have to take a day's leave, I've too much work on really, and ... I don't know ... I'm not mad about the idea. But I suppose we should go. I expect you'd get on with Miles – and you used to play tennis.'

'Wimbledon? How lovely! But – I don't know – you don't sound very keen. And what about Tommy? Who'll look after him? I can't just go off for the day like that. I suppose I could ask Mummy. She's been hinting about a shopping trip up to London for ages. Or there's always Reggie and Nanny Holt.'

Dinah couldn't help being impressed by the flamboyance of the large cream-coloured Austin that rolled to a halt beside them. The man who leant out of the driving-seat window also had a touch of flamboyance. He wore pale linen and a panama hat and was a type familiar from her life at home. Her father had friends like Kingdom, an unflappable Englishman with a dry laugh and encased in unshakeable confidence.

A little girl stumbled out of the passenger seat. Kingdom also stepped out of the car. He raised his hat and held out his hand to Dinah. His clasp was firm and dry, his hazel eyes very bright.

'At least the weather's cheered up. No rain today, I think. This is Judy. My god-daughter. I persuaded her mother to let her take French leave from school – just one day can't do any damage, eh, Judy?' He squeezed her shoulders.

Judy smiled and held out her hand. 'How do you do.'

'You'll sit in the front, Mrs Wentworth, or in the back with Judy?'

Dinah wondered why the girl's mother wasn't of the party. She knew Alan would prefer the front and sensed that Kingdom wanted her to sit with the child in the back, so she did. She would have preferred a different arrangement, but men always hogged the front seat.

Kingdom wheeled the car round and set off for West London. It was exciting to drive through the streets and watch London stream by. She could see the schoolgirl was thrilled too. She tried to talk to her about her school, her work and whether she played tennis, but the girl was very shy. She must be about twelve or thirteen, but in her cotton frock with a sash and her short white socks and button shoes, she looked, if anything, younger.

As soon as they reached the grounds of the All England Tennis Club Dinah caught the decorous excitement of the event. The china-blue and white sky, the surging green of trees and grass and the sedate flocks of spectators walking towards the entrance were a thrill, and when they reached the Centre Court the atmosphere had a special mixture of tension and relaxation.

The first match of the day, between two Americans with peculiar names, Ham Richardson and Budge Patty, lasted for five long, thrilling sets. Budge Patty was the reigning champion, but in the end he lost. Dinah felt sad for him as he shook hands with the young man called Ham, who had wheat-white hair and looked as though he'd come straight from Kansas.

Judy concentrated so hard that her knuckles were white. 'I'm glad Ham Richardson won,' she said, 'he's so handsome, don't you think?'

Miles Kingdom, turning towards Dinah, smiled. 'Wonderful volleying from Patty, wasn't it? I'm rather sorry he lost.' And then: 'Why don't you take Judy for an ice cream. The match was quite exhausting, I expect you're a bit bored now, aren't you, Judy.'

Dinah slightly resented being handed the role of Judy's chaperone and it was clear the child wasn't bored at all, but she rose obediently from her seat. She felt stiff and perhaps it was a good idea to stand up and stretch one's legs. 'Let's go and mill around, shall we, Judy? There might be an interesting match on an outside court.'

They queued for ice cream and then, with their little tubs of strawberry and vanilla, strolled out, edging between the spectators on the outside courts and hearing the thud of the balls and the shouts of 'out' and 'fault' and the implacable voice of an umpire calling the score through the bright air. She could smell grass and rubber and the sun was warm on her back at the same time as the chilly wind nipped round her legs and tugged at her hat. She held it on with her white-gloved hand and then couldn't be bothered, and pulled it off. Out here the crowds were more informally dressed anyway and the hat felt silly.

Alan stood with Kingdom at the debenture bar. It was typical of Kingdom to be a debenture holder. The long match had exhausted Alan. He despised all sports, as did all his intellectual friends, and had found the match unendurably boring, while at the same time tense, but he did his best to sound enthusiastic.

'Wimbledon is quite an interesting social occasion, isn't it – hovering somewhere between Ascot and Twickenham, perhaps? Very English, anyway.'

'I don't know about that,' said Kingdom. 'Not any more. It's completely dominated by foreign players. The Americans, the Australians – no sign of the new Fred Perry. All part of this country's decline, I suppose.'

'But you said Drobny might win and isn't he a British citizen now?'

Kingdom was having none of that. 'Even if he does win, he's still Czech. He didn't learn his tennis in this country. Our whole training system's hopeless.'

They stepped onto the terrace with their drinks. Kingdom turned towards Alan. 'I'm glad we've found time for a chat.'

Alan was quite certain that Kingdom would never mention Edith in front of Dinah, he'd never behave as crudely as that, yet all day he'd felt nervous, for there were subtler ways of sowing doubt and suspicion. Now he was additionally nervous, because he feared this 'chat' was going to be about Colin. He decided to pre-empt the interrogation. 'I haven't seen Harris for a while,' he said, hoping he sounded casually unconcerned. But Harris was not what Kingdom wanted to talk about.

'The interview you did with Konrad Eberhardt. What's happening about that? Montagu Palmer said there might be some delay.'

Montagu Palmer was near the very top of the BBC. Alan was taken by surprise. And then thought he shouldn't have been – because Kingdom was the kind of man who knew the Montagu Palmers of this world. But what a relief that Harris wasn't the focus after all! 'It hasn't gone out. The old man rambled so much – I don't think we'll be able to use it. We might do a more extended programme on him, I suppose. He was so bloody confused, I didn't really twig at the time, which was stupid of me, but I think his mind must have been going a bit. In any case, it may be sub judice now.'

'I wondered if there was anything he said … that might have had a bearing …?'

'A bearing on what, exactly?'

'Well, he knew Klaus Fuchs, didn't he. I know he wasn't in atomic research, but – you know …'

'He never said anything about that. Some of the things he

said were a bit wild. There was all this talk about his autobiography, as if it contained all kinds of secrets. He didn't seem
suicidal, if that's what you mean.'

Kingdom shook his head with an indulgent smile, as if
suicide was far too simple an explanation. 'An autobiography!
That would make interesting reading, I should imagine. But the
point is, I'd be awfully grateful if I could have a sight of the full
transcript. Of the interview.' Kingdom was smoking, looking
out over the terrace.

'I don't see why not. Mind you, it's a complete mess. But ...
isn't there a police investigation?'

'They're useless. No imagination. They're not even particularly interested. I can't *tell* you what a low opinion I have of
CID.'

They drank, looking out at the view of the suburbs bathed
in late-afternoon sun. After a while Kingdom said: 'I'm rather
glad the Eberhardt interview hasn't gone out yet. As a matter of
fact, it might be a good idea if it didn't go out at all.'

Alan glanced sideways at his host, who continued to stare
blandly ahead. Could he really have said that? 'It's not my
decision,' he said coldly.

'Well – think about it. Do what you can.'

Why don't you talk to Palmer, then? was the retort that
crossed Alan's mind, but he thought it wiser not to say it.

Soon after six, when the sun was sloping over the Centre
Court and the fans were milling around outside the players'
entrance, Kingdom called it a day. Dinah would have stayed
until nine o'clock and Judy begged to stay longer, but Kingdom
insisted: 'Must get you home to your mother at a decent hour.
I promised we'd be back before eight.'

Kingdom dropped her off at a big house in Primrose Hill. He
got out to escort her to the front door and bent down to kiss her.

'Thank you so much for taking me, Uncle Miles. I've had
a lovely day.'

'Remember me to your mother – I won't come in.'

'You seem very fond of her,' said Dinah, thinking how nice it was he took an interest.

'Lovely little thing, isn't she,' said Kingdom as they drove off. As the cream-coloured car cruised up Rosslyn Hill he said: 'I've no children of my own and they've had a hard time, she and her mother. Her father was captured by the Japanese – Singapore. Died on the Japanese railway. Rotten luck.'

'It's hardly bad luck to be killed in battle. I thought killing people was the whole point of war.' Dinah heard her own voice sounding shrill and aggressive, but it made her so angry.

But Miles Kingdom just laughed. 'My dear Mrs Wentworth,' he began and then the sentence tailed away into a kindly silence of infinite condescension.

eighteen

V ICTOR JORDAN PASSED HIMSELF OFF as a British businessman concerned with the development of the new, postwar Germany. He invited McGovern to meet him for lunch at a club originally set up for officers and officials of the occupying forces. As soon as McGovern saw it, he realised it was Frieda Schröder's place of work, but as he glanced round the dining room there was no sign of her. Nor did he really expect to see her. She presumably worked in a back office somewhere.

The Occupation was winding down, Victor Jordan told him and the officers' club would be closing soon. In the meantime it continued to provide an excellent lunch.

'The currency reform was a godsend,' said Jordan as they settled at their table. 'Bonn's a stuffy little place, but the Federal Republic has really picked up, it's properly established now. Of course there's been hardship for the Germans – two million unemployed at the end of last year and they grumbled like mad about the way prices went up – but in the long run they'll be thankful. The whole of West Germany will be like the Ku'damm. Not that the Krauts are grateful.' He ordered drinks from the obsequious German waiter and looked beadily at his guest. 'I don't know that your cover's that brilliant, you know. Journalist is too often a code word for secret agent. Look at Guy Burgess – he was a kind of journalist at one time. God, what a bloody mess that is. What were they thinking of back in Whitehall? What has our mutual friend got to say about that?' He stared at McGovern accusingly. Our mutual friend meant Kingdom, he assumed.

'Pretty shocked, I think.'

'Pretty shocked! A bit late to be *pretty shocked*. We've known about the information leak for some time. Most of my colleagues and the Foreign Office wouldn't admit it, couldn't believe it, utter disbelief. But – since Klaus Fuchs was arrested, anyway – we've had to bite the bullet. There is a ring of agents in Britain. American intelligence, the Venona project in West Virginia, told us that. But our friend will have put you in the picture.'

McGovern knew that Kingdom was not to be mentioned by name. 'Not entirely, sir.'

'Oh?' Jordan raised his eyebrows. 'We were on to one of them, very close. Guy Burgess behaved so outrageously in America – open anti-Americanism, provocative statements, drunken driving, insults, picking fights – he'd have had to be brought home anyway …' His words petered out in a shrug.

This, McGovern knew, was tantamount to admitting that the two missing men were Soviet agents. But everyone knew that now. The only question was, how it could have taken so long. It seemed incredible. 'I'm here because it seems possible Colin Harris could have had something to do with the getaway.'

'Piffle.' Jordan frowned. 'I've had my eye on Harris ever since he arrived in 1948 and I can tell you he's a lamb to the slaughter so far as anything to do with espionage or skulduggery of any kind is involved.' He stared in an unfriendly way at McGovern. 'Are you telling me that's really why you've been sent over from the Branch? Very irregular. And pointless.' And I also don't believe you, he seemed to be saying.

McGovern hadn't warmed to his host, a tall, bony, lantern-jawed, public-school specimen of a type he'd too often encountered in the war, full of militaristic confidence in his own rightness at every turn. He wasn't surprised to be patronised – MI6 looked down on everyone else – but he wasn't quite ready to be insulted. Nevertheless he kept his temper.

'I know it's irregular,' he said politely, 'and obviously I'm not up to speed on all sorts of things. It's simply that it was thought a fresh eye might be useful. I'll certainly not be invading anyone's territory. Harris was planning to return to England with a German girl he wants to marry. There's a bit of concern about that. Only now it seems he's changed his mind. So perhaps my presence wasn't really needed, after all.'

'Your very presence is an invasion, old chap.' With that there was a bleak silence until the waiter served their food. Then Jordan continued: 'If the German woman wants to move to England, to that extent it could be interesting. She could be a spy. Half the refugees who cross over into West Berlin are spies. It's a massive problem. There are so many of them the chances of picking them up are infinitesimal,' he said bleakly. 'Well, we'll talk more about that later. But tell me your first impressions of Germany.'

'I've only been here a wee couple of days. They seem to be doing a lot.'

'The determination of the West Germans is extraordinary. Admirable. The Allies have done a lot too. But it changes all the time. At first it was education. Education in democracy, education to get the country going again. Now we're rowing back on the whole education policy effort, it didn't work, no support from the Americans. Now it's more *cultural* policy. We're trying to de-Nazify the Germans by putting on Shakespeare. As if they didn't have enough bloody culture of their own. And look where it got them. You know, the Beethoven-loving Nazi, the SS Obergruppenführer who weeps as he listens to Mozart. A caricature, but accurate.'

McGovern thought of Feierabend and his love of opera.

'My other contact introduced me to a Dr Hoffmann, who knows Colin Harris and arranged for me to meet him.'

The way in which Jordan's face almost imperceptibly rigidified told Jack that this was significant and unwelcome news. 'Your other contact being?'

'Theodor Feierabend.'

'Feierabend.' Jordan carefully cut some meat from his shank of pork. He munched. 'Delicious. Is yours good?'

'Excellent, thank you.'

'Feierabend,' repeated Jordan. 'Well, well.'

'Why – is he unreliable?'

'It makes perfect sense, I suppose, as a way of getting to meet Harris. But beware of Ulrich Hoffmann. He's about to become a little too well known,' he said. 'His secretary was arrested last week.'

'I didna trust him at all.'

'Sound instinct.'

McGovern waited to hear more, but Jordan lifted the wine bottle. 'Another glass? German reds are insufficiently appreciated, in my view. The cherry note in this one is very attractive. You can't compare it to a good Burgundy or a claret, even a Côtes du Rhône, but pleasant enough all the same.'

McGovern was not a wine drinker. His father drank beer and the occasional wee dram of whisky. Lily's parents didn't drink at all. Nevertheless McGovern found he was enjoying the light, soft flavour of the wine. 'It's good,' he said.

'Let me tell you something,' said Jordan. 'Do you know there are more kidnappings in West Berlin than in any other city in the world? This is kidnap capital, McGovern. Now, there are different kinds of kidnappings. Type one: immediately after the war Russian agents would snatch people who were, or who were believed to be, Nazi war criminals. Often as not they were helped by Germans in the Western sectors and the Americans simply allowed it to happen. We were all against the Nazis then, weren't we? War crimes suspects? Let them face a firing squad or rot in a Russian labour camp.

'That didn't last. Then we move on to type two. It wasn't long before CIC – the American Gestapo, as the natives call the American intelligence corps – realised how badly they needed some of these Germans. So the game became more complicated. The Germans began to realise what was in it for them and it wasn't long before they were offering their services on all sides. West Berlin's the best place in the world for spying on the Russians. That doesn't surprise you, does it? And it's rapidly becoming the best place to spy on *us*. That's part of the point of the so-called German Democratic Republic. It's fast developing into the Soviet's intelligence arm.'

'Does this have to do with Hoffmann?'

'I don't know why his secretary has been arrested. Perhaps he had nothing to do with any kidnappings. But he's certainly not to be trusted.'

'So why is Colin Harris mixed up with him?'

'Good question. But as I said, Harris is an innocent abroad. God knows why he wants to marry some German girl, but I'd bet he's doing it for the most honourable or even charitable reasons. A more interesting question is, why is *she* doing it?'

'Hoffmann introduced us. She just wants to get away, that's the feeling I got.'

'You met her, did you?' Jordan eyed McGovern as if surprised at this evidence of enterprise. 'And Hoffmann introduced you. Interesting. But if she's so keen to get away, why doesn't she just go, claim refugee status?'

'I think she's terrified of her father.'

They ate in silence until Jordan said: 'How long have you worked with our friend?'

'About eighteen months.'

'What do you think of him?'

The question completely threw McGovern. He had no

idea what on earth he was supposed to say. It was the sort of question you just shouldn't be asked. He struggled to put into words his complex feelings about the man he admired and to some extent tried to emulate. 'He seems very able.'

'He is.'

McGovern ventured a question of his own. 'Have you worked with him?'

'At the end of the war. He was here then. A brave man. Awarded the MC for some wartime exploit, I can't remember now what it was. His job here was sifting through the refugees. He was the absolutely best interrogator we had. He was outstanding. The Americans liked him because of that. And even before they got hold of the idea, he was one of the first to see how very useful some of our erstwhile enemies might be. He had the Cold War mentality right from the start. He was criticised for it at first, but in the end of course we all came round to his point of view.' Jordan signalled to the waiter. 'You'll have pudding? They do very good fruit tarts.' As the waiter cleared their plates Jordan continued: 'Yes, he was viewed with suspicion at first, was our friend. He was the Robespierre of the Allies – you know, purer than the pure and yet the most fanatical of the lot.'

'Fanatical?' This didn't at all fit in with McGovern's image of Kingdom.

'Our American friends were shipping everything they could lay their hands on back across the Atlantic, silver, grand pianos, art works, you name it, and that was quite apart from all the low-level stuff – drugs, cigarettes, money and so on. Kingdom very much disapproved of the occupying forces who got involved in the black market. Found it all very *infra dig*. And the way women were treated. What the Allies did to women isn't something to be proud of, you know. The Russians were the worst, but everyone did their bit. Although I have to say we were considered a bit more decent than the others. Well,

Kingdom was rather strict about all that, which didn't make him exactly popular. As a result there were one or two attempts to float rumours about him.'

'Rumours?'

'That he wasn't quite what he seemed. Either that he was lining his pockets like everyone else or that he had some other line of activity that no-one knew about. But no-one could ever stick anything on him. Nothing *to* stick. And anyway all those rumours died down when it became clear how useful he was. Absolutely bloody indispensable. I do wonder, though, if he's lost his touch a bit now. He does seem to have a bit of an *idée fixe* about Harris, wouldn't you say, he does seem to exaggerate his importance. I don't understand that. In no way is Harris agent material. For either side.'

'Harris certainly spoke out very much against it when I met him.'

'Well, he would, wouldn't he. But in his case I believe it's the truth.'

McGovern lay in bed in the Hotel Am Zoo, restless and unable to sleep. It wasn't just that he couldn't get used to the peculiar eiderdown with no sheets and the mattress which was far too soft. He could not stop thinking about the lunch with Jordan. The muted hostility hadn't surprised him, but Jordan's hints and innuendoes had been unsettling, to say the least.

Next morning he sat for a long time over breakfast, reading a copy of *Der Spiegel*, in which there was a brief, factual report of the disappearance of Burgess and Maclean. He had nothing to do until his rendezvous with Harris at the hotel in the afternoon. The city waited outside to be explored and he was free to wander round it. That was an intriguing prospect. It was a long time since he'd had such an opportunity. It would also allow him to see if he was being followed. He set off with enthusiasm.

He found a bookshop and spent an hour browsing the shelves, trying to interpret the mood of the nation (or rather the half-nation) from the new novels laid out on the tables at the front. He sat in a café for a while, and then walked again with no determined purpose. There was nothing to make him feel anyone was shadowing him. From time to time, in the bookshop and the café, he attempted to get into conversation, but his fellow customers were guarded and he didn't get far.

West Berlin was a discordant mixture of bomb site and building site. Impossible to settle down to an interesting walk because at every turn you were jarred by the destruction and thwarted by dead ends. In other places your ears were battered by the tumult of building sites with their wrecking balls, tractors and cement mixers. To get away from it all he went into a church that had survived the bombs because he saw the poster outside advertising a lunchtime concert of string quartets by Brahms. There was just a small audience scattered along the pews to hear the music, which was unfamiliar to McGovern. He found it tragic and uplifting at the same time, but also soothing, beautiful.

As the time drew near for his meeting with Harris he made his way slowly back to the hotel, still watchful, but plotting what questions he could ask the Englishman without arousing suspicion. He even wondered if Harris would turn up, so it was a relief to find the Englishman waiting for him in the foyer.

'Mr Harris. I'm delighted to see you. It's good of you to spare the time.'

They shook hands.

'Let's get out of here. This place makes me feel uncomfortable. Full of profiteers, I should imagine.'

McGovern couldn't help grinning to himself. None of his dad's Communist Party friends had had the impeccable upper-class accent with which Harris spoke. These patrician Reds mystified him. Yet it was too easy to dismiss them all as futile romantics or malcontents trying to work off some grudge against the system that had nurtured them so richly.

'We'll find a café somewhere,' said McGovern soothingly.

The place they found on the Kurfürstendamm could hardly have been more congenial to Harris than the Hotel Am Zoo, but he sat down resignedly enough and took out his cigarettes.

'Have one of mine – they're no so easy to get hold of here still, I understand.'

Harris smiled. 'I was in London recently. I brought my own supply back with me, but thanks, anyway. So what do you want to find out about Berlin?'

'Whatever you can tell me.'

Harris looked at the tip of his cigarette. 'The people? The place? The politics?'

'Anything,' said McGovern amiably. 'Your own impressions and, of course, how you yourself came to be here. There must be a story there, too.'

'Not really. Well, to start with the people: they've shown tremendous resilience. They don't think about the past. They just look forward. The Nazis – swept under the carpet in the West. But that's a strength in a way. I was in London recently and honestly it depressed me. The British are so weighed down by the past; we're shucking off the Empire, but in the worst possible way, cutting loose and leaving a mess – and at the same time there's all that triumphalism about the war. We stood alone, we won the war, all that. It was the Russians who really won the war, but no-one gives them any credit.'

'So what you're saying is all in all you prefer Berlin.'

Harris smiled rather grimly. 'Well, there are problems here too.'

'Tell me about them.'

Harris was well informed, but he painted a rather abstract picture. He was keen to emphasise the benefits of the new

East Germany, yet his account was shot through with hints of criticism.

'Very interesting, but my paper will be wanting the odd wee personal story or two, to flesh out the statistics. Not just that production's soared, but what that means for the people with jobs, how your neighbours cope with the housing problem.'

'I tried that line myself, I thought I could sell a few articles to *Picture Post* or something like that but, as I said, the Germans prefer not to talk about themselves. They haven't time and many of them have too much to hide. Even in the East.'

'It must be complicated,' said McGovern, and his sympathy was genuine, 'and for you too.'

Harris shook his head. 'It's impossible to settle here – there's so much under the surface, undercurrents. I didn't feel at home in London any more, but I don't feel at home here either.'

Who can say why two individuals take to each other? But the two men had. McGovern had not forgotten about his task, but now his wanting to know more about Harris was no longer simply an informational exercise. The man intrigued him.

'That's difficult. But, for example, what about your fiancée? She must have an interesting story.'

'Frieda?' Harris frowned. 'What about her?'

'Well, for example, she and her father were refugees. Where did they come from? That could be interesting. Back home we've rather lost sight of all the refugees and what they went through.'

'Well, naturally, there's not much sympathy for the Germans.'

'Some of them were victims too. They weren't all dyed-in-the-wool Nazis.'

Harris sighed. 'They did come from an interesting part of Germany. From Thuringia, they lived near an industrial town called Saalfeld. Down there they hadn't really experienced much of the war until fairly late on, in some rural areas they'd really been quite protected from it, or that's what Frieda's told me. It wasn't until right towards the end, spring 1945, that things got bad. The Americans arrived and bombed the town and the people fled and hid in the wood and in tunnels that were there because of the iron-ore mines. But the Americans moved on because it had been decided Thuringia would be part of the Soviet sector. So they became refugees, Frieda, her sister and her father. Her mother died the year before, I think. Her aunt, her father's sister, was supposed to be living in Berlin, so they came here instead of crossing over into Bavaria, though they never found her. But they got here at least. It was very hard. I don't know how they survived. Frieda won't really talk about it. Well, she met a British colonel who took an interest in her, she admitted that, but she's never ... I don't know what sort of relationship it was, but you can guess. Then her little sister died and they moved back into the Soviet sector. That was unusual – the movement's all the other way, so it's possible Schröder was up to something in the British sector. He probably had some black-market stuff going on, but he wouldn't have been alone. Perhaps the authorities got wind of it. He has a past too, I expect, though of course it's never mentioned and then again so many have a past. Funnily enough, whether he was some sort of Nazi or not, he's managed to worm his way in with the communists. God knows how. I think he knows something about some of what they got up to in Thuringia – there was a settling of scores down there – social democrats murdered, that sort of thing. That might even be why they moved across to the East, he wangled a room in a flat through his new friends or something. I thought of trying to get in touch with Colonel Ordway when I was in England – that was the British officer she knew – to see if he knew anything about it, but I just didn't have time.'

'That is an interesting story,' said McGovern, 'but I'd need to know more, to flesh it out a bit.'

Harris leaned towards him. 'Frieda's frightened of her father. He's a very unpleasant man. She deserves something better,' he said, 'and if I decide I'm staying here, at least I'd like her to still have a chance—'

'You think *I* could help her?'

Now Harris's smile was embarrassed. 'Well … I didn't mean exactly … But she just has to get away from her father.'

'So you're minded to stay here yourself?'

Harris smiled, but it wasn't a happy smile. 'I left England under something of a cloud. And I told you I was a member of the Communist Party there. I thought it would be a fresh start in a new, socialist country. Unfortunately I got into a bit of trouble here as well – a … a thing with a boy. It's not exactly illegal over here, but the authorities don't like that sort of behaviour, so the quid pro quo was it could all be brushed under the carpet if I kept an eye on Schröder.'

'But I thought you said he's on good terms with the East Germans.'

Harris smiled. 'He is. But that doesn't mean they trust him. No-one trusts anyone. That's one of the reasons I'm not happy here. There's too much surveillance. In Schröder's case they thought *he* could do a bit of informing. Anyway, they don't like him quite as much as he thinks they do. I can't stand the man, so in one way I don't mind keeping an eye on him. But it's not a pleasant situation, it's not how things should be.' Harris looked at McGovern with another of his grim smiles. 'And the fact is I'm damn lonely. The only person I can talk to is Frieda and of course she doesn't really understand.'

Harris, his pent-up misery unleashed, talked in a raw, unguarded fashion, describing his isolated, uncertain existence, a stranger in a strange land. When they parted, he gave McGovern his address.

'I'm afraid it's unlikely I'll be paying a second visit.' The detective felt almost guilty, as if he were letting Harris down.

'Well, if you do, you'll look me up, won't you. But all things considered I probably shall go on with my plan to return – when things have died down a bit. I just don't know what to do really. If I don't help Frieda get away I'll feel rotten, but – God, I don't know what to do. Go or stay. God knows. What do you think, Roberts?'

McGovern purchased a second postcard from Kurt's kiosk in the foyer. 'Your friend,' said Kurt, 'the one I saw waiting for you earlier. A German gentleman came enquiring about him – after you left. You want to be careful, sir. It's so easy for someone to disappear in Berlin.'

McGovern ate in the hotel dining room and afterwards sat sunk in one of the deep lounge sofas with a German lager, the taste of which he didn't much like, in front of him. Harris was a baffling enigma. So open about working for the East Germans, pouring out his troubles like that to a journalist – that was hardly the behaviour of a spy or a double agent. Perhaps he truly believed that he could shift his sense of responsibility for the German girl, for his fiancée, on to a stranger.

McGovern tried to imagine how Kingdom would have interpreted it. And the more he thought about it, the more disturbed he became. He remembered Victor Jordan's sugges- tion: that Frieda Schröder might herself be a spy. So Kingdom would probably have drawn the conclusion that the whole of the Harris sob story was nothing but a ploy to get Frieda safely into England to do whatever she was told to do.

But Kingdom was a cynic. McGovern, for all his years in the police force, was not. And he had taken to Harris. It might be a hard-luck story or he might be a noble failure, but McGov- ern's instinct told him the man was too transparent, too naive to have been completely lying.

Frieda though – that was a different matter.

nineteen

M CGOVERN STOOD BY THE WINDOW in DI Slater's office. The room was superior to his own, because the window looked out on an actual side street, not a light well. It was also larger than his own punishment cell of a room. He still in some ways preferred his little secret den, because it was hidden away from casual visitors. Also, the assignment of rooms wasn't a slur on him personally. It simply proved that the Special Branch in general was held in low esteem. And yet what they did was more important than ordinary detective work: defence of the realm.

He'd returned from Berlin only the previous evening and still felt bewildered and unsettled. He'd by no means got a handle on his impressions, but it couldn't be discussed with Slater. He badly needed someone to confide in, but he hardly knew Slater, who was genial enough, but seemed unwilling to put himself out unduly. McGovern had been completely frank with Jarrell, but the sergeant was too inexperienced to give him real moral support and anyway he knew even less than McGovern.

'Cushy number. A nice little trip to Berlin in the middle of the Eberhardt investigation. What was that all about?' Slater grinned. 'Like I always say, the Branch don't know they're born. Sitting about reading books one day – off to foreign parts the next. But Berlin – outside the normal Special Branch remit, ain't it?'

McGovern smiled.

Slater gazed reflectively back at his new colleague, but when it became clear he wouldn't get any more out of him, said: 'What can you tell me about Konrad Eberhardt then? I'm not familiar with the political side of the case.'

'I don't know if there is a political side, other than that Eberhardt was originally a political exile. And that he was a scientist, not involved in nuclear physics, but who knew Alan Nunn May. And Klaus Fuchs. Why don't you just run through it for him, Jarrell?'

Manfred summarised the German's history in a few concise sentences. He ended with: 'I expect you know, sir, that he was going senile, his idea of going back to Germany may have been a sign of that.'

Slater nodded. 'But what's any of this got to do with someone slinging him into the canal?'

'Perhaps someone wanted to stop him going back to Germany,' said McGovern. 'He talked about going back, but if his brain was giving out, that could have been some mad idea that bore no relation to reality. All the same, someone might have thought he was planning to return.' He paused, working out how much to say about Harris. 'Two Communist Party members were seen with him at the funeral at Kensal Green Cemetery after which Eberhardt was found in the canal nearby. They can't be ruled out as suspects. We saw them talking to Eberhardt. They wandered off among the graves out of sight and later we saw the two of them, but by that time Eberhardt was no longer with them.'

Slater said: 'You're assuming Eberhardt died without ever having left the area, then?'

'Seems a reasonable assumption.'

'So these Reds of yours could definitely have had something

to do with it. Well – everything to do with it. They didn't want him going back to Germany and so … That makes it sound almost like a kind of assassination.'

'Assassination's a bit strong. And there's a problem with the motive. We've been told they, or one of them at least, *wanted* him to return to East Germany. And it seems a wee bit unlikely they'd murder Eberhardt at the funeral. Very risky.'

'Could someone else …? Who was at the funeral? Whose funeral was it?'

'Bill Garfield? You know – the writer. A radical, well known, so it was quite a large gathering, lots of literary types. He and Eberhardt were friends. And there was nothing suspicious about Harris being there either. He'd met Garfield in Spain, both of them were there in the civil war.'

'Why would anyone murder someone at a funeral? But he *was* murdered after the funeral,' said Slater. 'Christ! That means we have to try to interview everyone who was at the bloody crematorium. But there's no way of even knowing who was there. I've looked at the canal along there. The cemetery goes up to the edge of the water, there isn't a path that side. So the killer must almost certainly have come *from* the cemetery. That doesn't *prove* it was someone from the funeral he'd been to. He might have lingered on, he might have wandered around in a confused state and been attacked by some opportunist, for money—'

'There was no money in his wallet,' said Manfred.

'Right. So it probably was an ordinary robbery with violence that ended up as a murder,' said Slater, 'but what you say about your men – you'll interview them, won't you. Have them in for questioning.'

'We'll try. You'll still have to interview any of the mourners you can get hold of, though, won't you.'

'That'll be a hell of a job. You were there. How many of them were there, would you say?'

McGovern thought about it. 'Seventy? Eighty?'

'And how do we find out their names? Anyone can turn up at a funeral. God!' Slater stood up and stretched. 'Let's continue this over a jar.'

In the cosier surroundings of a pub popular with the CID Slater felt evidently more comfortable. Several CID turned up and there was no further discussion of the Eberhardt case. Slater appeared to feel he'd done enough work for the day. With a familiar sense of being vaguely out of place and slightly alienated, McGovern made his excuses. His next job, he decided, was to try to interview Alex Biermann.

Alan Wentworth had worked hard on the Eberhardt programme. He had edited and re-edited the transcript of his interview with the old man, but in the end everyone had agreed that it could not be broadcast. Instead he had cobbled together an *in memoriam* programme splicing slivers of the few more coherent bits of the interview into discussions of Eberhardt's work and reminiscences from friends and colleagues. It was to go out on Sunday. He was deeply dissatisfied with it, but at the same time pleased it would be broadcast, because he was convinced that Miles Kingdom had tried to make sure it wasn't.

He hadn't reacted at the time, but afterwards was furious to think that he hadn't challenged Kingdom's suggestion at Wimbledon that the Eberhardt interview might be spiked. The idea that the Secret Services might interfere with freedom of speech appalled him. In theory he knew that sort of thing happened, that information did get suppressed from time to time – and had to be. Perhaps his liberal outrage was just naive. But it was one thing to know about it in the abstract and quite another when it was a concrete fact and you were the person being asked to suppress the information.

He'd had a few dark moments when he'd imagined Kingdom

telephoning Dinah and just subtly raising the ghost of a doubt in her mind – as a punishment because he'd pressed ahead with the Eberhardt programme. Yet it all seemed so ridiculous. It could not possibly matter for the programme to go out. It contained nothing remotely subversive or secret.

Nevertheless, the fact remained that the programme as it stood was deeply unsatisfactory.

'Konrad Eberhardt left Germany in 1938 and arrived in England to a life of exile. He has described his childhood as completely uninteresting, a typical Prussian bourgeois family upbringing. Unlike many today, he had no time for the fashionable interest in childhood and its significance, rejecting the ideas of Sigmund Freud as romantic and irrelevant, above all as completely unscientific. Yet that stern and highly moralistic upbringing stood him in good stead and gave him the courage to resist the Nazis when so many of his compatriots were dazzled by the Führer.'

McGovern was seated in his dusty sitting room. He listened attentively to the broadcast, hoping for useful information. Fragments of an interview were spliced into the narrative, which told of Eberhardt's promising career, a career that stalled once the Nazis came to power. Yet he had not left Germany until 1938, when he finally came under suspicion for having, he claimed, helped some Jews to leave the country. At that point he managed to get away, a dangerous journey with his wife, Gerda, first to France, then to Britain.

The whole progamme was jerky and disjointed. There were inconsistencies and gaps. McGovern gained no clear idea of the dead man's scientific career, why it failed to flourish once he was in London, or why he was released from internment so swiftly. The snippets of interview with the old man and his hoarse, heavily accented, tobacco-laden voice, struck

McGovern as both poignant and pointless. Towards the end, asked about Germany as it was now, his feelings about it and whether he wished to return, he almost shouted: 'Return to Dresden? Dresden no longer exists! Dresden is a pile of rubble.' And then, in a completely different tone of voice: 'I still have family there. My aunt – to survive the Dresden fire storm and still live to be ninety! They want me to return.'

Finally, Eberhardt spoke of an autobiography and how it would 'spill the beans'.

The programme over, McGovern switched off the wireless and went for a walk. It was odd that the programme had failed to mention Eberhardt's suspicious death, but then it was surprising the programme could be transmitted at all when the case was ongoing, but perhaps the format had been chosen for just that reason: it was a general assessment of his life and work, not an investigative piece about a murder.

The McGoverns lived in a grim, redbrick mansion block in Eastcastle Street, near Oxford Circus. Some of the flats were used by the BBC, some by government departments. Others were rented or leased to odd households, mostly old inhabitants who'd been there since before the war. There was something secretive about the silent stairwells and clanking lift shafts, but it was convenient – within walking distance of Whitehall – and Lily loved its proximity to the shops and, more importantly, art galleries and museums.

On this Sunday evening Oxford Street and its side streets and alleys, so busy on weekdays, were deserted and silent, yet free of the withdrawn and sullen atmosphere of parts of Berlin. There was hardly any traffic and even most of the pubs were shut, devoid of custom on the Sabbath. McGovern felt particularly lonely. He walked towards the Tottenham Court Road until he came to the Academy Cinema, but he didn't feel like going to see the French film that was showing, or, indeed, seeing any film on his own, so he turned back and walked north past Broadcasting House towards Regent's Park. The day was still and light, but he hardly noticed. He was sunk in something that hardly qualified as thought, ruminating on Colin Harris and Konrad Eberhardt.

As he walked he puzzled over the old man's autobiography. They'd found no such manuscript among his papers. Perhaps it didn't exist; an old man's senile rambling. Perhaps, on the other hand, Harris had it. Perhaps some secrets were hidden in the document. Perhaps it really was a bombshell waiting to be lobbed into the public realm. He should have somehow got hold of it when he was in Berlin, but how could he have? He hadn't known about it then.

Later, alone in the flat, he tried to assemble the information he'd gathered into coherence.

One: Harris and Eberhardt had known each other and done some sort of business together. The communist, Biermann, was mixed up in that too. The two of them were the last persons – or so it appeared – to have seen Eberhardt alive. McGovern hadn't risked a mention of Eberhardt's name to Harris when he'd talked with him in Berlin. That was a pity, but couldn't be helped. He had to bear in mind that Harris might be Eberhardt's murderer, but, if so, why? To prevent the old man's return to Germany must be the obvious answer. Yet Biermann had prepared the tickets.

Two: Harris's main preoccupation had been – or apparently been – to get Frieda Schröder away from Germany. That might be because she was a spy … As a seasoned investigator McGovern knew he should discount anything Harris said – about his doubts, his misery, his sense of dislocation. It was probably all a smoke screen to disguise his true purposes. And yet …

Three: Kingdom had specifically asked that McGovern be involved with the Eberhardt case. He'd instructed him to attend the mortuary and discuss the case with forensics. McGovern felt fairly sure Kingdom had not told the truth, or the whole truth, about the reason for his interest in Harris. The Burgess–Maclean connection wasn't credible; therefore it had to have to do with Eberhardt.

Four: and that led on to something that McGovern found most uncomfortable: Victor Jordan's reservations about Kingdom. He'd praised him to the skies as the war hero and great interrogator, yet everything he'd said had subtly undermined that praise. To liken him to Robespierre, the French Revolutionary leader who might have been incorruptible, but had unleashed the Terror – that was strange. Ruthless. A committed anti-communist. That picture was rather at odds with McGovern's Kingdom: cool, cynical, sceptical. Jordan's attitude had also, subtly, communicated something different from his actual words. However, just as McGovern disbelieved in the theory of Harris as murderer, so he equally didn't accept Jordan's view of Kingdom as less than outstanding at his job.

Five: then there was the question of the dubious Dr Hoffmann. The reason Feierabend had put him in touch with McGovern was clear, indeed it was the only thing that was clear: Hoffmann had been in a position to introduce him to Harris. So what was the connection between Harris and Hoffmann? Was it simply through Frieda's father? And since Feierabend seemed to have his finger in many pies, couldn't he have managed to introduce him to Harris himself?

Six: Frieda had had a British 'protector', a Colonel Ordway, with whom Harris had thought it might be useful to get in touch. Perhaps that *would* be a good idea. Perhaps the Colonel had had something to do with Schröder's alleged black-market scheme. But Gorch would never agree to that. To attempt to delve into Frieda Schröder's past was by some distance a step too far.

Seven: Eberhardt had mentioned an autobiography. A book that would 'spill the beans'.

McGovern wrote it all down and read it through. At first it seemed not to help at all. Nevertheless, when he read it through a second time he recovered a memory. When Harris and Biermann had been talking at the cemetery with Eberhardt, a parcel had changed hands. Eberhardt had had a package he'd given to Harris, who'd slipped it into his briefcase – a briefcase, which was an odd thing to bring to a funeral.

Perhaps that was the autobiography. The autobiography might be the key.

twenty

CHARLES HALLAM CAME HOME after lunch on Sunday to find Aunt Elfie's Old Etonian boyfriend seated with the family in the garden. It felt peculiar, as if Kingdom had been there all the time, a fixture since Charles's earlier weekend leave.

This leave was only twenty-four hours, but soon he'd be free of the Navy altogether. Oxford was just about appearing over the horizon and he was feeling happier than he had for many months. He was finally beginning to make romantic headway with Christopher. More importantly, his mother was home again.

Dad had written to say she'd left hospital – but where was she? Not in the garden. It was not his mother, but the tall, blond Englishman who lolled in the hammock, which looked as though it might collapse under him at any moment.

Charles had a horrible, hollow feeling in his stomach as he greeted the little group with a perfunctory wave. Perhaps Vivienne was still in the asylum, perhaps she hadn't come home after all. Looking at his father, he said rather desperately: 'Where is she?'

John Hallam stood up. 'She's resting. She'll be so pleased to see you, Charles.'

And Vivienne was pleased to see him. She was in her old

place, reclining on the chaise longue in the ground-floor drawing room. A little more haggard each time she came home, a little thinner, and her black hair was streaked with grey, her eyes wells of vagueness; she lifted her languid arms. 'Darling! How absolutely wonderful to see you.'

'It's wonderful to see you too.' Charles bent to kiss her and the movement turned into a rather desperate hug, so intense that he felt close to tears. But as he moved out of the embrace to sit by her feet at the end of the sofa sadness overwhelmed him, for he knew that there was just somehow less of her than there used to be. She was still lovely, marvellous Vivienne, whom he loved so much, but part of her personality seemed to have drifted away, so that she became forgetful and as if nothing, not even he, her son, meant as much as in years gone by.

'I did terribly well in my Russian exams,' he told her, 'and soon I'll be shot of the whole boring business of National Service.'

'That's marvellous, darling,' she said, but her gaze wandered away from him and vaguely round the room.

'How are you feeling?' He watched her, full of apprehension.

'I'm feeling fine.'

They never talked about the hospital.

'I interrupted your rest,' he said.

'I'm glad you did, darling. It's so nice to be home. But now, if you don't mind, I'll carry on dozing a little longer and then I'll come down to the garden and join you all.' As he reached the door, she said: 'Who is that man who was here at lunch? I've met him before, haven't I, only I can't remember—'

'I think Dad's hoping he'll propose to Aunt Elfie.'

'Oh ... what an idea.' Vivienne giggled. 'But what does he *do*? No-one told me what he does or who he is, you see.'

'He's a journalist, I think.'

In the garden Aunt Elfie and Judy cleared the coffee cups and the glasses and Charles's father went to phone the hospital where he worked. Kingdom stood up. He offered Charles a cigarette. Charles, who did smoke, refused, because there was something patronising in the gesture with which the older man proffered the silver cigarette case. It seemed silently to suggest that Charles was to be treated as an adult, but only out of the goodness of Kingdom's heart.

'So your days on the Russian course are nearly over. How did it go?'

'I did okay, actually.'

Kingdom looked at him, appraising him, Charles felt. 'Tell me about it – your impressions, what you've learned.' He sat down again, this time on one of the wicker garden chairs, and gestured at the seat beside him.

Despite himself, Charles was flattered by the attention. He tried to make his account sound both modest and amusing. Kingdom was, after all, not patronising him. He was genuinely interested. After a while, when Charles ran out of things to say, Kingdom rose to his feet once more, extracted a card from an inner pocket and handed it over.

'I know it's much too early – you've your years at university in front of you, but if you ever feel you might like to have another chat, do get in touch, won't you.'

'Thank you very much, sir.'

'You obviously have a gift for languages. Pity not to use it really. But maybe you'll end up preferring to stick to the Roman Empire, rather than dealing with ours or what remains of it.'

Charles smiled politely at this odd remark. Only later did he work out what he thought Kingdom was actually hinting at.

It was Sunday and a hot one at that, and McGovern was to meet Kingdom by the Round Pond in Kensington Gardens.

'Sorry I'm late. I was having lunch with friends. An idyllic scene, don't you agree?' Kingdom gestured at the little boy poking with a stick at his toy boat bobbing just within reach, at the nanny rocking a pram the size of an Edwardian pony carriage, and at a whole family, well dressed, dark, olive-skinned, whose three children, all with curly hair like bunches of grapes, tumbled their expensive clothes in the dust. One of the women in the group reminded McGovern a little of Lily.

Kingdom was staring ahead. 'You've seen the detective in charge of the Eberhardt investigation? What's going on? I heard the broadcast. I was bloody furious it went out the way it did. That bit at the end about an autobiography – what the hell's that about?'

McGovern decided for the moment not to mention the parcel that had been exchanged in the cemetery. It might not be the autobiography and if it was, he should have remembered about it sooner. Further, Kingdom might blame him for not having managed to get hold of it, for not having asked Harris about it, and for not having informed Kingdom. So he merely said cautiously: 'We found no manuscript in the house. Maybe there isn't one. Perhaps it doesn't exist. It might be a delusion, part of Eberhardt going a bit senile.'

'Possibly. You may be right. This friend of Harris, Biermann? Was that the name? Have you interviewed him? He might well know about it.'

McGovern knew he should have already made enquiries. 'It's possible he has the manuscript. If it exists, of course.'

'Yes. If it exists. But have you seen him?'

'I only got back on Thursday. I've not had the time. I had to see CID about it, it's technically their case, after all.'

'Oh – CID.' Kingdom gestured dismissively and dragged on his cigarette as he gazed out over the pleasing vista of parkland, the green lawns and trees thick with foliage. The noise of traffic was muffled, just soothing urban mood music for the peaceful-ness of the scene.

'What sort of information might the autobiography contain?'

'Oh, use your imagination, man,' said Kingdom irritably. 'What the hell do you think? Nuclear stuff …'

'But he wasn't engaged in nuclear research.'

'No, but he knew Fuchs. He may have got hold of all sorts of bits of embarrassing information. But anyway – what about Harris? What do you really think he's up to?'

McGovern hoped he sounded more confident than he felt. 'I don't think he had anything to do with the Burgess and Maclean business, if that's what you mean.'

'The Burgess and Maclean *business*, as you call it,' said Kingdom wearily, 'is a hell of a lot more than just another *business*, another little irritation in the vast and interminable locust plague of life's little irritations. It's not a mosquito bite, you know. It isn't the common cold. More like bubonic plague.'

'I didna mean—'

'What Harris is up to is part of what you went to Berlin to find out, isn't it.'

'I managed to get an introduction. I met him a couple of times. It seems like he's changed his plans. He's not so keen to come back here any more. Harris did mention Burgess and Maclean. He was very disapproving. Spying has nothing to do with communism, he said.'

McGovern was hoping for some praise for his success, but Kingdom only said: 'Did you believe him?' He flung his cigarette away and immediately lit another.

'Yes, I did. Naive, idealistic, a wee bit out of his depth. I met his girl as well. She's upset about his change of plan. She's still desperate to leave Berlin, come to England.'

'You met her?' Kingdom raised his eyebrows. 'You didn't tell me that.'

'There hasn't been an opportunity. I haven't seen you since.'

Kingdom uncrossed and recrossed his legs. 'Of course. Well, what about her? What did you think of her? What was your impression?'

'She's beautiful.'

'For Christ's sake. That wasn't what I meant.'

'She's had a hard time—' McGovern began to rehearse the story she'd told him, trying to convey his sense of her victim-hood, but Kingdom soon interrupted him.

'Look, old chap, I don't want to seem heartless, but they all have a sob story. Always a mistake to get taken in by a pretty face. It was chaos in 1945. People did what they had to do to survive, but afterwards they like to embellish it a bit. That's always the way. And perfectly understandable. You have to be able to live with yourself. Or so I imagine.'

'I don't think I was taken in,' said McGovern quietly, but he was offended by the slur. 'I'm just reporting what she told me. She just wants to leave Germany because of all that happened. Her mother died in 1944 and not long after the war her sister died too. I met Victor Jordan. He told me there were hints her father was up to – I don't know – the black market, I suppose, but anyway something illegal. He seems to be a rather sinister character. Mr Jordan thought he must have had links with someone in the occupying forces. He told me all the things going on at the end of the war, the black market, the way the Allies treated the women – but he was very complimentary about you. He said you'd not have anything to do with any of that. He said that didn't always make you very popular. They were all at it themselves, they were so corrupt they couldn't believe you didn't have some wee scam of your own.'

'He said that?'

'It was by way of being a joke, sir.'

Kingdom frowned. 'To tell you the truth, the stories about the black market were exaggerated, in my view. So far as we were concerned, that is. Of course the Germans were doing whatever they could to survive, but I'm surprised Jordan should have made those sorts of comments about the Allies.'

'He also said you were the best interrogator.'

'Did he? I didn't send you there to discuss me.' He smoked in silence. After a few minutes McGovern found the silence intimidating. Opaque. Unfathomable. But then Kingdom spoke.

'You know all that talk of having a good war? You had a good war, all things considered, didn't you? Badly wounded, but you were able to get away, have a new life. Well, I had a good war too. In fact my war was absolutely fucking brilliant. I enjoyed active service. Loved it. And afterwards – in all that chaos – I'm proud of what we did in Germany, restoring some kind of sanity. The Allies did a bloody good job in Berlin – and Jordan shouldn't be running it down. We *saved* the Germans and they were only too pleased to do what we wanted. You shouldn't believe everything Jordan says. He did all right himself, I shouldn't wonder.' He stood up. 'I'll be in touch soon. You might need to go back to Berlin.'

'Gorch will never—'

'Forget Gorch.'

The early evening sunlight slanted across the lawns. McGovern walked slowly in the opposite direction from Kingdom, towards Bayswater. He puzzled over the autobiography. He couldn't understand why it worried Kingdom so much. Eberhardt had no nuclear secrets. His secrets, if any, must be of some other kind. But what other secrets could be troubling Kingdom? And what had he, McGovern, said that had annoyed Kingdom so much? For something had certainly ruffled the agent's sangfroid.

twenty-one

C⋙つ

T HE ONLY ASPECT OF THE CASE that was going well was
Manfred Jarrell's relationship with Doreen of the Progressive Travel Agency. Jarrell had convinced her that he had Alex
Biermann's interests at heart, that he wasn't under suspicion,
that no-one wanted to arrest him and that his, Jarrell's, sole
interest was in Eberhardt's murder. As the relationship developed
he learned more about Biermann's visit to Yorkshire. It was
because a northern comrade was suspicious about a group of
Ukrainian immigrants who had settled there after the war and
who, it was rumoured, were engaged in illegal fascist activities.
Some of their neighbours even alleged that they had fought
for the Ukrainian Waffen SS and against the Russians. These
suspicions had been passed on to Biermann in the belief that
he could get them into the *Daily Worker*. Could there not be an
exposé of settlers who were effectively enemy aliens? How had
they been allowed in? Hadn't they been vetted? Why weren't
they in prison in Germany or the Soviet Union? Although no
longer working for the communist newspaper, Biermann had
travelled up to Leeds, suspecting that the claims might be due
more to anti-immigrant prejudice than to any reality. Jarrell
didn't know if he'd found out anything about them.

Alex Biermann lived in a small block of flats at the end of
a terrace of lumpy Edwardian artisans' cottages that straggled

down towards the river Lee. The modern block seemed to have been built on a piece of spare land adjacent to a sawmill factory. A continual sawing sound grated and whined as the policemen approached the flats and, although he could not see it, McGovern felt sawdust in the air. His throat was dry and his eyes stung.

'I can't make head nor tail of Hackney, sir,' said Jarrell. 'It just doesn't seem to have a centre.' In the late afternoon they had struggled through the rush hour by crowded overground train, bus and foot into the shapeless and meandering districts that seeped out towards the marshes, the reservoirs and beyond, through miles of terraces, bomb sites and factories, towards Epping Forest. Now, having reached their destination, they looked up at the shabby flats. The concrete façade was cracked; the curved ocean-liner windows carried a faded memory of the seaside, but far from gleaming white in sparkling south coast sunshine, the building, stuck between the sawmill and a railway line, was a dingy shade of grey.

'So what do we know about wee Alexander Biermann, Jarrell?'

McGovern had sent his junior off to see if Special Branch had anything on Biermann, and, sure enough, as with so many communists, they had.

'Born 1926 in Dresden. Came over here with his family in 1934. His father was a pastor who opposed the regime, his mother came from a wealthy landowning family. Junkers, they were called, sir.'

'*Yoonkers*, Jarrell. It's pronounced *Yoonkers*, not like junket. J is pronounced like a y.'

'Sorry, sir. Well, I think a lot of them, the *Yoonkers*, supported Hitler, but she stuck by her husband and followed him over here. She had money too, and he eventually managed to get some sort of teaching job. They're not hard up, live somewhere just south of London, sent the son to private school. In 1944 he was conscripted, saw action in Italy, was meant to go to university after he came back, but seems to have rebelled against his family, instead he joined the CP, very active in the Young Communist League, became a Party organiser, wrote for the *Daily Worker*, don't know what he's doing now he's left the Travel Agency. No arrests or convictions, by the way. I cross-checked with Eberhardt's file. He knew Eberhardt since childhood. Eberhardt was a friend of Biermann senior. Before the war, at least. So all that's true.'

'Let's see if Mr Biermann's at home. And don't forget, we're CID, not Special Branch.'

A dishevelled young woman in blue trousers and a man's shirt opened the door in answer to the bell and smiled at them, pushing aside a messy tangle of dark hair.

'Hullo!'

'Mr Biermann at home?'

'I'm afraid not. He's just nipped out – but he'll be back soon.' She appeared delighted to see them. 'Can I say who called? Or can I help you in any way?'

McGovern flashed his card, but that didn't disturb her. She gestured them into a cramped, chaotic living room.

'Can I get you some tea or something?'

McGovern declined. The young woman cleared a space on the settee, which was piled with papers, and sat looking at them.

'What's Alex been up to now?' she enquired brightly.

'You tell me, Miss—'

'Bridgenorth, I'm Alice Bridgenorth.'

'We're sorry to bother you, miss. Perhaps you could just let Mr Biermann know we're investigating the murder of Konrad Eberhardt, who was a friend of his and of his family, we understand.'

'Oh yes! He'd known him all his life,' interrupted Alice. 'He'd been a friend of the family, although I believe they'd fallen out. But Alex kept in touch with him. It was a terrible shock, him dying like that. Alex was dreadfully upset.'

'Is there anything you can tell us about him, anything that might help us understand exactly what happened? I mean, what did Mr Biermann say? We know he saw Mr Eberhardt shortly before he died.'

'Yes, they were at a funeral. He'd persuaded the old man to go back to his family in Germany, because he thought he wasn't in a fit state to look after himself any more, he's all alone here, you see. He even thought it might have been his fault, somehow, that he – died. Look, are you sure you won't change your mind about the tea? It must be awfully thirsty work being a policeman.'

'Well, thanks. Some tea would be nice.' It would give them, McGovern thought, time for a quick nose round the room, but Alice Bridgenorth returned with the tea tray before they'd found anything interesting.

'You were saying Mr Biermann thought Mr Eberhardt's death was somehow his fault?'

Alice laughed. 'Oh, only in the sense that they met at the funeral of another writer, as you said, and they talked for a while, but then Alex lost track of him. He said one minute he was there and the next he'd disappeared. Alex worried about it, but then he thought, well, Mr Eberhardt had travelled up from Deal on his own and could presumably get back again without accident. Only he didn't.'

'Can you tell me any more about this going back to Germany idea? It was simply for the old man's good?'

'Of course! What else could it have been?' She picked up a packet of cigarettes and offered them, before lighting one for herself.

'I've no idea. I'm not suggesting there was any other reason. Did you know the old man yourself?'

'I'd met him. We went down to Deal together to visit him

one time, but it was pointless my being there. Alex thought I could tidy the place up a bit while the two of them were talking, but Mr Eberhardt got quite angry when I started to touch his things, so that didn't work.'

'Did Mr Biermann mention other people at the funeral? You can appreciate there being so many people near the scene of a crime, people who may have known Mr Eberhardt ...'

Alice Bridgenorth laughed, put her hand to her mouth. 'It's awful to laugh, isn't it, but that's so odd, someone being murdered at a funeral. Why choose a funeral to murder him at? It's macabre and so risky you'd have thought with so many people around. But someone really did kill him?'

'I'm afraid so.'

'Actually, Alex said in a way it wasn't so surprising because he'd quarrelled with almost everyone.'

'What had he quarrelled with them about?'

'I don't know really, but Alex used to say Mr Eberhardt and his friends from before the war were always rowing about what went on in Germany then, whose fault was it Hitler came to power. Alex said they lived in their little world of exiles and couldn't stop fighting old battles. That's why he thought Mr Eberhardt would be better off in Germany, he'd be living in the real world.'

'One sort of real world.'

'Alex is very much against living in the past.'

'These quarrels, Miss Bridgenorth. How serious were they? Did Mr Biermann ever suggest that the dead man might have made serious enemies in the exile community?'

The girl gazed at him. 'Well, how odd you say that, because Alex did say there were rumours. Alex said it was all spite, but Mr Eberhardt had told him some of them thought he was an informer. But what would he inform about? I mean, it doesn't make sense, does it?'

Recalling that Eberhardt had known Klaus Fuchs, McGovern

didn't answer her question, but Jarrell said: 'Would you know the names of any of these individuals who thought he was an informer?'

'Oh, but you don't think any of them could have – I mean they're all old, they surely wouldn't *kill* anyone – that's just absurd. Alex jokes about it. They crossed swords, a lot of former comrades, he says, but writers and intellectuals don't go round murdering each other.'

'I hope not,' said McGovern, 'but you understand we have to look at all possibilities.' He looked at his watch. 'You said Mr Biermann would be back soon. We don't want to take up more of your time.'

'He'll be back any minute,' insisted Alice Bridgenorth.

'We'll wait a little longer then.' The girl was so open that it was worth risking a few questions about Biermann, he thought. He began by asking how long she'd known him.

'I met him at a party. He's a communist, you know. I'm not. Of course I agree with his ideas, most of them. But I'm not what he calls an activist. He'd like me to be, but I don't have the time. I'm training to be a teacher and the comrades always seem to be so busy. Alex used to work for the Party. Wrote for the *Daily Worker*, but he found a lot of it a bit grey and bureaucratic. Not much vision, he said. There were too many constraints. Then he worked for a travel agency, but that was just an interim solution. Now he's signed up to work for the buses. They're desperately short of manpower, he says. I'm not sure it's such a good idea to do that sort of work. It's manual work, really, isn't it and he's so educated. But he says that way he'll find out how things work, what life's really like for ordinary people. That's the problem with the Party, he says, they're a bit out of touch with ordinary workers. And he'll get involved with the union. Then later on he'll go back to writing, he'll be able to write about the lives of ordinary people.'

Rather, thought McGovern, as though 'ordinary people'

were a different race from intellectuals. But Biermann was young and idealistic. And ideals weren't a bad thing, after all.

The sound of the front door opening was followed by: 'Hullo! Alice?'

'We're in here.'

Alex Biermann stood in the doorway, as untidily dressed as the girl and in similar clothes, but unlike her, he seemed deeply suspicious. 'What's this all about?' He advanced into the room, but remained standing.

McGovern and Jarrell stood up. 'We're investigating the death of Konrad Eberhardt.'

Biermann examined their police cards closely, then sat down abruptly on the arm of the sofa, close to Alice. 'About time someone's doing something about that. You don't seem to have taken much notice of it so far. How many weeks is it now?'

'We're doing our best. We wondered if you could tell us about the last time you saw him, at Bill Garfield's funeral.'

'Oh, that's it. I see. I suppose your lot were crawling all over the funeral, spying on the Reds to see what they're up to these days. Which in the case of that lot is nothing very much. I wouldn't even have called Garfield a socialist any more, if he ever was one.' He looked down at his girlfriend with a look McGovern interpreted as one of affectionate resignation. 'What have you been telling them, then?'

'We were just talking about the dead man,' said McGovern quickly, 'and how fond you were of him.'

'I'll get some more tea. You'd like some, wouldn't you, Alex.' She gathered up the cups and left the room.

'I suppose she's been talking a lot of nonsense,' said Biermann ungraciously.

'We came to talk to you about the funeral. With so many people there it's difficult for us. In theory any of them could be a suspect.'

Biermann snorted contemptuously. 'They're all talk, that lot. A few of them probably hated Konrad, but … no.' He shook his head.

'Do you know any of them? It would be helpful to have some names.'

Instead of answering the question, Biermann said: 'I knew Konrad since before I left Germany with my family. Got on with him better than with my own father. I suppose you think I might have had something to do with his death, but you're wrong. I was really cut up about it.'

'Why should we imagine you had anything to do with it? You and Colin Harris were among the last to see him alive, but why would you kill your old friend, Mr Biermann?'

'Oh, is this all about Colin? For God's sake, why don't you leave him alone?'

'It's all about solving a crime, Mr Biermann. And Konrad Eberhardt was a controversial character, wasn't he? Former friend of Klaus Fuchs suddenly returning to East Germany? He had a reputation as an anti-communist. It seems very odd he wanted to go back, doesn't it, Mr Biermann?'

Biermann's glance sharpened. 'Do detectives usually bother with things like that?'

'Things like what, Mr Biermann?'

Biermann shrugged. 'Well – ideas, I suppose. Politics. Other than that you're the arm of the state. I suppose you saw him as a subversive.'

'Leaving aside the politics, Mr Biermann …'

Biermann smiled. 'Is it possible to do that?'

'We're just interested in his murderer. Who may have been at Garfield's funeral. We're simply interested in who was there.'

But Biermann said he hadn't noticed who was there. He'd spoken to Eberhardt about the journey to Germany. The idea was Eberhardt would travel with Colin Harris as far as Berlin, but he couldn't get the old man to concentrate on these plans.

When the mourners were dispersing, he looked for Eberhardt, but couldn't see him. He went back to the wake. Mrs Garfield – Georgina – had persuaded him to stay on long after the others had left. 'She was a bit upset and we had some more to drink and I tried to comfort her and – well, things got a bit out of hand. I suppose I'd drunk rather a lot. She certainly had. Old Garfield had been ill for a long time, you know, and I don't suppose … anyway he was much older than her … and when people are upset, they can behave a bit unpredictably, can't they? I feel bad about the whole thing now. I shouldn't have let Konrad out of my sight. I thought he could look after himself, but he obviously couldn't.'

'Did Colin Harris go to the wake? You and he left the cemetery together.'

'Oh, so you *were* there. No, he didn't. Said he didn't like that sort of occasion.'

McGovern decided to call it a day. 'Thank you for talking to us, Mr Biermann. If you do remember the names of anyone there, it could be very helpful.'

He was almost out of the front door when he suddenly turned back. 'Just one last thing – what about the autobiography? He mentioned an autobiography in the radio broadcast that went out last week. What's that all about? He gave Harris a parcel. When you were all in the cemetery.'

Biermann took it like a slap in the face. 'That's nonsense. There isn't one.'

'There wasn't a book, a manuscript in the parcel?'

'No. As if it's any of your business.'

'What if it wasn't an autobiography? Or if it was an autobiography that included political information or possibly information about scientific activities that would be useful to East Germany?'

Alex Biermann stared at McGovern. 'You people live in

some kind of fantasy land. You see traitors everywhere.'

The two detectives walked up the straggly little street to the main road.

'He knew who we were, didn't he,' said Jarrell. 'He knew we weren't just ordinary CID.'

As McGovern sat in Slater's office to discuss what had so far been achieved, his irritation level had within minutes mounted to the point at which he was going either to have to leave or to lose his temper. Slater's response when McGovern reported on the interview with Biermann was an unhelpful, 'Why don't you bring him in for questioning? Rough him up a bit?'

'He could be a suspect,' piped up Jarrell, 'except that he seems to have been the only person in the world who actually liked the dead man.'

'He was the last person to see the dead man alive, for Christ's sake. Along with this subversive you were supposed to be watching. Your surveillance doesn't seem to have been very successful,' said Slater. 'A murder was committed while you were actually shadowing a potential suspect.'

'Thanks for pointing that out.' McGovern gritted his teeth.

'But Biermann has to be on the list,' said Jarrell, changing tack, perhaps just to annoy his superiors. 'He was present at the funeral and he had an interest in persuading the old man to return to Germany. Suppose the old man suddenly changed his mind—'

'Again.'

'And that didn't suit Biermann,' Jarrell continued. 'Which would suggest Biermann had some special reason for wanting him back there – for example, that he was in contact with the East German government, that he was working for them.' Jarrell looked at his audience triumphantly. 'And then there was this red herring, when he suddenly told us about his ... his *dalliance* with the widow, Garfield's wife.'

'Dalliance!' Slater burst out laughing. 'Are you some kind of bloody poet? He was having it off with Garfield's widow? My God, she's a bit past it, isn't she! He's half her age.' The idea seemed to scandalise Slater.

'I think she's only in her forties.'

'Well, she looks older.'

'It's irrelevant. Jarrell's right, it could have been meant to divert our attention, but it doesn't lead anywhere. Other than that, he didn't tell us anything we didn't know already. What about the mourners you've seen?'

The project of interviewing the mourners would get nowhere, McGovern knew. At best it would involve hours of work for almost no reward. He was glad it was largely Slater's job rather than his.

'We've interviewed five so far,' said Slater. 'Needle in a bloody haystack. And probably there isn't even a fucking needle. None of them would have known for certain Eberhardt would even be at the funeral. Which means it wasn't premeditated.'

'Anything useful?'

'Not much. Of the five, three were no use at all. Then there was a woman who hinted she had an affair with him, didn't speak well of him, but it was all a long time ago; and there was another émigré exile, a writer called Theodor Strauss. He certainly knew Eberhardt. And he definitely disliked him, wasn't at all complimentary about the old man. Didn't like Garfield either, described him as a phoney hero, full of bombast and posturing about Spain, claiming to be the great International Brigade hero, when almost all the real heroes were dead. Strauss seemed to think Eberhardt dying at a funeral was rather a joke or even poetic justice, although he didn't say why. He described his relationship with Eberhardt as the result of exile, feverish, exaggerated. But the interesting thing from our point of view is he said no-one could ever trust Eberhardt. He wasn't reliable. He was always changing his views. And he said one thing to your face and another behind your back. They were interned together, but Eberhardt got out very quickly and Strauss said he always suspected him of being an informant. Reporting to the authorities about other internees.'

'An informant: that's interesting. But that was just during the war. Unless he was now informing on Alex Biermann – or on Colin Harris ... but he was confused. He was unlikely to be much use as an informant any more.'

'A funeral seems a rum place to murder him. If there really was a *plan*, if it was premeditated, why not do it in his home in Deal?' pondered Slater.

'Yes,' chirped up Jarrell. 'There he was, he lived alone, it wouldn't be difficult to break into the house. His murderer may have been known to him. He might have let him in.'

'But he wasn't killed in his own home, so that's irrelevant,' snapped McGovern.

McGovern pictured the confused old man wandering about in the cemetery and perhaps accidentally straying out onto the edge of the canal beyond the rusted gates. If someone had followed him, he might not have noticed the hostile intent when that person approached him. But the confusion raised again the question of whether this really was a murder. 'Someone who was confused could possibly have somehow tripped, fallen over, knocked his head and then fallen into the canal.'

'We've been through all that,' said Slater. 'The white coats are still insisting it's unlikely.'

'There's one thing you didn't mention, sir,' said Monkhouse, Slater's sour-faced sergeant, with whom McGovern had clashed what seemed like weeks ago. 'Strauss said he looked round some of the graves and noticed someone loitering around nearby.'

'Thanks for reminding me. Yes, I left that out. A big man,

there was nothing special about him, he said, but somehow he didn't look like the other mourners. Which makes me think,' concluded Slater with an air of triumph, 'that it *was* just a robbery after all.'

Which meant, thought McGovern, that his colleague wasn't going to put himself out unduly to solve this particular crime. A body in the canal was nothing unusual after all. A crime that often went unsolved – although less so, when an identity was established. Slater would haul in a couple of villains, try to stick it on one of them, and if nothing came of it, well, Eberhardt had no relations and seemingly no friends and the whole thing would soon be forgotten. He left the office in a grim frame of mind. Things were going nowhere and he had to report again to Kingdom. He'd at least have the stuff about Biermann to show for his efforts.

twenty-two

T HE RENDEZVOUS WAS AT the Natural History Museum on a wet Wednesday afternoon. McGovern found Kingdom in a distant deserted room devoted to reptiles. Stuffed snakes were displayed in frozen, writhing positions in glass cabinets. No visitors had penetrated this far, and its dusty specimens amounted to nothing but a surplus of useless information. McGovern disliked snakes and their petrified malice preserved beneath glass in this forgotten corner of the vast building made his flesh crawl.

Kingdom leaned against a wall by the window. 'I've spent hours with that fucking pansy, Blunt, but I can't pin him down.' He brought out his cigarette case. 'You've seen Biermann, then?'

This time McGovern owned up about the parcel he'd observed change hands in the cemetery. 'But Biermann categorically denied any knowledge of the autobiography.'

'Why the hell didn't you tell me this before?'

'I personally doubt any autobiography exists.'

'The fact that Biermann denied it makes it all the more likely it *does* exist, in my view. And if it does, Harris has it. Well, now you'll definitely have to make another trip to Berlin. If there's a manuscript, we have to get it back.' His eyes flickered, darted to and fro as if an unseen enemy lurked even in this cemetery of serpents.

'The Super will no stand for me having another wee holiday in Berlin.'

'He will if I ask him nicely.'

'About the Eberhardt case,' said McGovern, 'I've talked to CID. They've interviewed several individuals who were at the funeral, but they're no closer to finding the murderer.'

'I don't give a fuck who murdered Eberhardt. What's important is what he was up to.'

Kingdom's brutal indifference to the death startled McGovern, but he ploughed on. 'Someone Slater, the CID man in charge of the case, interviewed suggested Eberhardt might have been an informant. I thought – is it possible he was working for the East Germans after all? We had him down as an anti-communist, but if he really did want to return, then perhaps he was working for them all along.'

'An informant?' Kingdom paced round the cabinets looking or pretending to look at the snakes. 'It's an interesting idea, but I doubt it. But if it were true, of course, then the autobiography would become more important. A possible coup for the Russians, or the East Germans.'

'That's not the way information would be passed on, though,' objected McGovern.

'But if it were some kind of propaganda coup. That's what "spilling the beans" would mean, isn't it? Something intended to be published, to make a splash, create a scandal.'

McGovern knew he didn't want to believe in the autobiography. He didn't want to believe that Harris could be mixed up in something like that. If Harris was really the courier in charge of a damaging document to be given to the East Germans, then in McGovern's eyes Harris would become a kind of traitor. But Harris was an idealist. In *his* mind it wouldn't be treason. In his eyes it would be … what would it be? An exposure of the corruption of Cold War politics on both sides? A plague on both your houses?

'Well, McGovern?'

'You may be right.'

'Well, see to it you find out. And do the necessary.' He was silent for a while. Then: 'What else about Biermann?'

'He's a busy wee man. It was he who planned Eberhardt's return to Germany. Now he's joining the workers on the buses. He's even investigating some Ukrainians in the north because a fellow Party member suspects them of being fascists who fought with the Waffen SS.'

'How very fanciful.' Kingdom moved restlessly along the display, gazing into the cabinets. 'Look at this one. One wouldn't want to meet that in the jungle. Were there snakes in the desert? I suppose they were frightened away by the noise.'

'When you say "do the necessary", what exactly do you mean?'

'You know what I mean. I told you from the start. See he doesn't return. And find out as much as you can about his fiancée's unpleasant-sounding father.' He walked to and fro. How restless he was. 'I want to know what Harris is up to with the woman's father. Is it just that he happens to be the father of the woman he loves – if we can believe that? Or is the real connection with Schröder *père*?'

'Harris talked about Thuringia. Schröder came from that part of the world.'

'Really?' Kingdom's gaze was as penetrating and opaque as ever. And then he smiled. 'You know what Thuringia is famous for, don't you?'

McGovern shook his head.

'Uranium. That's where the Soviets get the uranium to make their bomb.'

When Lily heard that McGovern was to return to Berlin, she made a brief trip to London. They spent an intense day at the Festival of Britain, she trying to conceal her anxiety, he trying to reassure her. The breeze whisked them across the bright, chilly open spaces between the exhibition buildings. A fountain spouted at intervals, its jet blown about by the wind. There was something flimsy about the light, efficient structures to which they were directed along a pre-chosen path by the Festival programme. If you do it in the wrong order it won't make sense, the brochure warned. They dutifully queued for the Dome of Discovery; in fact, there was a lot of queueing, and McGovern felt it was all a bit too didactic, almost preachy. They were being told to have fun and it wasn't spontaneous. He didn't feel at home among the low-rise buildings, the self-consciously modern murals, the spindly furniture and manicured spaces.

But the Festival lifted Lily's mood. For a while she forgot to be anxious. She loved the clean buildings and bright colours. 'At least they're trying,' she said. 'It's a glimpse of the future, isn't it. An end to austerity.'

McGovern tried to match her mood, but only when they made love late that evening did he briefly lose himself in their mutual surrender. And even then, afterwards, sleep wouldn't come, for his thoughts circled round the remembered figure of Frieda Schröder; the gaunt face of Colin Harris and all his confused attempts to do the right thing; the ebullient Alex Biermann, so full of hope and energy; and Kingdom. Most of all he thought about Kingdom and about what Kingdom expected of him. Once it had seemed clear, but he could no longer read Kingdom's moods. Perhaps he had never been able to, perhaps he had never understood him. But he was determined to do what he'd decided to do before he left for Germany; and resolved to make it count when he got there.

twenty-three

ᴄ𝄢ᴐ

THE SUN BEAT DOWN out of a hot blue sky as McGovern
and Jarrell cruised through the south London suburbs and
onto the Brighton road. It had taken McGovern many hours to
locate the man he was looking for, but his success had buoyed
him up. For weeks he'd felt himself a pawn in a game he didn't
understand, but now he'd taken the initiative in seeking out
Frieda Schröder's former 'protector', Colonel Ordway. With
luck, no-one would know, but if they did, so be it. He didn't
care if it got him into trouble later.

Jarrell drove and McGovern had the map. After Haywards
Heath he started to give instructions. They turned off the A23
and were soon driving along winding lanes between high
hedges. Jarrell's driving, poor at the best of times, became even
more erratic, but the whole landscape was deserted and they
encountered not a single oncoming vehicle. The land slumbered
in the Sunday sunshine. McGovern found the lush green countryside almost too rich in its overpowering greenness, the trees
sinking under their weight of foliage.

'Here it is, I think.'

The ancient house, made of rosy brick and rust red tiles,
stood some way back from the road and was approached by a dirt
track. They bumped along until it widened into a gravel drive.

The man waiting by the open front door was tall and lean.

A brown tweed cap perched forward on his head to shade his eyes. He stepped nimbly forward and held out his hand. 'Inspector McGovern?'

'Aye.' He shook hands. 'And this is Sergeant Jarrell.' Ordway invited them into the dark panelled hall and thence into a long drawing room, also panelled. They eased their way past ancient sofas and rickety side tables and out into the sunlight again. The Colonel had evidently been seated at a garden table reading the *Sunday Telegraph*.

'I'm drinking whisky,' he said. 'What about you?'

Jarrell refused. The Colonel poured him plain water from the jug and strong doses of the finest Islay single malt for McGovern and himself. 'As a Scotsman you'll appreciate this.' He drank. 'What's all this about then? Berlin after the war, eh? Old history now. Don't you have enough to do in London? I hear the whole place is chock full of Jamaicans these days. God knows we didn't fight the war for that. Still, you know what you're doing I suppose. Fire away.'

McGovern began carefully. One foot wrong and the Colonel might kick up a fuss. That mustn't happen, because neither Gorch nor Kingdom knew that he and Jarrell were here. 'It's a delicate matter, sir. And it's strictly off the record. We're investigating the murder of a German who'd been living in this country for many years, since before the war, an anti-Nazi. He was apparently planning to return to East Germany when he was murdered. There are links to Berlin and in the course of our investigations we've run up against a family there, well, a man and his daughter, Thomas and Frieda Schröder. I understand you knew them when you were in Berlin with the occupying forces after the end of the war. We wondered if you could tell us anything about them and particularly the father.'

Colonel Ordway looked extremely taken aback, but he recovered in double-quick time. 'Little Frieda Schröder? Good God. I always wondered what happened to her.'

'I'm sorry to bring it up, sir, but we're interested in Schröder's activities at the time.'

The Colonel sipped his whisky. 'You probably know I had a brief liaison with Frieda Schröder. My wife's at the church rearranging the flowers for evensong. Can't stand all that bloody claptrap myself, but women like it. In any case, I've got no secrets from her. She's no fool. She knows what happens in wartime. It was a rotten show having to leave Frieda like that. But what could I do? I told her to apply to the work scheme, the North Sea scheme it was called, for German women in West Berlin. There were private employment agencies too. I might have wangled work for her through one of those. She seemed to like the idea, but then all of a sudden her father and she decamped to the Soviet sector. Extraordinary thing to do.' He drained his glass and refilled it. 'He worked at Buchenwald, you know, the concentration camp, during the war. They lived down in that part of the world, Saalfeld inThuringia. Buchenwald wasn't far from the town.'

'I didn't know that.'

'I see you're shocked. You're wondering why he wasn't prosecuted, hanged or at least sent to prison. But there were so many – and a lot of them got away with it. Some of them were just doing what they were told, of course. But he was one of the ones who thoroughly enjoyed it. That's the impression I got, anyway. He was a cruel man. A crook as well. He had something going in the British sector, Frieda used to drop hints; he was hand in glove with someone, the black market, I suppose. Well, I thought I should try to do something about it, but then, all of a sudden he moved them back into the Russian sector, and the North Sea scheme was only for females in the Western sectors, so that was that. Never could understand why he moved them back like that. Thinking about it though, maybe he knew I smelled a rat. Possibly he had friends in high places. Who knows? Or Frieda may have let slip I was on to him, I don't know. It's a long time ago now.' He sighed, puffing out his lips in a gesture of – defeat? Regret? Guilt? McGovern couldn't tell.

The Colonel leaned forward. 'But what exactly is it you want to know? What's behind all this? What's it got to do with this old bird who's died?'

'It's a security matter, sir. The security services are on high alert after the missing diplomats business. I'm not at liberty to go into the details, but we believe the man, Schröder, may be relevant to our enquiry.'

'Burgess and Maclean. Bloody fools. Something rum going on there. Never trust a queer, that's what I say.' The Colonel brought out a pipe and was carefully filling it with tobacco from a shabby leather pouch, pressing it down into the cup of the pipe, lighting it, starting to puff. 'But that doesn't entirely explain it. What could have induced men like that? Siding with the Reds! Unbelievable. Mind you, I voted for Attlee's lot myself in forty-five. Thought we needed a change, Labour government, something different. Never cared for Churchill myself. Yes, something different was needed. But now they've gone bloody mad. I've never dared tell the local Conservative Party. I'd be out on my ear, court-martialled in short order, I dare say.' He laughed. 'I think it had something to do with what I saw in Berlin, in Germany, back then. Bit of a shock to the system, as a matter of fact. But that's a far cry from betraying your country, although some of my neighbours around here wouldn't see much difference. But I'm sorry – you were saying—?'

'Is there anything more you can tell me about Thomas Schröder? You're suggesting someone in Allied command was protecting him?'

'I wouldn't go that far. It was just a thought. More likely he just fell through the net. Impossible to prosecute everyone, old chap. We did our best, but ... the ones that got away were many and various. Or it's possible he *was* interrogated, but managed to conceal his past ... or—' he paused and frowned, sucking his pipe. 'You see, as soon as the Russians ceased to be our glorious allies and were enemy number one again, which happened pretty damned quickly, the secret services were on the lookout for anyone who could help when it ceased to be a matter of bringing Nazis to book and became all about the crusade against communism: Nazi intelligence officers who had useful information, or Ukrainians and Latvians and all the rest of them from the SS Waffen divisions in that part of the world.'

Jarrell had been very quiet all afternoon, but now he sat up: 'Ukrainians?'

'They hated the Russians,' explained Ordway. 'Saw them as occupiers, hated them worse than the Germans. All about nationalism, you see. Some of them were patriots, some of them were hard-core Nazis themselves. None of that applied to Schröder, of course.'

McGovern said: 'So what you're saying is that when Allied interrogators came across Nazis who could be useful against the communist threat, they let them go in return for their cooperation.'

'Yes. I don't know how that would apply to Schröder. He was just a slippery customer. It wasn't as if he'd been in Nazi intelligence or anything useful like that. But perhaps he was useful in some other way.'

'The black market?'

'Possibly. I don't know. I used to think there was something going on. Frieda was very cagey about things, but you got the feeling things weren't right.' The Colonel sighed. His pipe made a little popping noise. He smiled apologetically. 'Brings it all back, you know. Lovely girl. I never could understand why she didn't just get out when she could. But, as I say, I got the feeling Schröder was up to something. So possibly things got too hot for him in the British sector. That may be why he cut and run. You know, we treated them decently on the whole, the Huns. Most of them – well, the last thing they'd do was move to the Soviet sector. I tried to make a few enquiries about Schröder, but there was so much going on, so many much bigger problems, basic things like food and water, we were trying to set up an administrative regime – in the midst of all those atrocities, starvation, ruin, corpses ...'

'So what Schröder did – move out of the British sector and into the Soviet one – wasn't usual?' McGovern knew this already, but he asked the question anyway.

'It certainly wasn't. I told Frieda she didn't have to go with him.' He paused again. For a second McGovern thought the older man was close to tears. 'Look – there are things, events, mistakes that come back to haunt you. And Frieda was one of those. I always felt I could have done more to help her. But in the end I just said goodbye and came home.'

'Perhaps I will have a wee drop more after all.' McGovern wanted to gain time. 'She wants to get over here now,' he said, 'she's desperate to get away.'

'*What?*' Ordway's eyes were very round and blue.

'There's an Englishman she wants to marry.'

Ordway snorted. 'You can bet your bottom dollar her father's behind that too. He'd sell his daughter, he'd sell *himself* if there was a few bob in it for him. He's probably in with the commies now, he's probably done some crooked deal with them.'

'You mean she might be sent here on some sort of spying mission?'

'Don't know about that. More likely her father thinks he'll get over here on her coat tails. If he's not in with the East German government. Poor little girl.' The Colonel's pipe popped and puffed. It went out. He poked it with a pipe cleaner, lit it again. 'You know,' he said, 'she did hate her father ... and yet in a way she didn't. She *could* have got away if she'd really wanted to.'

twenty-four

◖✦◗

THE RECEPTIONIST AT THE Hotel Am Zoo, a middle-aged man who looked like a professor and had only one arm, recognised McGovern. 'Good day, Herr Roberts.' The thin smile was a concession, a recognition of McGovern's status as a returning patron. 'You have a room at the front. A Herr Harris has left a message to say he will meet you here at six o'clock.'

A room at the front: McGovern saw himself in a room at the front in a different sense. Here he was on the front line of the Cold War, staring out of his window at the fault line between East and West. He did not feel that he personally was walking that tightrope, although he'd again carefully searched his room for signs of anything suspicious, but he now understood why the Berliners were as they were. It was about more than survival after defeat. Their war had not ended. The men with a voice, the politicians and ideologues on both sides, talked of good and evil, black and white, but Berliners lived in a world of grey shadows. Life here was an uneasy balancing act. It was an act, a performance and that's why you never knew where you were with anyone.

Harris was waiting for him in the bar. 'Thanks for getting in touch. I thought you said you probably wouldn't be back.'

Someone was playing the piano in the adjacent lounge. Its crystal notes fell like drops of water from a fountain.

'There's been a change of plan. Let me get you a drink.'

'Just some coffee, thank you. I suppose they have decent coffee in a place like this. Coffee's almost impossible to obtain over here.'

McGovern had already decided what he was going to say. It was against everything he'd been taught. He waited until the coffee had been served. Then: 'I'm not actually a journalist. You've been very frank with me. I shall be frank with you. I'm investigating a crime. The death of Konrad Eberhardt.'

As Harris listened, his puzzled look morphed into a frown. 'You took advantage of me, deceived me.' He stood up, an angry, clumsy movement, knocking the coffee table so that the cups rattled and spilled. 'What crime am I supposed to have committed now? Are you going to arrest me?'

'Sit down. Of course I'm not going to arrest you. You saw Eberhardt shortly before he died, at Garfield's funeral, at the cemetery, but I don't believe you murdered him. Why would you do that? What would the motive have been? But I am interested in the parcel he handed you when you and Alex Biermann talked to him there. There was a radio interview – he mentioned an autobiography. Was that what was in the parcel? The manuscript?'

Harris didn't sit down again, but he didn't leave either. 'I trusted you.'

'You can trust me. The fact I've told you who I am proves that, doesn't it? I'm not here to harm you. But perhaps you can help me. Do you have any idea why Eberhardt was murdered?'

'Why should I know why Eberhardt was murdered?'

'It must concern you, though. The most likely explanation is that someone wanted to stop him shipping the manuscript out of the country.'

Slowly, Harris sat down. He still looked angry. 'How did you know about the manuscript?' Harris's mood seemed to slip into resignation, defeat, fatigue. 'I knew I was being followed. I was certain of it.'

McGovern ignored the question. 'Tell me about the manuscript.'

'Alex was fond of Eberhardt. God knows why, he was a horrible old man, but Alex was sorry for him, I suppose. The two of them used to argue about politics, but they enjoyed it. Then I got a letter from Alex, telling me that Eberhardt had made some sort of confession. He'd admitted he'd informed on fellow exiles and people he still knew who were communists. Alex was horrified, naturally, but then he got this idea that it all had to be made public. He encouraged Eberhardt to write it all down. Eberhardt was vain as well as everything else. It sounds crazy, but he rather liked the idea. He'd confess and be admired for it. When I was over there I went down to see him to talk about it. I was meant to collect the manuscript, but it wasn't ready. I was pretty sceptical about the whole thing, actually, and when I visited him I could see he was wandering a bit. I didn't really believe the book existed, but Alex said he'd seen it. Eberhardt had written a whole section on his childhood months or even years before and now he was bringing it up to date with all the stuff about his years in exile. Alex said he'd be coming to the funeral and would bring it with him then. And I'd bring it back here. Alex believed he was doing the right thing, the book would expose the betrayals of the West, how Konrad was used. Then he got this mad idea that the old man should return to East Germany. Eberhardt had complained about being lonely, he had said to Alex he was homesick, so Alex thought it would be a wonderful *coup de théâtre*. Famous scientist sees the light, returns to his new socialist homeland and denounces the Western spy system that manipulated him, while his book reveals how he was put under pressure to become an informer and betray his friends. To be fair, Alex was also genuinely worried about him, he wasn't looking after himself and Alex thought he'd be better in Dresden, he'd be looked after by his family. But even that wasn't realistic, his family hadn't been in touch with him since before the war. It was a sort of fantasy on Alex's part. He was always a bit hare-brained.'

'So why did you allow yourself to be involved?'

'I suppose I got a bit carried away by the whole idea too. Look—' Harris leaned forward. 'Eberhardt was interned, although he was an anti-Nazi. The German anti-Nazis weren't treated very well, they were banged up just like the fascists. *With* the fascists. And if he'd been pressured to inform – on communists, not on the Nazis, mind you – I thought it was fair enough to expose it. So I was to bring the manuscript back, because Alex knew, really, deep down he knew that Eberhardt wasn't ever actually going to get back to Dresden. So I was to bring it back here and work on it.'

'He bought the tickets. Why did he do that, if he didn't think Eberhardt would get there?'

'You don't know Alex.'

'So you have the manuscript. And is it damaging? To British interests, that is?'

A smile cracked Harris's gaunt face. 'As soon as I started to read it I realised it was nonsense. It was confused, it was – well, rubbish. Most of it anyway. Completely useless. The early part, about his childhood, was more or less coherent, I think he must have written it some time ago, but the rest – hopeless, I'm afraid.'

'Whoever pushed him into the canal was hoping to get the manuscript? That could have been the motive. That could explain why someone got rid of him. Though why there – on that particular day—'

McGovern had been concentrating so intensely on what Harris was telling him that he'd forgotten his surroundings, but now he became aware once more of the discreet sounds, beer poured, the distant piano, low voices.

So there was no damning manuscript. That would please Kingdom.

'Ironically, of course, from my point of view it's rather a disaster. I'd hoped to make some money out of it. If it had been a big publishing success. You see – so I am a traitor, after all. Only I don't see it like that.'

'How *do* you see it? I got the impression you're nae so impressed with East Germany.'

'I change my mind from day to day. If the Eberhardt thing blows over, I still may return to England. Do the right thing by Frieda.'

Did that mean, McGovern wondered, that Harris was to get her into Britain where she could operate as some kind of spy? Victor Jordan had said Harris was a lamb to the slaughter, but it was beginning to seem more complicated than that. McGovern wished he didn't like him. 'Frieda still wants to leave? Get away from her father?'

Harris nodded. 'But there's a complication. Schröder's been back a couple of times to his old hunting ground, Saalfeld, where he came from. They want me to go with him.'

'They?'

'The East Germans. They want to know exactly what he's up to. And they think I'm in his confidence, that he trusts me. He actually doesn't trust anyone, but he's happy for me to go with him. I think it's because he thinks if there's any trouble I'll take the brunt of it. And I'm quite keen to go, because there's a hell of a lot going on down there. Things that shouldn't be going on in a socialist country. Unrest among the workers. If I get a look at what's really going on, it may help to make up my mind. It's a pity you're not a journalist, you could have come with me and perhaps you'd have got a scoop for the Western press.'

'They'd nae let a foreigner within a hundred miles of the place.'

'That's true.'

'Not that I wouldn't be interested. I'm told there's uranium in the region.'

'You knew that, did you? Who told you that?'

McGovern didn't answer, but merely shrugged and Harris continued anyway.

'You're right. There is. And a lot more than that. That's partly why I wanted to go on my own account, not just to keep an eye on Schröder. Mind you, anything that gets him into trouble is good news in my book. If he could be brought to trial ...'

'Would Miss Schröder be happy to stay here then, if that were to happen?'

Harris frowned. 'I don't know about that. No – on the whole I think she'd still want to get away.'

'So tell me what's going on in – Saalfeld, is that the name?'

'Saalfeld's most important industry is the Maxhütte steel mill. It's the most important in the Soviet zone, so they're expanding it as rapidly as they can. The Soviets have been mining for uranium in the ore mountains of Western Saxony since 1947. They need it for their own atom bomb. It's all under their direct control.' Harris paused and glared at McGovern. 'I suppose you don't think the Soviet Union should have an atom bomb. But as the West has one—'

McGovern put up a hand to halt the flow. 'Let's leave that out of it. I'm not here to debate the rights and wrongs of the atom bomb. I'm interested in what you're telling me, that's all.'

'We don't get to hear about what's going on down there. But there have been rumours. I need to see what's going on with my own eyes. Then I suppose if I did decide to leave it could get me back into work in England. It would be a big scoop. I don't know if I could quite bring myself to do that, though.' Abruptly, he stood up and held out his hand. 'I'm off tomorrow. No chance of seeing you again before I go. I hope you sort out the Eberhardt business.'

Once again, McGovern was alone with only the soft murmur of voices for company. The pianist no longer played. Little as he liked the German beer, he signalled to the barman for another.

He knew less than ever what to make of Harris: one moment a disillusioned Red, the next working for the East Germans. He supposed that his tactic of honesty with Harris had worked. But what he was supposed to do with Harris now he had no idea.

Feierabend had suggested a rendezvous in the Zoological Garden as it was such a fine day. The warm, brown eyes, the lock of hair, the rosy lips were all in place, the mask of the Berlin survivor. He was friendly as ever, smilingly delighted to see his old friend McGovern, yet McGovern detected a slightly disturbing flicker of uncertainty.

'I have arranged for you to see Herr Dr Hoffmann again, at his office,' he said. 'He was unfortunately not free to see you this morning at your hotel. His chauffeur will meet you at the crossing point.'

McGovern remembered Victor Jordan's advice from his previous Berlin trip. 'I've been warned not to see him in East Berlin again. I was told that would be risky.'

'Oh ... I don't think you should worry, Mr Roberts. You are a British citizen, after all.'

'Very well.' McGovern decided to accept, because if he got cold feet later, he could always decide just not to turn up.

'I saw Harris again. He told me he's going to a mining area in the east of the country. He said something about some unrest?'

'Oh – in Saalfeld, Thuringia. He is to try to go there? That will be very risky for him, I believe.'

'Why is that? What's been going on?'

'Where should I begin? Rumours are rife over here on this side. We know there are many problems in the region, due to the expansion of the steel mills and the uranium mining. The Russians have drafted in hundreds of extra steel workers from all over the place to add to the many refugees from further east who were already there. It's become almost a forced-labour situation, and frantic efforts to raise productivity – anything from piece rates to coercion – have failed. This is what we have heard.'

'We never hear anything about this in the West.'

'You surprise me. It would make excellent propaganda. It's hardly an advertisement for socialism. You see, the result of the influx of workers has meant unbelievable shortages of everything, from food to housing, and the predictable resulting resentment of the local population. And now there's unrest in the countryside as well, with compulsory food levies in order to feed the newcomers. There's been black marketeering, of course, like everywhere else. This is not what the East Germans want just when they are in the middle of trying to create the new socialist state.'

'You seem to know all about it.'

'Well, it is very interesting. Of course everyone wants to find out what's going on. And that's always easier when the people are angry and starting to rebel. It hasn't been well handled. There have been arrests, interrogations, officials being purged. They say it is like the American Wild West down there, an East German Klondike, drunkenness, whoring and fights. The whole place is a tinder box. It is all building up to a strike or something worse, a riot, even a full-scale uprising.'

'Do you have an idea why Schröder and Harris are going there?'

Feierabend smiled. 'It is obvious, is it not? Schröder is up to no good. And Harris is a fool.'

No-one spoke well of Schröder, he was seen on all sides as a thug, so McGovern was happy to accept that, but it was harder to swallow the idea of Harris as a fool. He was an intelligent man, an idealist, misguided perhaps, but ... to put himself in danger by going to Thuringia was more than foolish. It seemed like the action of a madman.

twenty-five

⟨✦✦⟩

MANFRED JARRELL AND DI SLATER walked towards the block of flats where Alex Biermann had lived. The sunlit street was silent and dreamlike as they approached the building and saw the black police Wolseley sedan and the ambulance. Jarrell counted five bystanders, neighbours, three in front of their front doors and two staring out from upper windows, shielding their eyes from the sun with their hands. They too seemed locked into the silence of the place.

Biermann's body lay slumped face downwards on the floor in the hallway, where he'd been shot.

'A professional job?' Slater looked at the pathologist. 'It looks efficient.'

'Possibly.'

Slater squatted down and looked closely at the dead man sprawled against the skirting board. He shook his head and stood up again. He turned to Jarrell. 'We'd better have a look around.'

'His girlfriend wasn't here?'

The uniformed sergeant looked at Jarrell. 'What girlfriend?'

'There was a young lady living here as well.'

'How do you know that? She's not here now.'

'Obviously not.'

The sergeant lost interest, the body was hauled on to a

canvas stretcher and Jarrell and Slater were alone. Leaving
Jarrell in the untidy living room, Slater made a rapid first recon-
noitre of the rest of the flat and returned.

'We'd better do a search,' he said grimly. 'There's just a
small kitchen and bathroom and a bedroom, that's all. You
search the bathroom and bedroom. I'll start in here. After that
we'll talk to the neighbours.'

Jarrell began with the bathroom. There was nothing to
interest him. The rickety wall cabinet contained only routine
chemists' remedies: milk of magnesia, aspirin, some antiseptic ointment and some plasters. Neither basin nor bath,
grey-rimmed from the hard London water, had been cleaned
for some time. Toothpaste smeared the glass shelf below the
mirror. Jarrell looked at his own reflection with distaste, but
the general disorder offended his fastidious nature even more.
What a couple of bohemians they were! It was a painful contrast
with the comfortable, orderly home in High Barnet he shared
with his parents and younger sister.

It was also depressing to be indoors on such a lovely day.
The glass in the small, half-opened window was of a familiar
frosted pattern of fleur-de-lis; the metal frame was rusted. He
stared out at a white wall and when he turned away the pattern
continued to throb, floating hotly in front of his eyes. He shook
his head and forced himself to move on.

The bedroom was obviously shared. The bed was unmade.
On each side of it stood a packing case serving as bedside table
and each holding a small lamp. The clothes crushed into the
narrow wardrobe were both men's and women's. Several pairs
of boots and shoes were tumbled at the bottom. The top of the
chest of drawers was crammed with books, papers, a packet of
condoms, some make-up and a biscuit box containing jewellery,
some of which looked valuable, because the rings were neat
and small, the thin chains obviously gold. They reminded
Jarrell of his grandmother. Papers were stacked on the floor:

newspapers, what looked like typed articles and notes, mixed with Communist Party leaflets and booklets.

Jarrell pulled out each drawer and searched thoroughly among the sweaters, shirts and women's underwear. It would be necessary at some point to read through at least all the typed notes, yet he was convinced he'd find nothing that he didn't know already.

'Come and look at this,' called Slater.

Leaving the stacks of papers, Jarrell obeyed.

'I've found his diary.' Slater waved a small, leather notebook. 'And some research of some kind in this folder. You'd better have a look. It's more your area.'

'It's a shame DI McGovern isn't here,' murmured Jarrell, 'he'd be much better at this than me.'

'Take a quick look – we'll take it away with us if it seems interesting and you can go through it properly later.'

Jarrell sat down on the sofa and opened the black ring-folder Slater had handed him. The top sheet was a hand-written letter from an address in Yorkshire and began, 'Dear Comrade'. The letter concerned a local association of resettled Ukrainians and the writer was writing to Biermann in his former capacity as a reporter on the *Daily Worker*, assuming, or hoping, that he would pass the information on and that the paper would investigate what he claimed were fascist interlopers in the Dales.

Biermann had evidently followed up the information. There was a stonewalling letter from a government department, notes and some cuttings from local newspapers, and a petulant handwritten letter from someone who seemed to have been part of the postwar refugee-vetting operation. There was also a name, Mihaili Kozko, written on a sheet of otherwise blank paper.

'Biermann went to see Eberhardt a number of times,' said Slater, who was reading through the diary.

'We know they knew each other,' said Jarrell wearily. 'Don't we need to talk to his girlfriend – if we can find out where she is? We'll have to tell her—'

Ignoring this, Slater said: 'Let's take as much of this stuff as we can carry away with us and go and talk to the neighbours.' As they left, Jarrell made sure he had the Ukrainian material and he also slipped Biermann's diary into the bag.

The small block had three floors with two flats on each floor. It didn't take them long to work through them. Most of the occupants were out on this beautiful weekday afternoon – or had chosen to lie low behind locked doors – but an elderly woman, in the flat below Biermann's, said she had heard a 'funny noise' and someone running down the communal concrete stairs. Pressed, she admitted she had looked out of the window and had caught a glimpse of a man walking away towards the main road, but she'd seen only his back and couldn't describe him other than to say he was 'biggish' and wearing 'rough clothes'. She spoke warmly of Alice Bridgenorth. 'She's ever so kind, poor thing,' said the old lady. 'She goes to the shops for me sometimes. When I'm feeling poorly. She said she was going to stay with her parents. They live in the country somewhere.' Then with that special expression Jarrell had noticed women used when imparting morally dubious news, she added in a stage whisper, 'Mind you, I don't think they were married.'

They crossed the road and knocked on the doors of the little houses opposite. The three women and two men who'd been watching the scene as Slater and Jarrell arrived all denied seeing anyone. No-one had heard a shot and they'd emerged onto the pavement or looked out of a window only when the siren of the ambulance had alerted them to the drama playing out across the road.

Slater insisted on going for a drink. Jarrell had no objection to working with Slater while McGovern was away and since Slater's sergeant, Monkhouse, had fortuitously been suspended after a serious accident while driving a police car, the arrangement had become almost inevitable. What Jarrell did object to was what he viewed as Slater's lax approach. Still, he was pleased to be at the heart of the investigation. But instead of discussing the case, as he'd hoped, Slater was soon laughing and exchanging police gossip with another colleague. Jarrell sipped his Rose's lime juice.

'I found an address for his girlfriend's parents,' he said. 'Might she be staying up there? It's in Northampton. I could phone the local constabulary, or phone the parents. There's a number as well.'

'Why don't you toddle off and do that, Jarrell. Instead of sitting there like a constipated virgin.'

'Thank you, sir.'

'Yeah, yeah, off you go.' Slater waved him away with a genial smile, but Jarrell heard merriment behind him as he crossed the saloon bar. No doubt they had him down as one of the weird Special Branch nutters, but he didn't care.

He took the underground to Sloane Square. From there he caught a bus to World's End and thence to a pleasant house behind a high wall in this Fulham backwater. Slater hadn't noticed that Jarrell still had the bag of papers from the flat but anyway he wouldn't (unlike the protocol-mad Monkhouse) have been too bothered that Jarrell was enough of a work-obsessed fanatic to want to work on them at home. But before studying the papers Jarrell had decided to talk to Mrs Garfield.

It took rather a long time for Mrs Garfield to open the front door in response to his ring and when she did it was clear to Jarrell, with his hyper-sensitive teetotaller's antennae for alcohol, that she'd been drinking. But she was coherent and friendly and soon he was seated opposite her in yet another chaotically untidy living space, this time a high-ceilinged drawing room with chintz armchairs and sofa and a huge gilt mirror over the marble chimneypiece.

Mildred Garfield gestured to the sofa and raised a half-empty bottle of wine in an invitation to Jarrell to join her. So insistent was she that in the end he was forced to declare himself an abstainer.

'Good heavens, how very amusing. I thought the police all drank like fish.'

'I'm the exception that proves the rule,' he replied, not untruthfully. 'Look, I'm afraid I've some very bad news,' he said. 'Someone who was at your husband's funeral has been shot – murdered, in fact. Alexander Biermann.'

Mildred Garfield stared at Jarrell with her large, watery blue eyes. For a moment she seemed not to take in the information, but then she murmured: 'Oh ... oh ... but that's terrible.' She drained her glass and poured more wine into it. 'How on earth ... oh, what a dreadful thing to happen.' She sat staring in front of her.

Jarrell tried to choose his words carefully. 'I don't suppose you knew him well, I suppose he was a friend of your husband, was he, but I wondered – when was the last time you saw him?'

'It was only the day before yesterday,' she murmured and now her large eyes began to fill with tears.

'I'm really sorry to upset you, Mrs Garfield,' said Jarrell, 'but it would be very helpful if you could tell me how he seemed. Was he worried about anything, for example?'

Mildred Garfield shook her head. 'Alex wasn't the worrying type,' and she smiled. 'He was always full of what he was doing, his enthusiasm of the moment. We talked about Konrad – Konrad Eberhardt. He knew Konrad well, had done since childhood and Konrad was a good friend of my late husband. Mind you, they'd had disagreements recently, but ...'

Maybe it was a waste of time, but Jarrell asked anyway. 'What sort of disagreements?'

Mildred Garfied was still dabbing tears from her eyes with an already sodden handkerchief, but she managed a watery smile. 'I shouldn't mention it, I suppose. Of course, it was a secret, but – well, poor Bill isn't here any more and ...' She paused. 'They were both very much against Stalin, you know. I suppose you'd call them anti-communists, they were very caught up in all this Cold War business. Bill was a bit obsessed, I thought, I told him so. Myself, I think they're all the same in the end, left, right. Well, anyway, politics bores me. They do nothing but argue. All those arguments, oh, how boring they are, I get so sick of all the opinions ... but Konrad and Bill – they thought they were doing the right thing – you know, passing on information to the authorities, about people they thought were pro-Russian, friends of theirs, you understand. I thought it was a bit ... well, not quite the done thing, I suppose, but ... you know, it was always impossible to argue with Bill and—' The sentence faded away into a shrug. After a pause she continued: 'Bill worked for intelligence during the war and he knew one or two people and he used to drop the odd hint now and then, that's all it was. Of course he – we – continued to move in those sort of ... you know ... circles, and people trusted him, so ... he thought he was doing the right thing, of course.'

Her tone implied that although some might take a different view, words such as 'informant' or 'treachery' would be too harsh.

Jarrell was fascinated to hear that Bill Garfield, the well-known, even famous, leftish writer had been grassing up his friends, but he didn't want to lose the thread. 'Was that what he and Dr Eberhardt disagreed about?'

'No ... on the contrary, Konrad and Bill were all in that together. In fact, Konrad worked more closely with ... you know ... the secret services than Bill. He felt very strongly about some of the things communists had done and he was very argumentative, he always thought he was right and he could be quite vindictive as well, I honestly didn't like him very much – and once his wife died, after Greta passed away, he was always a bit smelly and unkempt.' She smiled again. 'Oh dear, that's rather an awful thing to say. Let's just say he was a bit lost after she'd gone.'

'Did you know about Alex's plan to get Dr Eberhardt back to Germany?'

'That was what Konrad and Bill argued about! They fell out over that. Konrad kept changing his mind about every-thing. Bill thought he was mad! I secretly thought he might be happier if he went back to Germany, but Bill – well, so far as Bill was concerned, Konrad had betrayed all his anti-communist ideals.' She lifted the bottle, but it was empty. 'If you'll just excuse me for a moment—'

When she returned with a fresh bottle, Jarrell watched her walk unsteadily across the room. She was eccentrically dressed in a long skirt with a fringed hem that looked like a curtain and a clashing Tyrolean sweater and had bound round her shoulders an embroidered Chinese shawl.

'Are you *sure* you won't join me?'

Jarrell shook his head firmly. 'Did Alex Biermann talk to you about his work at all? He was interested in some refugees, refugee communities in the north of England?' He looked hopefully at Mildred Garfield, but with a bewildered expres-sion she pressed her hand to her breast. 'I just can't believe he's been – *murdered*, you said. Who on earth would want to murder Alex? He was just the sweetest, oh, the *sweetest* boy.'

And Jarrell, although he was only twenty-five years old, knew without a shadow of doubt that this was the moment the truth about Alex Biermann's fate had finally hit her. He wasn't going to get any more information out of her, for now she finally burst into floods of tears.

twenty-six

◠⚬◡

A S SOON AS MCGOVERN CAME alongside the car he knew he'd made a mistake. But it was already too late. There were three of them. The rear door was opened and they bundled him into the back before he had time to retreat. One moment he was there, free, stopping, looking at the black sedan, deciding to turn back; the next he'd been grabbed, kicked as he was shoved into the car, held down and blindfolded. He'd been hit with the butt of a revolver and now his head was held downwards against a pair of knees clad in rough material. He was in near agony from the cold, greasy metal of the gun pressed against the jawbone behind his ear. He dared not even try to raise his head. He smelled dust, metal, petrol, cigarette smoke.

Berlin accents; they were discussing a football team. Laughing. It was humiliating, pressed double against some man's knees. One of them poked him. The gun shifted against his head. He heard a tram pass. The car slowed down, turned, stopped. There was shouting; a gate clanged open.

He was pushed out onto concrete. One of them hauled him roughly to his feet. Seized by the arms. Still blindfolded. One on each side of him, frogmarched until there was a creaking door. Clanged shut behind them. Another door. He was pushed forward. The blindfold whipped away. They slammed the door. He was alone.

The interrogation room had grey cement walls and no window. The only furniture was a table and three chairs. He tried the door, but it was locked, as of course he'd known it would be. He sat down at the table. He held his hands clasped in front of him to stop them shaking. He knew he had to stay calm. Whatever was coming would be unpleasant. A pulse seemed to twitch all over his body, jumping from place to place like a flea. He tried to concentrate on what he might say, but his thoughts kept slithering away to what had just happened. The visit had been a set-up, an obvious trap – a trap set by Feierabend or Hoffmann or both. Both. Hoffmann – he must have alerted the East Germans. But what use was he, Jack McGovern, to them or the Russian military?

Harris. Had Hoffmann contacted Harris? Had Harris betrayed him?

They'd taken away his watch. The lack of time disoriented him. He already seemed to have been in this room for a very long time.

The key turned in the lock. The mixture of relief and dread knotted his stomach.

The two men looked like bureaucrats. Each had the greyish skin so many Germans had, each wore spectacles, each had receding hair, each wore a cheap suit made out of material that looked more like cardboard than cloth, one blue, the other shit-brown. The only difference was the blue suit was thin, the brown suit was paunchy and fat. McGovern knew they were German, not Russian, before they spoke – to say that they would speak in German since Herr Roberts knew the language so well. They seated themselves opposite him.

'I'm a British citizen. I demand—'

'A British citizen has no right to spy on the citizens of another country, you'd agree, wouldn't you, Kommissar McGovern?'

They knew who he was. This was bad. Harris had told them. Must be Harris.

'My name is Roberts. I'm not a spy. I have not been spying on anyone. I'm a journalist.'

'But you have been in contact with Colin Harris. The two of you are both spies, perhaps.'

Not Harris, then. Unless it was a bluff.

'My reason for meeting Mr Harris has nothing to do with Germany. It is an internal British matter.'

'Both you and Mr Harris have been in contact with Ulrich Hoffmann. We should like to know about your connection with Dr Hoffmann and what your business with him was.'

'I don't have to answer any questions. You're holding me here illegally.'

'You're not aware that Hoffmann is under judicial investigation in West Germany?'

Instinct and training told McGovern to let nothing escape, to tell them as little as possible, not to show his surprise at this news, not to betray his fear, not to show any emotion, not to engage at all. He stared at the table, trying to appear calm.

'What was the purpose of your meeting Dr Hoffmann here?'

'You've seen my papers.'

'You claim to be a journalist, so why has no-one heard of you? The foreign press agencies in Berlin. No-one knows anything about you.'

They must have rung round. While he waited in this tomb they must have made enquiries. Or perhaps earlier. Soon after he'd arrived in Berlin. Well, he had only himself to blame for that. He should have contacted the press, made himself known, strengthened his cover.

'Why pretend, Herr Kommissar McGovern?'

If his cover was blown, all the more reason to stay silent.

'We were told you claimed to be reporting on aspects of

cultural life in postwar Berlin. Well, Herr Dr Hoffmann would hardly have been of help there.' The thin man in blue smiled. They were just taunting him now. 'Who introduced you? The Americans?'

'No comment.'

'What happened then? He turned up at your hotel and introduced himself? That sounds very improbable. How would he have known you were there? How would he have known about you at all?'

So perhaps it was Feierabend who'd got him into this mess: *we've been told ...* McGovern mentally raced through the possibilities: that Feierabend was some kind of double agent; that Harris was involved; that Hoffmann was behind this and that he was, after all, trying to get him kidnapped, a possibility McGovern had previously dismissed as absurd. 'I have nothing to say. I've done nothing wrong. You have no right to detain me.'

The two Germans looked at him. Then they suddenly stood up and left the room without a further word. The door clanged again. This was disconcerting. McGovern stood up too and walked around the cell. He was thirsty and in need of a piss.

The silence was profound. He walked up and down. At least his footsteps broke the blanketing silence, but he decided that sitting down would be a better way to control the ever more urgent pressure in his bladder.

He rested his head on his arms and tried to doze off. Perhaps he had, but he couldn't be sure, for when he became aware of his surroundings again there was no change.

It wasn't that time dragged. There was no time. There was just a vacuum, airless, suffocating.

Eventually he got up again and looked round in desperate hope of a basin or a drain. But he already knew there was none. He had reached the point at which he knew he was soon going to have to urinate on the floor, which would be humiliating and would increase the power of his captors over him, when they returned.

He sat down again, rested his head on his hands.

The sound of the key. He raised his head jerkily.

Now there was a third man with them. The third man had broad shoulders and arms as thick as telegraph poles.

'You can go, Herr Kommissar McGovern. We're taking you back to the British sector.'

He could hold on until then.

The third man shoved him along a corridor and out into a yard. McGovern saw to his astonishment that it was now quite dark. A van was parked by the door. McGovern was shoved inside and the third man followed him in. In his relief McGovern relaxed and lowered his guard. He was utterly unprepared for the vicious punches as soon as the motor started. The first caught his jaw, the second landed on his stomach. His bladder opened, his trousers were soaked, he buckled with the pain and humiliation. He was punched again as he lay on the floor of the van in his own pee and the stranger kicked him repeatedly, shouting obscenities.

The van drew to a halt. 'Get out!' screamed the German, but as McGovern painfully tried to move, to crawl to a sitting position, he was seized from behind and flung from the back of the van. A final vicious kick and punch. He vomited, dizzily hearing the van rev up. He raised his head from the ground. The van accelerated forward, gained speed, but then abruptly went into reverse, back towards him. It was going to run him over. A surge of panic: he rolled away – not quick enough – dragged himself sideways and knocked against a sack of rubbish. The van jolted backwards, was almost upon him as he frantically managed to kick the sack under the wheels. Within inches of his head. He lay as if dead, waiting for the driver to get out and examine his handiwork. But the driver didn't get out. The van bumped over the rubbish and at once began to move forward again.

As McGovern listened to it driving away into the night his terror folded into exhaustion. He must have passed out. He became aware of the darkness of the empty, unlit street. He didn't know where he was. He dragged himself to his feet. His sodden trousers clung uncomfortably to his legs and crotch. The pains in his shoulder, jaw and back were acute, he had a splitting headache. He could barely limp. He staggered along the empty street, past the ruins and shells of buildings until he came to a wider but still deserted avenue. He limped on and saw the giant Red Cross candle Hoffmann had shown him on that first visit, which seemed like years ago. At least then he was in the West ... but of course they'd dump him this side of the city as a message to the Western authorities for which the East would deny responsibility. He struggled towards the woman in the kiosk ... and tried to speak to her. His tongue seemed thick. He could hardly say the words. The woman looked at him in disgust.

'Bloody drunk. You ought to be ashamed of yourself. Look at you – German manhood, what a rotten joke – you men, you got us into this mess and now you can't get us out of it.'

'The Hotel Am Zoo,' he croaked.

'Hotel Am Zoo! That's a laugh. They won't let you in there. That's for the profiteers and the Amis, not for scum like you.'

'The Ku'Damm – please—'

She looked at him more closely and seemed finally to take pity on him. 'You're in a bad way, aren't you. You're not far off – it's just a way further on, ten minutes'll get you there.'

In the state he was in it took him closer to half an hour. He managed to pass through the lobby without attracting attention, his hat pulled down to conceal his face, and was glad he'd kept his room key with him. The East Germans had returned it with the rest of his possessions – his wallet, passport, watch and fake press card.

He peeled off his filthy clothes, every movement agonising.

He moved like a man of ninety. He ran a hot bath and soaked for a long time. It was only when he lay on the bed wrapped in a towel that he realised the room had been searched. Nothing was quite as he'd left it. It could have been the maid, but he didn't think so.

Lily had insisted he bring a basic first-aid kit, as if you couldn't obtain plasters and aspirin in Berlin, like anywhere else. Well, perhaps you couldn't; things like that were probably in short supply here. Now he was glad he had them to hand as he gingerly rubbed antiseptic ointment on his face and swallowed some codeine. He dropped naked into bed and fell into a feverish sleep.

The following day he stayed in his room. He felt too ill and was in too much pain to move. He locked his door, dozed, drank a lot of water and towards evening, when he felt slightly better, telephoned Victor Jordan.

twenty-seven

ᕮᕮᕮ

THE NEXT DAY HE STILL FELT TERRIBLE. He feared the sinister pain in his back, where the gorilla had kicked him, could indicate damaged kidneys, but he hadn't passed any blood, and was thankful that although his jaw was slightly swollen, it wasn't broken, nor had he got a black eye, which would have been horribly conspicuous. He knew he'd actually been very lucky. He was just bruised and sore all over but no longer felt sick and dizzy. He struggled down to the hotel dining room, where he tried to swallow the German breakfast of hard-boiled egg, cheese and cold sausage. The coffee was real, but came with evaporated milk. He read the *Berliner Zeitung* he'd purchased from Kurt in his kiosk, but it was difficult to concentrate when his mind was in turmoil, a slightly hysterical feeling of relief at war with a sense of ongoing danger and threat.

A waiter approached his table. 'Someone to see you, sir. They're waiting in the lobby.'

'Ask him to join me here, please.'

'It's a young lady, sir.'

She crossed the dining room uncertainly, watched by the few guests, mostly solitary men, still eating breakfast at this late hour.

'Frieda!' He clambered painfully to his feet and manoeuvred stiffly round to pull out a chair for her.

She glanced nervously around, conscious perhaps that her shabby clothes looked out of place. But, he thought, they only enhanced her beauty.

'Coffee?' He looked round and took a cup and saucer from the next table.

'Real coffee?' she said. She drank. 'It's good.' She leaned forward. 'I need your help, Mr Roberts.' She hesitated. 'But – what happened to you? Did you have a fall?'

'You could say that.'

She looked at him, a look he couldn't interpret. 'Do you know who did this?'

'Never mind about that. I'll survive. But why have you come to see me? How can I help you?' He looked searchingly at her. She gazed back. Her eyes were deep as a well. The faint frown that twisted her winged eyebrows made her look severe.

'You saw Colin, didn't you? Before he and my father went away? Did he say anything to you?'

'About why he went, you mean?'

She shook her head. 'They have gone for some stupid reason.' Her head drooped. 'No, I wanted to know what Colin said to you, whether he still doesn't want to go back to England, whether he really wants to stay here.'

'Has he not talked to you about it?'

'He has got so involved in what is going on down there, or in what he thinks is going on. He is not interested in me.'

McGovern watched her. For all her gloomy, almost sullen manner, she had a very direct appeal. She was surely just profoundly unhappy. He couldn't believe the whole story about England was because she was a spy. 'I don't know that much about it, but I'm not thinking it'd be so very difficult for you to get work in England, to emigrate on your own. It should be possible, at least.'

'Is that really true?' She looked doubtful. 'I don't know,' she muttered, 'I don't think ...'

McGovern let the silence linger on. He continued to watch her, now again assailed by doubt, wondering if she was really as desolate as she seemed and if it was only that she wanted to get away from Germany. Perhaps she too was playing a double game, like the other Berliners he'd met, who played ambiguous roles, roles that were sometimes poorly rehearsed and uncon-vincing, as if the actors themselves had little belief in them, but which still managed to generate a fog of uncertainty over everything.

'Tell me how I can help you,' he said. 'But you must be honest with me. You've not told me much so far.' He spoke softly. 'That your father worked at Buchenwald, for instance. You didn't tell me about that.'

'You know about him? Who told you? Colin doesn't really know. At least, I never told him.' She stared at him specula-tively and for the first time McGovern wondered if her every word, her every move was calculated. She shrugged dismis-sively as if she despised his ability to be so easily shocked. 'Do you think there's anyone who hasn't some dirty little secret from the war?'

He refrained from the obvious reply: that working in a concentration camp wasn't just any dirty little secret.

Unexpectedly her mood seemed to lift. 'My father is away,' she said, 'and Colin has gone with him. So I can do what I want. Perhaps I could show you something of Berlin? On Saturday? We could go for a bicycle ride. Then we could discuss your suggestion. Whether it is possible for me to leave on my own.'

The man on the desk at the hotel had told McGovern with a pitying smile that bicycles were in short supply, but Kurt had got hold of one for him in return for a generous tip. He'd dreaded the thought of hoisting his bruised body onto the machine, but he was strong and his powers of recovery considerable, so that now as he followed Frieda out past the Olympiad stadium and towards a lake where she said you could bathe, the dull aching of his torso was quite bearable.

They turned off the main road and onto a lane, on each side of which stood large villas, some merely neglected, some in ruins, all partly screened by plane trees so that they rode along through stripes of light and shade. After following the lane for about half an hour they reached a lake surrounded by trees. They chained their bikes to a wooden railing. Beyond that there was a grassy slope and then a rim of sand. McGovern had no bathing trunks. Nervously he saw that Frieda was pulling her dress over her head to reveal a swimming costume underneath. He'd heard about nude bathing in Germany, before the war at least. 'I'd like to swim,' he said, 'but I've not got a bathing suit—'

Frieda laughed at his discomfiture. She seemed a different person out here in the woods by the lake. 'No-one would mind if you swam naked, or you could wear your underpants. They'll soon dry in the sun.'

He crept self-consciously down to the water's edge. The water was cold and he tried to swim with vigour, but that made his back hurt. He reached the centre of the lake and turned, treading water and watching the girl as she approached the edge.

She swam decorously out to meet him, but he was too cold to wait and set off again, his crawl sending up sprays of water. Frieda slithered like a fish through the water, her arms raising barely a splash. McGovern had a sudden memory of bathing in Loch Fyne long ago. Here the sun glittered on the lake's surface, but the still, dark water soon chilled him. He swam back to the shore, shook himself like a dog and wrapped himself in one of the towels Frieda had brought. With his knees up to his chin he watched her distant head above the lake's surface.

It was Saturday and there was a fair sprinkling of bathers, some in the water, others lounging on the shore. The curious thing was that so many of them were blond and bronzed, fit young male and female bodies. It was a dreamlike scene, as if he'd suddenly been transported back to the thirties, so that he briefly felt he was in Hitler's Germany with its cult of Aryan beauty and athletic physique.

They moved to the little café, hardly more than a shed, at the side of the lake. There they sat at an outside table and ate vanilla ices followed by coffee. 'So Mr Harris has gone with your father.'

'Do you have any cigarettes?'

'Of course. I'm sorry.' As he held the match flame he looked at Frieda's lowered head and longed to stroke her dark hair.

'Workers not being properly treated, Colin said, I don't know much about it and it's better not to talk about things like that. But Colin was angry, he has always said he is a communist and a socialist, but he said this wasn't socialism.' She smiled. 'Of course it's not socialism, socialism is just a word.'

She stood up. She had tied her towel sarong-style round her hips, but her dark blue costume revealed the swell of her breasts. 'I should like some more coffee. I will get it. If you give me the money.'

She returned with the cups of coffee on an old tin tray. 'Things are always so complicated with Colin. He has such high ideals, but no-one can come up to them, neither people nor politicians. He told me something of this old man he knew, who was killed. He was afraid your police thought he'd been in some way involved. And then there was something about a book. He was supposed to give it to the authorities here. But now he's lost interest in that and can think only of finding out what is happening in Saalfeld.'

'So he was working with the East Germans?'

Frieda played with her coffee spoon. 'He didn't exactly

tell me,' she muttered, 'but I don't think he had a choice. I think they thought he could be useful. And they – they had something on him. There was some trouble with a young man. I didn't understand at first, but now I don't know how I could have been so blind, so naive, because the fact is Colin isn't really interested in women. It was kind of him to be prepared to marry me, to get me away, but he didn't *want* me. But there was this thing with a boy and so ... yes, he has helped them a little. Through my father he got to know Herr Dr Hoffmann. Officially that was because he was a lawyer and could help with our marriage, but actually the real reason was to spy on Hoffmann.'

Her words did no more than confirm what Harris had already told him, but now he was more interested in her reaction. He watched her and wondered if she truly loved Colin Harris. Her wistful sadness, her anxious eyes ... He decided to risk a direct question.

'What was your father really doing at the end of the war? Immediately after the war, that is?'

Her manner changed immediately. Now he'd worried her. 'Why do you ask that? What has that to do with what is going on with Colin? Why are you always asking these questions? Why can't we just be here and enjoy ourselves?'

'I'm just interested, that's all. I went to see Colonel Ordway.'

Frieda dropped her cigarette and bent down, picked it up, then changed her mind and ground it out with her foot.

'Don't you remember Colonel Ordway?'

'He was an old fool,' she muttered.

The change in her manner was startling. 'Didn't you like him? Wasn't he kind to you?'

'He tried to get involved in things that were none of his business.'

'What sort of things?'

'Why did you go and see him? He was just a stupid old man who thought he was helping me. But he wasn't.'

'In what sort of way was he trying to help you?' He couldn't decide whether she was angry, or fearful, or merely resentful. Displeased, certainly, but why he didn't know.

'He tried to help me get work in your country. But it's all in the past. I don't want to talk about it. It doesn't matter. Please.' And now her smile was so soft and so pleading that he almost hadn't the heart to go on.

'Why didn't you go? I thought that was what you wanted.'

'It was ... too difficult. You wouldn't understand. There was a man ... Anyway we moved to the Russian sector after my sister died.'

A man she was in love with, then. It was obvious she didn't want to talk about it, but he had to pursue it.

'You were in love with this man?'

She shook her head.

'And your sister died? How did that happen?'

'I don't want to talk about it.'

'I'm so sorry. That's terrible. I know it must be painful, but – she *died*? She was ill?'

'Yes, and there wasn't enough food.'

'How dreadful.'

He knew he'd come up against a wall. She just wasn't going to talk about it. They sat in silence. After a while Frieda put her hand on his. 'I don't think Colin is going to help me get away from here and from my father. But perhaps you can help me. You said you would try.' She turned away and stared into the distance, her elbow on the table and her hand supporting her face.

'I will try,' he said, as much to placate her as anything. And yet he meant it. He said: 'I think there's more about your father you haven't told me.'

Frieda shook her head. 'Why do you say that? He's just a brutal bully who worked in Buchenwald. That's all in the past now. I just want to get away.'

'Okay. I'm sorry. I didn't want to upset you.'

She drew another cigarette from his packet, which was lying on the table. He lit it for her, she blew out the smoke. After a while she said, 'We shouldn't quarrel.'

'I didn't know we were.'

'This is as far out as you can go,' she said and gestured towards the trees. 'The other side of the lake is enemy territory, for you, East Germany. There's barbed wire and everything behind the trees. Of course *I* could go there, any time I want, but then I'm not really supposed to be here. But never mind. Let's just enjoy the sunshine, shall we, since we *are* here, and forget about all our problems for a while.'

She threw another half-smoked cigarette away onto the grass and leaning close to him, she pulled him into a passionate embrace.

twenty-eight

Cᵥᵥᴖᴐ

MANFRED JARRELL TOOK THE number 5 bus to St
Olave's hospital. This part of docklands was as much
a foreign land to him as Hackney. He'd memorised the route
before setting off. It didn't look good for a detective to be
studying a map as he walked along. It made you look vulnerable and you were, because if you were peering at a map you
wouldn't be on your guard.

He scoured the grimy, noisy streets as he walked. The district
was a formless mess of workshops, hangars, garage repair shops,
newsagents and factories, crisscrossed by the railways. Every
kind of enterprise huddled under the arches close to the river.
There was even a park so small and blackened that it seemed as
artificial as the surrounding shabby buildings.

In spite of his careful preparation he took a wrong turning
and it was some time before he reached his destination. The
Ukrainian Seafarers Association was housed in a Victorian
terrace, but set apart by its gothic façade. Its front door was
shut, but opened when Jarrell pushed it. Inside, he looked
round the dark hallway, then knocked at a door on the left. A
voice shouted something in a foreign language.

The man who faced him across a huge desk looked him
over. Jarrell returned the stare with a diffident smile. The man
was intimidating, a big man with short hair *en brosse*, a shabby

jacket welling over bulging shoulders and an open-necked shirt revealing a thick neck.

Jarrell explained, in what he hoped was a convincing German accent, that he was looking for a friend. 'We knew each other in Germany, after the war. I met him in a DP camp.' He was observing the room as he spoke. A double door to his right was half open and he could see into the back section of the double room. It was furnished with sofas and easy chairs. The walls were covered with notices, a calendar and posters, all in a language he assumed was Ukrainian.

'I was told this is a place Ukrainians meet, not just sailors. Refugees, expatriates.'

'You were? Who told you?'

'I'm anxious to get in touch with my friend. I just want to make sure he's okay, you know, have a chat about old times, share some memories.'

'Who is this individual you imagine will want to talk about life in a DP camp?'

'His name is Mihaili Kozko.'

The Ukrainain stood up. 'How strange, my friend, that you do not recognise me. And I certainly do not recognise you.'

Jarrell's wits couldn't get him out of this one, but he soldiered on desperately. 'You certainly look different. But we were all starving wretches then, weren't we.'

The man who said he was Mihaili Kozko smiled. 'What do you want with Mihaili Kozko? Why are you wanting to talk to me about the past? Raking over the ashes? Settling scores?'

'I haven't any scores to settle.' Jarrell was losing his German accent and tried to retrieve it. 'I wish to speak to many refugees. I told you, I am writing this book on the life in the camps.'

Kozko shook his head. He was smiling. He moved round from behind the desk and towards Jarrell. Jarrell retreated. 'You better go, I think. Ukrainians, we don't like strangers here. This is Ukrainian home for us, this place. Go. Get out.'

Jarrell retreated, crossed the road, walked a little way and leant against a wall. As his adrenalin level sank he felt shaky and slightly sick. What rotten luck to have chanced on the very man – he'd never thought Kozko might actually *be* there. He'd almost mentioned Alex Biermann by name. That could have been a disaster – although Kozko might not know that Biermann had been making enquiries about him. Then it occurred to him that, after all, there was a positive side to the encounter. He now knew what Mihaili Kozko looked like. He could find out more about him if he hung around for a while.

He looked round for a spot from which he could watch the Ukrainian Seafarers Association and found a covered passage from which he could see the building. After an hour, Kozko left. Jarrell followed. The journey led to a pub in Jamaica Road, Bermondsey. Kozko entered the saloon bar and after some hesitation Jarrell risked the public bar, hoping they weren't in completely separate rooms and that it would be possible to see from one into the other.

In fact, the two sections were separated only by a latticed wooden screen and the circular bar itself. Jarrell cowered against a pillar from which he could peer round into the other bar. He couldn't see Kozko. But when a figure he recognised stood on the threshold, astonishment jolted through him. It was Miles Kingdom.

twenty-nine

CᴡᴡƆ

ON A REALLY HOT, DRY DAY like this Monday, London glittered in a dusty, metallic haze. Women flowered into cotton frocks in cottage-garden colours and men in light suits brought a holiday sparkle to the sober streets, yet everyone grumbled that it was muggy, humid, unbearable, and expressed their desire for some good British chilly fresh air.

Dinah, too, felt tired and listless in the heat. On the bus, she tried to think of the work she'd be doing at the Courtauld, but her thoughts kept slipping back to yesterday's lunch with Regine and William. They'd sat in the garden. Alan and William had talked books. William was trying to interest Alan in one of his firm's publications with a view to a slot on the Third Programme. Dinah had sat on a rug on the grass with Reggie beside her and the children close by.

'How are you?' Regine had asked. 'You look a bit tired.'

'I'm fine,' Dinah had replied brightly, but she hated it when people said things like that. Tired meant you looked unattractive. 'Why do you say that?'

'No reason … just … nothing. I thought you seemed a bit … quiet, that's all.' And Regine had fiddled with the lovely white broderie anglaise of her skirt.

'No – tell me. There is something.'

Regine had leaned back to get at the packet of cigarettes on the low garden table behind her. 'There isn't, really. William said ... oh, I don't know, something about Alan being a bit out of sorts, having some problems at the BBC. But he seems fine. Look, he's laughing away.'

'Yes. That's nonsense. The Third Programme's absolutely marvellous for him. There *was* an interview that didn't go well, but that's all blown over. It wasn't serious.'

'I expect that's it. William just said he'd heard something ... nothing, really. I expect he got the wrong end of the stick. He's not much good at gossip.'

There was something wrong with this conversation, Dinah knew. 'Gossip? Who's gossiping about Alan?'

'No-one, darling, of course they're not. I haven't the faintest idea what William was talking about and it's all rubbish anyway. Just one of his silly authors, I expect. Now they've started that poetry series – I don't know, the poets seem to be so bitchy. I expect Alan wouldn't broadcast someone's work on the Third Programme or something. Writers are so malicious. They're all jealous of Alan's success, you know. Sometimes I almost wish I was back with Neville and his boring curator friends.' She laughed. 'Not really.'

But Dinah was puzzled. 'Perhaps it had something to do with Konrad Eberhardt, that old German living in Deal, the one who died. Alan interviewed him, but the broadcast had to be postponed and I think that may have put the schedules out a bit. Something like that. They had to alter the timing. Alan was very disappointed, because the interview had been such a lot of work. Alan had planned it all so carefully. He stayed overnight down there in order to have enough time.'

'Overnight?' repeated Regine. 'Is Deal that far away? I suppose the trains are very slow.' Having lit her cigarette, she had blown out a long plume of smoke.

Now that Dinah was seated on the bus with nothing to do, she remembered the conversation too clearly. Reggie wasn't stupid. By even mentioning something so trivial she'd made it more important. She must have known that at the very least it would niggle. Perhaps she hadn't let it slip out by accident at all. Perhaps it had been deliberate. Perhaps she'd been fishing, hoping for more information from Dinah.

Dinah hadn't given a moment's thought to Alan's staying overnight in Deal at the time. He'd said he'd need at least two sessions with the old man. But Reggie's surprise had jolted her into recognising that it was more than a little odd. It wasn't as if Deal was a long way away.

She and Alan had returned from Reggie's in the early evening, drunk with the sun and white wine and she'd repeated a part of the conversation to Alan. He'd nearly bitten her head off. 'What on earth are you talking about?' he'd almost shouted. 'Reggie just can't resist, can she! And she's got a mind like a sewer.' Later he'd gone to the pub to get cigarettes and had been away an awfully long time. She'd asked if he'd met someone he knew at the William IV and stayed to have a drink and he'd just said, 'I wasn't gone long, was I?' But it had been nearly an hour. 'For Christ's sake, Dinah, do I have to account for every minute of the day?' He'd been so irritable.

It was his bad temper that still depressed her now. Perhaps she tried too hard to please him. Perhaps she took his moods too seriously, took it to heart too much when he was fed up, as if it were always her fault, when usually it had to do with his work. She tried to cheer herself up by resolving to be more resilient, firmer, to not let it get her down. Yet she reached the Courtauld in a low mood and wasn't looking forward to her day's work, her day of independence. Miss Welsh in the Library was more tiresome than usual. Dinah went to lunch with Jeremy and Polly, as she did most Mondays; they were at the Courtauld all the time and their chat about people she didn't know left her out. She was just on the sidelines, and the way they gossiped like mad was almost as irritating as Miss

Welsh, continually looking disapproving as if she had a prune in her mouth.

In the evening there was a BBC party.

'We needn't stay long, need we? I'm feeling a bit tired.' Dinah was brushing her hair in the bedroom while Alan sat on the edge of the bed.

'No, darling – it's just one of the high-ups. I have to show my face. Or of course if you wanted you could get a taxi back here and I'd follow later.'

She shook her head. 'Would you so much want to stay if I came home?'

'No – no, of course not. It's just that it's work, for me. You do understand that, don't you? I mean, you don't have to come at all, Dinah, perhaps you'd rather not, I assumed ... I know it's a bit miserable for you, at times, when I've been working so late all the time. I thought you'd enjoy it.'

She smiled. 'Of course I want to come.'

The party was at a pretty stucco villa in St John's Wood, grander than the flats and houses of most of Alan's BBC friends. She heard a soft hubbub of voices as they approached the house. The French windows on the raised ground-floor room were open so that passers-by saw the guests standing with glasses in hand. As Dinah and Alan reached the steps the noise of the voices was closer to a roar, the sound of sociability soaring up on a wave of champagne.

She saw she was not quite smart enough in the new chintz frock she'd thought was so pretty, for many of the women – and most of them were older than she was – wore silk or something at least more obviously expensive. She was still the ingénue wife after all, when she'd so much hoped she'd grown out of the role. Still, her skin was clearer and brighter than most, and the pink and black dress did suit her. They pushed through tightly knotted circles and couples conversing on important-sounding matters and reached the drinks. Glass in hand, Alan turned to survey the crowded room, lifted a hand in greeting, touched Dinah's elbow and said: 'Come and say hello to the chaps.'

Again they eased themselves past the guests, brushing against Savile Row suits and brocade cocktail dresses. They reached the group of three men and one woman, the rather plump, blonde poetess, Edith Fanshawe. She'd been at that other party they'd been to not long ago. Then to Dinah's surprise she caught sight of Reggie and William standing by the window. She broke away to say hello.

'Darling!' said Reggie, 'I didn't know you'd be here. Have you caught sight of Dylan Thomas yet? I think he might be in the garden – possibly passed out in the undergrowth. I believe he's been sick already. And over there, look, the acting contingent – Gielgud ...'

But as Dinah looked round what she saw was not John Gielgud, but that poetess, the Fanshawe woman, standing close to Alan. And now she was laughing up into his face and she put her hand on his arm in the most proprietorial fashion. Dinah's heart knocked against her ribs, but for a moment her mind went blank. Until Alan looked down at the woman with a smile that was so familiar to her.

And she knew.

In the taxi going home neither of them spoke. Sentences formed in her mind, but none could be spoken. Who was that woman you were talking to? You're having an affair with her, aren't you? Why did you take me to the party when you knew she'd be there? You must think me such a fool – did you really think I wouldn't notice, that I haven't got eyes in my head? The monologue raged relentlessly in her head, but the silence refused to be broken. Alan gazed calmly out of the window. Dinah felt as if they were two prisoners being driven towards some unknown fate. She knew what he'd say. Don't be ridiculous, Dinah, just because she touched my arm. You're behaving like a child. I can't stand jealous women. No, of course you can't, she retorted silently, because they interfere with what you want to do.

The taxi dropped them at the bottom of the cemetery and they walked in velvety darkness up to their cottage. Alan took her arm and steered her along. So far as he was concerned, she realised, nothing was the matter.

She rang for a taxi for Mary.

'You haven't asked how he was.' Mary's surprise showed in her voice. 'He went off like a lamb.'

Dinah shut the front door after Mary. Alan was in the best of moods. 'Well, darling, did you enjoy it? Who did you talk to?'

'I hadn't expected Reggie and William to be there.'

'Oh, you know Reggie – that sort of thing's her meat and drink. She'll start giving parties herself again soon, she might even resurrect her salon, now the twins are older and she's feeling so much better.'

Dinah swallowed. 'Alan.'

He'd already started up the stairs.

'What? Come on, darling, I'm exhausted. All that talking shop. I can't stand it,' he grumbled, but he sounded very cheerful.

Something about his good humour cut off the possibility of speaking. I saw that woman touch you on the arm. You must be having an affair with her. And the furious response: are you mad, Dinah? What are you talking about? She followed him up the stairs.

In bed he put his arm round her and kissed the back of her neck, but she curled away from him and said she was terribly tired. That he'd wanted to make love to her after spending all evening with *Edith Fanshawe* made her angrier than anything else. Long after he'd fallen peacefully asleep, she lay rigid with anger. The remembered images played and replayed like a maddening film. Her hand on his arm and the way she looked up at him – and then he'd moved back ever so slightly so that they were no longer touching. But was that for fear of being seen or a sign of rejection? The film, played and replayed, became less and less distinct until she no longer knew what she'd seen and what was imagined, but that did nothing to stop the raging accusations that went on and on and round and round in her head.

Tommy was cramming scrambled egg into his mouth. Alan came into the kitchen in his tatty old dressing gown.

'Who was that woman you were talking to last night?'

'What woman?'

'You know, that poet woman, Edith Fanshawe. You seemed to be awfully friendly.' She rather expected an angry response, but he just looked at her blankly. 'The way she looked at you. I thought – is she in love with you or something?'

Alan's stricken look sent a stab of fear through her. It felt like a physical pain. 'Don't be ridiculous. It's just, well, we've been working quite closely together recently.'

'You didn't tell me that.'

'Well, you're not interested in all the Beeb gossip, you're not that interested in what I do there.'

'I *am*.' Now Dinah was indignant. 'How can you say that? And what do you mean by working closely with her?'

'Nothing. We've just worked on some poetry programmes together.'

'Well, you didn't tell me, you usually talk about your friends, you went on and on about Stanley and all those men—'

Now he did seem annoyed. 'What on earth is this? Some kind of inquisition? What's the matter with you, Dinah?'

He'd stayed overnight in Deal. And now she suddenly remembered the scrap of paper she'd found in a book in his study, with scrawled on it 'See you at the seaside'.

'She went to Deal with you, didn't she!'

Alan's jaw literally dropped, at least, his expression was blank, but his whole face seemed to slip slightly. 'How did you know?' The words seemed to come without his having willed them. He sat down at the table. 'You know – these things happen – you're a grown-up woman, Dinah, you're a woman of the world. Don't you remember, before we got married you said you didn't expect me to be faithful, couples shouldn't be jealous—'

'Then it's true.'

thirty

⌒⊶⌒

VICTOR JORDAN WAS WAITING for McGovern at the Hotel Am Zoo bar.

'You're looking rather the worse for wear.'

It embarrassed McGovern to be bearing the scars of what looked like some drunken brawl. He also felt foolish because he'd failed to take Jordan's advice.

'I took up Hoffmann's invitation to pay a return visit to his office. He wasn't there, but some other people were.'

'Don't tell me you went. I warned you. You bloody fool. I told you not to cross into their sector again. So what happened? Someone else was there – who else?'

'I don't know who they were.'

'And you got roughed up. You should have taken my advice.'

'I wish I had. I got more than roughed up. They tried to kill me. I only just missed getting run over. They beat me up, then they drove over onto this side of town, hurled me out of their van and tried to run me over.'

'You're out of your depth, McGovern. What the hell was your boss playing at, sending you out here in the first place?'

'He's not exactly my boss—'

'Whatever your relationship, it's not helpful to us to have you messing around out here. He must have completely lost

his touch. Do the authorities in West Berlin know about this?'
McGovern shook his head.

'On the whole I think that's just as well.'

There was an uncomfortable pause. McGovern knew he had to defend his presence in Berlin, but he was no longer sure why he was here. 'I know the reasons for sending me out here after Harris weren't very clear. To begin with it was supposed to have something to do with Burgess and Maclean, but it was obvious Harris had nothing to do with their defection. And the marriage with Fräulein Schröder was considered suspicious, because Harris is supposed to be a homosexual.'

Jordan shrugged impatiently. 'Oh, *that*. I long ago gave up being surprised by anything anyone gets up to in bed.'

McGovern took a deep breath. 'Well, you're probably right, but it was felt to be a wee bit strange. It was even suggested that Fräulein Schröder might have been some kind of spy, that that was the reason for her attempting to enter Britain.'

The vivid memory of their kissing by the lake flashed up and of her long legs and sinuous body and her dark eyes beneath winged eyebrows in her pale, sad face. Thank God it had only been a kiss. He'd not have forgiven himself had he let it go further. As it was – but he dragged his thoughts away from that and back to his self-justification. 'Look, I realise I've not done so well. I've made a fool of myself. I should have taken your advice.'

'Does our friend in London honestly believe that if the East Germans were grooming the Schröder woman as a spy, we wouldn't have got wind of it? For God's sake, does he think we're utter idiots? The whole thing stinks. You were badly briefed, in fact it doesn't sound as if you were properly briefed at all. So much for MI5 and their meticulous attention to detail. There isn't the slightest chance Colin Harris was involved with the disappearance of Burgess and Maclean and MI5 knows it. That was just an excuse. So what's the real reason you're here? I think you'd better tell me.'

So Jordan thought that the whole thing was a cover and that there was a secret, hidden agenda.

'You're saying I'm lying? That I have some other reason for being here? That isn't true. I've been straight with you. I'm here to find out more about Harris.'

'But what does our friend really want to know about Harris? Why is he interested? We don't regard Harris as important. So why does he?'

A closer examination of Kingdom's motives had been something McGovern had been trying to avoid. It was too unsettling. But he knew Jordan was right. He'd asked the same questions himself.

'He was interested to hear that Harris was travelling with Schröder to Thuringia. That made him sit up, because he said there are uranium mines down there.'

'Indeed. We're well aware that Schröder has been to the Saalfeld region. In fact, he is there at this moment. There is trouble brewing there, I can tell you, by the way,' said Jordan. 'Saalfeld is also where the Schröders lived, after all, throughout the war, when Schröder was working at Buchenwald. Do you know anything about that area, other than there's uranium?'

'Well—' McGovern recalled what Colin Harris had told him. 'I heard there was a wee bit of unrest in the region. Dissatisfied workers. The East Germans wouldn't like that, I can see.'

'Damn right, they wouldn't. But whose side is Harris on? We're pretty clear about Schröder. He and Hoffmann have worked together for a while. At least, Hoffmann has used Schröder when it suited him. But Harris – we were never that interested in him until you came along. When you were here a few weeks ago everything you told me convinced me our friend in London's losing his touch. He seems to be panicking. I suppose the question we should be asking is, why is he panicking? Perhaps there is genuinely something to worry about.' He laughed. 'Well, of course there is. There's always something to worry about. But what particularly in connection with Harris?'

He lifted a hand to attract the attention of the barman and ordered a further round of whisky.

'In the meantime I have another surprise for you. I don't believe it's been reported much back home, but Dr Hoffmann's been arrested. So it's hardly surprising he wasn't in his office when you went to see him there. If you'd informed me beforehand that you were planning to visit him I could have alerted you and then all this wouldn't have happened.'

'The men who interrogated me told me that. It was a bit of a shock, I'm telling you. But are you saying Feierabend knew that? He arranged the visit deliberately so that I'd be – what – *killed*?'

''Fraid so, old man. Roughed up at any rate. He must have done. So he dropped you in it, didn't he. That monkey's full of tricks. Wouldn't trust him further than I could throw him.'

'Why is Hoffmann under arrest?'

'Ah, it's a complicated story. No-one comes out of it well, but that's normally the case in Berlin. Well, Dr Hoffmann, as I think you know, lives in the British sector, or did, yet he had his legal office in the East. What you probably don't know is that he was in the Abwehr – Nazi intelligence – during the war. Pretty high up too. On several occasions he invited individuals to his office with the promise of work for them. Several prominent ex-German army and Abwehr men, old wartime friends of his, have disappeared in the last few years after accepting an invitation from Hoffmann. At the time of these disappearances – kidnappings in fact – the families of the missing men raised the alarm, tried to get something done about it, but any enquiries there may have been ran into the ground. The occupying forces weren't that bothered; in fact they actively hindered the widows' campaign. When the Americans were in charge of all things to do with the law, they were content to turn a blind eye to many things, especially at the beginning, before the war on communism took centre stage.'

'So Hoffmann was working for the Russians. But he was in Nazi intelligence during the war.'

Jordan smiled. 'Plenty of Nazis have changed sides pretty damned quick. In many cases, of course, they weren't even that keen on the Nazis in the first place, but they just went along with whoever was in power. However, it was always felt that as Hoffmann was an important figure in the Abwehr – he ran things in Norway for a while – he must have been a signed-up Hitlerite.'

'So it's been fairly easy for people to cover their tracks? That's shocking.'

'Good God, man, what do you expect? With all the chaos when the war ended it was easy for them to slip away and then with the development of the Cold War, priorities changed.'

'I've heard that explanation, or excuse, but even if it's not surprising that more Nazis haven't been brought to trial, I still find it shocking.'

'In that case you'll be pleased to hear that in Hoffmann's case retribution is at hand, or seemed to be. Because recently everything has changed. With the creation of the new West Germany has come the setting up of a separate, autonomous West German judicial system.

'As soon as this happened two of the widows of the vanished men – well, one has to assume they're widows – launched legal actions against Hoffmann. The independent West German legal system is keen to show its muscle. As a result, Dr Hoffmann was arrested by the West German authorities and charged with the kidnappings of these two men. Remember I told you this was the kidnap capital of the world? One of them has disappeared completely, someone claims to have seen the other one in some Russian labour camp, but no-one knows whether this is true. The story that's emerging is that they were war criminals and were wanted by the Russians, who've continued to be rather more zealous in their pursuit of Nazis than we have been since the political priorities changed. The kidnapped men were members of the Abwehr. And because Dr Hoffmann had also been an Abwehr officer he was able to entice former comrades into the Soviet zone, where they were arrested and immediately deported, charged, murdered or sent to a labour camp. Charming show of loyalty to your old war comrades.'

McGovern felt out of his depth. 'So he must have changed sides. He *is* working for the Russians.'

'Ah – but that's what's so interesting. I don't think so, because CIC, the Americans, that is, are furious. They have challenged the legality of the steps taken by the West Germans and are trying to get Hoffmann out of prison. Now, why should they do that unless he was working for them? I have my contacts in CIC, of course, but I haven't been able to get much out of them, they play their cards bloody close to the chest. Not the most obliging allies, I must say, but it seems clear he was working for them, well, working on both sides up to a point, but mainly for them. He threw the regime in Berlin a few titbits, some of his former Abwehr friends, but he was actually working predominantly for CIC. And one thing they didn't tell me, but which I've found out by other means: he had visited the uranium mines, he and Schröder together. One presumes they were trying to find out as much as they could about that for the Americans – quantities of ore, how quickly they're getting it out, all that sort of thing.' Jordan paused and eyed McGovern. His look was not entirely friendly. 'But where does Harris come into all this? How did he come to be so closely involved with the two of them, with Schröder? If there's one thing we know it's that Harris is a committed communist.'

Now McGovern could at last justify his existence and feel less of a fool. 'I don't think he is any more. I've managed to talk quite a bit to him. I managed to gain his confidence. I liked him. He's fundamentally decent, but the East Germans semi-blackmailed him into informing on Schröder for them. I think he's pretty disillusioned with the regime.'

'I see, one of those. Not so starry-eyed any more about the East German sector's Stalinist regime, found out it's not the socialist paradise he was expecting. That figures. He did want to return to Britain, after all.'

'He'd changed his mind, but he'd not be happy there or here. He told me he was going to the Saalfeld region to find out exactly what's happening down there. The East Germans think he's spying on Schröder, but in reality he's spying on them. Or possibly a bit of both.'

'So he's gone to Saalfeld to spy for and against the East Germans at one and the same time. That's twisted, even for Berlin.'

'I feel sorry for Harris. He's an idealist.'

'There's no place for feeling sorry in this business, I'm afraid. Absolutely fatal to get bogged down in pity. So many people we come across have got into trouble through a series of mistakes and poor judgement and bad luck and stupidity. There's no end to it if once you start feeling sorry for everyone. No room for idealism either, I'm sorry to say. Least of all in Berlin.'

It was McGovern's turn to signal the barman for more whisky.

'Let me tell you something.' Jordan looked around the bar, but there was only one other couple, a man and a woman, seated at the other end of the room. He'd spoken quietly all along, but now he lowered his voice further. 'You see, our relationships, with one another, with the other side, are delicate and complicated. The web of information isn't quite how it might seem to an onlooker.'

'I'm nae an onlooker,' said McGovern.

'Well, that's the problem, you are and you aren't. You're half in and half out. Here in Berlin, at least. No doubt it's different at home. But here you're an anomaly, McGovern, and what I'm curious to know is why the anomaly? But you'll have to ask your MI5 friend about that. Our system here works pretty well on the whole. It's not really, or not wholly, a question of concealing information from the other side or wrenching their secrets from them by fair or foul means. That's what the general public imagines, but it's more that it acts as a system of keeping the equilibrium going with an *exchange* of suitable information. The situation is self-perpetuating. It's checks and balances essentially. Secrets are leaked to forestall worse dangers. They get in a panic about something. We reassure them it ain't going to happen. Someone at our end gets paranoid about the Red Army crossing the border; they tell us nothing doing. Normal service as usual. That's how it works, McGovern. So we don't really like it when someone like our friend in London sticks an oar in. Could be very dangerous. More particularly because the Russians are in the process of setting up the East Germans as their major spying system against the West. We're monitoring it very closely. The last thing we want is someone from MI5 butting in just now. Extremely irregular. I think when you get back to London, you should do your damnedest to find out what his game is.'

'Don't think I've not asked myself these questions.' Yet, and it made him angry with himself, McGovern knew he hadn't asked as many questions as he should have done.

Jordan stood up. McGovern, assuming it was the agent's parting shot, stood up as well and stuck out his hand as a prelude to saying goodbye. But Jordan patted him on the shoulder. 'I'd like to invite you round for a meal with some friends this evening, if that suits you. I think you might get on. You might find them interesting.'

♦ ♦ ♦ ♦ ♦

At six, Jordan collected McGovern from the hotel. They took a tram to Charlottenburg and on the way Jordan revealed there was a purpose in the visit.

'It's not just a social occasion, although they'll be pleased to meet you, I'm sure. Major Black has been in charge of a section of the refugee work here since 1946. They're still flooding across the borders, I don't know if you realise that. His wife was working with the Allies in the refugee camps directly after the war. That's how they met. They were especially concerned with children and while we were talking earlier today I remembered something. I didn't mention it then, because I wanted to check up on it, see if I got my facts right. Not that there were facts as such, but there were a lot of rumours. There was rape of course, we all know that, and prostitution, but there was also child prostitution and that was very murky. They'll tell you about it.'

'Child prostitution?'

'There were murders too, or unexplained deaths. But I remembered there were a couple of murders of children which did cause a bit of a stir even in the midst of the chaos.'

McGovern was too surprised to react, other than with a shocked: 'I'd not thought of that. Of children being exploited.'

The devastation in Charlottenburg was less than in some parts of the city, but there was still a vast flattened area of cleared rubble next to where Jordan's friends lived, a pompous, late-nineteenth-century block, with heavy plaster swags and pilasters that had been chipped and cracked. They rose to the first floor in a creaking lift, and waited on a dark landing.

To McGovern, Celia Black looked more German than English. She was tall and her blonde hair was pinned into an elaborate braided bun with plaits running round from the front of her head to the back. She had cold colouring, a pale skin and very light blue eyes and her effect on McGovern was of a clear, cold glass of water. Yet her smile was welcoming enough. Her full skirts rustled as she stepped aside to let them pass into the salon. This was a high-ceilinged and once splendid octagonal room, with inset gilt mirrors, but there were cracks in the plaster of the walls and a raw wound on the ceiling where a chandelier must once have hung. The room with its heavy bourgeois furniture had seen better – much better – days.

The Major was a worried-looking man with receding hair. As they sat over drinks – a local aperitif – he spoke wearily of the immense task presented by the unending stream of refugees from the East, speaking with what seemed like genuine concern for what so many had suffered. 'You should write about it,' said the Major, for Jordan had suggested it would be better if McGovern became a journalist again. 'Which paper did you say it was?'

'The *Scottish Herald.*'

'People at home have forgotten all about it. Since the Berlin blockade no-one thinks about all this any more. I don't think they realise there are still thousands and thousands of DPs – displaced persons.'

The food was good, a tasty fish in wine sauce and sautéed potatoes with peas in cream, and McGovern couldn't help wondering why he'd had more good food here in Berlin than seemed available to the victors in London. As they ate Celia Black described her work immediately after the war. She and her husband had met in Berlin where both were members of the army of occupiers and survivors trying to restore order to chaos. She was a trained nurse, employed by UNRAA in an administrative capacity. There were so many different medical problems. 'And the children,' she said, 'so many had no fathers, no parents at all, surviving in whatever way they could, living in the ruins. It was a terrible problem, trying to deal with the children. Many knew they were orphans, many didn't know what had happened to their parents. We had to try to trace them – make every effort. It was easier in a heartrending way when the children definitely knew their parents were dead.

'We soon became aware that there was an enormous exploitation of these children, separated from their families, who were being used and ill-treated in all sorts of ways. Some of them simply ran errands or worked with the women clearing the rubble, and that wasn't so bad, others were messengers or couriers in the black market, others were thieves – and many, of course, were sexually exploited, made to prostitute themselves or even did it willingly.'

'In one sense it wasn't surprising,' said Major Black with a painful smile. 'If everything else, then why not that? If you think about it, why wouldn't children be sexually exploited?'

'Mr Roberts is trying to get an angle on all this,' put in Jordan. 'Isn't that so, Roberts?'

This was McGovern's cue. 'I've met someone, a woman called Frieda Schröder. It's complicated to explain, but it could be an important story. Her father worked in a concentration camp, but although he was interrogated he never came to trial.'

'I'm afraid that's happened in a lot of cases,' said the Major. 'So many people were involved, it simply wasn't possible. Even those involved with the camps – with the Jews – I'm afraid there are many Germans who got away with it, whatever they did. And of course some of them did nothing, nothing wrong, that is.'

'This man, the woman's father, seems to have been involved in something after the war, probably the black market. He seemed to be settled in the British sector and his daughter had a relationship with a British officer, but then they suddenly moved East. I think it was after her sister died.'

Husband and wife exchanged glances. 'Her sister died? What did she die of?'

'Fräulein Schröder just said she was ill. I suppose they were semi-starving.'

'Probably not, if her father was involved in the black market,' said the Major, 'but many children died. Terrible things went on, bodies would be found and some of those deaths were not accidental. It was impossible to investigate every case. It was often just a matter of another body found among the ruins, impossible even to tell why they'd died. There were some incidents that caused more of a stir, when it was quite clearly murder. Once or twice people in the district thought they knew how it had happened and who had done it and pointed the finger. I remember one case at least. Some neighbours denounced a local man who was very unpopular in the district. The little girl had been violated. I don't remember the man's name, though, but there was certainly some talk about him. I think the authorities thought there might be grounds for an investigation, all the talk and gossip.'

'Now the West German judicial system is up and running,' said Jordan, 'do you think there's any possibility they could open an investigation on this sort of case? Following their triumph with Hoffmann? I've heard a rumour they're reopening some of these cases. Or rather, investigating. Because the cases never were opened in the first place.'

'In the case of the little girl who was murdered,' said the Major, 'in the end nothing was done, or could be done, because he'd spirited himself away.'

The story made McGovern very thoughtful. He must see Frieda again. There was so much he must ask her. A dark suspicion was beginning to unfold.

thirty-one

⟨⟩

'**Y**OU CERTAINLY BELIEVE IN taking the initiative, don't you, Jarrell. Who told you to go charging off in search of this Ukrainian?'

'I thought, sir—'

'It wasn't me, was it, Jarrell. Have you somehow been in contact with DI McGovern?'

'No, sir.'

'Well, who the fuck gave you permission to set up your own investigation? Which is what it more or less amounts to. If Monkhouse hadn't driven like a bloody maniac and got suspended, this wouldn't have happened. I wouldn't have been saddled with you, God help me. I thought he was a pain, but you're a frigging nightmare. Now I've got another fucking maniac on my hands. He was a maniac for doing things by the book and you're the bloody opposite. And the result is this individual you've decided is a suspect knows all about you. And how's that helping the so-called bloody enquiry?'

'I've done some research on Mihaili Kozko, sir. I've followed him up. He's got form. GBH, assault. He's not that popular in Yorkshire, even among his own. That's why he's moved down here.'

'So why isn't he banged up? What's he doing down here, if he's a convicted criminal?'

'The conviction was quashed on appeal, sir.'

'Oh, really.'

'I followed him, sir. I know where he lives. We could bring him in for questioning.'

'On what grounds, may I ask?'

'We could think of something. You can always think of something, can't you, sir.'

Jarrell thought the inspector was going to hit him. Instead he took a step backwards. 'What makes you so certain he killed the Biermann kid anyway?'

'Just a hunch, sir. But Biermann was investigating him because there were allegations he'd been in the Waffen SS, that he's a war criminal. He's an obvious suspect.'

'Biermann was a commie. More likely *he* was up to something.'

'If you say so, sir. But this isn't like the old man, is it. I mean – a body in the canal. Happens all the time. But a shooting, even in Hackney, we have to get a result sir, don't you think? I mean, it was almost more like a gangland killing. We don't want any more of those, sir.'

'Stupid of Biermann to have got involved. I can't stand amateur sleuthing. He had it coming to him.'

Slater was red in the face. Jarrell was well aware he was playing with fire, but he couldn't resist taunting the man who'd so often sneered at him. Particularly as what he said was true, and Slater knew it. He needed to get a result.

What Jarrell didn't mention was the man whom Kozko had met in the pub on the Jamaica Road. That was the shocking link that could explain everything, but Slater wouldn't understand and anyway couldn't be allowed to know. The person who should know was McGovern, but Jarrell didn't know how to get in touch with him. He was on his own.

thirty-two

ᴄ᙭ᴐ

THERE WERE TWO PEOPLE McGovern had to see before he left Berlin. He tracked down Feierabend at the Eldorado. 'I want an explanation.'

Feierabend was perfectly friendly. He was working now, he pointed out, but they could meet the following morning in the gardens of the Charlottenburg Schloss.

Next morning Feierabend was sunny as ever. 'Wonderful weather. It's always hot at this time of year.'

'It certainly is hot.' Lily would have loved it, for like her father she missed the heat of India in the perennially rain-streaked streets of Glasgow. But there was no time to miss Lily now. He gestured towards a seat beneath a tree.

'Sit down. There's some things we need to get straight. You set me up, didn't you. It was deliberate. You sent me to Hoffmann's office again, where I was meant to be got rid of. You were never working for us, for the British. You were always on the other side.'

Feierabend looked genuinely horrified. 'This is not true. This was not what I thought was meant to happen. It wasn't my job. To hand you over to be killed.'

'Well, what exactly *is* your job? I thought you were one of our informers, a go-between, a useful contact.'

'But precisely that is what I am. It was I who put you in

touch with Hoffmann, for example, so that you could meet the Englishman, Mr Harris.'

'But the second time was a trap.'

Feierabend stopped in his tracks and turned to face McGovern. 'Absolutely not. I still do not understand it. In the first place, I did not then know that Hoffmann had actually been arrested. Secondly, I could not see any reason for your ill-treatment. Someone had an interest in your being given a warning – or even murdered, although ...' He shook his head. 'No, I really can't see how the East Germans gained anything from that. If Hoffmann set it up, it wasn't to please them. But I don't think it could have been him, because he was already arrested. You have other enemies, perhaps.'

'Well, it's perfectly obvious I do, do you nae think, seeing I was nearly murdered. But who they might be I have no idea.'

'I have certainly not been told to harm you. Look, it all started originally when someone made contact with me. It wasn't someone I knew here in Berlin. The story was you were concerned with Mr Harris. Hoffmann knew Harris through Schröder, so that seemed a good way to set things up. That was the end of the matter, so far as I was concerned. I have contacts with the East German police, yes, you shouldn't look so surprised – and I heard nothing about them wanting to see you, arrest you, anything like that.'

'I don't understand what game you're playing,' said McGovern. 'Do you play both sides against the middle, like everyone else in this city?'

Feierabend laughed. 'Why should you think that? I've played straight with you, Herr Kommissar McGovern. My job was to put you in touch with Harris, and I did that through Hoffmann.'

'But you know my real name.'

'Of course. The truth is, there are many people like me in Berlin. For me and many of us there are no sides. There is only survival.'

'So you knew Hoffmann.'

'I know many people, and so did Herr Dr Hoffmann. In both East and West. In the German Democratic Republic they were rightly concerned once they suspected that Hoffmann was spying on their uranium production. They were trying to use your friend Harris, but I don't think they'd worked out quite how he could be useful. Perhaps they first of all have the idea to get him to go back to England, but what could he have done when he got there? He wouldn't have had access to any useful information. Then they thought he might spy on Schröder, but unfortunately when he discovered the situation in Thuringia his idealistic soul was wounded and now he has probably ended up making more trouble for himself and everyone else. I expect he went down there with Schröder in good faith. Of course he isn't a Western agent and perhaps – probably – he doesn't realise that Schröder is.'

'Schröder works for the West?'

'Perhaps only in the sense that he has been working with Herr Dr Hoffmann. But they, the East Germans, who may in any case believe Harris is some kind of double agent, will of course be able to use his presence in Thuringia in any way they wish. Or even if they don't think that, it will suit them to say they do. So what he's doing is very risky and stupid. I expect that like so many of you in the West he wants a better socialism. He is shocked when he hears that conditions for the workers aren't quite what he expected. But idealists like him are not realistic. These are difficult times, you understand. Here in Germany we recognise the freedom of necessity. The East Germans aren't trying to do what the West is doing here, create a consumer society. They want to build an equal society, in which there are jobs, housing, free education and health for all. They truly want that. They may even believe it will be an equal society, though of course it won't really be if only because their leadership is so hierarchical. Most of their leaders spent the war in Moscow and unfortunately they are thwarted by their own experiences and assumptions. They are completely out of touch. And what is worse, they do not trust the people. *Das Volk*, Herr Kommissar, has done so many terrible things that they cannot be trusted any more. They have to be told what to do and how to think and they have to be watched very closely. But it's possible things will improve in that direction too, when the foundations of a socialist society are in place. I am enough of a progressive socialist to believe that.'

'Or so you tell yourself,' said McGovern nastily.

'Oh, that's unfair, Herr Kommissar.'

'So what's going to happen to Harris?'

'He will go to prison, I'm afraid. Unless your government gets him out. But I doubt if they'll do much about it. They have enough problems with Burgess and Maclean, they can't afford another international embarrassment. And it won't be so easy to explain what he's done, back in England, do you think? A known communist who's been living in the Soviet sector for several years – and then suddenly he sides with the strikers, if that *is* what he did. Well, perhaps it is not so difficult to explain. If it can be made to seem he has been working for the British government, there might be a surge of support. In the meantime I imagine he's probably already been arrested. And you know what the East German government will do, don't you? They will buy off the workers, or some of them, and crack down on anyone who can be portrayed as anti-socialist, against the state and all the rest of it. And Mr Harris will fit very well into that category.'

McGovern was under no illusions about the situation Harris had created for himself. An idealist, a utopian – but surely just because he was unrealistic and reckless, he shouldn't, couldn't, just be left to rot in an East German jail. But he did not know what he could do about it. He could talk to Victor Jordan, to Kingdom, but he doubted they would be keen to help. In fact they might blame *him* for not somehow reining Harris in. Or they might even say he should have manufactured some excuse for getting Harris arrested in the British sector, so that he could be quietly booted out of the country and returned to Britain. Of course there was no way he could have done that – although the British agents in West Berlin probably could have if they'd wanted to.

The only way to create any interest would be to leak it to the press, to make sure it wasn't hushed up. 'But perhaps,' he said, searching for a more hopeful angle, 'now that Hoffmann's been arrested, when he's tried, couldn't a case be made that Harris was trying to prove he was up to no good? Might the East Germans relent and release him?'

Feierabend laughed. 'Ah, but you haven't heard the latest. Hoffmann won't be tried. Something very strange has happened. He's disappeared, been spirited away. The rumours are he'll soon be in America, possibly under another name.'

'You mean the Americans—'

'He must have been very important to them,' said Feierabend. He stood up. 'I shall have to go soon. I am due to start work at lunchtime.'

'So whose side are you really on?' McGovern wasn't ready to let him go.

Feierabend smiled. 'I told you. I'm not on anyone's side. Or rather, I'm everyone's friend. And I have a suggestion to make, to prove it to you. Tomorrow they are hosting the World Youth Festival of Peace and Freedom in East Berlin. A million young people are going to march for world peace, against the Korean war and against colonialism.' His tone was slightly satirical. 'In spite of the propaganda it will be a sight worth seeing, I can assure you of that.'

'I know all about that. They don't like it over this side and are trying to stop the delegates from arriving in East Berlin. They think it's an attempt to spark off some sort of uprising.'

'They are unarmed young people!'

'Perhaps they are secretly armed.'

Feierabend shook his head, smiling. 'It could be, but they are delegates from all over the world – South Africa, the socialist countries, China … I could take you across,' he suggested. 'As I say, it will be something worth seeing.'

'What, so that I can get kidnapped and roughed up again?'

'That won't happen, I promise you. Not if you're with me.'

It was a risk McGovern thought it unwise to take, although he would have liked to see the parade.

In the event he saw it anyway, because Jordan managed to get him included in a group of Western diplomats who had been invited. Most of them refused, so there were plenty of spare places.

That was how, the following day, he found himself standing at Jordan's side behind a window looking out over Marx Engels Platz. Fireworks crackled and spat and shot their garish blue and magenta into a sky that rapidly turned smoky red. Flags waved and fluttered everywhere as thousands of doves were released into the air and a Soviet plane tore across the city above them, while below, headed by a giant statue of Stalin carried like a god at the head of a Hindu procession, column after column swept forward. Wave upon wave of delegates followed the juggernaut, their banners proclaiming they came from all over the world. When showers of leaflets rained down on the march-past they appeared to cause some disturbance among the cheering crowds, but the parade continued relentlessly forward, wheeling and turning as it circled the square and then marched away to the East, a demonstration of the onward march of communism.

Harris would have been proud, McGovern thought, his doubts put to rest. But later some young pioneers broke away from the parade and, evading the police, raced across the border into West Berlin and streamed towards the glitter of the Kurfürstendamm.

thirty-three

༄

CHARLES WAS ALONE IN the house when the bell rang. He'd reached home in a state of euphoria. Finally the Navy was behind him. And in an unexpected celebration on the last night, Christopher, the man he'd been besotted with for months, had finally and amazingly succumbed.

At first he was too caught up in his memories of everything they'd done to notice the piece of paper on the hall table. It was only when he'd called out his mother's name, had looked in the drawing room and then run up the stairs to her room and discovered the whole house was empty, that he'd made a more careful search for clues and found the note, which baldly told him Dad had had to take his mother back to hospital that very morning. 'I'm sorry there wasn't time to warn you.'

She'd never relapsed so soon before. Charles was frightened, with a fear too deep to contemplate, and which manifested itself simply as a kind of paralysis. He sat silent and motionless on his bed for a long time and then decided to telephone his old school friend, Oliver. Anything to take his mind off it. He looked at his watch. It was nearly four. Perhaps they could even play tennis. But the effort of descending the stairs to the telephone was too much for him. He continued to sit on his bed. He was nearly, but not quite, crying. The lump of tears was stuck in his throat.

He was still seated on his bed when the front doorbell rang. He took his time descending the flights of stairs through the lofty house, walking slowly, slowly downwards, hoping that whoever it was would have given up and gone, but when he opened the door he saw it was Aunt Elfie's boyfriend.

Kingdom looked quite disconcerted. 'I didn't realise you'd be at home. For good now, is it?' He entered the house without waiting to be asked. 'I was expecting to find Judy here. I'm very sorry to hear your mother's unwell again. Rotten business. Your aunt telephoned to say they'd be staying here for a while. You don't mind if I come in and wait. She won't be here until later, she asked me to entertain Judy, who'll be here very soon. She's coming straight round after her tennis lesson. I thought she'd be here already. I brought some ice cream.' He handed Charles a damp parcel wrapped in newspaper. 'Would you mind awfully putting it in the fridge? I don't know my way around,' he said, advancing relentlessly into the drawing room.

Seized with dull resentment, but incapable of objecting – as if he could have anyway – Charles did as he was told and then climbed wearily back up from the basement kitchen. He drifted into the drawing room. His only wish was for the man not to be here. But he *was* here. He wasn't going to budge. He was waiting for Judy and then for Aunt Elfie. He'd be here for ever. Charles knew he couldn't stay himself, because they'd have to make conversation and the conversation would inevitably be about his mother. He had to get away, get out. Still, out of pride, he made himself act in a proper way as host.

'Would you like a drink, sir? I'm sure there's some about. A whisky and soda perhaps.' He couldn't believe Kingdom didn't sense his violent resentment. Kingdom, however, seemed pleased, utterly unaware of Charles's near-hysterical tension.

'Thank you. Very kind.'

Charles produced the drink from the sideboard in the

dining room. 'I'm afraid I'm going to have to go out, sir. Meeting a friend.'

'Don't worry about me. Judy will soon be home and she can keep me company. It'll be a chance to get to know her better.'

'If you're sure you don't mind, then ...'

'Of course not, of course not. You go along. By the way, you haven't forgotten what I said to you last time we were both here?'

'No, sir,' Charles said, wondering what it had been.

'You've plenty of time to play the field – in all senses of the word – while you're up at Oxford. But after you come down I really did mean it when I said come and see me. I'm sure we can find you something.'

As Charles hurried along Regent's Park Road towards Camden Town he saw Judy coming in the opposite direction. She was wearing a white tennis dress and gym shoes and carrying a racquet.

'Hullo, Charles!' Her face lit up. He could see she was thrilled to see him. 'I'm so glad you're home. I didn't expect you to be here. I didn't really want to have to stay here again, moving about all the time's such a nuisance.'

'Well, as you see, I have to go out. But your mother's friend, Mr Kingdom, called round. He's still there, so you won't be alone.'

'Oh?' She looked surprised and then she smiled. 'That's nice. Uncle Miles is awfully friendly, I don't really feel shy with him.' She twirled her racquet as she spoke.

'Have a good time,' said Charles carelessly. 'I'll be back later on.'

But when he returned, drunk, some hours later, the situation had unexpectedly changed.

thirty-four

❦

ALAN WAS SUSPICIOUS OF the club environment. He regarded himself as a pub rather than a club man and disliked the lethargic atmosphere of Kingdom's club. The brown room slumbered in the amber light of early evening and contrasted painfully with the vitality of the Gluepot or the Stag's Head.

Kingdom was late. When he finally arrived he made no apology: 'I think I'll order a bottle of champagne.'

'*Champagne*! Is there something to celebrate?'

Kingdom laughed. 'It's my birthday.'

'Personally I've reached the age when the last thing I want to celebrate is getting older.'

'Believe me, it can only get better. You feel younger all the time,' said Kingdom with manic recklessness.

'You seem bloody pleased with yourself.'

'Actually, there is some bad news. So we might just as well get drunk. Colin Harris has been arrested.'

'Don't tell me – not in East Germany.'

'I'm afraid so.' Kingdom let it sink in.

The barman brought the champagne. They watched the ceremony of its opening. The cork was extracted silently, with only a whiff of smoke from the bottle.

Alan watched, mad with impatience. As if he hadn't enough to worry about.

'How did it happen?' He listened with near horror as Kingdom described the situation: the strike, the cautious response of the East German government towards its own people and their tactic of blaming Western infiltrators. It had been a simple matter to target Harris as an example.

Alan groaned. 'Oh, God! The imbecile. He was always such a fool.'

'Well, now he's in real trouble. Very convenient for the East German government. They can use him for their own ends. A bloody great propaganda coup.'

Alan gritted his teeth. 'Is there anything I should do?' The last thing he wanted at the moment was to have to undertake a mercy mission to the German Democratic Republic.

'Our people over there will give him every assistance. They'll do everything they can to keep it under wraps, they want to avoid a diplomatic incident at all costs. They'll be nego- tiating. It would only complicate matters if you got involved. There wouldn't be anything you could do. You wouldn't be allowed to visit him, which might have cheered him up a bit, I suppose. Good of you to think of it, though. But look, I've had to tell you, for obvious reasons, but for God's sake, keep it to yourself. We don't want it in the news. Well, not more than it has to be. If it gets linked with Burgess and Maclean the balloon will go up.'

'But it isn't linked ... is it?'

'No. But what I mean is, the press could construct a link. That it's spurious wouldn't help. It would look bloody terrible for us.'

'By "us" you mean your outfit.'

'Of course.'

'That's all you care about, isn't it. You don't care about the country. Your reputation, that's all that matters.' The momentary flash of insight came from Alan's relief at having

got away with an expression of goodwill that entailed no conse-
quences, which was offset by the acute irritation Kingdom's
bombastic good spirits was causing him.

'We *are* "the country". Without us, this country would
have been overrun by communism long ago.'

This was so absurd that Alan forgot his ill humour, forgot
Colin and forgot his troubles with Dinah long enough to taunt:
'So why aren't the missing diplomats behind bars?'

'That was an accident. We trusted them. We couldn't have
known. Good God, Wentworth, Burgess and I went to the same
school!'

So that was how it worked, Alan thought. With breath-
taking arrogance and wilful blindness. Pointless to argue with
such stony self-assurance.

'Everything possible will be done to help Harris.'

'I certainly hope so.' It was an effort to say it, but he added:
'I want to do what I can. I'm sure there is something I could
do. Even money ...'

'Don't get ideas about publicity. Don't start thinking that
stirring things up at Broadcasting House will do any good.'

Alan smiled. 'I hadn't thought of that. But I must say it
seems like rather a good idea to me.'

'It isn't.'

'You say publicity will only make things worse. But I don't
agree. It can only help, surely. Colin's a romantic. He could
be portrayed as an idealist, fighting for the heroic strikers,
fighting for the true socialism the East German government
has betrayed. Or simply against the Stalinist state.'

Kingdom refilled their glasses with champagne, but his
celebratory mood had evaporated. 'Be careful, Wentworth. It's
so easy to go too far. Don't taunt the beast. It's dangerous.'

Alan tried to frame a defiant reply, but before he had thought
of anything, Kingdom added: 'How's your wife these days?'

It gave Alan a grim satisfaction to be able to reply: 'She

could be better. She found out I was having an affair.' It was as much as to say to Kingdom: you've got no hold over me whatsoever now. Not that you ever had really.

Kingdom raised his eyebrows faintly. 'Unfortunate,' he murmured.

Briefly Alan considered the possibility that it had been Kingdom, after all, who'd somehow alerted Dinah. But no – she'd found out for herself, no doubt with the help of bloody Reggie. He only hoped Reggie hadn't told her about the time he'd made a pass at *her*.

Alan took the Bakerloo line to Great Portland Street station and walked along Bell Street to Edith's flat. He'd reached a decision. He had to end the affair. Irrationally, he blamed Edith for the turmoil in his marriage. She was too demanding ... possessive ... her behaviour at that party. He'd thought Dinah hadn't a clue, but she was no fool, he'd underestimated her. He'd make it clear to Edith – perhaps he'd wait until they'd made love though ...

To his surprise Edith was dressed in a cool, blue linen dress and looked as if she was about to go out.

'Darling! How very formal! It makes you look so prim. I can't wait to take it off.' He approached, put one arm round her and engulfed her in a kiss as with his other hand he undid her top button and roughly pushed his hand inside to squeeze her breasts.

Edith pulled herself out of his grasp and stepped away from him. She smiled her cat-like smile. 'You're so impatient. Sit down, I have something to tell you.'

Alan's stomach lurched. Oh Christ! Pregnant. Just when he'd decided ... He lowered himself uneasily onto her hard little sofa. 'What is it, darling?'

'I'm getting married.'

Married ...

'Well – say something, darling.' Her smile was more provocative than ever.

He sat staring at her. Eventually he croaked out: 'Who to?'

'The banker, Sir Avery Pearson.'

'*What*! I don't believe you. You're joking. You're having me on.'

She shook her head indulgently. 'On the contrary. We're getting married at Chelsea Register Office on Friday.'

Fury drove him to his feet. 'You bloody bitch! What are you *talking* about! You never even told me you'd met him. Why didn't you tell me? Two-timing little tart.' He surged towards her.

Her air of triumph held steady, but she put out a hand in front of her to ward him off. 'Don't be ridiculous! You have no rights over me. Who are you to talk? You were never going to leave your wife, were you.'

He swung out blindly and slapped her face. They both recoiled, she with a hand to her mouth, he angrier than ever, but now with himself as much as with her. He flung round furiously and slammed out of the flat.

He made for the nearest pub and sat numbly smoking. He'd been a bit drunk. He really shouldn't have hit a woman. Yes, he must have been drunk. All that champagne with bloody Kingdom. His generalised rage, embracing Kingdom, Colin, Edith and Dinah gradually seeped away into self-pity until he was empty, completely drained.

Half an hour later he trudged up the path alongside the cemetery, dreading what he would find at home. 'Hullo,' he called uncertainly from the hall.

Dinah had had an unexpected encounter with Dr Blunt at the Courtauld. As she climbed the splendid Courtauld staircase to the landing where it divided and then surged upwards in two stony curves, she was close to tears. She had cried a lot since the awful row with Alan. You would have thought you'd run out of tears, that the ducts would dry up, but no, on the contrary, there were always more. She despised herself for it, but she couldn't stop. Her head was down, her lips pressed together, her face distorted. She almost bumped into someone running down. It was Dr Blunt.

'Mrs Wentworth! Dinah! Is something the matter? You look rather pale. You're not – is it another—'

She laughed rather miserably. 'Oh no, I'm not pregnant.'

He took her elbow and steered her swiftly back up the stairs to his office and soon Dinah to her own amazement had poured out her sorry story of a wife betrayed. As she talked she knew Dr Blunt was lapping up the gossip and drama, but she also felt his sympathy was sincere. He offered no practical advice, but it was a relief just to talk about it.

For, to her surprise, there'd been no-one she could talk to. She'd thought she had staunch women friends, but at this moment of crisis there'd been none to turn to. Pride had prevented her from unburdening herself to Reggie. Of the others, one, a psychoanalyst, would, Dinah felt, have been too 'psychological' about it, seeing Alan's as well as Dinah's point of view; another lived in the country; she didn't know the peace group women well enough; while of course to mention it to her mother would have been unthinkable.

'Shall we ask Miss Lefebvre to bring us some tea?'

The tea came, with some of Miss Welsh's cakes as well. Dinah watched Dr Blunt. Although he was so tall and so thin, he was large-boned, as his wrists, which protruded from the too-short sleeves of his shabby jacket, proved and it was rather endearing, the clumsy way he arranged the cups, handed her a plate and poured the tea. And he seemed to be too tall for his chair, swung one leg over the other and folded himself like a retractable ruler. His flannel trousers weren't properly creased, but his black lace-up shoes gleamed like ebony. Dinah wondered that a man could be such an aesthete, so intensely sensitive to the beauty of works of art, yet so indifferent to his own appearance and surroundings. Jeremy, one of the few to have seen the inside of Dr Blunt's flat at the top of the building, had reported that it was more like a barracks than a home, 'positively spartan'.

Here in the ramshackle study the Poussin painting glowed on the wall behind them, with its depths, its light and shade, the intensity of its yellow, and the richness of mysterious blue, a powerful, numinous presence.

Dinah sat in the shabby armchair at right angles to Dr Blunt's.

'You really must come back to us full-time in the autumn,' he said. 'You must have an independent life of your own.' A smile stretched his papery face and revealed surprisingly large teeth.

'I think that'll be really difficult with the baby,' she said. 'He's over a year old now, you know, and he's so active. He's walking. He's almost a toddler.' But she stopped, for she felt sure Dr Blunt wasn't interested in babies.

'The longer you put it off the more difficult it will be. You'll probably have more children, your husband will grow more and more used to your being at home—'

She knew it was not that he rated her especially highly as a student. It was not even that he was particularly interested in her. It was rather that he wished for her to experience to the full the matchless opportunity of studying at the greatest art-history institution in Britain, perhaps anywhere. Polly complained that he didn't care about the women students, but Dinah didn't criticise him for that. A fair number came from upper-class families for whom the study of art was an appropriate preparation for the future wife of a rich man who would cherish family heirlooms and add to them with judicious new purchases. It was the men who would be the curators and who, trained by Dr Blunt, would carry his legacy into the museums of the future.

Polly, set on a serious curating career, was an exception. Dinah felt that she herself was more a kind of anomaly, a girl who, for some unknown reason, Dr Blunt had decided to take under his wing.

Perhaps Dr Blunt needed someone to talk to as badly as Dinah did, because he began to reminisce about the 1930s and Dinah, listening, knew that he was as agitated about the disappearance of the missing diplomats now as he had been on the day the news had broken. He talked about the rise of fascism all over the world – 'it wasn't just in Germany or even Europe, there was Chiang Kai-shek in China—' the Soviet Union had been the only hope. She could tell from the way he talked about Guy Burgess how important the friendship had been to him. Burgess was the one who had influenced him towards communism and whose disappearance had … hurt – angered – frustrated him? After a while he stopped talking and lay back in his chair, seeming shattered.

'You look rather tired, Dr Blunt.'

'These endlessly pestering MI5 people – I'm absolutely exhausted. There's one in particular. He remembers everything I say and then if I say anything – *anything* – that seems to be inconsistent *in the smallest degree, the minutest particular*, he picks me up on it and we go all the way back to square one and start again. And it's all completely pointless, because I don't know anything. They've wrung me dry. I'm a limp rag.'

She couldn't believe it was still going on. 'But they surely must know you had nothing to do with it. Just because you knew them—'

'They still think I helped them get away. And if I did that it means I knew more about them than I let on.'

'That's just absurd, Dr Blunt.'

Dr Blunt smiled his twisted smile.

And in the charged silence, for a moment there was an electric current charging the atmosphere with expectation. As if he was about to say something extraordinary, as if—

'Don't let's talk about it any more. I'm sorry to bore you with it. Especially when you're having such a beastly time.' He laughed. 'Oh, what a bore it is, feeling sorry for oneself. We're both feeling sorry for ourselves today, aren't we. I think perhaps we should move on to gin and tonic.'

Dinah hardly ever drank gin and certainly not at 11.00 a.m., but she accepted a small one. He raised his glass.

'To you, Dinah. I'm looking forward to seeing you back here full-time in the autumn. Don't let anything stand in your way. You owe it to yourself – and to your son – to make the best use of your talent. You have a real feeling for the work.'

She smiled, embarrassed, but she knew it was the highest compliment he could offer, more than offsetting, in his eyes at least, the tiresome banality of an unfaithful husband. And to hide her pleasure, she simply said: 'I must get back to the library. Miss Welsh will wonder where on earth I've got to.'

'There was one other thing,' said Dr Blunt in a different tone of voice, unfolding himself and standing up. 'Your father's a lawyer, I believe.'

'That's right.'

'If ever I needed to discuss this business with someone ...'

'Oh, I'm sure he'd be only too pleased to help. But it won't come to that, will it?'

'I don't expect so.'

Dinah was still thinking about Dr Blunt's words when Alan came home.

'I bought some gin on the way home. D'you fancy a drink?'

She didn't tell him she'd had some earlier in the day.

Drink in hand, Alan swallowed. 'Look – Dinah—'

She stood at the sink, her back towards him.

'I've – I've behaved so badly. It didn't mean anything, you know. It was just – it was nothing. She – I was stupid, thoughtless, I never cared for her – please …'

Dinah turned towards him and leaned her back against the sink. 'Then why did you do it? If it meant nothing to you. You knew it would hurt me so dreadfully.'

Alan raised his hands in a helpless gesture. 'I've given her up. I told her I couldn't see her any more. And I *didn't* think.'

'Well, you should have thought.'

'But when we first met we talked about what being married meant and how we shouldn't be jealous and possessive. You said that. You agreed.'

Dinah pressed her lips together. She wasn't looking at him. 'Well, I was silly and inexperienced. I had *no idea*. I don't care what I said then. I understand things differently now. I'm a mother now. That changes everything.'

He stood with hanging head. 'I'm so sorry.'

'It mustn't happen again, Alan. I couldn't stand it. It's not fair on me, or on Tommy.'

'Of course, of course. I promise.' And as he said it, he meant it, overcome with affection and pity. Tommy. And he did understand that he'd hurt her, although it was beyond his imagining how much.

'I think it's important that I go back to the Courtauld in the autumn. Go back properly, I mean, as a full-time student. Dr Blunt wants me to.'

'But what about Tommy? If motherhood's so important to you.' Already he was in danger of becoming truculent.

'We'll have to have a nanny. Or I may be able to make a different arrangement with Mary. I'd like to help Mary. Her real ambition is to be a nurse, but she hasn't any education. If we pay her properly she'll be able to save up – she may need to do some courses, I don't know, I'm going to find out about it.'

'But Dinah—'

'I don't want to argue about it. I just want to do it. You do what *you* want. All the time. Don't you. And now I want to do what I want for a change.'

An awful sense of dismay and something he couldn't put a name to welled up in him. He put his arms round his wife and murmured, 'Of course, of course, whatever you want,' sincerely determined at that moment to be a better husband and to make Dinah happy.

thirty-five

⌒⋙⌒

MCGOVERN WAITED FOR FRIEDA outside her place of work, as he had done when Hoffmann had taken him to meet her the first time. She saw him and crossed the street with that curiously sideways walk of hers, as if she were drifting away, evasive and yet drawn to him.

'I thought you might come,' she said. 'I hoped, anyway, but I was afraid you might have left. I was going to come to your hotel. I need your help now. You are going to help me? Tomorrow is my last day at work here. I won't be coming across any more. They make it more and more difficult. You are supposed to promise not to. It is seen as unpatriotic. I shall have to find work there, on the other side.'

'I'd like to take you somewhere nice,' he said, wanting to be kind to her and at the same time dreading the conversation they must have.

'To your hotel, perhaps.'

He shook his head. He wanted to avoid anywhere where they would be alone and she might tempt him into doing something he'd regret. The scene by the lake had to be forgotten. In any case, the evening with Celia Black and the Major had changed everything.

'You heard about Colin and my father?' She spoke without emotion.

'You must be worried about them,' he said, stupidly, almost forgetting for a moment that she hated her father.

'Worried? How stupid it was of them to go there. But at least one thing is clear now. It is quite certain that Colin cannot help me. But you will help me now, won't you.'

They walked in the direction of the Kurfürstendamm.

'Let's go to the Kempinski.' He didn't know where else to take her. He was still a stranger here, shut out from the secrets of this black city. He longed to get away from the place altogether, but he had to talk to her first, had to know if his theory was correct.

'You will help me, won't you.'

He still didn't answer.

'Please.'

'When I get back to London – I go back tomorrow – I'll try,' he said, not knowing if he could, or would.

He was becoming bold. He asked the waiter to recommend a wine and they were brought a slender bottle of Riesling. He needed it to give himself courage.

'I met some people here who were working with all the abandoned children right after the war. What they told me was very interesting.'

Frieda looked at him. 'What was that?'

'They talked about the way children were exploited, when everything was chaotic, in the hunger years. They talked about child prostitution, children murdered, even.'

To his annoyance the waiter interrupted them with the menu.

'You'd like something to eat?' He assumed she was probably hungry. She nodded and he ordered a plate of sausage, bread, some salad.

She drank. 'The wine is very nice.' He poured her more.

McGovern continued: 'I was told about rumours, rumours about your father and about someone in the occupying forces.'

'I know nothing about this.'

'Why did he suddenly move into the Russian sector?'

'How should I know? Do you think he ever thought he needed to explain himself to me? It was just: Come. We're going. But why do you talk about this now? It's all in the past.'

'I think it's important, Frieda. You see, they worked with children, these friends of my friend. And, like I said, they said bad things were happening to some of the children, abandoned children, homeless children, children with no parents. They were ill-treated, exploited, one or two were even murdered.'

Frieda put her hand on his arm. She was looking at him in that way of hers that was hard to resist, not imploring, nor seductive, but as if she saw deeply into him, as if she understood him. 'Please don't let us talk about the past. I want to talk about the future. Because I really need your help, Mr Roberts.'

'But it isn't in the past, is it, Frieda. I was told the new West German government might even investigate some of these murders.'

McGovern only had Victor Jordan's word for this and doubted it. It seemed improbable that, of all the iniquities that must have gone on, this should have been chosen for a further investigation. The Hoffmann case was different. It was already a scandal and the widows of the men who had disappeared were significant members of society, or at least their husbands had been. One dead corpse of a child among the ruins where so many corpses lay – that was unlikely to be given the same priority. True or not, however, McGovern could use this 'information' as a lever to get Frieda to talk. But perhaps that was too subtle, because it wasn't working.

She shrugged. 'This has nothing to do with me.'

'Frieda. You want me to help you. You mustn't lie to me. You must tell me the truth. My coming here to Berlin in the first place was to find out what Colin was doing. You were part of that because you both wanted to return to England. Or that was what we thought at first. Then Colin had second thoughts or changed his mind, but you're still desperate to get away.'

'Wouldn't you be desperate if you were me? With a father like mine?'

'But Colonel Ordway told me he could probably have helped you. Yet you didn't go then. If you want me to help you get away you have to tell me what happened after the end of the war. You didn't tell me your father had worked in Buchenwald. Are there other things you're not telling me? I think there are.'

She fiddled with a button on her red cardigan. It was loose on its thread.

McGovern leaned forward. 'Your father – what was he doing?'

She wouldn't look at him, but she straightened up and drank more wine. 'We made it to the British sector here in Berlin, when everything was still in chaos. We had no way of living at first, of even getting food. But my father was very clever. He had had all kinds of arrangements in the camp and he knew how to—'

'How to what? Exploit the situation?'

Frieda nodded. 'I suppose you could put it like that. He knew how to use people. He understood their weaknesses. He was clever in that way.'

'So he got involved in the black market?'

'Not exactly.'

'What, then?'

'Well, yes, in a way. And then – I'm not sure, but I think someone from Buchenwald, a survivor perhaps, recognised him. I don't really know, but that's what I suspect. Anyway he was interrogated. But nothing came of it, there were no charges, nothing. He was very ... I don't know ... confident after that, and, well, things went on as before. May I?' And Frieda slid a cigarette from McGovern's packet, which lay on the table between them. He lit it for her. She smoked. She wasn't going to say any more. He let the silence continue for a time, but then he made another attempt.

'Things went on as before; what does that mean? What things?'

She shrugged and made a face. 'Oh ...'

'Was your father exploiting children? Was he involved in some sort of child prostitution racket?'

She tried to maintain her look of indifference. 'By then I had met Colonel Ordway. I had a job, I wasn't there much. I don't know anything about that. What makes you think he would be involved in such a thing?'

The food arrived, but she only picked at it.

'You were not actually living with the Colonel, were you? You must have known something about what was going on.'

She shook her head, swallowed. Her eyes swam with tears. 'You don't understand what it was like.' She put a hand on his, and her look was hard to resist.

McGovern had thus far held back from mentioning the sister. It was his strongest card, perhaps his only card. But it was based on pure supposition and guesswork. 'You must have known what happened when your sister died. What happened, Frieda? How did your sister die?'

She shook her head. 'No-one knows exactly. Her body was found. No-one knew how it got there, on a bomb site.'

'Frieda. You're lying.'

She stood up. 'I have to go now.'

McGovern also stood up. 'Sit down. Remember I promised to help you if you told me the truth.'

She might be lying, but he was lying too and she must surely know it. She wasn't stupid. The uglier the truth she revealed, the less likely her escape; unless, that is, she believed she had wholly ensnared him. He had to gamble on that. 'I'd do anything to help you, Frieda, you know that, don't you,' he said. 'Please. Sit down.'

She acquiesced. He refilled their glasses and then took her hands across the table. 'Whatever it is you've done, I'll help you – you'll be able to make a fresh start in another country.'

'You really mean that?'

He nodded.

'If I tell you, will you promise to help me? Truly help me?'

'Of course I will, Frieda. I promise.'

'Well, in a way you are right.' She spoke in hardly more than a murmur so that he had to lean forward to hear her words. 'There were all these children. I don't know how it started. I suppose he himself ... as I said, he could always find out people's weaknesses, he was very good at that. He used to boast about it, when he worked at the camp, how easy it was to get people to do what you wanted if you knew what *they* wanted. That was the key, he used to say, find out what they want. Of course he used violence as well, but he always said, psychology, that's the clue. Some people will do almost anything to satisfy their desires. And once we were here in Berlin, the occupation was a wonderful opportunity. He knew there were soldiers – he found out there were men who wanted what he could give them. Not so much the Russians. The Russians raped every woman in sight, but they were nice to children. But some of the others. And there was someone from the interrogation team who came to see him, who liked what my father called green fruit. Many men like that, he said, it's quite normal.'

'Tell me more about this man. What was he like? What did he look like?'

'I don't remember much about him. Tall ... fair ... well dressed. You could tell he was rich. We were not rich. My father did all right in the war, but we were still common people. Other people in our village envied us, because we had more than them, but sometimes really important men came to visit my father and then you could tell the difference. The difference in their clothes, their shoes – and they always had those extra things that those sort of men have: a signet ring, a heavy watch, a silver cigarette case, even a special implement to do something to their cigars. It's not that those things are useful, it's what they tell the world. And he was like that. He had everything always right, the watch, the ring, the cigarette case ...'

'Would you recognise him again?'

'I should think so,' she said, but without much interest.

'What about you and your sister?'

'I was fifteen, nearly sixteen, I was already too old for these men and besides I had met Colonel Ordway.'

'Did you never think of telling the Colonel what was going on?'

'My father would have killed me.'

'And your sister? Did she know? Was she involved?'

Frieda's expression had become closed in and she was muttering in an almost dreamy way. 'Sabine was very pretty, but she was so stupid. The man I mentioned, the interrogation man, he liked her. But she wouldn't do as she was told. Something happened. I don't know what it was exactly, but I think she tried to run away, she threatened them, she said ... I don't know if she said she'd go to the authorities – if she even knew who they were and what good would that have done anyway, so ... One evening I came home and *der Vater* said she was missing and then when she didn't come back, after a while he said perhaps she wasn't coming back. And the body was found, and people started to talk. So we moved to Prenzlauerberg.'

'Did many men visit your father? That would have been very risky, surely?'

'Only the one I spoke of. And he didn't come for ... *that*, not there, where we lived. He had a car ... No, normally there would be a meeting place – there were so many places in the ruins – and it would be done like that. There would be an arrangement.'

'So you knew all about it. How were these arrangements made? You must have had an idea. There must have been some sort of go-between. Your father could never have done it all himself. Did he make contacts with the members of the occupying forces who wanted that sort of thing? Did the man who visited him put him in touch with likely clients? And who found the children? It seems to me the most likely person to entice the children would have been a woman, a girl, someone not much older than them. Isn't that right, Frieda?'

And finally Frieda smiled. 'You are not stupid, Herr Roberts. But what could I do? That was life in the hunger years. I went searching in the rubble, in the ruins for the ones who had no-one to look after them. I promised them food and somewhere better to sleep and sometimes I gave them some little thing, a trinket, a toy that my father had got from somewhere or had found. The children weren't frightened of me. And then I'd take them to the rendezvous. The man would give me the money and I would take it back to my father.'

'That must have been an awful thing to have to do.' He watched her sensuous lips, her sad eyes, her dreamy expression.

But she looked straight at him now. A burden seemed to be lifted from her, she sat up, and with the lightness and freedom of at last speaking the truth, she said: 'I didn't really care. It stopped my father beating me. And the children were starving. It was a good bargain for them. They got food and some chocolate, didn't they.'

thirty-six

❧

I N THE COURSE OF HIS WORK a policeman encounters a
disproportionate number of violent, stupid, malevolent and
self-destructive individuals. This can lead to a jaundiced view
of human nature. McGovern had always fought against the
occupational hazard of disillusionment, had kept an even keel
and rejected the cynicism that led some of his colleagues to an
unremitting contempt for the whole human race.

His conversation with Frieda had nevertheless shaken him
in more ways than one. He was glad to get away from Berlin.
As the plane rose above the city, he looked down at the grey
honeycomb of bombed buildings and new constructions and
began to attempt a coherent understanding of what he now
knew. But it was hard and the drone of the engines sent him
into a doze in which he was back at the youth march on Marx
Engels Platz, only now it was Kingdom who was his companion
and kept telling him this is the future.

Events had moved quickly in London, as McGovern discovered
when he reached the office. Mihaili Kozko had been brought in
for questioning. At first it hadn't gone well. Slater had fumed.
But fingerprints were taken and turned out to match a set on
Konrad Eberhardt's wallet.

He was to be questioned again today. McGovern and Jarrell were to be present.

'You've been very active while I've been away, Jarrell.' McGovern suppressed an unworthy feeling of professional resentment that his sergeant had done so well. He knew it was ungenerous and did his best to suppress it. 'Well done,' he said, more heartily than necessary. 'That was good work, tracking down the Ukrainian.'

'It was just luck. A hundred to one chance he'd be the first person I saw at the sailors' union, which is what the association is, really. It's a sort of community centre for Ukrainians. I went through Biermann's notes, the ones that were in his flat. He'd done a lot of investigation. He'd discovered Kozko's known by more than one name and has quite a reputation up north. I spoke to detectives up in Leeds, sir. They were glad to see the last of him.'

'You didn't expect to link him to Eberhardt.'

'That was the big surprise, sir. It hadn't occurred to me he might have killed Eberhardt. I thought it was all to do with Biermann. We might get him to confess to Biermann's murder as well, but we haven't any evidence for that. I feel bad about Biermann. Looking through his notes, I felt I really got to know him. He was very thorough.'

'Sounds as if he'd have made a good reporter. Shame he didna stick at that instead of getting a romantic idea of mucking in with the workers and solving crime into the bargain.'

'He'd still have got in trouble if he was trying to nail Kozko.'

'We'd better go down. Slater's starting the interview at ten.'

'Before we go, there is one other thing.'

'Okay. Make it quick.'

They were standing, ready to go, but when McGovern heard what Jarrell had to say he sat down again, causing his chair to swivel round, unsettling him even more.

'You saw this Ukrainian with *Kingdom*? How did you know it was him? You've never met him.'

Jarrell's smile hovered between creepily sly and sickeningly modest. 'I followed you once, sir. One time you were going to meet him. I thought it might be useful to know what he looked like. And it was.'

McGovern was winded. 'You cheeky wee devil! You'll go far, Jarrell. If you don't get cashiered first.'

'Inspector Slater doesn't like being kept waiting, sir.'

'Shut up, Jarrell. Just give me a moment. I need to think about this.'

When McGovern arrived home from Berlin, his first act on reaching his flat had been to try to ring Lily, but his second had been to try to arrange a meeting with Kingdom, only to be told that Kingdom had gone on holiday. What he would have said had they met, he wasn't sure. He had only suspicions. Kingdom might not be the interrogator of whom Frieda had spoken, her father's sinister contact in the ruins of postwar Berlin. Yet if he had been, if some infernal deal had been made, it would explain why Schröder had gone free. Yes, Schröder had gone free; that didn't prove it had been Kingdom who'd interrogated him and let him go in order to fulfil his own desires. McGovern did not ultimately believe that Kingdom *could* have been that man, but he fitted Frieda's description and McGovern was racked with suspicion and uncertainty. To be told that Kingdom was on holiday had come as a relief, but it only delayed the confrontation there must be.

Now there was this new and horribly unexpected link with the man who had almost certainly murdered Konrad Eberhardt. McGovern sat, winded, for a few minutes, but then he stood up and pulled himself together. 'Yes, we'd better go.'

Mihaili Kozko lived up to the caricature of a thug, with his near-shaven head and truculent expression, his muscular arms and stocky build. At first he denied everything. He couldn't remember what he was doing on the day of the funeral, but he knew he hadn't even been in London. He'd never heard of Konrad Eberhardt. Presented with the evidence, his tone didn't change at first, but gradually Slater's interviewing style, of straightforward bullying that stopped just short of physical violence – McGovern wondered if he'd have been as restrained if he and Jarrell hadn't been present – began to break Kozko down.

Eventually the Ukrainian said: 'It was an accident. It was job for me. I not mean to kill him. I am supposed to get a parcel from him, give him fright so he not go back to Germany. He got angry. This I did not expect. He try to hit me. So then I hit him and he fell down. Unconscious. I took money from his wallet. Then he start to wake up and grab me by the foot, so I break free and kick him in the water.'

'What do you mean, it was a job?'

But Kozko, while admitting he'd been employed to recover the 'parcel', refused to say by whom. 'I not been paid, because I have no parcel. But I did what I am asked. Is not my fault if no parcel. I still owed money. I get him. He pay me in the end.'

'You'll have got your own back if you tell us who he is,' said Slater craftily.

But Kozko was having none of that. 'I don't care about that. Getting revenge. Is only important the money.'

Slater roared with laughter at this. 'Well, you're not going to be seeing any money, are you, you stupid bastard, because I'm charging you with manslaughter, so you're going on remand and I doubt your paymaster is going to visit you in Brixton prison.'

thirty-seven

A MONTH PASSED. McGovern could not reach Kingdom. The agent was taking an unusually long vacation. McGovern returned to normal Branch duties. He met up a couple of times with Slater, but the detective had nothing new to report. Kozko continued to refuse to admit he'd had anything to do with the Biermann shooting.

It was late August now, the dog days of summer. Some mornings there was an autumnal mist in the air. Lily's father was sinking fast. Soon, McGovern knew, he'd be travelling north for the funeral and after that Lily and he would be together once more.

Gorch called McGovern into his office. 'Kingdom has been suspended.'

This was startling. Yet, as the news sank in, McGovern feared this meant the confirmation of things he should have known or guessed all along, half-doubts and – since Berlin – the darkest of suspicions that he couldn't wholly admit because they caused him so strongly to doubt himself and his judgement. He'd rated Kingdom: his style, his panache, his *certainty*.

'*What*?'

'He wants to see you. You know how to get in touch.'

'Why has he been suspended?'

'It might have something to do with Burgess and Maclean?

I ain't been told much. They've made such a hash of things, he may have got caught up in it.'

The shock was chilling, but slowly a sense of relief seeped through him, his body relaxed and he was inwardly thanking God that it wasn't after all about something to do with Schröder.

'He'll probably tell you himself.'

McGovern turned off the main road, passed a park and playing field on the right and crossed an iron bridge. Beyond this a path shaded by trees on one side with, on the other, a wire fence protecting derelict sheds and boathouses soon broadened out into the open and ran beside a ditch bordered with reeds. He was beginning to feel disconcerted. In the past they had often met in the open air, but this was different and seemed far from civilisation.

Kingdom had told him he'd be waiting by the gate that led onto the marshes.

McGovern looked round. At first he thought he was alone. Then he turned and saw Kingdom's hatless figure emerge from the short tunnel under the railway.

'You found the place all right? Let's walk, shall we?'

They set off across the open field, which stretched emptily forward beneath an evening sky of unearthly yellow barred with dark, banked cloud. McGovern had never been here before and in fact had had no idea such a rural wilderness existed in the middle of London's vast labyrinth. There was not a human being in sight, nor even signs of human habitation. Had he known what a lonely place it was he might not have come and his initial feeling of surprise was starting to curdle into apprehension.

As if reading his thoughts, Kingdom broke the silence. 'An eerie place, isn't it. Or should I say uncanny? I can never remember the difference. Is eerie when something that should be there isn't and uncanny is when something that shouldn't be there, *is*? I think that's it. In which case uncanny is the correct word, isn't it.'

'It's a wee bit spooky.'

Kingdom laughed. 'Uncanny.'

'So what's here that shouldn't be?' McGovern surveyed the land, deserted on all sides. Not even someone walking a dog.

'*Us*, of course, McGovern. You and I.' Kingdom laughed again and McGovern shivered. For the first time he wondered if he should have brought a weapon.

'Did you want me to report on Berlin, sir?'

'Not much of a success, was it.'

'No. I'm sorry, sir.'

'Although *actually* it's at least achieved the result of getting Harris out of the way. No thanks to you, it has to be said. He's been the author of his own undoing, and they've arrested Schröder as well. Neither of them will see the light of day for some considerable time. And they certainly won't be turning up here.'

'He's still a British citizen. Surely something can be done.'

'Don't go soft on me, McGovern, for God's sake. We can't take another international scandal on top of fucking Burgess and Maclean.'

'So from your point of view, the whole thing's been a success. Even though the success wasn't down to me.'

'Not entirely a success. Your second visit was meant to bring about a different result.'

'What result?'

'It doesn't matter now. Events have moved on.' He put a hand in his inner pocket, but it was only to pull out the silver case. McGovern accepted a cigarette. He needed it to steady his nerves, because Kingdom was jittery and his mood was contagious. McGovern's distrust was darkening into dread. 'I don't think we'll be working together any more,' said Kingdom.

'Then why are we here? What's the purpose of this meeting?'

'I wanted to clear a few things up.'

'There are some things I wanted to ask you, too.'

Kingdom glanced sideways at him almost flirtatiously from under his lashes. 'Yes, I thought you'd eventually begin to add things up.'

'You told me to go to the Garfield funeral. You said it was on the off-chance Harris would be there. But I believe you *knew* he'd be there. I believe you somehow knew he'd be meeting Eberhardt and that he'd be given the manuscript to take back to Germany.'

'Yes, that's true. Harris was stupid enough to talk it all through on the phone we tapped at his hotel. I'm amazed Biermann didn't tell him to be more careful. He must have assumed Harris was using a safe phone.'

McGovern continued: 'And you told me to view Eberhardt's body at the mortuary. But no-one knew it was Eberhardt then. But *you* knew. So that means ...'

'That I knew who killed him? Very good, McGovern. Only that thick-headed Ukrainian wasn't meant to *kill* him. He was meant to get the manuscript. He was too late, of course. Eberhardt had already passed it on to Harris. But if I'm honest, it's just as well the old man's out of the way. Think of it – distinguished scientist returns to East Germany, publishes his autobiography with a grovelling confession of how he informed on his friends and was hand in glove with British intelligence – what a propaganda coup for the Reds.'

'There was no autobiography,' said McGovern. 'Harris told me.'

'How ironic. I should probably have realised that too. Of course Harris may have been lying to you.'

McGovern shook his head. 'I'm sure he was telling the truth.'

'*Really?*'

'Harris isn't a liar.'

'You believe that? Well, actually you're probably right. More fool him. The art of lying is the greatest of the arts.'

'There was something I wanted to ask you, sir. Victor Jordan told me you were a brilliant interrogator,' he began.

'Yes, you passed on the compliment. Very gratifying to have praise from that quarter,' said Kingdom drily.

'I wondered if you'd interrogated Kozko in the DP camps, if you were the one who'd given him clearance and let him into this country.'

'Wrong there, I'm afraid, old chap. But I got to hear about him and he's been useful on a few occasions. Useful, that is, in the way a vicious dog is useful.'

'Did you instruct him to shoot Biermann?'

'Biermann was trouble. He was a loose cannon. He was mixed up with Eberhardt and then he started poking his nose into what was none of his business. I could do without him. But Kozko had it in for him anyway. Kozko is a very patriotic guy. That was a bit of private enterprise by Kozko on his own. He didn't take kindly to people nosing around in his affairs.'

'What's patriotism got to do with it? And why were Ukrainian fascists allowed into this country anyway?'

'That was all a bit of a cock-up, to tell you the truth. Long story. Although some of our former enemies are very useful now we're not so fond of the Reds. My enemy's enemy is my friend.'

That was one puzzle out of the way or partly resolved, even if the answers were horribly unsatisfactory. But: 'What I don't understand is why you sent me off after Harris. I don't see the point of it. You never believed he was part of getting Burgess and Maclean out of the country.'

'Well done!'

'I'd rather you didna patronise me, Mr Kingdom. I may

have been fooled, taken in, whatever you want to call it, but Superindent Gorch agreed the operation.'

Kingdom shrugged. 'He owes me one or two favours. Don't worry, nothing dubious. Just bits of information he was able to use. So I knew he'd agree to send someone.'

'So why did I go? What was it meant to achieve? And why choose me?'

McGovern had hoped and even expected that the explanation would involve a flattering reference to his talents, but Kingdom simply said: 'I knew Gorch would agree. I have a feeling he chose you because he thought he was doing you a favour. He thought he was giving you a leg up, that it would be good for your career. And then – didn't you think it a little odd that no-one ever asked about your background? About your father, the shipyard militant, the Clydeside Red? I found out all about that. And I thought it might just come in useful one day, that sort of information is always invaluable. I had it in reserve, in case you found out too much, in case you got awkward.' He went on: '*Of course* I never believed Harris had anything to do with Guy Burgess and Donald Maclean. At first I just wanted to find out more about what he was up to in London. Largely idle curiosity on my part, although … I don't know, maybe I had an instinct … They knew about him over there, of course, in Berlin, but he didn't seem to be up to anything much, just sitting around feeling sorry for himself.

'At that point I didn't even know Harris had met the Schröders. Then a friend of his – who I ran into completely by accident – told me Harris was going to marry Frieda Schröder and bring her back here. I must say that was rather a blow. If she came, her father would try to follow. At all costs I didn't want Schröder over here—'

So – McGovern felt the adrenalin rising – Kingdom had known Schröder already … in the past … after the war …

Until that moment McGovern hadn't been 100 per cent

sure; 90 per cent perhaps that the tall blond interrogator with the watch and the silver cigarette case had been the man at his side now; but not 100 per cent sure. He'd still clung to a scrap of hope, but now he knew for certain.

Kingdom seemed not to notice his companion's agitation. He continued: 'And then the Eberhardt business blew up at the same time. So now I had two problems. Eberhardt couldn't be allowed to leave the country and Frieda Schröder couldn't be allowed in. They were essentially two completely separate problems. Except that the person linking them was Harris.'

They reached the end of one field, crossed a ditch and passed into another desolate tract of land. McGovern looked all around, in the hope that he might see some other human being, but they were alone.

'The first time I sent you it was simply to find out about Frieda Schröder and what was going on at that end. But Thomas Schröder's no fool. He soon guessed you were up to something. He had the nerve to get in touch. He reminded me of the old days. Said his daughter would soon be coming to Britain and he'd make sure to follow. And what would have been the end result of that? Blackmail. That's when I got the wind up. I panicked. That's always a fatal mistake, McGovern. I'm telling you, don't ever panic. Fatal in my line of business. Means you've lost your touch.'

That was what Victor Jordan had said: Kingdom must have lost his touch. The sun had sunk below the viaduct, light was fading from the sky and shadows had begun to cobweb the deserted marshes.

'Hadn't we better be getting back? It's getting late.'

'Yes, let's turn back. Can't drag this out indefinitely. Just putting off the inevitable. Postponing the evil moment.'

The evil moment. McGovern's heart missed a beat.

'But first,' continued Kingdom, 'you haven't asked what was meant to be achieved by your second visit to Berlin. And

I'm afraid the answer is it was meant to be the end of you. You see, when you came back the first time, I panicked again. Something you said convinced me you knew all about the Schröders and me. I was certain you knew what had happened. All those remarks about what Jordan had said and how I wouldn't have any truck with the black market – I read God knows what into that. I thought you were hinting you knew much more than you let on. And you did know, didn't you? You'd found out everything.'

'No, I didn't know anything. That evening in the park. I couldn't understand why you were so irritable. I thought I'd done something wrong, but I couldn't work out what.'

'I thought the best thing would be another Berlin visit, only this time you'd meet with an accident. It might have been simpler to get Kozko to deal with you in this country. I've so much on Kozko, he'd never refuse a request from me. But that would have led to an embarrassing murder enquiry.

'So I replied to Schröder's friendly letter. He was to fix something up with his East German friends. They were told you were a dangerous agent, up to your neck in all the stuff with Hoffmann. Then the West Germans arrested Hoffmann, but that was a bonus in a way, because it was all over the press over there, and no-one would notice you'd disappeared. Not for a while, anyway. And when they did, it could be passed off as a robbery or a hit-and-run, an unfortunate accident, that sort of thing.'

McGovern was listening, but he was also planning what to do in the next five or ten minutes. Did Kingdom have a gun? If he did, things looked desperate. If not … 'At that point I knew nothing about the Schröders. Nothing whatsoever,' he said. His own voice sounded toneless to him, leaden with the horrified disappointment that had gripped him. And the growing dread and fear.

'But you do now, eh?' Kingdom laughed. 'Well, that's

another irony, isn't it. But the biggest irony of all is that now it doesn't matter. It doesn't matter one fucking bit. I suppose you got Frieda to tell you in the end. And I suppose she turned it into a tragic story. When actually she was in it up to her neck.'

McGovern's revulsion towards Kingdom was cold because he could not understand the compulsion that drove the man, but his hatred of himself for having been so taken in was hot and shameful.

Kingdom stopped in his tracks. He smiled. McGovern's heart lurched.

'I've no regrets, you know. No-one got hurt.'

'Frieda's sister *died*. She was murdered.'

'Was she? Schröder could be violent, he had a nasty temper, but I thought he told me she fell down some crater in the rubble, I don't really remember. You know, it's all a very long time ago now, my dear.'

McGovern quickened his pace as they traipsed over the rough grass.

'Nothing to say, McGovern? You haven't asked me why I've been suspended, why we won't be working together any more. Too polite? Too timid? You were always a little in awe of me, I think. A little too deferential.'

'Gorch thought you might have been involved with the diplomats after all. That you'd bungled things.' McGovern's voice sounded hoarse.

Kingdom laughed. 'Oh God! That's so amusing. No. Nothing so pukka, I'm afraid.'

'What then?' Kingdom's taunts were getting to him. If violence was coming it might be his, not the other man's.

'If you must know, I've been charged with a serious offence and I'm lucky to have got bail.'

So the story had one more twist. McGovern had thought there were no more surprises in store. But – the truth – it landed like a blow to his chest – the great interrogator, the great anti-communist: he must have been a double agent all along. It wasn't just that Kingdom, in 'losing his touch', had made a mess of things. He'd actually been working for the Russians. There was no other reason he could have been charged. Yet if that were the case – treason – how could he have got bail?

'You were working for the Soviets.'

Kingdom seemed to find that even more amusing. 'You thought I was a double agent?'

'Why else would you be arrested?'

'You couldn't be more wrong. It's another case of my losing my touch, I'm afraid. Or was it that my sense of irony failed me? Irony: the perfect armour against the slings and arrows, etcetera. And irony is the perfect antidote against taking oneself too seriously. You take yourself seriously, don't you, McGovern. Always a mistake, I feel. But when it came to Sabine the irony slipped away. Irony's no defence against the passions. And now, again – it was just one risk too far. But she was such a sweet little girl, McGovern, you've no idea. If only she hadn't told her cousin, the silly child. And the little pansy told the mother. Who I'm afraid took it rather badly. She thought I was interested in *her*, you see, when all the time it was little Judy. God, I loved her.'

And now Kingdom stopped abruptly and turned to McGovern. 'The reason I needed to see you again was to apologise. I owe you an apology. You're a decent policeman, McGovern. I admit I used you. I even tried to get rid of you, but you didn't deserve to be sacrificed to my absurd loss of nerve.'

McGovern, his heart lurching, had perforce stopped when his companion had come to a halt. All he could do was be alert. The important thing was to watch for the slightest movement. Kingdom was dramatising, he was getting off on the situation, he was capable of – anything.

'You're my witness, McGovern. I want them to know I'm

ₒoing the right thing. I want you to tell them that. This way there won't be a trial.'

They faced each other in the gathering darkness. And then – it wasn't even dramatic. One moment Kingdom was standing there, the next – he'd gone. A flash – and the sound of the shot died in the still air.

thirty-eight

ON A GREY, HUMID SATURDAY in early September Dinah was helping Reggie prepare for the dinner to entertain Dr Blunt. Reggie was making mayonnaise with olive oil from Boots the chemist. Elizabeth David said you could get it from some shop in Soho, but Boots was nearer. The mayonnaise was to accompany the salmon one of William's authors had given him. ('I think he was hoping for a bigger advance.') Dinah sat at the kitchen table and peeled potatoes.

'How are things?' enquired Regine casually.

'Oh, much better. We had a lovely holiday in Cornwall.'

Regine was trying to regulate the flow of oil into the egg yolk and beating the mixture furiously with a wooden spoon. 'You know,' she said as she tried to stop the bowl sliding around on the table, 'I felt I should never have said anything to you at all.'

'If you put a damp cloth under the bowl, it won't slip like that.' Dinah no longer wanted to talk about her marriage. The time for that was past. It was repaired, like a piece of china stuck together and looking almost as good as new; but Reggie was looking at her, wanting reassurance. 'You didn't really say anything,' she said.

Reggie's rueful expression was less a plea for forgiveness from Dinah than an indicator of self-forgiveness, but she insisted: 'I sort of hinted. There had been rumours. I didn't know what to do. I thought it would probably all blow over and you'd be none the wiser, but then on the other hand ...'

'I think I had begun to wonder ... and I've thought and thought about how I went wrong, you know.'

Regine groaned, 'Oh, don't blame yourself. That's what women always do.'

'But I'm going back to the Courtauld as a full-time student in the autumn, I'm really excited about that.'

'That's wonderful, darling, that will be fun.'

'And he did give her up for me. So everything's fine.'

Regine said cautiously: 'She's married a banker, you know. Some old man.'

'That was quick. On the rebound, I suppose.'

'Yes, I'm sure that's it. William says she's a scheming witch anyway.'

Dinah was touched that Reggie had arranged the dinner especially, really, for her. It was a small one. The guests, apart from Dinah herself and Alan, were an art historian in his forties and his wife, a singer, and a youth whose presence was unexplained and who stood locked in indifference or shyness.

'You remember Charles Hallam, don't you, Dinah. He used to come to my Sunday afternoons. He's going up to Oxford in the autumn. Which college was it, Charles?'

'Magdalen.' He said it with a modest smile, which somehow despite itself confirmed his distinction, his effortless superiority.

Dr Blunt couldn't take his eyes off the boy.

Almost the only topic of conversation, the gossip that trumped all the other scandals they might have discussed – Burgess and Maclean (rather stale by now), William's lady author who'd run off with a man in a circus, Elizabeth David's wonderful new cookery book, the *extraordinary* way Georgina Garfield was behaving and Vivien Leigh's disastrous performance as Lady Macbeth – was Miles Kingdom's suicide that appalling event in some sinister region of East London, the result, as everyone knew, but only whispered, of his arrest for an unmentionable crime.

Charles assumed that was why he'd been invited.

To begin with his father had tried to keep him out of any further involvement, but he'd heard the agonised conversations, Aunt Elfie's distraught accusations and his father's attempts to calm her down. Judy had been sent to stay with friends in the country to help her get over what had happened, with instructions to mention 'the incident' to no-one. She'd hugged Charles very hard as he said goodbye and muttered, almost sobbing, 'Oh Charles, I feel so awful, I should never have said anything at all.'

And all he could think of to murmur had been, 'It'll be all right, Judy, you haven't done anything wrong. It's not your fault, really it isn't.'

His father had pleaded with Aunt Elfie not to go to the police. Charles had listened to the terrible arguments and in the end when his father tried to get him to leave the room had said: 'It's better if I know, Dad, everyone'll be talking – I won't blab, I swear, and anyway it was me she told.'

They raged to and fro. 'It would only be worse for the child,' said Dr Hallam, 'it's far better not to go to court, Miles Kingdom is very distinguished, they probably won't believe her anyway and—'

'He has to be punished.' Aunt Elfie sat rigid as a stone. 'I can't let him get away with it. To think he asked me to marry him – why, the *cheek*—' And she'd burst into tears.

'Don't do it out of revenge, Elfrida.'

'How dare you! How *dare* you suggest – how could you accuse me of that, John?'

'I'll see the girl gets to see a good psychiatrist – better by far in the long run.'

Charles hadn't been able to restrain himself then. 'You mean like it's been better for Mummy, I suppose.' He hadn't meant to shout, but his father had looked at him, stricken. There was a dreadful silence, an awful stretched-out moment before Dr Hallam returned to the fray. 'You can't ruin a man's career, Elfrida, for a – a lapse.'

'You call it a lapse to rape a twelve-year-old girl.'

Rape ... and his father had flustered and prevaricated and fallen silent.

Now Charles relived the scene as the adults of whom he wasn't quite yet one discussed it voraciously around him. Regine knew that Judy was his cousin, but was too tactful to mention it. She looked at him now and again as if hopeful he'd contribute, but he lounged back in his chair, ate masses of salmon, cheese and lemon soufflé and drank quantities of wine while watching Dr Blunt.

Dr Blunt raised his fastidious eyebrows when Alan said: 'Didn't he talk to you when Burgess and Maclean disappeared?'

'But of course, he had to, everyone knows I knew Guy very well indeed. And Kingdom was a brilliant interrogator. I'm sure if I'd had anything to hide he'd have wormed it out of me in the end.' Dr Blunt smiled at them all serenely.

'And to think all along, it was little girls,' murmured Reggie. 'His wife committed suicide, didn't she? Perhaps that was why.'

Afterwards they drifted into the drawing room. It was a warm, close night. The French windows were open and some of the guests stood in the darkening garden, glasses in hand, smoking. Charles found himself alone with Dr Blunt, who bent over him solicitously from his great height to ask: 'And what are you going to read at Oxford?'

'Greats.' Charles hesitated. Then: 'You knew Miles Kingdom quite well, did you? You see – I met him a couple of times

– actually, you probably know this, anyway, but my cousin was actually the girl ...'

'No, no ... I had no idea, really dreadful,' murmured Dr Blunt.

'The point is that's how I met him a couple of times, when he came to the house and when I told him I did the Navy Russian course, he seemed to think I might be interested later on in that sort of ... career, I suppose you could call it. He encouraged me to think about it. You knew him – and Guy Burgess – I expect you know something about it. D'you think that would be a good idea – is it the kind of thing one ought to go in for?'

'MI5, you mean? Well, I do know something about it. I was in intelligence myself, in the war.' Dr Blunt smiled kindly at him. He seemed to consider it. Then he replied serenely, 'I don't think so, on the whole, Charles, no, I don't think that would be a good idea at all.'

It was to be nearly thirty years before Anthony Blunt was publicly exposed. He'd after all been a Soviet agent all along. 'I met him once or twice,' said Charles to his companion – they were seated in a café on the Venice Lido at the time. 'I'm not at all surprised. I always thought he was probably a spy.'

thirty-nine

⤴

February 1956

MCGOVERN HURRIED AWAY FROM the Old Bailey at the end of a Monday afternoon and paused to buy an evening paper from the stand on the corner. The banner headline had caught his eye: BURGESS AND MACLEAN IN MOSCOW.

After five years the 'missing diplomats' had finally held a press conference in a hotel room in the Russian capital. They admitted being lifelong communists and Marxists, but: 'We neither of us have ever been communist agents.' They had left Britain once they realised that 'attempts to put Marxist ideas into practice are doomed to failure, so long as Britain and America are not serious about upholding world peace. We have come to the USSR in the hope of promoting better understanding between the Soviet Union and the West.'

McGovern walked slowly along High Holborn towards Chancery Lane, trying to take it in. So they'd been in Moscow ever since their dramatic disappearance. Why reappear now? Why deny they were spies?

It vividly brought the past back. Those days in Berlin ... Frieda Schröder ... the rendezvous with Kingdom ... McGovern needed to think, to digest it all. He dived into a dark little pub, paid for his half pint, found a table, sat down and read the news more carefully.

He'd crouched over the body in the dusk, felt for the pulse that wasn't there and a moment later, without conscious thought, had slipped his hand into an inner pocket and withdrawn from it the silver cigarette case. He'd never told anyone but Lily. Lily understood it wasn't a vulgar theft. He didn't use it; it lay, like a charm or a fetish in a dusty drawer, not a souvenir, but a reminder not to be taken in by appearances, to remember that even the handsomest, the richest and most brilliant might have a twisted mind or a dark heart.

Now he turned the pages of the paper, but instead of reading, he sat staring in front of him while the images unreeled compulsively and the memories flooded back.

Kingdom, he thought, would have appreciated the irony of Harris having lied about the Eberhardt autobiography, which had appeared in East Germany to great acclaim. McGovern had cursed Colin Harris for deceiving him about it. He'd been trying to organise a way of getting Harris out of the GDR, so the publication was a slap in the face. Soon, however, doubts began to be raised as to the authenticity of the book. It became another scandal in which the truth was veiled in a fog of uncertainties and rumour.

His glass was empty. He decided to return to Whitehall on foot. It was pleasanter than being crammed into a crowded bus and would, he thought, give him time to shake off the past. He was wrong.

He walked down Kingsway and along the Strand. Then, as he crossed Trafalgar Square he caught sight of a willowy woman walking slowly along the pavement. She was well dressed in a grey coat and skirt and stiletto heels. Her sideways, drifting walk was somehow familiar. He looked into her face. The long mouth, the winged eyebrows ... surely it couldn't be—

He hurried after her, stretched out and touched her arm.

She drew herself up. The faint frown was also familiar. He eased her aside from the sober British crowd, the flock of pedestrians headed home, with heads down, preoccupied, unsmiling, grey in this grey city.

'Frieda. How extraordinary.'

She reluctantly allowed him to lead her to the steps of St Martin-in-the-Fields.

'How strange to meet you again, Herr Roberts.' She spoke good English now.

He was gripped with curiosity. 'You got here after all! How—?' But what he most passionately wanted to know was the truth about *her*. Had she really been in it up to her neck? You couldn't trust Kingdom, but she'd spoken so coldly the last time they'd met. 'You must let me buy you a drink. You must tell me how you got here in the end. I know a bar near here—'

'That is very kind, Herr Roberts, but I'm afraid I don't have time.'

'You must at least tell me what happened.'

She shook her head slowly. 'I'm so sorry, I really don't have time. It's a long story. What would be the point, Herr Roberts? Ours was only an accidental meeting and – well, it's so long ago. And after all, it's not as if you kept your promise, is it. You had no part in bringing me here.'

Gently she disengaged herself, gracefully descended the steps and walked away across the north end of the square past the National Gallery. Her white-gloved hand shot up as she saw a taxi. It slowed by the kerb. She climbed in and a moment later the cab had slid away into the stream of traffic and was lost to sight.

McGovern stood rooted to the spot for a moment. Then he too went on his way.

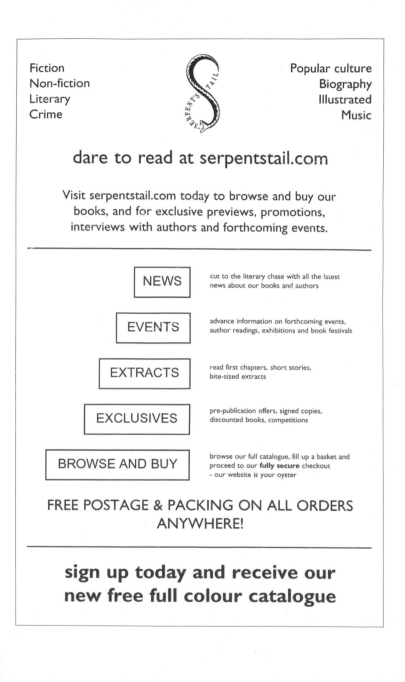